Brenda Dawson

Indian Blanket

Brenda B. Dawson

ISBN-13: 978-1470143022
ISBN-10: 147014302X

2Fires Publishing Co.
PO Box 673, Barnsdall, OK 74002
www.2firespublishing.weebly.com
2firespublishing@windstream.net
Cover Design by 2fires Publishing Co

Dedication

This book is dedicated to all the amazing people
who do not only see with their eyes, but also with their hearts.

In Memory Of

My husband, William J. Dawson, Sr.
and
My son, William J. Dawson, Jr.

"Rest in peace, my two Bills"

MY SINCERE THANKS

Annaraye Lewis, Cheryl Puryear, Bridgette Laramie
and
2FiresPublishing Co.

Your suggestions, support, and critiques
have kept me humble

Also by Brenda B. Dawson

Season of Magenta
Season of Regret

Coming Soon
Journey to Magenta

What are others saying about Dawson?

Barnes and Noble readers give *A Season of Magenta* and *Season of Regret* five stars!

"Fantastic!!! This book really grabs you from the start all the way to finish…."

"I just finished Season of Regret and it was wonderful! The Characters are very real, and Dawson writes in a manner that sucks you in…"

Amazon.com readers give *A Season of Magenta* and *Season of Regret* Five stars!

"Dawson has the ability to create pictures of her settings and characters with words that invite the reader to delve further into the intrigue of the story line…"

"Dawson creates a story of young love that sometimes makes the reader want to stop and say, "Wait, this has happened to me in the past." Brenda shares the good, the bad, and the ugly of young love…"

Kindle readers give *A Season of Magenta* and *Season of Regret* Five stars!

"I have read Season of Magenta TWICE. I loved it just as much the second time…"

"Keep them coming!"

Legend tells us of the old Indian blanket maker
who created colorful blankets so beautiful that
other Indians would come from miles to trade
for his creations.
Upon his death, God was so sad that the old
blanket maker's remarkable talent could no longer
be shared with his earthly brothers, that he created
a hearty little flower with all the vivid colors of
the old man's blankets.

The earthly flower was known as
Indian Blanket.

"Life's Journeys are as varied as the colors of the
Indian Blanket.

All are unique.

Some are tragic.

None are hopeless."
Brenda B. Dawson

Prologue

Colona, Illinois
May, 1970

"Stay calm, Danny love, we'll be fine." Jessie hoped the sound of her voice would calm the kicking and screaming child in the backseat. It didn't.

The flashing red lights whirled raging fury as they grew larger in her rear-view mirror. Over the screams of the child, the angry sirens of the black and white cruisers squealed their rapid advance on her bright yellow Fiat. She could have kicked herself for not having the second-hand Fiat painted black, blue, any dark color, anything but yellow. She'd planned to do this, but with Danny there was never enough money. Now here she was, the police cars chasing her through the depths of midnight, the yellow paint reflecting like a beacon to guide their way behind her.

Everything happened so quickly. There had been no time to come up with a real plan, and   barely enough time to gather a few clothes, secure Danny in a make-shift bed in the backseat of the car, and race through the darkness away from Colona. Then the police spotted her yellow car.

Sweat pouring down her face, jaws clamped rigid, Jessie gripped the ragged steering wheel and hung on for dear life. More terrified than a tiny rabbit with the hounds closing in, Jessie spoke more to herself than to the little boy. "We can't outrun them Danny, but maybe we can outsmart them." Danny kept screaming.

Recalling how the child would howl with laughter as she whirled him around her small living room to the blistering voice of Tina Turner in J.C. Fogerty's "Proud Mary", Jessie began to sing, "rolling, rolling, rolling on the river". Jessie was no Tina Turner, but as she sang, Danny's screams turned to soft sobs. She continued singing the phrase of the song over and over as she searched the road ahead for her turn off. As her mouth moved to the music, her brain was frantic with worry. Would the overgrown lane she searched for still be passable? Could she even find it?

"Rolling, rolling, rolling on the river." It wasn't much of a plan, but at least it was a plan, she thought as she sang, while racing through the night, and trembling in fear. She'd taken this back road out of Colona for a reason. The police knew all the streets and alleys of Colona, but they didn't know the back roads like she did.

"Rolling, rolling, rolling on the river." They were closing in on her and she knew it. She also knew that if she could outrun them for a short distance further, she could pull off the road onto a small overgrown lane she'd previously discovered when she was covering a news story for WKOB TV. Hoping to get a story on some rural marijuana growers, she'd driven this road in the dark many times using only her fog lights. Now she hoped she could find the concealed lane again. Finding that over-grown lane was her plan, her only plan.

"Rolling, rolling, rolling on the river." Jessie's eyes hugged the road as she raced onward, guided only by her fog lights. When the time came, she prayed that the police wouldn't realize she had shut off her lights and taken a dead reckoning detour onto the hidden lane. Actually, it was just an over-grown pathway. It certainly wasn't a lane and definitely not a road, but it was well hidden. *Oh where was it? Was that it up ahead? Oh, thank you, God!*

"Rolling, rolling, rolling on the river." Jessie turned onto what she hoped was the lane she'd once known so well. Bumping and spinning in the soft dirt, she forced her aging car onward through the over-grown brush until she found the abandoned shed she'd used as cover during her investigation. Driving her yellow Fiat into the safety of the shed, she sighed a huge thank you to her maker and prayed for their continued safety on their long journey home.

Danny must have sensed her relief because as she turned to look at him he laughed and gurgled up at her, his pudgy face and blonde hair illuminated in the moonlight cast from the shed's broken window. Love overwhelmed Jessie as she reached back and stroked the little boy's hair. "I love you, Danny. You're my son, and no one will ever take you from me. Be very quiet for a few minutes more, love. After those bad guys leave, I'll take you to meet your new daddy. One day he will love you as much as I do."

Jessie didn't kid herself that Jed would want either one of them in the beginning, not after everything that happened between them years ago. Still, she hoped this could be a new start for them. She was bringing Jed a son. Maybe he could finally forgive her for killing their son, Evan.

J&J Ranch
Oklahoma
May, 1970

"Looks like a damn dust bowl coming down the lane." Jed McClure growled, wondering just who'd be nuts enough to come flying down that rugged road slinging gravel, bouncing in the ruts, and tossing dirt half way to hell and back. He pulled the yellowed lace curtain back from his office window and glared. He knew his glare wouldn't be seen by the unwelcome intruder but he did it anyway.

It was a funny looking little yellow car, one he'd never seen anywhere near his hometown of Tahchee, Oklahoma. This car was one he'd surely remember if its stupid owner ever had the nerve to come near his ranch before, and by God they hadn't. Now here they came bouncing right up his driveway, dust and all, acting like they owned the place. Well, he'd see about that!

Grabbing his aging Remington 870 shotgun and his worn straw Stetson, Jed headed out the front door of his ranch house wondering why that fool couldn't read the warning at the gate. It clearly said in big letters:

PROPERTY OF JED MCCLURE
KEEP OUT OR GET SHOT DEAD

Plopping his tobacco-colored Stetson down on his silver-streaked blonde head, the big man stared in awe at the rapidly approaching auto. Parking his large body in the middle of his gravel driveway, he dared that crazy fool to venture past him.

As he stood ready and waiting, he wondered how that idiot managed to get past the locked gate. You had to have a key to get past that lock and almost nobody had a key. He had one on his keychain, and one in his safe. Ben White, his bookkeeper and his cook, Simon Hanson, both had keys, but no one else had a key. Well there was one more he remembered. Oh hell, no! She still had a key? Oh God!

Jed took his stand in his driveway, legs spread defiantly, shotgun ready. She wouldn't dare run over him! Would she? Oh, crap! She would!

Jumping back as the ugly car skirted past him, Jed glared his most ferocious glare at his long-lost wife, but she ignored him and kept on driving to her favorite place, the room at the north end of the long rectangular ranch house. After Evan died, she'd said it was her place to do some thinking, but he knew better. It was her place to be shed of him.

Shotgun in hand, Jed tromped down his driveway toward the north end of the rambling stone house. He stopped abruptly as she threw open her car door and exited the car like she owned the place. She didn't! She gave up her rights to the home when she gave up her rights to him. Jed squinted into the late afternoon sun wondering about his wife. Who did she think she was to come trotting in here after.... how long had it been?

Jed felt the cold sweat breaking out on his forehead and the hot sweat under his arms. Icy cold and sticky hot at the same time. It was just like her. She always had that effect on him. Still did after all these years.

"What the hell are you doing here, Jessica?"

Ignoring the engaging figure of a man, Jessica McClure hurried to the back door of the small yellow car. As he watched her, he could have sworn he heard a baby crying, but he knew that was impossible. That was a long time ago. *Evan.*

With Jed staring in amazement behind her, Jessie leaned into the scorching hot car, sweat running down her face, her auburn hair pulled back into a straggled pony tail. Wrapping her strong arms around the screaming child, she gagged. Danny had pooped his pants right outside of Tahchee, and she hadn't been able to stop and change him. It would have been useless to stop anyway, because there were no unsoiled diapers and no means to clean him. She'd used her last clean diaper somewhere in Kansas. Well, it was sort of clean. Now poor Danny had been sitting in poop since they left Tahchee and he was not happy. Remembering what an awful trip it had been, Jessie thanked God that they were now home. At last they were safe.

Marching around the car, holding the baby slightly away from her, Jessie approached the fuming man. "Take him," she said and shoved the squalling child into Jed's free arm, the one that wasn't holding the shotgun.

Jed was so shocked he grasped the smelly child to him as he noticed dark baby poop run down his own arm. "Damn you, Jessica. What the hell do you think you're doing coming back here? And who the hell does this kid belong to?"

Grabbing two fully-loaded suitcases from the hatchback of the small yellow car, Jessie ignored Jed and hurried toward the end of the house. Taking out her keys, she unlocked the door to what used to be her sanctuary and hurried inside.

Dropping the two suitcases inside the door of the cool stone room, Jessie hurried toward the big man glaring daggers at her as he tried to hold on to the squirming baby and keep the baby poop from saturating his own clothes. Jessie glared back as she grabbed the child from his arms and hurried back to her private space.

"He's my son," Jessie McClure shouted from inside the doorway. "His name is Danny, and Danny and I have come home." Without another word, the door was slammed in Jed McClure's face.

Retreating in defeat back to his end of the house, he thought about his wife. Jessie was home all right, and as usual, he was covered in shit.

Lowering her son on to the variant native tiles of the ancient room, Jessie gasped in thankfulness. No one would find them here. Jed would take care of them. He wouldn't know he was protecting them, but he would.

"Lord, it's good to be home," she whispered. It had been almost five years since she'd been home and she had missed every inch of this old place. She had missed him, too, if the truth be known.

Lovingly, Jessie caressed one of the cool stones of the aged wall. When it had been built before Oklahoma attained statehood, someone had the foresight to build this room facing away from the warmth of the sun, so it would stay as cool as possible in the scorching Oklahoma summers. The two outside openings to the room were the door facing east and the window facing north. There was a sturdy deadbolt on the thick door, and as far as she knew, the window had been opened only once and that was over five years ago. No one could possibly approach them without her knowing.

Years ago someone had installed a country sink with hot and cold running water in the room. Why, she had no idea, because there was a bathroom next to the room and past the bathroom there was a modern kitchen. But this room, papa's room, had been her sanctuary since his death so many years ago. When he was alive, he used this room to do his experiments in plant cross- breeding, always searching for the perfect strain of hybrid wheat that would eventually save his dying ranch. He never found it, but through his gentle teachings, Jessie discovered the same love of the land that he had known.

Gently caressing the old wall, Jessie savored the musty smell of years gone by, so many memories, happy and sad. *Evan.* After Evan died, she'd put a small bed in here, her private place to grieve. There were so many lonely days and nights of horrible grief with no possible absolution. "Oh, dear God," Jessie whispered, more a prayer for the future than a memory of the past.

Jessie brought herself back to reality capturing the toddler before he could escape in his filthy diaper. While the big deep sink was filling with water, she wiped his soiled bottom as clean as possible and then placed him into the comfort of the soothing water. As Danny gurgled and splashed, Jessie settled on a stool and maintained a careful vigil over him.

"There is nothing I wouldn't do for you, Danny. Your new daddy doesn't want us here right now, but where else could we go?" Reaching for the warm wash cloth, she poured small drips of water over Danny's head and delighted in his baby laughter.

She hadn't wanted to run home to Jed after everything that had happened so many years ago. He wouldn't want them, she knew that, but he'd always been her safe haven. He just didn't know that. She'd always loved him, too. He didn't know that either.

Jed McClure tucked his clean shirt into his equally clean jeans and rolled the blue chambray sleeves up his arms. He never took a shower in the middle of the day. Never! But there was a first time for everything, and things always seemed to change when *she* was around. *She* was what really ticked him off. *She* and her damn haughty attitude! *She* left him, damn her. He hadn't left her. *She* left him years ago! *How many years had it been?* He couldn't remember.

Grabbing a hair brush, Jed brushed his defiant hair. She'd always loved his hair, and now he wondered what she thought about his fading blonde hair aged with silver? Shoving his hairbrush back on the dresser, his mind wandered back to Jessica's baby. How could one little baby stink so much? Where'd she get that baby, anyway? She said it was hers, but that kid didn't look much like her. It had blonde hair. The kid looked more like him than he did her. That baby could have been his son, but it wasn't. His son had died years ago.

He knew she'd never remarried, because she'd never divorced him. He had paid an investigator to keep track of her over the years to be sure she was all right. He knew he was being stupid. She didn't need him. Still he worried she might need his money. She hadn't, but he thought if he could foresee problems for her, she wouldn't get into any real trouble out on her own. Snarling at the mirror, Jed remembered the little blonde-haired baby. *She'd gotten herself into a mess of trouble anyway.*

Did she take a lover and conceive a child with him? Jed wondered as he ran his fingers through his hair. She couldn't have done it by herself. She must have taken a lover. Jed felt the hair on his neck bristle with that thought and sensed an old familiar twinge of sadness.

"You left me, Jessie." Jed said to the vision of Jessie that was never far from his mind. "You went off and had a baby with someone else. How could you do that to me!"

Jed tried to shove the memory of his wife from his mind. She wouldn't leave. Was it Jessie, the young woman that occupied his mind? Or was it Jessie, the older woman that had his mind tied in knots? Probably both, he decided. It had been years since she left him, and she still controlled his thoughts.

"How many years had it been?" he asked himself. "Hell, I don't know," he answered.

Jed glanced at his own reflection in the mirror. He was lying, lying to himself. "Four years, eleven months, and sixteen days. That's how long it's been." He growled at his mirrored image. He had counted every single rotten day since she left him, and it hadn't been because of that stupid house law she'd found before their marriage. He really didn't care about the house anymore. He didn't care about the land under it either, but she was not going to trot her little ass back here now, take possession of this house, and leave him again like she did the last time. No, he wasn't going through that hell again, ever.

"Oh, she was a smart cookie," Jed mumbled to his mirror. Nobody could deny that. She knew she'd lose the house if she hadn't returned in time. That's the only reason she came back. The only thing she ever wanted was Evan, the stupid house, and to prove her father's wheat was viable. She sure as hell didn't want him! If he had half a brain, he would bulldoze the stupid house. Yes, that's what he should do! Somehow though, in a tiny corner of his mind, he knew he never could tear the old place down. There were too many memories inside the old pile of stones. Good memories and bad memories. Still, he could never let them go.

Jed sighed deeply, speaking softly as he thought about the wasted years without the only woman he had ever loved. "What happened, Jessie? Didn't you know you were all I ever wanted? You and Evan were my whole life. Didn't you know I was grieving every bit as much as you were when our son died?" Jed's sad mood was overcome by the anger used to disguise his pain as he continued his tirade against her. "Didn't you have any remorse running out and leaving me here alone in this empty world? How could you leave me, Jessie? I can never forgive you for that." Scowling at the mirror, the mirror scowled back.

Jessie carried Danny from her old room through the bathroom and into the kitchen. "Yeah, I know my big boy is hungry," she said as she rummaged through one of the cabinets and found a stash of crackers to tide Danny over while she found something to make for his supper. Placing the boy on a small mat on the kitchen floor, she pulled the refrigerator door open and searched the contents. Scrambled eggs were his favorite food and would be an easy fix. As she pulled the eggs from the carton, she heard the door open from the dining hall. It was Sunday, the ranch hand's day off, and she knew exactly who opened that door. She could almost feel the heated hostility across the room.

"Oh, just make yourself at home, Jessica. Don't wait to be invited!"

Jessica didn't need to turn around. It was him. "I have every right to be here. This is my house, too."

"And this is my land that your house is sitting on."

"Are you still harping on that, Jed? That was settled years ago. My Lord, give it up!"

"Why are you here, Jessica? What do you want?" Jed eyed Jessie with great caution. He knew why she'd come back and he would give her warning that he was on to her."Oh yeah, I do know why you're here. Your time's almost up, and you figure I'll bulldoze this damned old house."

Jessie shook her head in wonder. What was he talking about? Leaning down to find a skillet in a lower cabinet, she remembered. On the tenth of next month, it would be five years since she'd left this house, voiding her rights to the house. If he thought that old house ruling was why she came home, then so be it. That was as good an excuse as any.

Out of the corner of her eye Jessie spotted a diapered imp toddling across the kitchen, arms outstretched toward the voice. She heard her son plop his tiny body down on the floor in frustration and begin to wail. Jed had closed the door before Danny could get close to him.

Well, what could she expect? She knew he didn't want her back and he certainly didn't want her child.

It seemed as though he'd just fallen asleep when Jed heard the car door slam followed by the sound of a car barreling down his lane. She was leaving.

Quickly, he crossed over to his window and watched as the yellow car grew smaller in the moonlight traveling the distance of his long driveway to the main county road. She had left as fast as she'd arrived, and he knew he would have his normal life again. Settling back into the comfort of the bed they once shared, he felt a hollow helplessness engulf his being, a drowning in a world of despair and pain, an aching loneliness for only one woman. This was his norm since she'd left him.

At about five that morning, Jed gave up and got out of the bed. He'd done no more than toss and turn since he'd watched her leave him this last time, and he knew staying in bed was just prolonging his pain. Dressing quickly, he walked through the various rooms, through the dining hall, and into the modern kitchen. He nodded to his rotund cook, as he poured himself a cup of coffee and went to stare out the tall kitchen window, the warm colors of the Indian blanket flowers reminding him of the bleakness that settled about his heart.

Next year he was going to plow all those old weeds under, he decided, but that's what he'd told himself every year since she left him. She had always loved those silly weeds. She said it delighted her to welcome the little purple, red, and yellow daisy-like flowers every spring. They were hardy and tough, needed no upkeep, survived in the worst possible soil, and yet they spread their warmth across the land like their namesake, Indian Blanket. The only time he could remember that the Indian blanket hadn't bloomed was the year Evan died, but then he didn't remember much about that year. Or maybe he just didn't want to remember that awful year.

As Jed thought about that time so long ago, he remembered the deep sorrow, the incredible loss when their son died, and later the searing pain when she left him. She had brought back all those old memories. Now she was doing it again, leaving him just like before. Ready to start ranting to Simon about her nerve in coming home, to Jed's amazement, he spotted the little yellow car as it neared the house. The harsh lines in Jed's weathered face softened as the car became larger, eventually stopping and parking by the room where she'd claimed her space. She was back.

As Jessica exited the car, she pulled her sleeping child from his bed in the backseat and hurried into her room. Soon she returned for the supplies she'd bought in town; and as Jed watched, he wondered why she went to town in the middle of the night. Why didn't she wait until daytime when she would have a selection of stores to shop? The only shopping available in the middle of the night was that big monster store. Surely she'd want go to town during the daytime when she could see some of her old friends. Wouldn't she? What was Jessica up to this time?

"Simon?"

"Yeah, Jed?"

"Better set another place for breakfast."

Simon set down the bowl of pancake mix he'd been stirring and hobbled toward the window to see what held Jed's interest.

"Thank God," Simon murmured. "She's back."

"Yep, she's back all right. Oh, and Simon, she's not alone." Jed realized he'd been talking to himself, as he spotted Simon racing his wobbly old legs along the driveway toward Jessie.

When Jessie spotted the gnarly old man hobbling toward her, she dropped her bags and raced toward him throwing her arms around his thickened waist. Since her papa had died, not only had Simon been the household cook, housekeeper, and wrangler when need be, but to her, he had been nursemaid, childhood playmate, and dear friend. He'd always been the one she'd turned to when things went bad, and a lot of bad things had happened in the past. Smiling down on her as he was now, Jessie knew she really was home.

"Well, aren't you a wonder for my tired eyes, sister." Jessie smiled. Simon had called her "sister" as long as she could remember even after she married Jed. Never could she have imagined that it could sound so comforting. Jessie snuggled into his familiar girth as he patted her back lovingly. "It's been too long, sister. You should never have left here in the first place."

"I had to leave, Simon. You know that."

"And what did it accomplish, sister? He's been miserable every day of his life, and you don't look all that happy." Simon eyed her carefully. "I wrote you. I begged you to come on back home."

Jessie shook her head, picked up her packages and handed two sacks to Simon. Simon's eyes skimmed over the many packages of diapers and he gasped. "Sister, what have you done? Why didn't you to write me letting me know you were having a baby?"

"I didn't actually have him, Simon. Danny's mine. That's all I can tell you for the time being."

Both Simon and Jed had been worried sick over Jessie when she left them, and both of them had sought to protect her in their own way. Jed had a private investigator watching over her, sending him monthly reports about her activities, but Simon knew his family in Colona had their *own* ways, better ways of finding out about people, and nothing had been said about Jessie being pregnant.

"Jessica Maire McClure! What sort of trouble have you gotten yourself into? Whose baby is this? Good heavens, sister! Did you kidnap someone's child?"

Jessie ignored the old man's questions and hurried toward the door of the kitchen where she could hear the first sounds of Danny waking. Simon followed her into the room he'd kept clean all those years, knowing that one day she'd come home where she belonged. He just never expected her to come home with a child, but he knew that after everything which had happened in the past, anything was possible.

That was such a bad time back then, bad for everyone. It destroyed the love Jessie and Jed had found together. Well, it nearly destroyed it. It was still there. He was sure it was still there. They just needed to find it again, like they did before.

CHAPTER 1

Keegan Ranch
Oklahoma, 1961

"You did what?" Jessie gasped in disbelief.

"I told you, Jessie. While you were away at that fancy college learning to be the *perfect lady,* Carl stopped to snicker, then continued, "I sold those pitiful acres to McClure. He's been after this ranch for years."

"That's a bald-face lie, Carlino Barone. Jess McClure doesn't want this ranch, but I do! My house sits on that land.

Carl grinned at his stepsister. "Well, sister dear, I guess you've got a bit of a problem. You own a house with no land to set it on. When my father died, he left all this land to me!"

"Yes, and when my papa died the house legally became mine. Papa put the transfer for this house in his will right after I was born."

Carl Barone dusted a piece of lint off the shoulder of his cheap sports jacket. He had come of age last month, and it was way past time to sell this sorry little ranch. He was no rancher, never could stand the smell of cows, and the land wasn't worth a piddling damn. It was dried up and dead; nothing would grow. Let that sucker, McClure, deal with it. It was his headache now. So was Jessie.

"Carl, you're my brother for God's sake. Don't force me from my home!"

"Stepbrother, dear heart. I'm your stepbrother only because my father married your mother. There has never been any love between us and don't try and say there was, Jessie."

"Please Carl, I love my home. What will I do if you sell it?"

Oh yeah! What was Jessie to do? He didn't really give a damn. She could live in her old truck as far as he was concerned. Carl grinned at that thought.

"Well, Jessie, you can always fight McClure for this damned old pile of stones, and that's all it is, Jessie. Damn, girl! It doesn't even look like a real house."

"Carl, I've explained the history of this house to you many times. My family ancestors settled here before Oklahoma became a state. In fact, papa's room housed their entire family until they prospered and were able to...."

Carl interrupted Jessie, sick of hearing the same old story. "Yeah, and I told you how stupid it was of them to add on the rooms with half the rooms made of different colored stones. Hell, it looks like an old flophouse motel!"

"My ancestors were workers, Carl. They didn't have the time to search for the perfect stones to build another room. It was a matter of using what was available."

"Well Jessie, all I can say is your family sure had taste for shit!"

Jessie couldn't believe her ears. Was this the same boy she'd tutored every night so he could pass his classes? Was this the same boy she'd insisted was clean when he went to school?   Well, she tried to make sure he was clean, but he looked dirty even when he got out of the bathtub. His neck was always shaded and grimy, his black hair was greasy and messy, and he *wore* dirt under his fingernails. Still, she had tried to take care of him. No one else wanted him.

When Jessie was fourteen years old, her mama had married Carl's father, Rico Barone, in Boston while she was on a trip to visit her wealthy family. Shortly after that, Rico and his eight-year-old son came to live with them on their broken-down ranch. It was obvious Rico was shocked when he saw the place, and Jessie could only imagine what sort of story Mama had fed Rico. It seemed he thought they were wealthy ranchers, but the truth was that they were as poor as church mice. When her mama married Rico, she thought Rico had money and he was the answer to their problems. He wasn't. He was as poor as they were.

After he got over the initial shock of the run-down ranch, he discovered the small amount of life insurance money her mama had left. The two of them raced through it like the money would last forever, traveling constantly, leaving the children in the hands of anyone who would put up with them. *Thank heavens for Simon.*

Two years later her mama and Rico were killed in an auto accident, and Jessie was left to turn her spoiled brat stepbrother into a decent person. It was a lost cause and never more obvious than it was right now. "Jess McClure has never shown any interest in this land." Jessie said. "Besides, this is *my* home."

Carl smirked as he watched the sweat break out on Jessie's anxious, unusually pale face. She wasn't as sure of herself as she usually was. "Do you suppose that will count for anything when McClure takes possession next week?"

Jessie gasped. "Next week? My God, Carl! Jess McClure doesn't want to move here. He has a fine home on his own ranch."

Carl openly laughed. He was enjoying watching Jessie squirm. Her old man had left a fat college fund for Jessie's education. He hadn't been left a damn thing from his father but that lousy ranch, and even that was a quirk of fate. What a joke on her when he sold it without her knowing one damn thing about it. Carl snickered again. "Yeah, McClure does have a nice home, and that's why he plans to bulldoze your house, Jessie. Jed McClure sure as hell doesn't need this old dump."

Jessie couldn't believe what Carl was saying. She thought she had heard him wrong. "Jed McClure? Are you talking about Jess McClure?"

"Oh, he goes by Jed McClure now. Guess someone said he had a sissy name so he changed it. Didn't want people to think he was a faggot."

Jessie thought about that for a moment. Jess McClure was a pest when they were kids. He was a nuisance, a tease, but no one could ever say he wasn't the epitome of a rough and rugged young boy.

Grabbing her truck keys from the hallway table, Jessie started out of the door leaving Carl laughing behind her. She knew that Jess McClure wouldn't do this to her if he understood that the house was *her* house. It was all she had left of papa. As ornery as he'd been when they were kids, he had always been a kind, considerate boy. Surely, he'd understand what the house meant to her.

Climbing up into her old truck, Jessie turned the key, and started down the long lane away from her home. Recalling the torment Jess McClure inflected on her when they were kids riding home on the school bus, Jessie tugged unconsciously at her hair. It all started when she was around ten and he was twelve. She remembered their ages because it started before Papa died. She had complained to Papa about Jess, but he just laughed and said Jess McClure was sweet on her and she should be flattered. She wasn't. He drove her crazy.

No matter where she sat on the bus, Jess would manage to sit behind her. Sometimes he'd ask other kids to change seats with him so he could sit behind her. Then the torture would begin.

He would play with her hair.

If she wore it in a pony tail, he'd twirl it around his fingers. If she wore it hanging down her back, he'd slip his fingers around the seat and stroke it. He never hurt her, but it was annoying. He was annoying! He had no business touching her hair and she told him so, but he wouldn't stop. Then one wet spring morning about two years later, everything changed.

The two of them had been waiting for the school bus at the tin lean-to shelter someone had built for the kids to keep dry during bad weather. It was an unusually rainy season that year, and all sorts of nasty, squiggly creatures erupted from the ground. While she and Jess waited together, she discovered to her horror that Jess McClure had to examine every single one of those gross, slithery creatures.

"Hey, look at this, girl." he said as he approached her with a creepy red worm slithering around his hand.

"Get that thing away from me, Jess McClure! I swear I'll hit you with my book bag if you come any closer to me," Jessie gasped, holding her bag in front of her to warn him away.

The book bag threat didn't deter him as he unconsciously moved toward her, head down, examining the fine worm. "That's stupid, girl. This here's a red worm, sort of unusual around these parts. Folks pay good money for these worms. Bet I could get rich if I dug me up a bunch of these babies and sold them to folks to use in their compost piles. Take a good look at him, girl. You'll see...."

Jessie had enough of him and his worm and flung her bag at him. When the book bag hit him in the chest, he flung his hands up and the worm went flying through the air landing in her long dark hair.

"Jess McClure! Get that thing off of me!" she screamed, feeling the slimy worm slithering down her neck onto her blue sweater. As she grabbed the shoulder of her sweater to shake the worm off, it fell inside her sweater. She was still screaming bloody murder as Jess raced toward her. The next thing she knew, Jess had his hand down inside her sweater searching for the worm. As Jess pulled the worm out of her sweater, she noticed his face was redder than the red worm.

He didn't say a word after that, just stomped away from her and put the worm outside the shelter. He stayed outside of the shelter, too, even though it was pouring down rain. Jessie knew it was an accident and told him he could come back inside the shelter, but he wouldn't. After that day he avoided her and never again sat behind her again on

4

the bus, but for some reason that she could never understand, she had missed him.

Then, several months after her papa died, Jessie remembered seeing Jess again. He was strolling up the long lane toward her house, carrying a bouquet of Indian blanket flowers. She knew he'd brought them for her and was delighted when she saw him coming. It had been a long, sad, lonely summer.

Pulling the old Reo truck to a stop, Jessie pulled out onto the main road that led toward the McClure Ranch. Once again her mind drifted back to the one and only time Jess McClure had come near the Keegan ranch. It had been a day just like today, Jessie noted. It had started out as one of those days when the early morning frost iced over the windows, but by afternoon the sun burst through with such a heated fury that it confused animals, birds, and man alike.

Mama had not bothered to get dressed again that day and was still wearing that shiny black and red kimono with the wrap-around tie that she wore every day. No one ever came to visit them anymore, so Mama said there was no reason to get dressed. The neighbors used to come. They had tried to help after Papa died, but Mama hated Oklahoma and its docile people, and was so rude to them that everyone gave up trying to help them. Jessie didn't blame them.

Now, here came Jess McClure strolling up the lane, as though he had no clue about Mama. Mama scowled out the window and Jessie hoped she could spare him. "I'll go see what he wants, Mama," Jessie said as she hurried toward the door.

"Oh no, you won't, Jessica! I don't want that boy to get any ideas he's welcome here, because he's not! I've got big plans for you, child! And that does not include any ignorant Oklahoma redneck!" Watching the lanky blonde boy walking the lane to their house, Mama's lips and jaw twitched something awful and Jessie knew what was going to happen. She felt so sorry for poor Jess.

Suddenly, there was a lot of pounding on the front door, and Mama swung open the door and stepped outside. Jessie couldn't hear what was happening, but from the window she could see how humiliated Jess looked after Mama got through with him, his face turning from a big grin to a somber scowl. Then he turned and left, racing away from their home, pitching his bouquet of Indian Blanket flowers on to their dusty lane as he fled.

Mama slammed the door and looked at her with a satisfied look on her face as she stomped toward her own bedroom.

5

"I'm going down to papa's room," Jessie called after her mother, but there was no answer. Jessie hurried from the house but could no longer see any sign of Jess McClure. She felt terrible about how Mama had treated poor Jess, and had hoped to catch him when she cut across the field to explain that she really appreciated him coming, but he was gone. All that was left was his wilting bouquet of the Indian Blanket flowers.

Squatting down on the dusty lane, Jessie picked up every one of those flowers, snuggled them to her bosom, and raced back to papa's room. Inside the cool cave-like room, she found a glass mason jar, put some water in it and tried to revive the dying flowers. They died anyway, so she pressed them inside a huge book on agriculture. She never had thrown them away, but Jess had never come near her house or her again.

As summer passed and school started in the fall, Jess completely ignored her, and she realized more and more how she had come to miss his attentions. His playing with her hair didn't seem to be such a burden after all, especially when the big bully boys got on the bus with their threatening glares. They never did anything to her while Jess had been sitting behind her, but she knew that without him, it was just a matter of time. Then, it happened.

Jess was about sixteen and she had just turned fourteen when Johnny Fackler, the biggest bully of them all, sat his big body down next to her on the school bus. She was scared to death of him and he knew it, and he loved it. Even though she inched as far away from him as possible, he kept pushing his legs farther apart to touch her. Then he leaned over and wrapped his arm around her shoulders covering her as he ran his hand up under her skirt. She was mortified but she knew that if she screamed, he'd deny he touched her, and she'd look like a fool. So she just sat there helpless against the big galoot.

"Get your hands off her, Fackler!" she heard Jess say from behind them.

Johnny Fackler removed his hand and twisted around to see who was there. "Kiss my ass, McClure! She's not your girl! I can do whatever I want with her." That was the last thing Johnny said before he was dragged out of the seat and tossed down the aisle.

"What's going on back there?" the bus driver yelled.

"Nothing, Mr. Reeves." Jess answered. "Fackler and I were just changing seats."

6

From that day on, Jessie considered Jess McClure to be her hero, and developed a horrible crush on him. He never did sit by her again, but then neither did Johnny Fackler.

As her mind wandered back to her younger days, Jessie recalled the time she'd run smack dab into Jess McClure in high school. She was an awkward sophomore with rounded hips and full breasts that embarrassed her to death. He was a gangly senior, all arms and legs with a questionable patch of blonde peach fuzz under his chin.

Both of them had been racing to class in opposite directions when someone called the name "Jess" and both turned to answer. In the confusion they knocked one another to the ground, him toppling on top of her. As he lay sprawled all over her, he stared down at her as though he'd never seen a girl before. She shoved at him to get off of her, but he didn't move. Not right away. After staring at her for a moment, he picked himself up, pulled her up with a mighty lunge and muttered something about being sorry. Without a second glance he raced off, not once looking back at her.

The last time she'd seen Jess was when his mother died, some years ago. When he came home for the funeral, he was no longer that long, gangly boy from high school. He had developed into a strapping young man, and much to her horror, she realized her girlish crush was still there. What was he like now, she wondered, as she geared down on the aging red Reo truck, her only means of transportation since she'd come home from school. As she pulled into the prosperity of the McClure ranch, she noted that it certainly was a different scene from her decrepit place. While the McClure ranch was thriving with cattle, wheat, beans, and alfalfa, the Keegan ranch was barren. Why?

As long as she could remember, Jessie had wanted to be a part of the activities of the Keegan ranch. She wanted to learn how to manage the crops, the cattle, and the ranch, but her mother had other ideas. "Don't you ever make the mistake I made, Jessica. I thought I cared for your father when I agreed to marry him, but living this crude lifestyle cured me quickly of those foolish notions! Marry a man for his money," Mama said. "You don't need to worry about the hard life of a ranch. Being a beautiful lady and charming a man for his money is all you need to worry about."

It seemed Mama would never stop preaching about money and men with money. After Papa died that's all she heard; that, and what a failure she was in her mother's attempts to make her into a lady, like her. "I have tried to teach you to be a lady, Jessica, a real lady like me, but you have failed my efforts! You have your father's penchant toward foul language which is totally unacceptable in a lady; you hang around your father's smelly old barn which no real lady would dare enter; and you dress in those awful cowboy boots which a lady would never be caught dead wearing! But then, what can I expect when your father promised me luxury and refinement if I married him, and he turned out to be no more than a lowly Irish Mick? And his friends! A black Nigra and an Italian wop! No wonder I can't train you properly! I have tried so hard to make you into a lady like me, Jessica, but to my great sorrow you have failed me. Fortunately for you, I have not given up on you. Not yet!

"I need to get you away from this horrible ranch, Jessica; away from these people and their crude influence. You need culture and polish. That is something the neighbors around this horrible old ranch certainly can't offer with their country barbeques and square dances. You need the finishing touch that only a fine ladies school can offer. Then you can have any man you want, a man with a high standing and lots of money." Against her better judgment, Devon's Finishing School for Young Ladies had been her education.

Now, here she was. She knew how to set a table for a seven-course meal, what wine to serve with what food, how to make a perfect soufflé and a more perfect meringue. She knew how to crochet doilies and tat delicate lace around fine hankies. She knew how to dress down for a game of golf and how to dress up for a formal evening. She knew what was in good taste and what was vulgar. She knew everything she didn't need or want to know, but the one thing she needed and didn't know was how to revive a dying, dead ranch?

Jessie pulled her truck in front of the well-kept garage that was adjacent to an even better kept house. The yard was neatly mowed, the bushes trimmed, and not one blade of grass lined the stone walkway to the two story house. The paint on the house was satiny white and the black trim provided a neat, tended appearance.

Far off in the distance, Jessie could see a big red tractor moving toward her, kicking up dirt as the blades of the cultivator worked the rich black earth. It had to be Jess, she decided, as she put her arms over her head and waved to him. She didn't see him wave back, but she knew he'd see her when he got close to the house, and that little thought gave her heart a slight flutter. She never had understood why he never came back to see her after Papa died. Had Mama's words

8

been so cruel to Jess that he was afraid to come near her? Maybe, she thought. Mama could be vicious when she set her mind to it, and she had definitely been in a vicious mood the day Jess McClure came to call.

Listening to the roar of the big tractor as it neared the house, Jessie noticed that the rows of green soybeans were healthy, neat, and straight without a weed to mar the growth. Looking past the cultivated bean crop, healthy fields of tall golden wheat flourished, so Jessie climbed up the fence to have a better look.

"Pretty, isn't it?" A deep male voice broke into Jessie's thoughts as she whirled away from the fence, catching her boot in one of the rails. Jed grabbed at Jessie so she didn't fall and Jessie grabbed at the air latching on to his shoulders.

"You okay?" Jed McClure asked as he helped Jessie gain her stance.

"Yes. Yes, I'm fine." Jessie was so flustered she forgot she was still hanging onto his shoulders.

Thinking she was glad to see him after such a long time, Jed pulled her close to him and grinned, straight white teeth gleaming through a wealth of dirty golden tan. "Did you come over here to fool around with me, Jessie? I'm busy right now, but I can come over to your house later on, and we can fool around all you want."

Trying to gain some composure Jessie pushed Jed away, trying to remember her practiced speech about her ranch. Fumbling for words, she watched as he shoved a lock of straight blonde hair under his mangled cowboy hat. The hat was pinched low in the front, rolled at the sides, and had been a tobacco color at one time. As he stood towering over her, his skin sweaty and golden from the early spring warmth, Jessie found herself so flustered her brain turned to mush. "Yes, uh, what did you say? I mean....no! No, I didn't come here to fool around with you."

Beaming a big smile, Jed moved closer placing his big hands around her waist. "If you didn't come here to fool around now, do you want me to come over later so we can fool around then?"

"I did not come here to *fool around* and I do not want to *fool around* later!" Jessie backed away from Jed again, blushing scarlet red, trying to ignore his muscled arms bursting from the torn off sleeves of his faded chambray shirt. "I, uh....I came here to discuss my ranch."

Jed slipped his hat down over his forehead and studied her. Her skin was flawless like fine porcelain, but over her aristocratic nose was

9

a smidgen of tiny freckles, and just above her full lips were minute beads of sweat. Her hair was worked into a dark auburn bun held severely at the nape of her neck by a heavy gold clasp. Regardless of that heavy clasp, Jed noticed numerous strands of dark hair had escaped down her back giving her an unruly, wanton look. She wore a yellow ruffled blouse, tucked into a pair of those new toreador pants all the girls were wearing. They were a lettuce-green color, and fit her little backside like a glove. Yeah, Jed thought, Jessie Keegan was as pretty as ever, prettier, if possible; she was sexy as hell, just like he dreamed she would be.

Expecting her to come and see him for some time, Jed wondered what took her so long to come and thank him. He had thought she'd be grateful to him for saving her ranch, but she sure didn't look very grateful. It didn't matter though. He was just glad to see her after such a long time.

"Jess," Jessie started to say, but Jed interrupted her.

"I don't go by Jess anymore, Jessie. It's Jed. That's what I'm called now." He didn't tell her that the day they collided in high school was the day he decided to change his name. With his name being Jess McClure, how could he marry Jessie? Jess and Jessie McClure? That just didn't sound right. Besides, her mama would laugh herself silly about their names being the same, just like she did when he went to see Jessie after her papa died.

That woman truly shamed him back then. She had made him understand he wasn't good enough for Jessie, but that didn't stop him in his life's plan to marry Jessie. He had ribbons from his valor in Korea, almost a college degree, and his own ranch was doing well. Surely, if Jessie's mother had been alive, she would approve of him now. Surely, she'd see him other than she'd seen him then, "Jess Hayseed, a useless piece of dirt".

"All right then, *Jed*, I found out today that you will take over the land next week that my brother, my *step-brother* Carl, sold you. I had no idea you would move so swiftly, and frankly, I'm not ready to turn over possession of my papa's land to a stranger."

"I'm no stranger, Jessie. My family has lived here as long as yours."

"Look, Jed, I didn't come here to argue genealogy with you for heaven's sake! I came here to tell you that I will not allow you to take my papa's land!"

Too late, Jessie, you should have known as soon as that brother, *step-brother* of yours, got legal age, he'd dump that place as fast as he could." Jed smiled hoping she'd let the whole thing drop without too much fuss. Didn't she realize he'd saved the ranch for her, for them, for when they were married? He didn't want to insult her by mentioning the foreclosure on her place. Why couldn't she just let it drop?

Jessie wasn't about to let it drop. "Good grief! You have a grand ranch. What in the world do you want with mine?"

"It's your step-brother's."

"What?"

"It's your step-brother's land and it's his right to sell if he wants. I want to buy it, so it's all settled."

"No, it's not all settled! For one thing, that was my papa's land and he left it to my mama!"

"And your mother died shortly before your step-father died, Jessie. Because your mama had no will, the land went to her surviving spouse, and even though he only survived her by a few days, the land was passed on to his son. Sorry, Jessie, but that's the way it is."

Humiliated beyond words, Jessie felt ferocious tears battling in her eyes that made her angry enough to continue. What happened to the kind young man she'd had such a crush on years ago. Didn't he have any feeling for her pain? "I can come up with the money, Jed! Just give me a few months and I'll buy my *step-brother*, oh hell, Carl.... I'll buy out Carl."

Realizing that Jessie wouldn't quit until he told her the truth about her ranch, Jed tried to speak with compassion. He understood her pain, but it was just a temporary problem. When they were married the ranch would be hers again, only it would be his ranch, too. "Jessie, it's not about just paying off Carl. I found out the bank was ready to foreclose on the place when I jumped in and bought it, so outsiders couldn't grab the place." Jed thought that warning her about the possible sale to outsiders would force her to realize what he'd done for her. It didn't.

Nearly snorting in anger, Jessie thought about Jed's words. The bank had never contacted her that the ranch was in foreclosure, and now she understood why. They had notified Carl. Had she known, she would have tried to stop it, to save it somehow, but now Jed McClure had bought it and all was lost. Jessie hated begging like a dog, but what else could she do but beg? "Jed, will you just give me two months? One month! Please, Jed, I'll come up with the money! Please, don't take my ranch from me. Please!"

Jed felt so sorry for Jessie. He wanted to pull her into his arms and tell her that in time, everything would be all right, but Jessie had worked herself into such a state he decided he'd better not push her. "I'm sorry, Jessie," was his only answer.

It was obvious to Jessie that this Jed McClure was a completely different man than the Jess McClure who had watched over her when they were kids. Here was a hard, mean, land grabber; one that would stop at nothing until he got what he wanted and obviously he wanted her land. Well, maybe he could steal her land away from her, but he could not steal her house. Not until she signed the papers and she had not done so, nor would she ever sell her house. Jessie put her hands on her hips and faced Jed squarely. "What about my house?"

"What about the house? It's part of the property, Jessie."

"It is not! The house and the property are separate, Jed McClure. My papa left that house to me upon his death!"

Jed pulled his dirty hat from his head and wiped his dripping forehead with his arm causing another dirty smear across his face. He was so deep in thought that he didn't realize it and wouldn't have cared anyway. When he bought Jessie's ranch, the contract didn't say anything about that old pile of rocks they called a house. He figured he'd bulldoze the whole thing and have several more acres to work. Jessie would live in his nice home with him after they were married. That's what he'd planned from the very beginning. Now he wondered if Jessie was just worried about having a place to live, so he came up with an immediate solution. "Okay, Jessie, I've got an idea. Why don't you marry me and you can live with me over here at the big house?"

Jessie couldn't believe this Jess....Jed McClure. The heat she'd felt in his touch a few minutes before was replaced by scorching anger at his conclusion to her problem. He had stolen her land, and now he wanted her to marry him? "Are you out of your mind? I'd sleep on the ground before I would ever consider marrying you!"

She needed time to accept his plan, Jed decided. He had the time. He could wait for her to accept it. "Jessie, listen to me. If you need a place to stay, you can stay here at my house. I won't bother you here, I promise. You can even rent from me if you want, but sweetie, your house has got to go."

12

Glowering openly at Jed, Jessie let him know just how furious she was. "Over my dead body, Jed McClure! And don't you ever call me 'sweetie' again, you arrogant ass! I'm not your sweetie, nor anyone else's sweetie! You got that Mr. Jed McClure?"

Tromping across Jed McClure's perfect yard toward her dusty truck, Jessie wondered how she could possibly have thought he would care that she loved her old house. He didn't give a hoot about her or her house. He couldn't wait to bulldoze the place! He'd said he was going to do it and she knew he would.

As Jessie crawled up into the tall truck she spotted Jed McClure watching her as though he were planning some big scheme against her. That's when she knew that if ever she needed help, it was now. He really was a snake in the grass, and somehow she had to find a way to fight him before she became his victim. Jed McClure was not taking her home away from her. *This was not over, not by a long shot!*

Jed watched his future wife as she jumped in her old truck. With as much power as the aging Reo could muster, it trudged out of his driveway and down the lane away from his house. He realized that his plan was not going to be as easy as he'd thought; but come hell or high water, he'd have Jessie as his wife.

Walking toward his big red tractor, Jed remembered back to years ago when he was a boy of fourteen and his determination to get rich selling red worms. Smiling to himself, he remembered Jessie Keegan's small warm breast he'd groped when he retrieved the ornery worm from under her blue sweater. That event haunted him for years. After that fateful happening, he became obsessed with breasts. He thought about her breasts every morning before he got out of bed, every day as he watched her from a safe distance on the school bus, and every night....all night. And then the day would start all over again.

Someday he would marry Jessie Keegan, he decided in his fourteen year old perception of life. When they got married, he would touch her breasts every day except she wouldn't scream and yell at him like she did at the bus stop. She'd be real nice to him, because he knew that's what happened between married folks. Tommy Sears had told him that. Tommy had a married brother who knew all about breasts and stuff like that.

Jed remembered when he turned fifteen years old, and as usual was thinking about Jessie's breasts as he walked the dried up creek bed that ran the length of his father's ranch and the adjacent Keegan ranch.

He was searching for Indian arrow heads, knowing he could sell them to the small Indian museum in Tahchee. They'd sell them to the tourists for twice as much as they'd give him, but that didn't bother him. At least he'd have some money in his pocket.

As he walked with his head down searching for the arrows, he saw something so unusual for his part of the county that he had to stop and dig down around it to examine it. To his amazement he found a *rose rock*, a perfect example, and he was thrilled. No fine sculptor could ever have carved a rose as perfect as the one he held in his hand.

The little rose-like petals were formed from circular plates of barite crystals and the dusty-rose color was from the sand where in its iron content gave it the unusual color. He knew this spectacular specimen would bring him more money than all the arrows he could find that day, and he couldn't wait to go into town and find out how much he'd make for his day's work. Then he decided that maybe he could find more rose rocks and he could become rich. As he prowled the rocky creek bottom, he wondered what he would do with all his money. Then he remembered there was a good looking pocket knife that had caught his eye at Skoll's Hardware the last time he was in Tahchee.

The Kamp King knife cost $1.25 and he knew that was an awful lot to spend, but it came with a leather pouch, had a leather punch tool, a bottle opener with a screwdriver, and even had a can opener. That knife would come in handy when he was out camping, searching for stuff he could sell. It was an investment he told himself, as he walked along carefully scrutinizing the dried creek bank that could become a raging river with a sudden downpour of rain.

All day long he searched the creek bottom for rose rocks and arrowheads. He found one more arrowhead, but he never did find another rose rock. The rose rock that he'd carefully carried in his shirt pocket was the only one he knew he would ever find in this part of the state. He decided it had probably washed down from some other county with the spring rains. After scrutinizing it carefully, he was amazed that the rose rock had maintained its perfect shape as turbulent as the spring rains had been. However, it had survived completely intact.

It was a special rock of that he was certain. As he thought about that lone rose rock, he realized that it was worth more than money to him. It deserved to be given to a special person. At first he thought about giving it to his mom, but he knew she had lots of pretty things. She didn't need it. Jess's mind immediately focused on the girl of his dreams. It had been a year since the incident with the worm. He was fifteen years old now, a man. No longer was he a kid like that day with the worm and Jessie's breasts. After that day, he gave up the worm business, but he never did give up thinking about breasts.

As he walked toward his home, he remembered that Jessie's father had died several months before, and he had never once ventured over to her house to tell her how sorry he was. He didn't know why he hadn't gone to see her, but he was pretty sure he'd forget and stare at her breasts and she'd get angry with him. But knowing how sad he'd be if anything happened to his folks, he decided that maybe the rose rock would help Jessie feel better.

By the time he had walked all the way to Jessie's house, he was hot, sweaty, and his body odor was questionable; but he knew this was something he had to do, and he had to do it without staring at her breasts. He would knock on the door; offer his condolences like a real gentleman, and leave. And if she put her arms around him to thank him, he would pretend he didn't feel her breasts. That's the way a gentleman would act. He'd watched Sheriff Matt Dillon and Miss Kitty of Gunsmoke on TV every Saturday night, and she sure showed a lot of her breasts, but never, not once had he seen Sheriff Dillon stare at Miss Kitty's breasts. But he had stared plenty, while his folks were at the neighbors.

As he walked along the over-grown lane to Jessie's house, he had run into a mass of purple and red flowers with tips of yellow growing alongside the lane. Someone had told him the flowers were called Indian Blanket and they were just a weed, but he didn't care. They were pretty. He decided he'd stop and pick a few for Jessie to go along with the rose rock. She would like that.

It was truly a funny-looking house Jessie lived in, Jess thought as he walked up the long lane. It looked like a bunch of little houses all put together. It was hard to tell which door you were supposed to use, but Jess picked one door and gave it a fierce knock, the rose rock wrapped in one of his mother's hair nets. The hair net was pretty. It was frilly and black. It smelled good.

After pounding on the door for some time, Jessie's mother came to the door. "What do you want!" she screamed at him.

"Sorry to bother you, Mrs. Keegan." Jess tried to make his voice sound deeper because that's what guys did when they were about

15

serious business. "I was wondering if Jessie was home." Jess could feel the rock burning in his shirt pocket as he tried not to look at Jessie Keegan's mother's breast.

Mrs. Keegan stared at him for what seemed like hours. Sweat poured down his face, and under his arms the odor grew stouter. "You're that McClure boy, aren't you?"

Jess wiped the sweat from his face and tried to push back the wet hunk of hair that always fell down in his face. It did no good. He just kept sweating and stinking, and the hair fell back in his face.

Stepping outside the house and onto the porch, Mrs. Keegan circled him as though he were a side of rank beef. After finishing her inspection of him, she faced him. She wore some sort of a shiny red and black kimono, tied at the waist, and Jess was certain she must be naked under that shiny kimono. Of course, every woman he saw anymore, he pictured them naked. He just couldn't seem to help it.

Mrs. Keegan's snappish voice brought him out of his personal thoughts. "What do you want with Jessie, young man?"

"My name's Jess McClure, Ma'am."

"Jess McClure? You mean like in my daughter's name, Jessie?"

"Yes, Ma'am."

Laughing hysterically, Mrs. Keegan didn't seem to be able stop. Finally, as she wiped the tears from her eyes, she got control of her chaotic laughter. "So now it starts. All you white trash will start sniffing around my daughter like a bunch of sorry dogs. Isn't that right, Jess Hayseed?"

"Ma'am?" Jess didn't know whether she was calling him Jess Hayseed to be funny or whether she had forgotten his name, so he reminded her. "No, ma'am. My name is Jess McClure and I have come to see Jessie."

Mrs. Keegan's face was covered with a scowl so ugly that it was hard to be sure she was the same beautiful woman he'd seen last year in Tahchee, but he knew it had to be her. Jessie had been with her, and besides Jessie looked just like her, except Jessie had smaller breasts.

"No, Mr. Jess Hayseed! You will not see my daughter! Not today, not tomorrow, and not next year! Never! Never will you see my daughter, you smelly, cow poking piece of dirt! My daughter is a lady and I have plans for her, and you and your kind will never get near my Jessica. You're not good enough to wipe the bottoms of her feet, you ignorant hayseed. Now get off my property and don't you ever come back. Jessica's too good for the likes of you or any of the low-life, ignorant ranchers around here. Do you understand me, Jess Hayseed McClure? Do you!"

Jess backed away from the porch and the raging woman. Spotting an old brass poker beside the door, he was certain if she'd seen it, she would have beaten him with it. "Yes, ma'am, I'm going."

"And take those damn weeds with you," Mrs. Keegan shouted as she slammed the door.

"Yes, ma'am," he murmured as he hurried back down the long driveway, away from that crazy woman and the strange rock home of Jessie Keegan.

When he was out of sight of Mrs. Keegan, he tossed the flowers into the dirt and walked slower, the rose rock still nestled safely in the black hair net inside his shirt pocket.

Chapter 2

Jessie roared her tired old Reo past the small town of Tahchee, Oklahoma, and over the county line into Tulsa. One of her friends from school, Ginny Kook, had a much older brother who was an attorney in Tulsa, and Jessie knew that surely he would help her with her battle with Jed McClure over her house. At their college graduation last month, both she and Ginny could see he had an interest in her. With that thought in her head, she was certain he wouldn't expect her to pay for his help. She just hoped he wouldn't expect her to pay in other ways. Edward Kook seemed to be a real gentleman: but if he wasn't, she'd set him straight on what he could or couldn't expect from her. She'd let him date her for awhile, and then she'd let him down easily.

Knowing her dirty old truck was severely out of place with all the Cadillacs, Jaguars, and autos so fine she couldn't identify most of them, Jessie held her head high and roared through the private parking lot of Kook, Kook, and Kook, Attorneys at Law. Finding an empty parking place, Jessie eased her big red Reo in next to a silver Rolls Royce and felt a tinge of sorrow over her sorry lot. Today was not the day to feel sorry for her losses, she told herself. Today, she needed to have all her wits about her and present her situation with as much dignity and decorum as she could possibly muster. She'd related her problem to Edward earlier that week on the phone and now they would work on her solutions. She could do this. She had to.

Slipping her feet out of her dirty cowboy boots and into a pair of what Miss Eleanor would have called "divine navy blue stilettos", Jessie slid out of the tall truck and patted down her short mauve and blue box jacket that matched her slender skirt. Glancing in the truck's side mirror she checked her matching pillbox hat and was delighted to see that it hadn't toppled from her bubble of dark hair as she had half expected it to do. The hairdo was supposed to look like Katherine Hepburn's in *Breakfast at Tiffany's*, but somehow Jessie didn't think hers looked so hot. Something was wrong with it: too high, off center, or something weird.

Leaning back slightly she tried to check her nylon seams but knew that was hopeless. They were straight when she left home. If they stayed half-way straight while that itchy garter belt was driving her crazy, then that was the best she could hope for. She removed her white gloves from the frayed bench seat and slid the short gloves onto her sweating palms, no easy trick in the miserable spring heat.

Feeling the sweat trickle down her dark eyebrows, Jessie hurried into the impressive brick building. Early that morning she had made up her face with thick pancake makeup, the brand recommended by Miss Eleanor. She dabbed on several shades of eye shadow, applied heavy black eyeliner, carefully glued the false eyelashes to her eyelids as instructed, perfumed and powdered her body, glossed her lips with white lipstick, and carefully tucked and teased her heavy dark hair into the Katherine Hepburn upsweep. Groaning under the weight of hairpins and hairspray, she sincerely hoped she didn't melt before she could get her business settled.

As the stylish blonde secretary ushered Jessie into the rich wood interior offices of Edward Kook, she heard the distinct sound of two male voices coming from inside the office. "Is Mr. Kook busy?" Jessie asked. "I could have sworn our appointment was for two o'clock."

The lady smiled but didn't answer as she knocked on the private door and then opened it. "Miss Keegan is here, Mr. Kook."

"Yes, yes. Send her in, Miss Dixon. Well, well, Miss Keegan. How wonderful to see you again so soon after your graduation. How have you been, my dear girl?"

Jessie couldn't answer; her eyes were on the man seated in the chair nearest the wall. He was dressed in a soft gray western-cut suit, a black shirt and a dark silver bolo clasp with a bright silver string tie. In the overhead lights, his golden hair shimmered like spun taffy and as usual, one straight shuck hung carelessly down over his forehead.

Standing tall and proud as Jessie entered the room, Jed watched as Edward Kook hurried around his desk to present a kiss on Jessie's cheek and wished he could lay a big smooch on her himself, but then he spotted her lips covered in some sort of chalky-white crap. And her face! What sort of goop did Jessie have all over her face, Jed wondered, and how did she grow her eyelashes so long? She sure didn't look like that the last time he saw her. She looked so much better then, in her tight green pants and yellow blouse with that dark hair disheveled in wanton strands down her back.

A small tremor running down his spine, Jed continued to observe his future wife. She must have hurt her foot, he decided, as he watched her struggle across the room in blue shoes with some sort of insane heels. How could any person walk in those shoes? Bringing his gaze up from her shoes, he allowed his eyes to linger on her legs, her hips and on her breasts a tinge longer than could be considered respectable.

He caught himself and continued his gaze up to her heavily made-up face: the darker than dark eyes, the ghostly white lips, and the monstrous beehive hair. He couldn't help but wonder why she'd done herself up like that. To him she looked like a vampire looking for its next feed. As he watched her flutter those bat-like eyelashes at Edward Kook, he noticed that even with the air- conditioning working its magic, sweat was appearing on her brow. If her forehead was wet, he was certain that little spot above her lips was wet, too. Someday, he was going to kiss that moisture away, maybe even ...."

Ed Kook's words to Jessie interrupted Jed's thoughts. "Jessie, I invited Mr. McClure here today so we could save some time. I know how busy everyone is with field work and so on."

Jessie couldn't get her brain around what was happening. She had thought Ed Kook would fall all over himself to see her. Now he was treating her like any regular client, except that he barely looked at her. She had been certain he'd had a crush on her at the graduation ceremony, or had she misinterpreted his attentions as more than they'd actually been. Hadn't she flirted properly? Not long enough? Too long? What happened? She had done everything she'd been taught by Miss Eleanor in her charm class. Jessie sighed in defeat. Maybe that's why Miss Eleanor was an old maid. She reminded herself of Miss Eleanor's insistence that she was not an old maid. She was an 'archaic', a single lady from a good family. In other words she was an old maid.

"Miss Keegan," Jessie jumped as she came out of her silly thoughts. "I found a ruling that's a bit unusual, but it's certainly legal. I have copies for both of you to read so there will be no misunderstanding.

"In short: Jed, you own the land under the house; Miss Keegan, you own the house that sits on top of the land. As long as you have resided at some time in the home for the past five years, which you have done with exception of school, Miss Keegan, Mr. McClure cannot force you from the home."

Jessie smiled. At least McClure couldn't steal her house from her like he'd stolen her land.

Jed wasn't taking the news at all well. "Now, wait just a minute, Kook! I bought the Keegan ranch fair and square. No one said anything about a ruling such as this."

20

Ed Kook was an astute lawyer, a rich man, and a clever one. "Maybe you didn't have a good attorney, Jed. Someone should have told you about this when you signed the contract."

Wiggling uncomfortably in the plush red leather chair, Jed knew what Ed Kook said was the truth. He hadn't bothered to have an attorney read over the contract. He bought the land for back taxes and was so delighted to get it, he hadn't bothered with the details. Now he knew he was going to pay for sure. "So, now I have a house on my property that I can't live in. That makes no sense!"

"Oh, you can live in it, Jed. You just can't make Miss Keegan move out."

Jed came out of his chair. "What the hell did you say?"

Jessie was laughing so hard her eyes began to tear. As she rubbed away the tears, she felt one of the false eyelashes come unglued.

Furious, Jed turned to glare at Jessie and as he did he wondered what was wrong with her? It looked like she had a spider hanging off her eye. He couldn't take his eyes off the strange sight as Edward Kook continued. "Again Jed, you can live in the house with Miss Keegan. You just can't make her move out."

Jed tried not to watch as Jessie fumbled with her eyelid, finally giving up and holding her hand over her eye. Forcing his vision from Jessie, Jed faced Edward Kook, a huge smile covering his face. "Jessie and me, unmarried, and living in the same house together? Now wouldn't that cause a ruckus out in our neck of the woods, Jessie? Yes, it would cause one hell of a scandal." Jessie smiled in agreement still holding her hand over her eye.

Her smile faded quickly as she heard Jed ask, "When can I move in, Kook?"

Jessie came out of her chair forgetting about the eyelash dangling down her wet face cutting webs into her thick pancake makeup. "Damn it, Edward Kook! Whose side are you on, anyway? You're my attorney. I'm paying you to take my side."

Ed Kook wanted to remind Jessie that she hadn't paid him a dime and wasn't likely to do so, but he didn't say anything. He couldn't. He was about to fall off his chair trying not to laugh at Jessie, her eyelash falling down her face, her hat flopping to one side of that monstrous hair-do, and somehow, from somewhere she'd gotten her dainty white gloves smeared with what looked like grease. As she flounced out of the room, it appeared one of her stockings had come loose from her garter and was falling down her leg. As she wobbled on those ridiculous high heels toward the door, she reached down, removed the hose and shoes, leaving his exclusive office barefooted. Then he remembered. Wasn't there one of the girls in his sister's class that hadn't passed that charm school they were required to attend? *Yes, it was Jessie Keegan, of course. Who else could it be? Someday, she would certainly make some man a spunky wife.*

Jed stretched his long legs under the heavy wooden table that had once fed many hungry ranch hands on the Keegan ranch. On top of the table Jed rested his elbow while his other hand twirled his Stetson around his finger. As he twirled the hat faster and faster the hat flew up into the air. With the same hand, he grabbed the hat before it could hit the ground. It was a game he played to dawdle away the time when he was bored, which was almost never. Today he was waiting for Jessie to return from Tulsa, and he was definitely bored; but he was certain the action would begin shortly. All hell would break loose when she came home and found him lazing around her table. Jed broke into a laugh. Wait until she saw his duffle bag sitting on the floor next to him. She'd have a fit. She did.

"What do you think you're doing, coming into my house, sitting at my table? You don't have my permission to be here, so get out!" Jessie's brown eyes turned a devilish black as she confronted Jed. Her arms were filled with brown paper bags and Jed figured she would have bopped him one, but she had to put the groceries in the kitchen first. Then she would come back and bop him.

He grinned. She snarled. After uttering a most unladylike remark, she slammed through the swinging doors that led to the kitchen. As fast as she left, she returned.

"I asked you a question, Jed McClure! What are you doing in my house? You're trespassing." Jessie stood staring at Jed and if looks could kill, Jed knew he'd be dead. He openly grinned as he noted her appearance. She had discarded her blue heels, her hat, jacket, and gloves, and finally her eyes looked normal without those dead spider claws on them. He also noted she'd lost complete control of her hairdo. Between the heat and the wind, no amount of hair spray could secure the toppled mess it had become. Now at last, she looked like *his* Jessie.

"What took you so long, Jessie? You left Kook's office before I did, and I still had time to run by my house and get my stuff." Jed knew she'd blow on that one and she did as he pointed to his duffle bag of clothes and grinned at her.

Jessie left through the door Jed had entered and returned in a heartbeat. In her hand she held a red umbrella with a dangerous looking point on the end. Quickly, Jed started toward her before she could do him some real harm. Jessie stood her ground jabbing at Jed with the long steel point of the dainty umbrella. "Oh no, you don't, mister! You get your filthy bag and your miserable person out of my house and be quick about it!"

Jed put his hands in the air in surrender until he could figure out what to do next. "Jessie, you know what Kook said not two hours ago. He said I could live in this house if I want, and that's exactly what I want, whether you like it or not."

Jessie tried to gain control of her anger. Miss Eleanor said ladies could win more with honey than with vinegar, so she decided to try the honey approach. "What's wrong with your house, Jed? You've got a much nicer place than I do. Heaven's sake," Jessie purred, "why would you want to stay in this old pile of stones when you have such a lovely home barely a mile down the road from here?"

"Five."

"What?"

"Five miles down the road, Jessie. My house is five miles away. That's why I want to stay here. It's too far to drive back and forth every day. I plan on getting this ranch up and running as fast as possible. I don't have time to run back and forth when you've got this house on my property with all these vacant rooms. I'm staying here."

Rolling his malleable hat back and forth in his hand, Jessie could understand why the hat looked like it was a squashed tobacco plant. It probably smelled like one too, she decided as she considered her next move.

"Jed, you know we can't live in this house together. As you said yourself, it would cause a scandal." Jessie batted her real eyelashes coyly.

"If you marry me, there won't be any scandal," was Jed's only reply.

Jessie threw up her hands in disbelief. "Take the damn room at the south end of the house if you insist on staying here, Jed. But I warn you, you're not welcome here!" Jessie didn't bother to tell him that room was the hottest possible spot in the entire house during the summer. A few nights trying to sleep in that misery would certainly cool his ardor for staying at her house. Smiling to herself, Jessie picked up her umbrella and left the room.

Jed wiped the sweat from his face and struggled in the heat of his twisted damp sheets. Pounding his pillow, he hoped somehow that would cool him. It didn't, so he sat up on the side of the bed and waved the sheets back and forth trying to fan his burning body. That didn't help either.

He was absolutely certain Jessie had given him this room because it faced the south. It did have a door facing east toward the driveway, but the windows faced south and west and the room got hammered with the heat all day long. She knew he'd be roasting alive, and he knew she was glad. She wanted him out of her house, but it wasn't going to happen.

Sweltering in the early summer heat, he was sure Jessie was cool as a clam in her rock cave at the other end of the house. She despised him; he knew that. She thought he stole her place away from her, but why couldn't she understand that he had bought the ranch to help her so she wouldn't lose her place?

He'd mortgaged his soul for her, and she wouldn't even give him a pillow for his bed. He hadn't expected her to make him a bed, but she could have at least given him a pillow when he asked for one. She didn't. In no uncertain words she told him that if he wanted a "damn pillow", he could go to his own house and stay there. He went there. He sure did. He went there, got the pillow and some bed clothes, and came right back to her awful house. She was not kicking him out. He was there to stay. She would accept him one day. He just had to wait her out.

Fanning the sheets, Jed realized he was simply getting hotter doing all that movement. As the sweat dripped down his face onto his chest, he thought about the glorious air conditioning his father had installed in their home when his mother became so sick. Even though the system completely depleted his father's bank account, Jed was glad he'd bought it. He couldn't stand to think of his beloved mother suffering with cancer in the horrid Oklahoma heat.

He'd been away on duty in Korea when his mother became ill, and because it was wartime, the Army only let him come home to see her when her days were finally numbered. Jessie was home on summer break then, and to his surprise she was with his mom the day he came

24

home. He later learned that Jessie had stopped by one day while he was away, and explained that she was a good friend of his, and wanted to help however she could. From that day on, his father said Jessie had come every day to help his mother. She would bathe her, change her into a fresh nightgown, brush her hair, and fill his mother in on all the local gossip, embellishing each story to make his mother laugh. Then Jessie would leave and return the next day. After his mother died, Jessie had even put her arms around him and kissed him. He thought that meant she had some feelings for him. Well, didn't she?

Trying to keep his mind off the sweat pouring down his head, he remembered when his father died, and how he'd received a sympathy card from Jessie. She said that she was in college and couldn't get home for the funeral. She signed the card, 'Love, Jessie'. What happened?

Before his death, his father had been completely taken with Jessie and said that without Jessie, he could not have made it through that awful time. "Jessie Keegan's a saint," the old man had said. Jed knew she might have been a saint to his parents, but as hateful as she'd been to him lately, he truly wondered about her sainthood.

After his mother died, it was a short time later when his father died, but it was a crucial time for a rancher, a rancher who cared to live. His father hadn't cared to live without the woman he loved. Jed had no idea how bad things had gotten at the ranch following his mother's death; but when he came home after the old man died, he found the place was in total devastation. The cattle were skeletal, the alfalfa was unplanted, the winter wheat rotted in the fields, and there was not a thing he could do to save any of it, because he was still on active duty. After the funeral, he sold the cattle, plowed the dead wheat under, put the house up for rent, and returned to active duty in Korea where war was raging between North and South Korea.

As time passed and the war raged on, he took every opportunity to read up on agriculture knowing there were new advanced ways of getting the best production from the land. To get his place to survive, he needed to learn how to care for the land in the modern-day methods. After his enlistment was up, the G.I. Bill and Oklahoma State University were the answer to his prayers.

Shuffling out of the bed, Jed poured a jar of water over his head. Even with the water running down his sweating body, he was still hot. If he had a few extra bucks, he could buy one of those small window air-conditioning units and keep the bedroom cool, but he knew that was a useless thought. It had taken most of his savings to get his ranch back on its feet; and although it was doing well enough now, it still was no moneymaker, not yet. By next fall, he was certain it would become profitable again.

Wiping his sweating brow, Jed poured more water over his head. The fall harvest was months away and he'd mortgaged his property heavily to buy Jessie's place. Now he was broke as a dam with a hole in it, and he still had a ton of improvements to make. And every day he got more tired. Why did he get more tired? Because he couldn't sleep at night in the miserable heat! Jessie did it to him. She wanted him out, but he wasn't leaving, heat or not.

Jed thought about his situation for a minute, and then yawned in near exhaustion. He knew he couldn't take care of Jessie's ranch if he couldn't get his rest. He needed a good night's sleep, and he would have it. He'd take out one of those new charge cards and get an air conditioner. That should really piss off Jessie, but it would be worth it. With that thought in mind, Jed fell soundly asleep.

"You beat me again, Ben." Jed noted by his watch that it was five a.m. and the old man was already outside working. Jed grabbed a bucket of grain and poured it into a deep trough as the few cattle gathered for their early morning feed.

"As you get older, you don't need much sleep, Mr. McClure." Ben White lifted another heavy bucket of grain and poured it into the same trough.

As he lifted the bucket, Jed noticed the strain on the face of the aging black man and knew Ben had to be at least seventy years old, far too old to be doing all that heavy lifting. "Ben, you don't need to do this heavy work. I can do it."

"Maybe I don't need to, Mr. McClure, but I want to. If I don't keep using what strength I have left, soon I won't have any."

Jed smiled at that sound reasoning. "My friends call me Jed, Ben."

Ben White grinned, his teeth glistening white against the brown wrinkled skin of his face. "Jed, it is, then."

Jed yawned as he grabbed a hose and began filling the horse tank used to water the animals. "Not sleeping very well, Jed?"

"It's too damn hot in the room Jessie *assigned* me. I'm pretty sure she picked the hottest room in the house, hoping I'd give up and leave."

Ben had been worried about this. He was afraid Jed had bought the dying ranch cheaply, intending to get some sucker to pay big bucks for the place and then abandon them. "Are you, Jed? Are you going to give up and leave?"

"Of course not, Ben, I own this ranch. I have every right to be here."

"That's not what I mean, Jed. This ranch will take an awful lot of work. Sean Keegan tried so hard to get it running again, but he died too soon. Then everything went to hell. Simon and I did not have the knowledge to keep it going, and Jessie was just a kid. It didn't take any of us very long to figure out that lazy man Mrs. Keegan married was useless *and* broke."

"I'm broke too, Ben, but I'm not letting that stop me from turning this place around."

"And just how are you going to do that, Jed? It takes money to make money."

"Ben, haven't you ever heard the saying 'borrow from Peters to pay Pauls'?"

Ben smiled and shook his head remembering his friend Sean had done the same thing. "I was afraid of something like that, Jed. I know it can work, but you'll surely need someone to keep a careful eye on your books. You don't want to get your Peters and Pauls mixed up."

"Yeah, you're right, Ben. So, is this an offer to take over the books like you did for Sean Keegan? I'll tell you up front though; I can't pay you any extra money."

"Now why would I need any extra money, Jed? What would I do with it, if I had it?"

Grabbing Ben's hand, Jed shook it gratefully. "You're hired, Ben. Hope you can work some magic with those Peters and Pauls."

"I did it before for Sean, Jed. I can do it again for you."

The roaring of Jed's dusty black pickup woke Jessie as she slept in the cool comfort of her cave-like bedroom. Quickly, she jumped out of bed and cursed herself for staying up so late reading. She really couldn't blame herself, though; it was such a joy to linger in the cool room knowing the world outside was sweltering in the heat, especially, Jed McClure.

Hurrying to the door, she cracked it open to see what Jed was doing and was immediately hit by the early morning heat. Today would be a real hot one, but she knew she didn't have to worry. She was cool

27

and content in her room. Most of the other rooms stayed fairly cool, but none of them were like her cave room. Jessie smiled as she thought about Jed sweltering in the heat in his room. That room was the last of the rooms to be added on to the house and the least insulated. Her father had told her that at one time, the room had been open, a sleeping room used only on the hot nights of summer. Then someone enclosed it. Now, Jed was sleeping there in enclosed walls of heat, but she doubted much sleeping went on at all in that oven-like room.

Cracking her door open further, Jessie leaned out of her door to observe Jed. He had parked by the door to his bedroom, and she watched as he walked in his long strides to the back of his truck and lowered the back gate. He pulled a large cardboard box from the truck bed, lifted it into his arms and walked toward his bedroom. Leaning out of her doorway she wondered about the words on that big box. Whirlpool something, it said.

Jessie stepped out of her door and skirted the distance toward Jed, trying to keep him from seeing her. "Hey Jessie, come open my door for me, will you?"

Jessie continued watching as Jed struggled to hold the big box and open the door. What did that box say? "Whirlpool Air Conditioner"? What was he doing? He couldn't put an air conditioner in that room. She wouldn't allow it, too much electricity, too expensive! Besides, he was foiling her plan to be rid of him.

"Hold it right there, McClure! What do you think you're doing?"

"This is a five-ton, single- room air conditioner, *Miss Keegan,* the last one to be had anywhere in Tahchee."

"You don't have my permission to run that thing in my house, Jed. Those things are very costly to operate."

"You, Ben, and Simon been enjoying all that *costly* beef I brought over from my freezer at the big house, Jessie?" Jed hated himself for smarting off to Jessie, but he had his arms full with the air conditioner, it was hotter than hell, and she was talking about the cost to help him maintain his sanity. Forcing a smile, he leaned against the wall supporting the heavy unit with one of his legs while he ignored the pain in his arms. "Jessie, please open the door!"

Knowing Jed had provided the means to keep her two loyal helpers fed, Jessie lunged for the door and shoved it open as Jed hurried past her and set the air conditioner down on the floor. The room was like an oven and she knew it served him right.

"Oh, to hell with you, McClure; I hope you freeze to death with the damn thing!" Jessie tromped from Jed's little sauna down to the kitchen for breakfast. She knew the vegetable garden needed to be tended before it got too hot, but suddenly she was starving to death. A good battle with Jed did make her hungry. She hadn't won this battle, but she let him know she was no pushover when it came to her house.

Ben walked from the barn toward the garden, where he knew he would find Jessie. "Miss Jessie, are you still working in that filthy ground without your gloves? There are all sorts of germs in that dirt."

Squinting up at Ben, her arm over her eyes to avoid the hot sun, Jessie smiled at the old man. "That's what soap is for, Ben. I love the feel of good rich Keegan soil. When I feel the dirt on my fingertips, I know I'm home where I belong."

"Yes, and one of these days you'll get sick and wonder why, and I'll say 'I told you so'." Ben White squatted next to her, his long brown fingers encased in a pair of jersey work gloves as he began pulling and pawing the pesky weeds of the garden. "So, how are you today, Miss Jessie?"

"I'm doing just fine, Ben. How are you feeling?"

"I'm tolerable, but this heat sure doesn't help."

"You and Simon don't have to sleep in the bunkhouse Ben, not when there are perfectly cool bedrooms in the house going to waste."

"It's not that hot out in the bunk house; it's made of the same stone as your house. It's just summer, and its hot outside. Besides, you know I can't sleep in your house. That wouldn't be right."

"Why, Ben? Because you're a black Indian sleeping in a white man's bed? That's a bunch of nonsense and you know it. Times have changed since the Tulsa riots, Ben."

"Maybe so, maybe not, but I'll not be the one that finds out."

Jessie shook her head and kept pulling weeds. They had been over this conversation many times and Jessie knew it was useless to try to convince Ben that things had changed since the reign of terror of the Ku Klux Klan. Some said the violence was still ongoing, but she had never seen anything to warrant such fear as Ben White seemed to hold.

As they worked along the rows of vegetables, Jessie wondered about Ben. She'd never quite understood the closeness between her father, Sean Keegan, and Ben White. Maybe being forced from their homes *was* the reason they were so close. She knew that as a young man, her father had left Ireland, escaping British rule and the turbulence surrounding the oppression of his people. Ben had escaped the overthrow of his home in the Tulsa race riots of 1921. As she thought about it, she realized their connection. They had both lost their homes and that's why they understood one another's heartache. That was why they were so close.

When Sean left Ireland, he'd begged his Irish father and Scottish mother to come with him, but they had refused. They weren't young and Ireland was their home with or without the bloody English, they'd said. So as a young boy, he'd come alone on his uncle's request to help work the Keegan ranch.

His uncle had lost his wife and children to illness two years before, and he was desperate for help. Eventually, Sean inherited the ranch; and as worthless and worn out as it was, he was determined to make it profitable, and he did for awhile.

Her father had said that one day out of the blue, Ben came wandering up to the ranch, dirty and tired, looking for a few months' work. He said he thought he had some distant relatives in Chicago and wanted to earn enough money to get there. That was over thirty years ago. Ben had never left.

At that time, Sean had said he'd been hesitant to hire a Negro into his crew of workers. He knew the racial unrest was rolling across Oklahoma gathering tar and damnation in its path faster than a snowball rolling down the hill of destruction, and he didn't want any trouble. But even with the threats from groups such as the KKK, Sean ignored them and their hostile ways. He let Ben stay for a few days to gather his strength before he was to move on to Chicago. Sean Keegan never did officially hire Ben White, and Ben White never did leave the home of Sean Keegan. They became friends. That's the way it was.

Her father said that Ben had been married at one time but she had never known what happened to his wife. He was a very intelligent man, obviously well-educated. His speech was impeccable, his manners flawless, and Jessie thought he must have been very handsome in his youth with his golden brown skin, high nose, strong cheekbones, and straight black hair.

When Papa was alive, Ben White had always been his right arm. He'd taken charge of the ranch bookkeeping which her father despised. He studied The Wall Street Journal as some people studied the Holy Bible, and in 1928 he insisted that Sean pull his money from his investments in the stock market. The next year the market had a historic collapse, and Ben most definitely saved Sean from bankruptcy.

One thing Ben couldn't foresee was the horrendous dust bowls of the 1930's that destroyed the land, starved the livestock, and bankrupted many of the smaller ranchers. Her father was a small rancher, but because of Ben's foresight, they survived, barely.... but they survived.

Occasionally, Jessie would hear Ben groan as he moved his aging knees to another row, picking and destroying the weeds in the glaring heat of mid-June.

"Miss Jessie, may I ask you a personal question?"

Wiping the sweat from her eyes, Jessie turned to smile at the old man, "Of course, Ben."

"Would you please tell me why you put Mr. McClure in that horrid hot bedroom at the south end of the house? You have several perfectly good bedrooms going to waste, and not one is nearly as exposed to the elements as the old sleeping room you forced Mr. McClure to use."

Jessie hesitated for a moment pretending to pull forth an unwilling root. "I don't want that man to get too comfortable with us, Ben. He stole my land. I can't forgive him for that."

Ben's aging knees finally gave out. He pulled his slender frame up and stood glaring down at Jessie. "Jessica Keegan, Jed McClure did not steal your land. It was a tragedy that your mama died before Rico and Carl inherited the land, but that had nothing to do with Jed. We're lucky he bought the place."

When Ben addressed her without calling her "Miss Jessie", she knew he was angry, but Jessie was angry too. Quickly she jumped to her feet and faced him. "How can you possibly say that, Ben?" After giving Jed's reason for buying her ranch a lot of thought, Jessie decided she had come up with the logical answer. "He bought this place so he didn't have to share right-of-ways and water-rights with anyone else! He knows that not all ranchers are as agreeable as the Keegans. All someone would have to do was cut off his right-of-way to the back of his property and then where would he be? He bought this place for that exact reason....that and the water that we've always shared. Now he's got it all and doesn't give a damn about us! All he's thinking about is taking care of his McClure ranch! And besides, if things get much worse, he'll up and quit on us anyway."

Ben frowned. "Oh Lord! How can things possibly get any worse for us?

"Ben, you don't understand. I heard that Mr. Jed McClure had only a few months left before he graduated from college, and he just up and quit! He never even bothered to take his final exams. Either he's stupid, or he's a quitter. Either way, we can't trust him."

"Yes, I heard all the rumors about him. Some people said that he was expelled from college; some said he couldn't pass the final tests. That I couldn't believe, so I asked him why he quit college. He said he went to school on the GI Bill to learn all the latest about agriculture. When he learned what he needed to know, he dropped out. It was planting time, and he needed to get his father's ranch back on its feet. And that's what he did, Jessica. He can do the same for us, if you will just give him a chance."

"You don't understand, Ben. He's come here to take over. Pretty soon none of us will have a say about anything."

"I don't believe that for one bit! I believe that Jed McClure is the answer to all our prayers. He's a tough cookie, a hard worker, and a fair man. If anyone can get this old ranch back up on its feet, he's the man to do it. Look what he did to his father's old place. That place was as bad, or worse than ours. Now it's rich with healthy crops, the cattle are getting fat, and the place looks like a good ranch should look. What's wrong with that, Jessica Keegan?"

Turning away from the old man, Jessie's lip quivered in humiliation. In the short time she'd been home, she'd tried to figure out how to get the place back on its feet, but the truth was she knew absolutely nothing about ranching. There was so much she needed to know, and none of it had anything to do with what she learned in school. Biting her lip until she tasted blood, she wondered why she had ever listened to Mama.

When she got home from school, she saw the deplorable conditions of the ranch and worried how she could possibly save them from inevitable bankruptcy. There were no cattle, no crops, nothing! Determined to save her ranch, she had quickly devoured books on agriculture hoping they could give her the information she needed to try planting her father's last hybrid wheat discovery. If she could get the grain to grow as her father had thought, she could market it and get the ranch out of trouble. That wheat could be the answer to everything, including restoring the respect of her father's name, which had been sorely drug through the mud by Rico Barone....and Mama. Then came Jed McClure, and that was the end of that.

Ben's tired voice softened. "Jessica, without your papa's hand to lead us, we have sunk to the bottom of the pot in the past years. We need the strength, the vision, and the knowledge this young man has to offer. You know what I say is true. Give him a chance to save us. Give the man a chance for all our sakes."

Walking away from her out of the hot sun, Jessie stared in disbelief at the back of the old man as his legs gave way and he fell to the ground.

Chapter 3

"If it's his time to go, there's no one who can save him, Jessica." Estelle Collins stroked Jessie's hand with her long slender fingers. Jessie hadn't seen Miss Estelle or Dr. Collins in several years. Time had passed so quickly from when she was a child and all the children would line up waiting for Dr. Collins and his graceful wife to perform the dreaded immunizations at school. Jessie remembered how Dr. Collins always wore a white jacket with a bow tie when she had to go to his office. Papa had said it was so that Doc wouldn't get pee on his tie when the boy babies decided to let loose while he was examining them. She thought that was silly.

Miss Estelle, as everyone called her even after she'd married Dr. Collins years ago, was always dressed in a nurse's uniform of crisp white cotton nipped in at her tiny waist, with an a-line skirt that flattered her long slender legs encased in white stockings. She wore her raven hair parted in the middle and pulled back into a chignon, and on the back of her head she wore a pointed nurse's cap that fit securely over that mysterious clump of raven rich hair. She always wore white shoes that never made a sound, even during her quick steps to her husband's side, given his slightest glance. It seemed to Jessie that the two of them were gifted by some magical mind-connection that was not of this world, a love that only a few were privileged to know, an undying love that Jessie hoped she would someday find.

"Of course, if anyone can save him, Dr. Collins will do it. He's a wonderful doctor, Jessica." Miss Estelle patted Jessie's hand, and smiled tenderly as her distinguished graying husband approached them. It amazed Jessie that Miss Estelle always addressed her husband as Dr. Collins, and wondered if she spoke to him like that at their home. Probably, she decided as she watched his eyes light up at the sight of his wife. Even though she hadn't gone into the room with Dr. Collins to help examine Ben, she still wore her nurse's uniform....ready if he needed her. That was true love, Jessie decided, as she wondered if Miss Estelle wore that white uniform to bed.

"I doubt Ben has seen a doctor in years, Jed," Dr. Collins said as he and Jed walked from the bedroom into the living room. "It's possible he's had a heart condition all of his life, but I don't suppose he knew about it. Things are different for people of color. They don't have the advantage of the white man's medicine until they're too sick for it to do them any good. But I think Ben will be all right for a while. He needs to take it easy, but getting him to take it easy might be a problem. I had to give him a shot to calm him down a few minutes ago. He kept trying to get out of bed, carrying on about sleeping in a white man's bed, so try and keep him calm with these pills I'm leaving for him."

Jessie breathed a sigh of relief and rose to greet Dr. Collins. Frowning as Dr. Collins was, Jessie didn't think he looked much like Cary Grant anymore. After seeing Cary Grant in the role of Dr. Noah Praetorius in the movie *People Will Talk,* she fell madly in love with Dr. Collins for one entire year of her life. That was the year Miss Estelle moved to Tahchee. It was the same year Miss Estelle married Dr. Collins. Jessie cried for one whole day.

Later on, someone told her that Miss Estelle and Dr. Collins had been sweethearts even when they were children. When Miss Estelle was around sixteen years old, her family moved from Tahchee, and they never saw each other again until she returned to Tahchee years later. That incredible love story thrilled Jessie and she immediately fell in love with her dentist. He looked like Paul Newman.

"How's our patient doing, sister?" Simon walked into the bedroom as Jessie spooned some broth into Ben's mouth under the watchful gaze of Jed.

"What are you asking her for, you old fool? I can talk. I'm not dead yet!"

Simon grinned seeing that his old friend still had his humor. "You could have fooled me, you old coot. You look like something that crept out of the swamp....after the alligator puked him up."

"Simon, stop egging him on. I'm having enough trouble trying to keep him calm."

"Ah, leave them alone, Jessie. They're just teasing each other." Jed said.

Jessie felt anger enraging her. Obviously, Jed didn't think she was qualified to feed poor Ben without his supervision. Now he was contradicting what she said.

"Don't you have something to do, Jed?" She asked.

"I am doing something, Jessie. I'm helping you with Ben," he answered.

"You are not helping me. You're getting in my way, so go away!"

Jessie didn't notice the look shared between Simon and Jed. "This old coot here ruined everybody's lunch with his shenanigans, so I reheated it for supper. Jed, you and Jessie go on over to the kitchen and eat before it gets cold. I got a feeling this old piece of alligator bait is ready for a nap and that big chair over there looks comfortable enough for me to take a nap, too. So, get on with both of you. Us old coots need our beauty rest. Oh, and Jessie, Doc and Miss Estelle will be coming back tomorrow night to check on Ben after they close Doc's office, so I invited them to come for dinner. I hope that's all right with you."

Jessie gasped in horror. "Miss Estelle and Dr. Collins are coming for dinner? Oh Lord! Miss Estelle is such a grand lady, she'll expect everything to be just so-so! That means I'll have to drag out all of Mama's fine linens and china, whatever there is left of them." With that, Jessie raced out of the room in a near panic.

"Women," Simon said.

"Women," Jed repeated.

Ben answered with a loud snore.

With the air conditioner roaring and blowing cold air over him, Jed felt he'd never had a better sleep in his entire life. He felt great, really great. Well, if he felt so damn great, he wondered, what he was doing waking up at three a.m.? Something was wrong. Something had happened, he could sense it. Maybe it was Ben.

Pulling his large body up to sit on the side of his bed, he scratched his head and stood. Ignoring his shirt and boots, he slipped on his jeans. Fearing an unwelcome intruder, he shuffled toward his door pulling it open slightly before checking on Ben. Not seeing any sign of movement outside, he pushed his door open until he could gain full sight of the yard and the long lane leading to the house. All was quiet, but the heat from the night nearly knocked him down. Then he noted a small figure sprawled on a bench under the cover of the connecting porch roof. Accustoming his eyes to the dark night, Jed could see that it was Jessie, and as he walked toward her, he could see she looked miserable.

"Jessie," he whispered. She didn't answer as he glanced toward her cave bedroom and noticed the door wide open. Trying to not wake her, he strode over to her door to pull it shut so it wouldn't let the warm night into the cool room. When he got to the door, he noticed the heat coming from the room and then he understood. Somehow with all the commotion of the previous day, Jessie had left her cool cave door open to the day's horrendous heat and her room was as insulated with the heat as an oven. It would never cool off until next winter, or he realized, until someone shared their air conditioner with her.

"Ah hell," he whispered as he picked up the exhausted Jessie and brought her back to his icy cool room. Lowering her down on his bed, he placed her damp head on his pillow and pulled a sheet up over her soft nightgown. "Sleep tight, my little love," he whispered. "You need to keep up your strength, so that tomorrow you can kick my ass for bringing you here to my room."

Jed grabbed his shirt and boots and quietly walked out into the heat of the night.

"Thank you," Jessie murmured the next morning at breakfast, remembering the strong arms that had carried her into that blessed cool room where she'd slept the night before. Jed wasn't really such a bad guy she thought between bites of scrambled eggs, hot cakes, and the most wonderful sausage she'd ever tasted, compliments of Jed's freezer. No, he wasn't some awful tyrant; he was actually very kind and thoughtful. But he had stolen her ranch, she reminded herself, feeling the anger that was too quickly dying away.

Jed lifted his eyes in acknowledgement. "When I get through with breakfast, I'll bring the air conditioner down to your room so it can cool your room." He didn't say anymore.

"Take it back to your room after mine cools down. Mine will stay cool, unless I forget to close the door again." Jessie kept her eyes down on her breakfast.

Openly staring at Jessie, Jed wondered if she was softening toward him a little. "It was an accident, Jessie. It could happen to anyone."

Nothing more was said. Jessie grabbed her empty plate and put it in the kitchen sink to soak. As she turned, she noticed Jed watching her, his breakfast clearly finished. Hesitating for only a moment, Jessie crossed back to the table, grabbed Jed's empty plate, and carried it back toward the sink.

That little chore was something that Jessie had never done for him before. It wasn't much, but he hoped that finally Jessie Keegan was easing down in her hatred of him. Giving her a short nod of thanks, Jed walked out the door and into the early morning sunshine of another hot day.

"You set such a lovely table, Jessica," Miss Estelle said admiring a tiny cup of Haviland china. "My mother had a complete set of Limoges, but it wasn't as valuable as this lovely set."

To Jessie's amazement, Miss Estelle was not wearing her usual white nurse's uniform, nor was her hair parted in the middle and pulled back in that mysterious stern chignon. Tonight she wore her dark tresses piled on top of her head with a few curly tendrils caressing her face and neck. She was beautiful, in understated perfection. Her sylphlike figure was clothed in a violet silk, mid-length dress with a short boat-neck, cap sleeves, classic pearls, and on her hands she wore white gloves. As Jessie marveled at the beauty of the elegant lady, her soft violet eyes and her long dark eyelashes, Jessie was reminded of the subtle beauty of Elizabeth Taylor and the unmistakable style of Jackie Kennedy.

With great care, Miss Estelle held one small dish up to the light and studied it. "Jessie, this china is hand painted Haviland, very valuable, truly antique china. Do you use it often for entertaining?"

Jessie gulped. She had no idea the china was so valuable, or that it was antique. Mama never said much about her pretty things, just that she wouldn't dare use them on the crude Oklahoma cowboys, or their wives. "No Miss Estelle, this was Mama's china. We never used it, ever."

"Oh, Jessie dear, I certainly hope you didn't feel you had to use your fine china just because Dr. Collins and I were coming?"

Jessie didn't know what to say. Of course, she'd used it for Miss Estelle. Miss Estelle had always been her idol, and she wanted Miss Estelle to think that she was a fine lady like her.

Somehow Miss Estelle seemed to understand. Smiling warmly herself, Miss Estelle put her gloved hand around Jessie's shoulders. "Jessie, you don't have to use fine china to impress me. You are a beautiful and kind young lady, and your mother was very fortunate to have you. I truly envy her for being blessed with such a good daughter."

Jessie held her head low, remembering her anger with her mother. "Miss Estelle, I really don't think I was such a good daughter to Mama. I would get really angry with her because sometimes she was downright mean to papa."

"Jessie, your mama was a very willful woman, and your papa knew of that when he married her. That's why he was always searching for his Irish pot of gold. He wanted to give her everything she wanted; but Jessie, I honestly doubt there would have ever been any pleasing your mother no matter what Sean did for her."

"And I didn't please her either, Miss Estelle. No matter how I tried, I let Mama down. She wanted me to be a real lady like her, but somehow, I could never be what she wanted me to be."

Miss Estelle laughed softly as she removed her gloves and stroked the serious lines on Jessie's face. "Jessie, my darling girl, didn't you know that being a caring and kind person is what makes a real lady. In our free clinic, we have many women volunteers who haven't the faintest idea what fine china is, or what fork to use, and could care less about that sort of thing; but Jessie they are good people. They radiate in their kindness and their concern for the welfare of others, and in my opinion, that is what makes a real lady. You have that goodness about you, too, Jessie, but sometimes I think you're afraid to let it show."

"But Mama always said I was gullible like Papa. She said that I needed to get away from this ranch. I'd never get anywhere in life if I wasn't like her."

"And aren't you really where you want to be, Jessie? You love this ranch."

Jessie frowned as she thought about that for a moment. Then she realized that Miss Estelle, in her infinite wisdom, had finally set her free. Her pinched frown turned into a big smile. "Yes, Miss Estelle, you are absolutely right. I am exactly where I want to be."

"Your mother was my friend, and I loved her, but she was not perfect; and Jessie, I'll tell you a little secret, you are a much finer lady than your mother could have ever been. You have the *heart* of a real lady."

Jessie was dumbfounded. Never in her entire life had she thought anyone would ever consider her a lady, especially after she failed that awful course in Miss Eleanor's Charm School.

"Well, your table is lovely, Jessie. Thank you very much for allowing Dr. Collins and me to be the first ones to use this lovely china with you and Jed. Maybe this can be the start of something new for all of us."

Jessie openly gasped. She'd forgotten about Jed and his big hands.

"Jed ran back to his room to change for dinner. He'll be just a minute, Jessie," Doc said as he examined the polished silver pieces on the side-board. "He's a nice young man, Jessie. Do you suppose there

39

could ever be anything between the two of you?" Without waiting for her to answer, he rushed on. "Just think, Jessie, if you married Jed this ranch would be yours again."

Jessie stopped dead in her tracks. She'd never thought of that. If she married Jed, she could get her ranch back. Of course, Jed would have something to say about that. He had mentioned marrying her a few times when he first came to live at the ranch, but he hadn't said a word about marriage in a long time. He'd lost interest in marrying and he'd lost interest in her, too.

Miss Estelle's comments interrupted her thoughts. "Oh wouldn't that be grand, Jessica? Jed is such a fine person and very easy on the eyes. You'd make the loveliest couple, and I know your children would be truly beautiful with the two of you for parents."

Dumbfounded, Jessie stared at Miss Estelle. What was she saying? Did she go along with this marrying thing? Had this been something she and Doc had discussed before they got to the ranch? Obviously, it was.

Doc turned from the side board and smiled at Jessie. "It certainly would solve a load of problems if you and Jed did decide to get married, Jessie. You must know the talk that's going around Tahchee about the two of you living together out here, not being married and all."

"Dr. Collins," Miss Estelle interrupted, "Jessica is a fine young lady, and Jed is an honorable young man. How could you possibly listen to such trite?"

Walking toward his wife, Doc placed his arm around her small shoulders. "Telly, you know I don't listen to that sort of garbage, but it is out there. No one would mention it to you, but they don't mind filling my ears."

"James Collins...."

Miss Estelle's words were interrupted by Jed as he entered the dining room. He hadn't realized this meal was to be such a dressy affair, until he saw Miss Estelle in a shiny purple dress and white gloves in this miserable heat; but he sure didn't want to downplay the work Jessie had gone to for this dinner, him wearing his jeans and chambray shirt. So for Jessie, who was wearing a white eyelet shirtwaist dress with a black belt and some sort of flouncy slip that whirled and swished as she walked, and for Miss Estelle in her purple finery, he'd gone back to his room and struggled into his gray suit, black shirt, and silver bolo.

Now, as the sweat rolled down his face, he wished he'd brought his air conditioner with him.

To Jessie's amazement, the dinner went quite well with only a few minor mishaps. Jed got his finger caught in the handle of the tiny coffee cup and spilled coffee onto the table cloth, but it was barely noticeable. What was really noticeable and almost funny was the look on Jed's face as he glared down at the size of the small dinner dishes being used instead of the big heavy plates they normally used. Jessie had to give him credit, though. He didn't say a word, just accepted his tiny portion and stared hungrily at hers.

Simon had insisted he would cook and play server for the dinner of four. Where he got his knowledge of dining etiquette was a mystery to Jessie, but Simon pulled it off without a hitch, including his fabulous version of Beef Florentine and his delicious Italian Tiramisu. As they lounged around the table sharing stories of years past, Sean Keegan's name came up frequently. Jessie had never known that Sean had been sweet on Miss Estelle when she returned to Tahchee, but Miss Estelle noted that he quickly lost interest in her, when he was introduced to Emma Lancaster, a young lady who was visiting from Boston. Everyone in town had laughed at Sean's determined pursuit of Miss Lancaster even though he was much older than she." Miss Estelle said as she remembered times gone by, "Whether he had worn her down, or whether she just gave in, no one knew."

Doc interrupted, obviously enjoying the conversation, "Some said she was in love with the idea of the old wild-west, and some said she really loved the wiry little Scotch-Irishman. Whatever the answer, several months later, Sean convinced her to elope with him."

Miss Estelle finished his next thought. "After the elopement, her family tried to intervene and get the marriage annulled, but Sean and Emma insisted they were in love, and her family eventually accepted Sean, the Irish cowboy they called him. The next year, you were born Jessica."

Doc spoke. "Even though the community had welcomed Emma as one of their own, when she married Sean, she never seemed to fit in. Some said she was a snob looking down her nose at hard working people, some said she was shy; but for some reason, Emma Keegan had never been happy living in the Oklahoma lifestyle."

"Obviously, it was not the life she had expected and certainly not the lifestyle she had wanted," Miss Estelle said glancing at her husband,

41

knowing she had interrupted his thoughts again.

Smiling at his wife, Doc continued. "Sean was always working on a project of some sort," Doc said, having been Sean's friend almost from the first day he arrived in Oklahoma. "He always hoped he could find a way to give Emma the life she yearned for: the finery, the travels, and the beautiful home. He was a highly intelligent man, full of dreams and hopes for a better life for his family. When he came up with the idea of cross-breeding wheat, he thought he'd found the answer. He had perfected his project, had the fields ready, and then he died suddenly of a massive coronary. He never had been able to give Emma the fine life he'd promised her. What a loss his experiments were."

"No!" Jessie said. "It's not a loss. After his death, Mama wanted to throw out all of Papa's work, but I wouldn't let her. I took the pots of wheat from his experiments and sealed them in big green canning jars, and I still have all of them. All I need is the chance to plant the wheat and I could prove papa was right. Mama thought papa was a failure, but Mama was wrong! He was not a failure!"

Miss Estelle leaned over and patted Jessie's hand. "Jessica, I truly believe that in her own way, your mother loved your father. Maybe she no longer believed in his work, but she stuck with him through it all."

Jessie wondered what choice her mother had. She lived so far away from her family in Boston, too proud to let them know her marriage was a big mistake. Mama was miserable, and with every one of Papa's failures, she became more bitter.

Doc interrupted Jessie's thoughts. "Well, Telly, it's getting late and ranchers get up early, and so do we. I think we should leave these fine people to their beds now."

"Yes, James. You're right, of course," Miss Estelle said as she rose from her chair. "This was such a lovely evening, Jessica. Thank you for your gracious hospitality, and please tell Simon again how delicious his meal was." Linking her arm in Jessie's as they neared the door, Miss Estelle whispered to Jessie, "If I had a daughter, Jessie, I would want her to be just like you."

Jessie sat on the porch swing as Jed walked Doc and Miss Estelle to their car, his flashlight ensuring Miss Estelle did not trip on any loose gravel. As she watched Miss Estelle hug Jed goodnight, she thought of the differences in her own mother and Miss Estelle. Miss Estelle was an absolutely elegant lady, whether she wore a nurse's uniform, or her beautiful lavender silk dress. Like Mama, she had come from a wealthy family, but she had given up all that wealth to return to the country doctor she loved. She accepted and even embraced the crude lifestyle of rural Oklahoma, because taking care of the people of Oklahoma had been her husband's dream.

Mama had never cared about papa's dream, and was constantly raving about what he had neglected giving her, shouting that he had brought nothing to their marriage but a bunch of useless promises. That might have been true, Jessie thought, but she had often wondered just what Mama had brought to their marriage.

Watching the flashlight as it neared the porch, Jessie thought about Jed, and remembered Doc's words about marrying him. She would get back her ranch if she married Jed, but what would Jed get from marrying her? All she had was a falling-down house and green mason jars of wheat. She'd be just like Mama: always taking, never giving, a selfish burden for someone else to carry. With that thought in mind, Jessie vowed that if she lived to be a hundred, she would never be like.

Glancing at Jed as he climbed the steps to the porch, she could see the sweat running down his face, but still he kept on his coat, his heavy bolo sealing his damp shirt to his body. He didn't sit down next to Jessie, but leaned against one of the porch posts, gazing out over the road as they both watched the lights of Doc's car fade into the distance. Finally, he turned toward her. "Jessie, when I was in your room today taking out the air conditioner, I noticed those green canning jars on the shelf. I have to tell you I snooped and took a good look."

Jessie was horror stricken. "Oh Jed, I hope you didn't open those jars."

"Of course not, Jessie, I just wondered what was in all those jars. Now I understand that those jars were your father's wheat experiments. It was too bad he died before it could be tested in the fields. What a loss."

Jed's interest got Jessie's attention immediately. "Well, Jed, it doesn't have to be a loss. Papa's wheat is well preserved. I saw to that." Jessie held her breath as she continued on about the feasibility of planting Sean's wheat, hoping Jed would offer to test-plant some of the wheat. He didn't.

Yawning, Jed loosened his bolo. "Your dinner was a great success, Jessie."

"Thank you, Jed." Jessie answered, her hopes for her father's wheat fading rapidly.

"But the next time...." Jed stopped what he was saying in mid-sentence.

Hoping Jed had reconsidered the wheat, Jessie quickly asked, "The next time....what, Jed?"

Jed didn't answer right away, drawing out her suspense. "The next time we have company for dinner, Jessie, do you suppose we could use bigger plates?"

With his arms stretched above his head, Jed thought about the evening's events as he savored the coolness of his bedroom. Jessie wanted him to test plant her father's wheat, he certainly understood that, but how could he plant Sean's experiment when he could barely afford to plant the Winter Wheat? No, he knew he couldn't chance it. Things were too uncertain right now. The Dust Bowl from years ago had devastated much of Oklahoma including the Keegan ranch, and Jed knew that until he could get some irrigation into the ground, little would grow on that ranch. He'd had just enough money left to install the irrigation system at his McClure ranch after he got out of college, and that's why his crops at the McClure Ranch were doing so well. That's why the Keegan-McClure Ranch was not. It was a damn tricky situation he'd gotten himself into and he knew it. He was walking a thin tightrope between success and complete failure and he had to be extremely cautious in whatever he did. Planting Sean's wheat was not an option. Not now.

Lying there in the cool breeze of his air conditioning, he thought of what a big worry growing Winter Wheat was. It was profitable, but it was still a worry. In the fall you worried that it might get too cold for the tender plants, then you prayed for snow to give protection and moisture to the plants. In the spring you worried about the hail that could destroy a whole field in a matter of minutes, and along with the hail you worried about lightning strikes that could fire up your field with the same devastating results. If your crop survived the spring, you had to be sure all the wheat was ready at the same time. Then you had to wait until the dew was completely gone from the plants before you could begin the harvest.

Being a rancher was a big pain in the ass. However, it was the most exciting life Jed McClure could ever imagine.

Exhausted, Jed McClure closed his eyes and was fast asleep. He smiled in his dreams as he watched Jessie Keegan dancing and swirling in an eyelet white dress with a black belt.

Chapter 4

"Jessie? Ed Kook, here."

Jessie positioned the big black telephone to her ear and wished the connection was better. "Yes, Ed. I'm here but the connection is not very good. There are a lot of scratchy sounds."

Ed Kook spoke louder, "Jessie, the reason I'm calling is that I've been trying to find more information for you on the ranch situation and possibly get McClure out of your house." Ed's voice became even louder, "Can you hear me now, Jessie?"

For some reason that she couldn't determine, the thought of being without Jed McClure's presence on the ranch didn't give her the great joy she had thought it might. Maybe she had just gotten used to him....or maybe it was the great meat on her table daily. "Go on Ed, I can hear you now."

"Jessie, I need to talk to you in person. I was thinking that maybe I could pick you up tonight, and we could drive into Tahchee for supper."

"Oh, Ed, I'm sorry, but I can't. Dr. Collins and his wife are joining us for supper this evening." Jessie didn't see any point in going into detail that Ben White had suffered a heart attack and didn't seem to be getting any better.

Jessie heard Ed Kook laugh softly and she could imagine the twitch of his small brown mustache. "What I need to talk to you about is very important, Jessie. Maybe I could come after you have supper with your guests."

"Why don't you plan to join us, Ed?" Jessie asked. Simon was serving a pot roast so there'd be plenty of food. "Could you be here around six?"

"I'll make a point of being there around six, Jessie. Thank you for inviting me."

Cautiously peering from his dark room into the night, Jed could see Ed Kook's long black Cadillac still parked in front of the main entry to the home. There was something about Ed Kook that he just didn't like. The man was smooth, too smooth, and he had monopolized the entire meal with his stories of his travels. Hell, the man had been all over the world...twice, it seemed. Each trip he talked about seemed to take longer for him to tell. The man was just plain boring.

Then Jed recalled how Kook had brought that bottle of wine like he was some big shot. Of course he knew he had some wine along with everyone else, but it would have been rude to refuse his wine. It wasn't very good wine, though. Kook claimed it was a fine port, a dessert wine, he'd said, but it was too sweet. It tasted awful. Jed was certain no one else liked it either, even though they killed the whole bottle. Well, what else were they to do? He knew everyone else was as bored as he was with Kook's big mouth flapping constantly.

Now Kook had Jessie cornered in the parlor and heavens only knew how long he'd keep poor Jessie up with his bragging and carrying on. Didn't Kook understand that they were ranchers, working people? They didn't keep banker's hours like those lawyers did. Why didn't he go home? What was so important?

Jed pulled back the shade in his dark room and peered out into the darkness again. Kook's long black Cadillac was still there. How could that man still be talking? Shouldn't he be hoarse by now? Jed flung back the shade and pushed the blonde chunk of hair out of his eyes as he thought of a way to save Jessie from Ed Kook's mouth. Maybe he should go into the parlor and interrupt, he thought as he peered out the window at the long black Cadillac. After all, Jessie needed her sleep. Yes, he decided, that was exactly what he would do.

"Jessie, I've done some digging into your father's business dealings in the past, and I wonder if you know a man named John Ross?" Ed's bushy brown eyebrows shot up as he waited for an answer.

Jessie thought for a minute. "No, Ed. I was close to my papa, but I never heard him mention someone by that name. Why do you ask?"

"There's a piece of property in Tulsa, which your father owned with this man, John Ross. I don't know if this man is even alive anymore; and there lies the question. If this John Ross is no longer alive, who owns this property? Are you, Jessie Keegan, the legal owner of that property?"

Jessie couldn't believe what Ed was saying. Was it possible she did own some property in Tulsa and never even knew about it? If so, that could be the answer to her problems. "Heavens, Ed. I doubt that I own anything like that. If my papa had any such property, he would have sold it a long time ago to help with the needs of the ranch. Besides, he would have told me about it, and there was nothing in his will about the property."

"That's because it was joint property, Jessie. When your father died, John Ross would have become sole owner; but there has been no transfer, and no one has come forth to claim the property. I wonder if perhaps this man has long since died and you are now the legal owner. I doubt that the land is worth much, but I'm certain I could get you enough money from it so that you could at least buy part of the ranch back from McClure."

Jessie gasped as she thought about what this could mean to her future.

Ed Kook stopped for a moment and seemed to be in deep thought. "Well, Jessie, because it's you, I would be willing to purchase the property from you straight out, so that you wouldn't have deal with the realtors, banks and so on. But, like I said, I doubt that the property is worth much. It's in such a decrepit location in Tulsa. However, if we find that John Ross is deceased and you are the rightful owner, I want the sale of the property to be done quickly so you don't have to worry your pretty little head about any of this and can buy your property back from Jed McClure as soon as possible."

Jessie knew nothing was that easy. Besides, she was getting used to having Jed McClure around to manage the ranch. "Ed, I sincerely doubt that Jed would agree to sell me even a part of this ranch. He's made arrangements for help on his other ranch so that he can spend most of his time here getting this ranch back up and running. Jed would never agree to sell me any part of this ranch. He'd never get rid of it, Ed. Not now."

"Oh, there's plenty of reason for him to rid himself of this place, Jessie."

"And what would that be, Ed?"

Stopping to clear his throat, Ed paused as he stared down at Jessie. "Jessie, I don't like to repeat information that I am privileged to, but I have it from a reputable source that Jed is almost penniless. He's dead broke."

Jessie's hand flew up to her mouth in shock. "What in the world are you talking about, Ed. Jed has talked about putting in an irrigation system here on the ranch! You have to have money to do something like that."

Ed sneered in disgust as he looked down at Jessie. "Talk, Jessie, that's all it is. I doubt he could borrow another cent for an irrigation system since Jed mortgaged his own place to buy yours. He's tricky, that Jed McClure, always wheeling and dealing. How he's gotten away with all his deals up to this point is a mystery to me; but I'll guarantee you one thing, it's just a matter of time before all his dealings blow up in his face. Now think about this Jessie, if you own even a part of this ranch, most likely you will be able to mortgage your share and buy the rest of the ranch back after the banks foreclose on Jed."

Jessie was shocked to hear Jed was in such financial trouble. She thought he had inherited a lot of money along with the ranch. Obviously, that wasn't true. If he were in such financial straits, why would he put himself into such jeopardy just to buy her ranch? She knew the right of ways and water rights were a necessity for him, but in truth, both were on his property as much as hers. No one could dispute that. From what Ed was saying, Jed took a chance on losing everything he owned to buy her place? Why did he do it? Was Jed McClure a snake or did he really care about her?

Ed interrupted her thinking. "Shall I proceed with trying to locate John Ross, Jessie?"

"What needs to be done to find him, Ed?"Jessie asked, hoping John Ross might be the answer. If she could sell her share to him, maybe Jed would let her buy back a small interest in her ranch. Now that she knew he needed the money, surely he wouldn't object to her offer.

"Well, Jessie, we will start by running some newspaper ads throughout the country, and of course, my office can begin a search in other areas."

"Oh Ed, that sounds expensive. You know I have no money."

Ed Kook smiled and patted Jessie's hand as he stood and walked toward the door. "I'll handle all the details through my office, Jessie. If we find that you own that property, you can pay me after you settle the sale. If you don't own the property, well then, I will have had the pleasure of your company and that is certainly worth it to me."

"Ed Kook, you are a fine man and such a gentleman."

Pulling Jessie toward him in a tender embrace, both were shocked as Jed came blundering into the parlor. "Hey Kook, I don't mean to rush you, but Jessie has to get up early tomorrow. She's been bugging me to teach her to drive a tractor, and I plan to teach her early tomorrow morning. I hate to have to remind you that we are ranchers, and for ranchers, this is very late in the evening."

Jessie was embarrassed all the way down to her toes. Jed knew it but ignored it.

Ed Kook smiled, his brown mustache twitching, "Yes, well thank you for reminding me that the time is late, Jed. Jessie, I'll call you during the week."

Jed smiled happily as he watched Ed Kook's big Cadillac start down the long lane, and away from all he loved.

Jessie wasn't so happy. "What was that all about, Jed? And since when will you allow me near your precious tractor?"

"The man's a bore Jessie; an obstinate, overbearing, bloated bore. Besides that fact, there's something I don't trust about him. I thought you'd be glad I came and saved you." Jed smiled.

Jessie didn't smile as she studied Jed's face, wondering if maybe Jed was jealous. Was he jealous of the well-traveled man, or was Jed jealous because of the relationship he thought she had with Ed Kook? She decided to test the waters. "He is not a bore, Jed! Ed's traveled all over the world. I think you're just jealous of him, because you've never been anywhere."

Jed thought about walking guard duty for hours in Korea during what was referred to simply as the Korean Conflict. "Oh, I've been places, Jessie. But, yeah, I didn't have much time for sightseeing. I was too busy trying to not get my ass shot off!"

Jessie flounced out of the room leaving Jed staring after her.

"You need more than a cup of coffee for breakfast, Ben." Jessie plumped the pillows behind his thin back and lifted the breakfast tray in front of him.

"I'm not really all that hungry, Miss Jessie, but thank you for your concern. You best hurry on out of here and finish your day's chores."

Both looked up as the door opened, with Jed quickly entering into the room. "Jessie, I told you that I would bring Ben's tray to him."

"He's right, Miss Jessie. Jed or Simon can bring my meals. There's no need for you to bother."

Jessie shook her head. "Eat your breakfast, you silly man. And then maybe you'll explain why you won't go to the hospital in Tulsa where they can have a look at your heart. Doc says...."

"Doc doesn't know what he's talking about! I've just got a case of the flu, nothing more!"

Jed settled himself on the side of the bed between Jessie and Ben. "Ben, you know she's right. Doc said there are all sorts of new

50

procedures they can do for heart problems. I even read about something called a pacemaker that...."

"I'm not about to have some strange device hooked up to me, Jed. If I live, I live. If I die, well so what, everyone dies. Now both of you get on out of here; you've got better things to do than to wait on an old man."

Jed grinned down at the old man's weary face. "No, we don't."

Jessie knew they both had a ton of work to do, but she anxiously agreed with Jed. Besides, she had questions she wanted to ask Ben. She just didn't want Jed around when she asked them, but it seemed that Jed was always around when she was alone with Ben. She couldn't help but wonder what that was all about. She knew he was jealous of Ed Kook, but he couldn't possibly be jealous of an old man who'd been like an uncle to her all these years.

"Are you coming, Jessie?" Jed held Ben's breakfast tray in one hand as he held the door open with the other.

"You go ahead, Jed. I need to talk to Ben for just a minute."

The door closed and Jed laid the tray on a table near the door. "I can wait for you, Jessie."

"I don't want you to wait for me, Jed. Just go."

Jed settled down in the big chair next to the bed. "I'll wait for you."

Ben nodded in agreement and Jessie decided they were both ridiculous. "What is it, Miss Jessie? What can I help you with?"

Jessie thought about Ed Kook's words about the property in Tulsa and the fact that Jed was nearly broke. With that thought in mind, she decided that it wouldn't hurt if Jed knew about the property. Maybe Jed could come up with some ideas to locate this John Ross. "Ben, I was wondering if you knew one of my papa's business associates by the name of John Ross?"

Ben began to cough uncontrollably, and Jed rushed to get him a glass of water. When Ben had composed himself, he settled back onto the soft pillow. "I've never heard your father speak of such a person, Miss Jessica."

Jessie wondered about that. Ben was as close as a brother to her papa. He knew everything there was to know about Sean Keegan's dealings. "Ben, are you trying to hide something from me? Are you trying to protect me from something in my father's past?"

Standing next to the bed, Jed spoke softly. "Jessie, don't bother the man anymore. He's sound asleep."

51

"Oh, I guess you're right, Jed. I keep forgetting how sick he is." As Jessie neared the door, she grabbed the tray as Jed opened the door for her.

As he looked back at Ben White, Jed noticed the old man watching them through half-closed eyes. Ben White knew a lot more than he was willing to let them know.

Jed took the tray from Jessie as they walked toward the kitchen. "Jessie, what's this story about your father owning some Tulsa property with a person named John Ross? I guess it's none of my business, but I just wondered."

"Oh Jed, it's no big secret. Well, I don't think it's a big secret. Ed Kook came out last night to tell me about the property and to ask me about this person, this John Ross."

Jed sighed in relief, knowing Ed Kook came on business and not because of an interest in his Jessie. With all Kook's fancy manners and expensive tastes, he could easily sway an innocent girl like Jessie into believing he was something he wasn't.

As they entered the kitchen, Jessie raced for the ringing telephone. "Good morning, Jessie." It was Dr. Collins, and Jessie greeted him cordially. Since Ben's illness, all of them had become good friends. "Jessie, I've been thinking about Ben. Some of his symptoms don't fit into the heart attack theory, so I'd like to do some more tests on him at my office. I know there's no use in arguing with him about going to the heart clinic in Tulsa. I've been through that conversation with him many times and he flat out refuses to go there. I can't blame him, though."

"Why would you say that, Doc? If he needs to go for more tests, then he should go to a place that can help him."

"Segregation, Jessie."

Not believing her ears, Jessie questioned Dr. Collins, "Segregation? What's that got to do with Ben getting the proper care?"

"Trust me, Jessie. It has everything to do with Ben. Now, will you please ask Jed to call me when he gets a chance?"

"Jed's standing right next to me, Doc. If something needs to be done about Ben, then I'm the one you need to speak to, not Jed."

Overhearing the conversation, Jed moved next to Jessie, and before she could say another word he took the telephone from her hand. "Yeah, Doc? What about Ben?"

Jessie couldn't hear Doc's side of the conversation, but she was furious that he had asked to speak to Jed instead of her. When Jed put the telephone back on the cradle on the wall, she let him know it. "So, now you've taken over the care of a man who's been like a part of my family to me! What's next, Jed? Will you take over control of me?"

Watching her flashing brown eyes, Jed began to laugh, and without realizing what he was doing, he pulled her into his arms. "Oh Jessie, my girl, I doubt there's a man born that could take control over you." To Jessie's shock, and Jed's too, he kissed her firmly on her lips. Quickly releasing her, he hurried from the room.

"Simon, will you please explain something to me?" Jessie asked as she snapped another green bean and tossed it into a large colander on the kitchen table.

"I will if I can, sister. What's on your mind?" Simon asked, wiping up the water from the wet beans Jessie was snapping and throwing into a colander.

"Well, why is it that Jed thinks he has to be present when I'm with Ben in the bedroom?"

Simon put the colander of dripping beans into a bowl to catch the water. He didn't answer so Jessie continued. "I swear, Simon, it seems like Jed is trying to protect me from Ben! Damn it, I've known Ben all my life!"

"Watch your Irish temper, sister. Remember your teachings from that fancy school you attended."

"Darn it, Simon, I don't need Jed to protect me from a helpless old man that I have loved all my life."

Tossing his dish towel over his shoulder, Simon walked to the tall kitchen window and peered out over the land. "Jed's not protecting you, sister. He's protecting Ben."

Jessie threw down a handful of beans. "Protecting Ben? Why on earth would Ben need protection from me? I love Ben!"

Simon turned from the window toward the young woman who'd led such a sheltered life out on the ranch. "Ah sister, it's all got to do with the Jim Crow laws."

Grabbing another handful of beans, Jessie continued. "Simon, you are making no sense! Who's Jim Crow and what has he got to do with Ben and me?"

Simon pulled up a chair and began to snap the beans with Jessie. "Jim Crow is not a 'who' Jessie, but it's a list of unofficial rules

53

regarding white and black people. To this day, some folks still believe that whites are superior to blacks; and in many places the local law will enforce this Jim Crow law."

"I don't believe a word of what you're saying, Simon. I've never seen black people being treated poorly by white people."

"How many black people do you know, sister? There's not one black family in Tahchee!"

"I went to Devon's Finishing School in Boston!"

"And just how many young black girls went to that fine finishing school you went to, sister? Oh, you don't have to answer, I know the answer. None, that's how many." Simon watched Jessie's face as she screwed it up in thought, just like she did when she was a little girl. His heart nearly broke for her. How could he ever explain the cruelty ordinarily nice folks could enforce in the name of priority. When something had been taught to you for generations, that's what you believed; and there was no changing it, not until society changed its rules. Maybe someday it would.

"Sister, did you notice that when Miss Estelle came out to the ranch with Doc last week, she didn't go into the bedroom where Ben was?"

"Oh, I thought she just wanted to visit with me."

"No, sister, I'm sure she wanted to visit with you, but most of all, she was obeying one of the old Jim Crow laws. It would have been highly improper for a white woman to enter into a black man's bedroom."

"Good Lord, Simon. Miss Estelle is a nurse!"

"Doesn't matter, sister. Rules are rules."

"Damn stupid rules, if you ask me! I never dreamed she'd give in to something so silly as a bunch of prejudiced lies. I always thought she was a fine lady!"

"Oh, sister, Miss Estelle is truly a fine lady. She's a kind and good person. She's the one who talked Doc into setting up a free clinic south of here. It's only available on Sunday afternoons because that's the only day Doc and Miss Estelle have off from their regular clinic in Tahchee. As soon as church is over, she and Doc treat the poor, including the Negros, and they don't charge them one red cent."

"Well, I don't understand that, Simon. She's allowed to treat a colored man in a clinic, but she can't treat him in his home? That's crazy."

"Well, I suppose no one says anything about it because the colored men come to their clinic for treatment. It's not like she's going into a colored man's bedroom, and besides, Doc is always with her. That's the difference, I guess."

"Oh Simon, if I didn't know you so well, I'd say you were lying to me."

"What I'm telling you is the truth. You grew up in a small town away from the big city ways and away from the silly prejudices that control men's thinking. Ben wasn't that lucky. He learned all about prejudice a long time ago when his home was burned. Now he doesn't dare allow anyone or anything to cast an evil eye on him. He protects himself. Jed knows that too, sister. That's why Jed always tries to be present when you go into Ben's bedroom. He's protecting Ben when Ben can't protect himself."

Jessie dropped her head down on her arm for a minute. Then she looked up at Simon. "I guess I just don't know much about life, Simon."

Simon thought about his own past and scowled. "Ah sister, there's some parts of life its best not to know anything about."

Later that day Jessie thought about what Simon had said about Jed protecting Ben when he couldn't protect himself, and she knew that was true. Jed was the sort of man who would protect what he cared about, and it was very obvious that he cared deeply for the welfare of the ranch and its people. Down deep inside, Jessie wondered if that unexpected kiss meant more than she had realized. Maybe Jed really did care for her.

Simon's voice broke into her thoughts. "Jessie, telephone for you. It's that lawyer fellow again."

Ed Kook studied the road that led him out of Tulsa and to Tahchee, Oklahoma. He'd hoped to get to the ranch earlier and miss the heat, but he had to attend Sunday church first, because it wouldn't look good for him if he skipped church.

Today, he welcomed this drive that he'd despised during the last two months of wining and dining Jessie Keegan. Today, this miserable drive gave him time to think, to sort out what he would tell Jessie to get her to sell the Keegan/Ross property to him. But the best part was that today would be the last time he made this miserable drive. He'd have what he wanted at long last.

From what he'd discovered, sometime after Sean's death Jessie's

55

mother had been notified of the property in Tulsa that Sean Keegan and John Ross co-owned, but she had never acknowledged the letter for some reason or other. He figured that was just about the time she went to Boston and met her new husband, too involved in her own personal life to care about what most people thought were Sean Keegan's many worthless investments.

From what he'd learned, John Ross had been killed during the Tulsa Race Riots of 1921. To ensure there were no claims on the property, Ed had legally done everything he could to locate any relative of John Ross. He'd put ads and legal notices in newspapers all over the state, and some in Texas, Arkansas, and Kansas. He'd spent quite a bit of his own money searching for any relative of this deceased John Ross and no one had claimed any rights to the property.

Since no one had answered his ads in the allotted time, legally Jessie could sell him that property, effective Wednesday. He'd get her to sign the papers today, using Wednesday's date, and he would give her the cashier's check he had processed previously, advising her to not cash the check until Wednesday. The little bit he was giving Jessie was almost a penance of the value he knew he would receive from the property, but once she signed those papers and cashed that check, the property was his.

With the opening of the interstate slicing through the black community of Greenwood, many small black businesses were being swallowed up by large corporations who'd undercut their businesses forcing them into ruin. The one major stumbling block in this big takeover was the entire city block owned by Sean Keegan's estate. It was worth a fortune by anyone's standards, and Ed Kook would be damned if he would let that sort of money slip from his hands regardless of who got hurt. As long as Jessie Keegan knew nothing of his deal, she wouldn't get hurt either.

Jessie Keegan was a sweet girl, but he knew she was definitely not of his class. The girl belonged out on a ranch in the country. She could never be the lady he sought to become his wife and run his home. Jessie might well fit into his bed, but never would she fit in with his associates, or his lifestyle. All that training at the finishing school was wasted on Jessie Keegan. She could never become a debutante, a socialite in training, as her pushy mother had planned. The girl had actually flunked one of the classes, the one called "Miss Eleanor's Charm Class." With that thought in mind, Ed broke down laughing, nearly missing his turn off into the small town of Tahchee, Oklahoma.

Feeling as though he was going to be sick, Jed watched the shiny black Cadillac as it made its way down the lane of the J&J ranch, the new name he'd come up with for the ranch. Even the few head of cattle he'd borrowed money to buy for the desolate ranch had the J&J brand. He'd called it by both their initials so Jessie might think more of him, hoping that maybe she'd finally realize he was more than a moocher on her property. It seemed to him that Jessie didn't care about him one way or another, or what he called the ranch. She was too busy dressing up all grand for the weekly dates she had with Kook, that rat fink lawyer of hers.

He knew Kook was spoiling Jessie rotten. He took her to the best restaurants in Tulsa, driving all the way out to the ranch to pick her up and then driving her all the way back to take her home. Then Kook somehow managed to get the best seats to performances that no one else could get a ticket. He knew that for a fact, because he'd tried to compete with Ed Kook for a short while. Hell, he remembered how he'd tried to buy tickets to Tulsa's local stage play version of *Westside Story* which he knew Jessie would love. The ticket agent laughed at him, told him the play had been sold out for six weeks. So where did Kook take Jessie on their third date? To see *Westside Story*, of course! Jessie still talked about that damn play.

Now, Ed was coming for their eighth date. Yeah, he knew it was their eighth date. He'd cringed every time he saw that damn black tank coming down the driveway, and he was still cringing as Kook pulled up in front of the main entryway to the home. Disgusted with Kook and mostly with himself, Jed turned and walked into his own bedroom so he didn't have to see the delight on Jessie's face when Kook announced where they would be going that evening.

Ben decided he'd been babied enough, babied half to death and he wanted to get up, get dressed and get back to work. Jed had allowed him to work on a few of the ranch books, but that was miserably uncomfortable: stretching, straining, trying to work in the dim light while lying in bed. It was time to get out of bed at long last, and no one was going to stop him.

Slipping out of a pair of his threadbare pajamas, he put on a crisp, clean work shirt, and slid his jeans up around his lean torso. Sitting on the side of the bed, he pulled on his clean work socks and laced up his worn brown work boots. With his brown belt in hand, he started from the room and entered the den on his way to the office. There he saw a man standing, one he didn't know. He was a white man! An angry white man! One with rage in his eyes!

"You son of a bitch'n black ass nigger! What in the hell do you think you're doing in Miss Jessie Keegan's home? Huh, nigger! Answer me now, before I kill you!"

Jessie threw down her dish cloth and she and Simon hurried toward the parlor, where they could hear Ben's pleas. "I'm sorry, mister. I'm sorry." As she raced forward, she could hear the sounds of angry slaps on bare skin and even worse, she could hear the pitiful pleading of the terrified old man. Who in the world would be hurting Ben?

As Jessie threw open the parlor door, she saw Jed grab the raised hand of Ed Kook stopping him in mid-air from striking Ben again with a thick brown belt. The back of Ben's shirt was shredded, and blood flowed freely down his aging brown back. "What the hell's the matter with you, Kook? What did this man do to you?" Jed yelled as he pulled Ben up from the floor and carefully sat the old man on a chair to examine his back.

Jessie gasped as she entered the room. "My God, Jed, what happened to Ben?" It was then she saw Ed Kook standing by the door with a heavy belt in his hand. "What happened here?" she shouted.

"I came to talk to you about your sale to me of that Tulsa Greenwood property, Jessie. When I saw the front door open, I walked in upon this nigger just wandering around in your house. I grabbed that weapon, that belt, away from him and confronted him."

Jed roared in anger. "Confronted him? How the hell do you confront a man when you're beating the hell out of him with a heavy belt! This man is a member of this family, Kook. You're not, so get the hell out of here!"

"My business is not with you, Jed!" Ed Kook shouted back. "I came to give Jessie a check for her property in Tulsa. I'm doing her a favor by taking that lousy piece of land off of her hands!" As Ed looked around him, all he could see was furious faces. Quickly, he crossed over to Jessie and put his arm around her possessively, more as a safe-guard for himself rather than for her. "I have your money, dear. Effective Wednesday, you may cash this check." Ed pressed the check into Jessie's hand.

Jessie shrugged his arm from around her back. "How dare you come in here and take it upon yourself to hurt a member of my family, Ed Kook! Jed is right. You don't belong here. You're not a member of this family. Get out!" Jessie knew she was throwing away all of their futures, but she couldn't help herself. She wadded up the check and threw it in Ed Kook's face. "And take your damned check with you!"

Ed picked up the check that had bounced off his face onto the floor. "Why are you causing all this commotion because of a useless nigger, Jessie?"

"Ben White is my friend, Ed! Now take that check and get out of my house!"

"My God, Jessie! Don't you realize that you'll never be able to sell that sorry piece of property to anyone but me? I'm trying to be your friend and help you to recapture your ranch." Carefully, Ed smoothed out the wrinkled check. "Look at this, Jessie! This is a cashier's check for ten thousand dollars made out in your name. All you have to do is sign this bill of sale and the money is yours. Your worries are over, and everything's all nice and legal."

Jessie heard a deep chuckle coming from the chair behind her. "Nothing's legal, *Mister* Kook. That check isn't worth the powder to blow it to hell!"

Ed Kook turned; ready to hit the old man with his bare fist, but Jed's fist was faster as it came down on Ed's nose, his horn-rimmed glasses shattering onto the floor. "Damn you, Jed McClure. Look what you've done to my new glasses!"

Ben cleared his throat as he watched Ed bend over to collect the papers that were knocked from his hands by Jed. "As I was trying to say, *Mister* Kook, Jessie is not the rightful owner of the Greenwood property. John Ross is still the legal owner of that property."

Ed glared at Ben as he stood. "Oh what the hell do you know about that property, you pathetic old black bastard? Who the hell are you anyway?"

"My name is Ben White, *Mister* Kook....but back in Tulsa in 1921, I was known as John Ross."

Smiling, Ben leaned down and collected the check that had dropped from Ed's hand. "Ten thousand dollars, *Mister* Kook? You offered our Jessie this peddling amount for property that's worth many times more than that? You really are a sorry, no-good crook. I knew your grandfather years ago, and you are just like him; and sir, that is not a compliment!" Ben took the check and threw it back on the floor. "Now *Mister* Kook, you heard what my *family* told you. Get out! And let me add, don't ever come back!"

As the black car raced down the driveway, all faces were not on the car but on the weathered face of Ben White. "Jessie, Tuesday we'll go into Tulsa, and I'll make claim for that property in Greenwood before it's considered Unclaimed Property and auctioned off to the highest bidder. The property deed was in my coat when I made my hasty retreat out of Tulsa years ago, the only thing I had on me when I came to the Keegan Ranch so many years ago. I've been watching the news reports about the property, and I know there are investors ready to buy at its rightful value. As soon as I make claim on it, I'll turn it over to you, Miss Jessie."

"Oh no, that property is yours Ben, or should we call you John?" Jessie asked.

"I've been Ben White for the last forty years. I can see no reason in confusing the situation any more than it is. I'll continue being Ben White."

"But you can't be Ben White anymore. Legally, you are still John Ross and you are a property owner, a rich one from the sounds of it."

Ben's voice softened as he allowed himself to use the familiar name he'd always wanted to use with the young woman. "Jessie, the only riches I have are what I've found here on this ranch in the security of my family. Knowing that I had this tremendous wealth that I couldn't touch, while I watched you and Jed struggle to keep this ranch afloat, well, that nearly killed me. I'm certain that's why I got so sick. It wasn't a bad heart. It was heartache from watching the people I loved hurting so badly, and I didn't dare help them when I knew I could."

No one said anything for several minutes, and then Jed broke the silence. "So you had this property for all these years. Why didn't you do something with it a long time ago, Ben?"

"I couldn't, Jed. Not unless I wanted to go to jail. You see, forty years ago, I killed a white man. I'm wanted for murder."

Jessie gasped in shock, then ran to Ben and knelt before him. "Oh Ben, it couldn't have been your fault. Something terrible must have

happened for you to take another man's...."

Jed interrupted. "Ben, I think it's time we heard the whole story."

Ben pulled himself up from his chair. "Yes, well, if I'm going to tell the story of my life, let's get a glass of iced tea and settle down some place comfortable. It's a sordid tale and a long one. To understand my past, you have to understand my family's early beginnings.

Chapter 5

Ben took a long sip of ice tea, and settled himself into a comfortable brown leather chair that had seen better days. Stretching his long legs out in front of him, he smiled warmly at the faces that had become his family. He would miss every one of them when he was cold and alone in a musky jail cell if he was lucky enough to see a jail cell before he was hanged. But he knew it was time....time to face what he'd been running from for the last forty years.

"My great grandfather was born a slave on a large plantation in South Carolina. I'm not exactly sure what year he was born as records of the blacks weren't accurate back then; but I know he was born some time during the early eighteen-hundreds. His name was Atu Wigfelt. Atu, meaning born on a Saturday, and Wigfelt was the plantation where he was born.

The black folk on the Wigfelt plantation were very fortunate people. The master saw that each family had an individual cabin for their home, that all had plenty of food on their tables, and that no family was ever torn apart by trades or sales to other plantation owners. The master, Mr. Wigfelt, was a great believer in education and decided that anyone who wanted to learn would be given as much education as possible. Education of the slaves was not acceptable to most of the other plantation owners, so this was never broadcast for general knowledge.

As I understand it, one of the young black girls born on the Wigfelt plantation, Odessa was her name, was born with a club foot. She seemed to be highly intelligent; but Master Wigfelt knew she would be useless in the plantation home or in the fields, so he saw that she was educated right along with his own daughter. The two girls became fast friends until Master Wigfelt's daughter succumbed to a weak heart and died several years later. When Miss Wigfelt died, Odessa's education stopped; but by that time she had a healthy grasp of the basics of education and soon became a teacher to any Negro child who wanted to learn.

My great grandfather, Atu, was one who craved knowledge, and in a way, that was his own undoing. When he read about life outside the plantation, he learned about being a free man, and he knew that freedom was what he wanted. He knew he had been given more than most Negros and he was grateful; but at night as he lay outside of his parents' cabin under the protection of the star-sprinkled heavens, the smell of ham, beans and cornbread lingering from the open doorway, he yearned to follow those stars into a world where he could make his own way in his life. But alas, he knew that day of his freedom would never be.

Then, one cold spring day when he was around twenty or so, Master Wigfelt gathered all his slaves together for a mass meeting. Everyone came. All work ceased. The master had something to tell them.

He was dying, he told his people as he stood amidst the cold rain, the soulful mourning and weeping, the denials and disbelief. He did not want them to be afraid, he'd said. He wanted them to be free. Upon his death, every one of them would be freed, and they would be given papers of their emancipation as proof that they were free people.

A few weeks later, the beloved master was laid in the ground, and as much as the other people worried about their fates as free people, Atu was delighted. Oh, he was sorry the master had died, but he had his freedom, or so he thought.

Master Wigfelt was no sooner in his grave than the new master came, his nephew John Wigfelt. John Wigfelt was every bit as cruel as his uncle was kind, and along with the disappearance of his uncle's kindness, the letters of emancipation also disappeared. The good black folk of Wigfelt plantation were slaves to the most brutal of masters. Young John Wigfelt was a tyrant, rapist, and murderer. Kitchen pots no longer bubbled with shanks of ham and beans, and cornbread was a luxury; children went to bed hungry, young girls bound their breasts to hide their maturity, and young men were beaten into submission. And more than ever, Atu dreamed of freedom.

Atu was a strong, strapping young man, and he knew that he could escape across state lines into Georgia where he could hide, but what of his father, mother, and sister? He couldn't leave them at the hands of a monster, so he hid away his dreams, only allowing them to surface at night as he lay under the same stars that had once promised his freedom.

Atu's sister, Efia, meaning born on Friday, was as beautiful as her name, and it didn't take long for John to discover the young brown-skinned girl. A child was more like it. She was barely developed when she was placed in the manor house as an upstairs maid. Sometime after that, it was discovered she was pregnant with John's child. Efia hated

John as all the slaves did, and she refused to have his child. Atu's and Efia's parents pleaded with her to accept her fate. She refused. They found her with a broken neck after she had jumped from the upstairs balcony to the marble floor below.

For what John Wigfelt had done to his sister, Atu nearly beat the cruel man to death when he found him alone in the woods. When Atu's parents discovered what had happened, they begged Atu to run, leave and find safety; surely he would be hanged, they said. After much arguing about honor, Atu did leave his family and began his long walk westward to freedom.

As Atu walked, he remembered the stories he'd read of the Indian heathens of the west, and he knew there were Indians in Georgia. Half afraid to venture forward for fear he would be scalped, Atu knew he had no choice but to smother his fears and keep on walking.

To pass the time as he walked, he wondered about the Indian people, and imagined they would live in teepees and wigwams as he had read about in the books; but after some time, he was amazed to see large plantations owned by wealthy Cherokee Indians. Studying the fine plantations from a distance, he wondered just who did the Indians have working those huge plantations? As he watched the rows of black people heading toward the fields, he spotted an overseer on a horse with a whip in his hand, and Atu knew who worked those fields. The blacks he'd seen were slaves for the Indians. With a quickened step, Atu changed his direction and walked north toward the Blue Ridge Mountains, hoping that there he would find freedom and peace at last.

After walking many miles, he discovered another community of the Cherokee people, and was amazed to see that they had adapted the style of the Europeans. The women dressed in the modern styles of the day and kept their log cabins clean and inviting. The men were farmers, hunters and fishermen. They built roads, schools and churches, and developed their own unique alphabet. Except for their black hair and red skin they could have been European middle class.

They were a friendly outgoing people. After seeing that Atu came in peace, was a willing worker, as well as an adept hunter, they accepted Atu into their community. During the Festival of the Corn, one young Indian girl, Agaliha, whose name meant "Sunshine", chose the handsome Atu as her husband; and Atu felt he had found his peace at last. Atu became Agaliha's hunter, and she in turn weaved him a marriage belt of river-read fibers, dyed red and black to identify him as a taken man. Being taken, belonging to his beautiful Indian wife, did not bother Atu one bit. He loved her dearly. A year later Agaliha presented Atu with a son she named Unaduti, whose name meant wooly head, because of his great head of black-wooly hair like his father's. When Unaduti became a man, his father would give him another name. It would be one of strength and honor as was the custom amongst the tribe.

All went well within the community for some time, and Atu discovered that being married to the beautiful Indian girl gave him more than joy. It gave him his freedom legally. He would no longer be considered a slave; he was husband to the Indian girl who was a free person, thereby making him a free person. He also learned that the Cherokee people had been allotted this land in Georgia in 1791, by a treaty made with the U.S. Government. The Principle People, the Cherokees, were considered an independent nation, and managed to hold onto their lands and to govern themselves in spite of so many other Indian tribes being forced from their lands. He had a real home. He had found peace, or so he thought.

One day it was announced to the people of the tribe that gold had been discovered on the land of the Cherokees, and that the white people of Georgia were trying to take the land from the Cherokees. That was the story they had been told, but Atu was certain the whites really wanted the fertile land that the Cherokees had been so successfully farming. Of course, the Cherokees protested legally, and in 1830 they took their claim to the U.S. Supreme Court. The Supreme Court agreed in favor of the Cherokees, but that didn't seem to matter one whit to President Andrew Jackson, a man as harsh and tough as his nickname, "Old Hickory".

In the year 1835, Congress forced the Cherokees to give up their land, and despite the opposition of Principle Chief John Ross, who was my namesake, the land was sold for five million dollars. Even though only a minority of the Indians had accepted this offer, Major Ridge, a Cherokee member of the tribal council, lawmaker and leader, signed the treaty with the government. In truth, Major Ridge and his son, John, had hoped there would be peace then among the Indians and the whites; but he knew when he signed that agreement, he had signed his own death warrant within the tribe.

As the years passed, Agaliha gave Atu a daughter and was again pregnant in 1838, when the federal troops were called in to *escort*, I believe that was the term used, about 13,000 Cherokee people to their *new* home in Indian Territory in the western part of the United States. Atu knew that Chief John Ross had done everything he could to help his people, but it wasn't enough. Almost 4,000 of these peaceful people died as they were pushed from their land and were forced to walk over 1,000 miles in the harshest of winters. There were no accommodations made for these people; they slept under wagons and on the ground, huddled together for warmth; and one by one they died, including Atu's beloved pregnant wife and their little daughter.

This horrible travesty of justice became known as "The Trail Where They Cried" or in later years, "The Trail of Tears". Some folks said the name didn't come from the proud Indians who refused to show their tears in this seemingly act of genocide, but rather, the name came from the tears of the white folks watching the injustice to this proud people as they buried their dead, and trudged on through the misery of winter, bayonets at their backs.

As angry as he was over the needless death of his pregnant wife and his little girl, Atu knew he must continue on for the sake of his young son. Often carrying the boy, sometimes pulling him along behind him, but always protecting him from whatever danger lurked near, Atu continued to walk. As they entered the Indian Territory which was later called Oklahoma, land of the Redman, Atu stopped his walking and gazed at the beauty around him. He stood in awe as he watched the clouds drifting in the most azure-blue sky, and settling in white puffs over distant emerald-green hills, but the most magnificent sight his tired eyes could behold were the fields of endless colors of purple, orange and yellow flowers. The colors were so vivid that it appeared as though someone had created a glorious, vibrant Indian blanket of warm-welcoming colors. He hoped that in this beautiful unspoiled land, they would find peace. That was not to be.

After they settled into Indian Territory, under the leadership of Principle Chief John Ross, the Cherokee people were sorely angry for the losses of their loved ones, and they immediately demanded justice against those who had sold them out of their own land in Georgia. The final act of the Trail of Tears was the execution of Major Ridge and his son, John, who agreed to the signing of the Treaty of Indian Springs, selling their land in Georgia to the U.S. government. Major Ridge's prophecy had been fulfilled.

Atu again married, this time to a Cherokee Indian woman who lost her husband and children on the long walk from Georgia to

Oklahoma. They had three children together after settling around the land that one day would became the town of Tahlequah, Oklahoma. Knowing how to read the white man's language from his schooling on the plantation, Atu became a teacher to the Indian children. He had finally found his long sought-after peace. His walk was done.

Atu and Agaliha's son, Unaduti, my grandfather, married an Indian girl and moved north with his family in 1860 to the settlement known as "Tulasi", which was later known as Tulsa, Oklahoma. In 1890, my father, John Ross, married my mother, Sara, a Negro woman, and they moved to the Greenwood Heights community of Tulsa where I was born."

Ben emptied his tea glass and stood. "Jessie, Jed, may we continue this story later? I'm very tired from sitting for such a long time. I need to stretch my legs before they start cramping."

"I'll fix us up something for supper, and maybe we can hear the rest of the story later this evening," Simon said as he walked toward the kitchen. Jed and Jessie were left staring at each other and finally they wandered out onto the porch.

Jed pointed toward the swing and Jessie took her place there, waiting for Jed to join her. It seemed so natural to have him beside her, she thought, as he eased his large body down next to her. It was a comfortable feeling. A feeling she missed when he wasn't around. Were those old feelings she'd had for him so long ago returning? Maybe, she thought, maybe those old feelings were always meant to be.

Ben settled back in the worn brown-leather chair. Jessie, Jed and Simon were ready for the rest of his story. "Where did I leave off?" he asked.

Everyone started to speak at once, reminding him that he'd left his story just as he began to talk about the Greenwood district of Tulsa.

In his deep, distinctive voice, Ben continued his story. "Years ago, Tulsa and Greenwood were almost considered two separate cities due to the separation of Negros and whites. Greenwood, the Negro section of Tulsa, was located north of the city and was a very progressive city. It was established at the turn of the century by a man named O.W. Gurley.

Having the same curiosity for knowledge as had his father and his father before him, my father quickly became a financial success and leader within the community. Greenwood had about 600 successful businesses and was referred to as the "Black Wallstreet" by some, and

"Little Africa" by a few, and worse by others. Let them call it whatever they wanted, but the truth was the stately homes of the affluent black people living there were said to be comparable in affluence to Beverly Hills, California; but even with the huge success of Greenwood, or maybe because of it, the racial tension between the whites and blacks ran high in Tulsa.

Many of the white people of Tulsa considered the black people inferior to them; and of course the ignorant white trash gobbled that up because they had to be superior to someone, even if it was only the lowly blacks. Now don't get me wrong, Greenwood had its share of niggers. Yes, Jessie, I called them niggers. The folks that I considered niggers were the drug pushers, the pimps, the thieves and any man that made his way in life off the frailties of human suffering, and there were just as many white niggers as there were black niggers.

"Still, there were some white folks who had been taught from childhood that the black people were inferior, no matter what they accomplished in life." Ben stopped talking, his astute mind deep in thought. "I have always wondered how a black teacher, doctor, or a minister of God, could possibly be inferior to some useless white bum, who refused to work, neglected his family, and spent his days shooting blarney over cheap whiskey with other white trash. Oh well, enough of that. We can't change the world.

"In my twenties, I was a dapper young man, certain of my good looks through my Cherokee and Negro background, and I had no doubt I was going to make a big difference in the misunderstandings between the whites and blacks of Tulsa. That was my goal in life; to bring better understanding between the two cultures. I had just finished law school, eager and excited to make my mark on the world, when I met the woman of my dreams, Aimee Despre.

"Aimee was from a French-Negro background down in New Orleans, Louisiana. I remember her grandfather said his family was too black to be white and too white to be black. They were Creoles of color, he'd said, mallatos lost in the shuffle of civil conflict. Shortly after the Civil War began, Mr. Despre moved his family west and made his fortune when oil was discovered on his land. Back then Negros were not allowed to own land in some locations, but Mr. Despre was French when he needed to be, Negro when he wanted to be, and he chose to be French when he purchased the land.

"I first met Aimee Despre at a swank coming-out ball in Greenwood. From the first moment I saw her, I thought she was the most beautiful woman God had ever made. Her skin was light caramel, soft and warm. Her eyes were an unusual green, more like the color of olives than an ordinary green. Her nose was slender and straight. Her chin was tiny, tilted up, proud and strong. Her lips were full and ripe, made for kisses, my kisses. Her willowy young body was lean where it was supposed to be and padded soft where it was needed. She was a goddess, my goddess.

"I chased her unmercifully until she gave up and accepted a date with me. Poor Aimee didn't have a chance of escaping me after that. I wined her and dined her, filled her home daily with bouquets of flowers, and blatantly made a nuisance of myself. Finally, she agreed to marry me. I'm still not certain that Aimee loved me the day she married me." Ben stopped and smiled, then continued. "I spent the first three nights of our honeymoon sleeping on a chair near the bed where she slept. I had always been so busy showing her what a success I was, I forgot to show her my heart, my inner love for her. When I did, she fell in love with the real me.

"Our married life was all I could have ever dreamed it would be. We had a grand home as fine as any home in Greenwood. We were respected among my business associates, and through Aimee's generosity and kindness, we were also respected by the poor living on the bowery of Greenwood. Because of Aimee's genteel background, I saw to it that we belonged to all the socially-elite clubs of Greenwood. Aimee said she didn't care about high society, but I did. Those were her people and I was determined she would not step down in society by marrying me.

"Our fourth wedding anniversary was on June 1, 1921, and I knew Aimee had some marvelous surprise she wanted to tell me at our anniversary dinner. I had to be out of town for the three days prior, but I promised her I would be home early on that day.

"Aimee had suffered three miscarriages over the last four years of our marriage, and both of us were devastated at our losses. We desperately wanted a child, but neither one of us talked about it anymore. What good did it do? Then one night, I noticed Aimee's normally flat stomach was becoming a bit round. She didn't say anything and neither did I. I just kept watching her girth grow larger as the weeks and months passed. Oh, how I wanted to ask her if we were going to have our baby, but I didn't dare mention it. I knew she'd tell me when she felt there was a good possibility our child would survive until full term. And I knew that was the big surprise she would tell me that night. I couldn't wait to get home."

Ben arose from his chair. "Excuse me please. I'll be right back." he said as he hurried out into the dark night.

Jessie started after him. "Ben, is there something wrong? Ben..."

Jed grabbed her arm before she could go after the old man. "Let him go, Jessie. He's reliving his nightmares."

Watching Ben leave, Simon was absorbed in memories of his own family in Colona: his devastating obligations, the woman he'd loved, his own unending pain. "I think I'll get a bit of air myself. You two young folks wait right here."

As Jessie watched Simon hurry from the room, she turned to Jed. "I don't understand, Jed. Why is Ben so upset? Maybe it's his heart."

"I think maybe it's a broken heart that he's remembering, Jessie." As Jed watched Jessie hurry toward the window, he wondered about the money that Ben said he would turn over to Jessie. Jessie could easily buy the ranch out from under him if he was late on even one of his payments to the bank. Needing to purchase Winter Wheat for fall planting and not having any money, he knew that was a big possibility. She would have her ranch again, and she wouldn't need him anymore. She'd be rid of him just like she always wanted to be. Jed felt sick.

The door opened and Ben and Simon entered the room. Ben took his place in his brown chair, Simon sat on a cane back-rocker, and Jessie and Jed shared the small sofa.

Ben cleared his throat and began again with his story. "Before I left to go out of town, I suggested to Aimee that we have the bedroom next to ours repainted. I didn't dare mention the fact that by now I was certain she was around six-months pregnant and our child most likely would survive. It seemed that as long as we didn't mention it, the child continued to grow; but the truth was, we needed a bedroom for this child that we were going to have, whether we mentioned it or not.

"Aimee quickly agreed, and I contacted a reputable contractor from Tulsa. He said he'd send one of his crew down to complete the job the next day. The following day was Memorial Day, May 30, 1921, and they would be closed through June 1st, he'd told me.

"As I returned home around noon on June 1st from my business journey, I had this horrible uneasy feeling. As I passed through the city of Tulsa and nearby Greenwood, I realized that I was returning to an uproar of confusion and destruction. As I pressed harder on the gas pedal of my Model T Ford, I could smell the smoke before the fires and devastation could be seen. As I entered Greenwood, I saw white people running, shouting and screaming death threats toward all Negros. I knew that interracial feelings had been running high for some time, but I had no idea it would erupt with such violence into what was later known as the Tulsa Race Riots of 1921.

"Driving down my street where there had once been fine homes, I witnessed skeletal remnants of burned-out shells of houses, and I prayed to God to let my home and my beautiful Aimee be spared. It was not to be.

"I barely stopped my car as I jumped out and hurried toward the front of my home which was still fairly unburned, not like the back side that was smoldering and ashen. As I raced toward my front door, I could see my beloved Aimee lying across the threshold in a pool of blood. She was alive as I grabbed her into my arms and headed back to my car. As I carried her to the car, she whispered the name of the person who had done this to her. Unlike the rest of the burning of Greenwood which was racial, this dreadful act was a personal one. The painter, Sam Downs, a white no good piece of scum who had been sent to our home to paint the room, had made advances toward my Aimee. Naturally, she had rejected him putting him properly in his place. The rejection from a black woman made him so furious that he came back later that day, hiding under the cloak of the racial tensions giving way in the streets of Greenwood. He told Aimee that he'd left something in the room that he needed to retrieve. When she let him back in the house, he attacked her. He beat her, kicked her in the stomach, and left her for dead as he poured turpentine around the back of the house and started it afire. With all the bedlam and confusion whirling around the area because of the race riots in Greenwood, no one even noticed my beloved wife lying on her own doorstep.

"I knew she had lost the baby, or was losing it as I raced toward the small Negro hospital, or to what used to be the hospital. When I got there, I saw the doctor working on the ground over a young boy, and as I hurried toward him, Aimee in my arms, I saw the doctor pull the sheet up over the boy. He was dead, but my Aimee was still breathing. I felt my heart in my throat, as the doctor threw down a sheet and I laid my Aimee on the ground. The doc motioned for me to stand back as he examined her. Then I watched in absolute horror as he pulled the sheet up over her beautiful olive-green eyes, still wide open as though searching the dark heavens for a reason for all this misery.

"The doctor didn't say another word to me as he moved on to the next person lying on his operating table, the filthy ground. I cannot remember when I felt such a mixture of emotion as I felt leaving my Aimee dead on the cold ground. All I knew was that I would have my revenge and I did. I found that sorry son-of-a-bitch, the white painter who killed my wife and child, and I killed him with my bare hands.

"Everything I loved was gone....everything. And the reason I had been gone when my wife needed me, the reason I was not there to defend her? I had gone out of town to make a purchase on that damn block of land in Greenwood. The deed to the land was still in my car as I raced away from Tulsa leaving my wife's family to deal with her body. I had dealt with her killer. That was enough. It was all I could do. And I was damned if I was going to hang for killing that bastard that took the one thing in this world that meant everything to me. Aimee was dead. She was in Heaven. God had taken away her pain and lifted her up into his arms. There was nothing left for me anymore.

"After I got about forty miles down the road, my Model T Ford gave out, and I started walking due north until I came upon the ranch of Sean Keegan: a white man, my best friend, my brother. He took me in, helped me heal in my grief, and after I told him what I had done, he never once judged me. After I got back on my feet, I asked Sean to give me a dollar to buy half of my property in Greenwood. With his name on the contract, no one would dare try and take the property away from a respected white rancher, so we post dated the sale back to June 21st. For all practical purposes, John Ross died in Tulsa. In Sean's will he left the property back to me if anything happened to him, but neither one of us ever suspected Sean would die so young. I was older than he, and we just assumed I would go first.

"So there you have it. That's my story. Tuesday, I will claim that property and sell it to Jessie for a dollar with the stipulation that she sell it immediately. I don't need, nor do I want that money. As far as I'm concerned, the money is Jessie's. I want no part of it. After that's finished, I will report to the sheriff and let him do what he wants with me. I've run as long as I can run, I'm finished.

Jessie raced over to the old man and knelt before him. "Ben, you can't do this. You're not a young man. Going to jail, to prison, that would kill you. We don't need the money that badly, do we Jed?"

"No, Jessie, you're right," Jed answered flashing a big smile, thankful Jessie wouldn't soon kick him off the ranch. "We can do without the money, but how could we possibly do without Ben's fancy bookkeeping?"

"No, Jed and Jessie. I thank you for your concern over my welfare, but my running days are over. Talking it all out, like I did this afternoon, has convinced me that I must face my fate if I ever want to be with my Aimee again. God doesn't look too mercifully upon murderers, so I'll do my time in jail and hope God will forgive me. Still, Jessie, the money is yours. Maybe you could use it toward the ranch."

Quickly leaving the room, Jed knew he was going to be sick.

Chapter 6

Deciding that she had put off this worry long enough, Jessie closed the door to her room and walked toward her old red Reo, her head low, her thoughts troubled. What was she going to say to the sheriff when she got to Tulsa? What if he accused her of harboring an escaped fugitive? What if he put her in jail? She wouldn't be able to help Ben one bit if she were incarcerated. Stopping in her tracks, she turned back toward her room.

If she told the sheriff what an upright citizen Ben had been all these years, would that make a difference, she wondered as she again turned toward her big truck. Everyone in Tahchee thought highly of Ben, didn't they? But, then, when was the last time Ben was in Tahchee? It was over a year ago, she remembered, because Ben hardly ever went to Tahchee. No one could vouch for him there, and the sheriff would think she, Simon, and Jed were lying in his defense. Jessie turned back toward her room, her mind soaked in sorrow, her heart heavy in grief.

"Are you going someplace, or not, Jessie?" Jed shouted as he walked toward his pickup truck.

Jessie hurried after him, as he ignored her and kept on walking toward his truck. "Jed, wait a minute. Where are you going?"

"I asked you first. You never did answer me."

"I need to go into Tulsa and see the sheriff."

"What for?"

"Jed, you know good and well I have to defend Ben of these murder charges."

Stopping so quickly Jessie nearly ran into him, Jed turned and glared at Jessie. "You have got to be out of your mind, Jessie. A white woman pleading the case of a Negro man? Those good ole' boys at the sheriff's office would laugh you out of the place! What in the world gave you that crazy idea?"

"Well, someone has got to defend him, Jed."

"And I am the one who is going to do it, Jessie. Not you!" For the first time that she could ever remember, Jed yelled at her, leaving her devastated and confused. Why was he so angry at her?

Jessie watched as Jed opened his truck door and got inside. Pulling out the choke, he turned on the ignition, gave two clops on the gas pedal, and pushed in the clutch. Quickly, she raced around the front of the truck to the other door and jumped inside. "Not without me, you're not going to the sheriff's office, Jed! I'm going with you."

"Well, you damn well better hang on, Jessie, 'cause I'm in a hurry!" Jed growled as he revved up the engine and let it go, hurling the small truck down the bumpy lane and on to Tulsa where the fate of Ben White would finally be settled.

Ben was free! And at long last, Jessie knew he could look forward to someday being with his Aimee. Daring not to look at Jed as they traveled the road back to the ranch, Jessie covered her mouth from the snicker lingering there. She just could not believe how brilliantly Jed had handled the situation at the sheriff's office. Without him, she would have gotten nowhere with that ornery sheriff, but Jed sure knew how to handle him.

At first when Jed said he was inquiring into the death of a Negro, John Roth, in 1921, the sheriff scowled at him in disgust and ignored both of them.

When Jessie told him how rude he was, the deputy glared at her in contempt. "If'n ya know what's good fo ya, ya'll will go on back to ya home and don't worry about no nigger business."

Stifling at the insult to Ben's people, Jessie interrupted. "And if you know what's good for you, you will give us the information...."

Grabbing her hand, Jed squeezed her fingers until they were numb, so she shut up and remained quiet. "Sheriff Tanner, this lady is from the East and doesn't understand how it is here in Oklahoma. Don't pay her any attention. You know how dumb those people are." Jed winked at the deputy and the deputy grinned in agreement with Jed. Jessie tried to squirm away from Jed's strong grip, but he held tight.

Flashing a knowing smile at the sheriff, Jed continued. "Actually Sheriff, we're here to inquire about the murder of Sam Downs on June 1st, 1921."

"What ya mean, Sam Downs' murder on June da 1st of 1921? What in tarnation would ya'll be a talkin' bout?"

"This lady here, Miss Priscilla Kennedy, is my cousin, on my pa's side, Sheriff." Jed stopped to sigh in disgusted resignation. "Her pa was third-cousin to Governor Winfred of New York City, New York. She wants to be a news-writer, a reporter. And she's looking to make her a big name for herself with a newspaper out of New York. My pa made me bring her down to see you, out of consideration for his sister, Matilda, because Cousin Priscilla and Aunt Matilda have come to visit us for a spell. I surely didn't want to bother a busy man like you, Sheriff, but Pa said he knew your reputation as being the finest sheriff in the state, and he said if I brought her to see you personally, you'd know just how to help her. She's doing some research on unsolved murders and Sam Downs' name came up."

Sheriff Tanner eyed Jed cautiously, sniffing out something he wasn't sure about. As he stared at Jessie and Jed in skepticism, Jed continued. "Pa said you'd probably get some pretty fine publicity from that New York newspaper if you helped their little junior reporter. Pa couldn't wait to call his cousin, the governor, and tell him how helpful you were to little Priscilla."

The sheriff's face lit up as he visualized his name in print in a fancy New York newspaper, and wondered if maybe they'd link his name with that Governor Winfred, whoever he was. "Well, if'n it's facts ya need, I'm da one dat kin find 'em. Ya'll go on an git ya self a cup of coffee over at the cafe, ya hear. Give me 'bout twenty minutes, 'cause I kin find bout anyting ya need." And he did.

Exactly twenty minutes later, Jed and Jessie returned. The sheriff was grinning at his findings. "Sorry, Miss Priscilla, but ya ain't got no unsolved murder. Dat fellow, that Sam Downs ya'll wanted to know about, he never died in 1921, but got hisself killed whilst he was in prison in Texas for murdering a nigger child in 1947. Nobody ever knew who killed him. Good riddance to bad rubbish, I'd say."

Jed stuck out his hand for the sheriff. "Thank you, sheriff. I guess Priscilla will have to wait till she gets back to New York City to find some unsolved murders. We take care of our own business down here in Oklahoma. Of course, we got the best of the best in sheriffs here. Oh, and sheriff, I know Pa will mention your name the next time he talks to Governor Winfred. Isn't that right, Priscilla?"

Jessie couldn't hold it back any longer, breaking down into a fitful laugh.

"What's so funny, Jessie?"

"Priscilla? You called me Priscilla? Good heavens, Jed. Couldn't you come up with a better name for me than that?"

Despite his anger at what was to come, Jed smiled as he pulled his truck into the driveway of the ranch and noticed Ben and Simon waiting for them in the front yard. Ben White was a free man: a wealthy man, a man who was giving his fortune to Jessie. As he stepped out of his truck, Jed wondered just how long it would take for Jessie to get rid of him.

Jessie threw her arms around Ben White. "You didn't kill Sam Downs, Ben, because he survived the beating you gave him. He was murdered though. He killed a child and was murdered while in prison for that crime. "

Ben couldn't believe what Jessie was telling him, nor could he believe that these two people cared enough about him to search out the answers when he could not do himself. Smiling, he was certain he could feel Aimee's soft hand touching him, and he knew that someday he would be with her, again. Nothing else mattered now.

"You're a rich man, Ben. I'll drive you into Tulsa tomorrow and you can claim the rights to your land before it's too late," Jessie said, releasing his arm.

"Jessie, as I said before, I don't want that property. I'll sell it to you for one dollar and you can do what you want with it. It should be worth a pretty penny after all these years."

Ben and Simon walked into the house leaving Jed and Jessie alone on the porch, Jessie deep in thought. "Jed, I was just thinking; with that money of Ben's, we could pay off the mortgage to the ranch if you would let me buy into the ranch."

"What did you say, Jessie?"

Jessie thought Jed didn't hear her, but the truth was he was dumbfounded and didn't know how to answer. He hadn't expected her to start trying to get rid of him so fast.

"I want to buy back into the ranch, Jed. That property of Ben's is worth a considerable amount more than Ed Kook offered and of course Ben knew that. So, what do you say, Jed? We can be partners."

"I don't know, Jessie. I have to think about that for a minute." In the beginning, all he'd wanted was to help Jessie so she wouldn't lose her ranch. Now he knew that the ranch was the only thing holding her to him. He couldn't give her up.

"Why do you need to think about it, Jed? It only makes good sense for Heaven's sake."

"Jessie, if you're trying to get rid of me by buying me out, then let me remind you, you don't know how to run a ranch by yourself. You may have the money, but you have to know how to use the money to the best means. No, I'm not going to give up my share of this ranch just so you can get your name back on the property and then lose it again."

"Jed, I'm not asking to buy the ranch from you! I just want to be a legitimate part of it. It would be a business deal!"

"Yeah, sure, Jessie, and then one day you will get all bent out of shape at me and force me out. Nope, that's not going to happen. I can make this place pay off. I just need some time."

"You need money, Jed. If Ed Kook didn't do anything else for me, he let me know you are broke up to your elbows. There's no way you can do all the things you plan for this place while carrying a mortgage on the McClure ranch and barely making payments on this one. You'll wind up losing everything, Jed."

Jed pulled his arm away from Jessie and started toward the house. She knew he was in trouble and he felt that was almost more than he could handle. "When it gets to the point that it looks like I'm going to lose the Keegan ranch, Jessie, then I'll sell it to you. Not until then."

"What's it going to take, Jed?" Jessie asked running to stand in front of the door of the house so he couldn't walk away from her. "What will it take to get my ranch back?"

Jed picked Jessie up and moved her from the doorway back to the porch. "I'm going to wash up for lunch, Jessie," Jed answered, feeling sick to his stomach. She'd get that ranch one way or another, he knew she would, and along with it, she'd get rid of him.

Frustrated with the obstinate man, Jessie stood on the porch glaring at him. "Jed! Stop walking away from me! I'm trying to talk to you!"

Ignoring Jessie, Jed walked into the house toward his bedroom and closed the door. The door flung open and Jessie stood staring at him. "We can have a contract drawn up, Jed. We can be business partners."

Why couldn't she understand how he felt, he wondered, turning to face her. "I don't want a business partner!"

Jessie hurried across the room and stood facing Jed. "Well, what do you want, Jed?"

"I want a wife!" Jed couldn't believe he'd actually said that, but that was what he wanted. He wanted Jessie as much as he'd always wanted her, maybe more. For the last few months he'd settled on just being near her, but that craving he had for her was always there waiting to throw him into a tailspin if given the slightest chance.

Without a second thought, Jessie answered. "I can be your wife, Jed. Being your wife will make our deal very legal!"

Jed couldn't believe what Jessie was saying. "You don't understand, Jessie. I want a wife who will share my bed; a wife who will give me a bunch of little brats running all over the place."

Jessie didn't flinch. She knew what was involved in a marriage. Did Jed think she was stupid or what? "I'm strong and healthy, Jed. I can share your bed, and I'm certain I can give you a bunch of little brats running all over the place just like you want. Marry me, Jed. That will seal our bargain."

Jed threw up his hands as he glared at Jessie. "Jessie, don't you understand me? I don't want a wife as a part of a bargain, and I sure as hell don't want a brood mare for my brats!"

Jessie glared at Jed, hands on her hips, defiant."Well, Jed, what more can I offer?"

"Are you out of your mind, Jessie?"

"No, I'm not, Jed. Think about it for a minute. We get married and I have my name back on the ranch, and you have the money you need to run the place. We've gotten along fairly well over the last few months, and I've come to accept you as part of this ranch. We'd make a good team, Jed."

"I can't believe you, Jessie. You'd do just about anything to get this old ranch back even if you have to marry me and have my brats! My God, woman! Are you nuts?"

"I know you think I'm nuts, and I don't care about that. You've been good for the ranch, Jed. I know with a little financial support you could bring this ranch back to life just like my papa tried to do. Think about it, Jed. Honestly, this could work for both of us."

Jessie didn't love him, he knew that, but he wondered if he loved Jessie enough to compensate for her lack of love for him. He knew he did, but what about the repercussions of such a marriage.

Jed thought about Ben's story, and how Ben had said that Aimee didn't love him when they first married. He said it took him some time, but she really did love him later on in the marriage. If Jessie got to know him better, maybe she would learn to love him. He'd be good to her. Oh Lord yes, he'd be good to her, but still, she had to give a little bit. She had to at least come to his bed. He'd be damned if he'd go begging at her bedroom door.

As though she knew he'd agreed to the marriage, Jessie placed her hand on Jed's arm possessively as though she was already his wife. "How long will it take us to get a license, Jed?"

"I don't know, Jessie." Jed answered, knowing he was taking a big chance. "As soon as everything is settled, we'll go into town and find out."

The wedding ceremony was about as cold as the marble in the Tahchee County courthouse and about as short as the narrow steps leading up to that ancient building. The bride and groom both wore washed out blue Levis, fitted Wrangler shirts, his in blue chambray and hers in red and white checked cotton, and Justin cowboy boots scuffed and scarred in faded brown-leather. The wedding ring the bride wore was the one her mother had worn on her wedding day, the same one the bride wore every day. The bride was not blushing, and the groom received no hearty teasing of the night to come.

Immediately following the ceremony, the marriage license safely tucked in Jessie's jeans' pocket, they walked to the Mercantile Bank across the street from the court house and opened a joint checking account in the name of the J&J Ranch.

The wedding dinner was hamburgers and fries at "Frank's Country Drive-In". Their ride home was Jessie driving her old dusty red Reo, and not Jed driving a shiny clean car with cans attached to the bumper announcing the joyous occasion of two lives joining into one. Still, they were married legally and that's all either of them cared about, each for different reasons.

Neither of them had told Simon and Ben about their marriage plans. Jessie knew there would be a big hassle about whether she loved Jed or not, and she really didn't want to hear it from the two old men, especially Simon. She'd made up her mind and that was that. Remembering the cruel things her mama had said about her papa confused Jessie. Was it love for Jed McClure that she felt, or was it love for her papa and what he'd tried to accomplish that drove her into this strange marriage.

Jed hadn't said anything about them getting married to Ben or Simon either. He hadn't been sure if Jessie would actually go through with the marriage, and he didn't want to look like a fool. With that thought in mind, he just kept his mouth shut, hoping she wouldn't opt out, and tried not to think about getting Jessie into his bed after they were married.

The bridal couple returned to the ranch mid-afternoon and noticing two stray calves roaming the lane to the ranch, Jed got out of

Jessie's truck and herded them on foot to the enclosure by the barn. Jessie drove herself up to the ranch without her new husband, and was left to make the announcement of the marriage to Simon and Ben. Whether she was a coward or just wanted to have Jed with her to share the news, Jessie didn't know, but for some reason she neglected to mention the marriage to Simon or Ben.

Jed thought his new wife had told Simon and Ben about the marriage when he returned to the ranch, so he said nothing about it. As he watched the sun dip behind the rim of his vision into the darkness, for which he'd been waiting, he wondered why neither Ben nor Simon said anything about the marriage, but he left it alone.

While Jed had been out herding the stray cattle home after the wedding ceremony, he came upon some of the flowers known as Indian blanket. He could have sworn the flowers were the exact same ones he'd brought to Jessie years ago when her mother kicked him off the ranch. Ignoring the strays ambling their way toward the barn, Jed picked a large bouquet of the colorful flowers intending to give them to his bride when she came to his bed later that evening. He thought that every bride should have a bouquet of flowers on her wedding day, even if they were just hearty weeds like the Indian blanket. Still, they were pretty. Those flowers and the rose rock he'd saved for her all these years would be his gift to his bride, his wife at long last. *Jessie McClure.*

Shortly after supper, Jed went to his bedroom to anxiously await his bride and the night to come. Grabbing a big glass jar, he filled it with water and placed the flowers in it. Scribbling out a note on a yellow piece of paper, he placed the aging rose rock on top of it. Eagerly readying himself for his bride, he showered with a scented men's soap he'd buried away in a drawer since college, shaved so close his face was like a baby's butt and even trimmed his toenails. He put clean linens on his bed, fluffed the pillows, and cleaned off his cluttered night stand. Then he lay down to wait for the arrival of his bride: *Mrs. Jed McClure.*

Jessie was as nervous as a bride and why not, she wondered. She was a bride! A bride who had been waiting for two hours for her groom to come to her bed! Where was he? Was he still out working? At supper Jed had said that he was really tired and sleepy. Was he *that* tired and sleepy? Was he so tired and sleepy he couldn't make it to his own wedding night? Or didn't he want her? Maybe that was it, she decided as she pondered the day's events.

After the wedding ceremony Jed had leaned down and kissed her, as though he was drowning in desire; and even though the city hall officiate did some serious clearing of his throat, Jed didn't stop the kiss until *he* was ready. After that kiss, Jessie thought things might be different between them; maybe they could have a real marriage and not just a business deal as they'd agreed upon.

Turning over, Jessie stared at the stars twinkling in jest at her through the windows of her bedroom. It was a crisp, cool September evening, one that promised the readiness of winter. The maple trees were turning from green to golden orange and the post oaks were shedding their leaves from their long scraggly arms. Labor Day was just around the corner and soon it would be time for the ranchers to sow the winter wheat. Jessie moved out of her bed and walked to the wooden shelf where green jugs of her papa's wheat samples laid dormant waiting for the opportunity to come to life, to prove Sean Keegan's dream, and to prove her faith in him. All these years she'd kept these big green jars of wheat sealed, labeled and ready for life. One of these days they'd be put in the soil and given the life they deserved. When? She had no idea, but someday it would happen. Frowning, Jessie crawled back into her lonely bed.

At 2:00 A.M., Jed gave up waiting for his bride to come to his bed. He thought about trotting down to her little cave and dragging her back to his room. She had promised him to be his wife, a bedded wife, and now she was welching on their business deal. Business deal! Oh hell! Was a business deal all he'd gotten out of this marriage? All he'd ever wanted was for Jessie Keegan to be Jessie McClure? Well, she was Jessie McClure now, and he still didn't have her as his wife. Not a wife willing to share his bed. She tricked him! She made him out to be a fool!

Jed kicked the sheets from the bed and wondered if there wasn't some law that said a marriage had to be consummated to be legal. Maybe he should tell her about that little item, whether it was true or not. That would get her butt into his bed fast enough. Yeah, a threat like that could make her jump his bones right out in front of the house with everybody looking on. But, was that what he really wanted, he wondered, as he pulled the sheet back up around him. Did he want Jessie to come to him out of fear or threats? No, he knew that he didn't want that. She had to come to him willingly, or not at all.

Caressing the empty pillow beside his, Jed gave up his angry thoughts about his wife. Jessie Keegan McClure was still the only woman he would ever love and he knew it. She didn't love or want him, but at least now, he could love her legally even though it was from afar. And then too, he wouldn't have to put up with the threats of some rascal like Ed Kook putting his hands on her. With that miserable thought in mind, Jed gazed at the jar of water filled with the bouquet of the Indian Blanket flowers and the rose rock sitting next to it. He was so stupid to think Jessie would want those silly weeds. They were just a nuisance. And the rose rock! Why in God's name would she want some ridiculous rock? Snorting to himself in his stupidity that Jessie would ever want him, Jed rolled over and turned off the lamp.

At 3:00 o'clock Jessie Keegan McClure gave up waiting for her husband to come to her bed. After doing some serious soul-searching as she laid waiting, Jessie realized that Jed was exactly the man she wanted, the same one she wanted all these years. He wanted her too, she was certain of that. What happened?

Shortly after three thirty, wearing only her nightgown, Jessie tiptoed outside to check Jed's window to see if his light was on. She hoped that he was waiting for her. Maybe they'd misunderstood the sleeping arrangements. Cautiously, she crept down the porch to his room. All was dark. The man was asleep, and here she was creeping around in the dark like some sort of female predator. Seethed in humiliation, Jessie crept back to her room and crawled into her empty bed. Punching her pillow in frustration, she decided that if Jed didn't want her, then she wouldn't bother him. With that miserable thought in mind, Jessie rolled over and turned off her lamp.

Jed glared as Jessie took her place at the round wooden table in the sunny kitchen. Jessie refused to look at Jed, and began to eat the breakfast that Simon set in front of her.

Simon had no idea what was going on between Jed and Jessie, but it seemed to him they must have had an awful fight. It had been going on for over a week, and every day it got worse. Oh, they both acted normal to him and Ben, but he knew there was something very wrong going on between them. They never spoke one word to one another when they were in the same room, and yet they both looked like they were ready to explode. That made for awfully uncomfortable meals.

Simon tried to think up something to say that would break the hostility between them. "It's gonna be another hot day. If this heat keeps up, Lord knows when we'll be able to start planting winter wheat."

"Yeah, and that damn air conditioner that I bought isn't working worth a crap, either." Jed scowled at his breakfast as though the air conditioner problem was his breakfast's fault.

Maybe that's what was wrong with Jed, Simon thought. Not getting sleep could do that to a man; make him all cranky and irritable. "Call Jensen's repair, Jed, they'll fix you right up." No one said anything so he continued in his efforts to get Jed and Jessie talking. "How are you sleeping in this heat, sister?"

Jessie didn't look up from her food. "I'm sleeping just fine, Simon," she said with a snip in her voice. "I don't have to rely on some silly air conditioner to keep me cool. I'm not stupid."

Jed's blue eyes grew large, laced with pure anger. "So, now I'm the stupid one! You're the one who forced me to sleep in that damn room with no insulation! It's hotter than hell in the summer, and I'm sure it's as equally cold in the winter!"

"Nobody forced you to sleep anywhere, Jed McClure! Why don't you go on back to your big house on your fine McClure ranch and sleep there instead of screaming at me because you can't sleep here!"

"You knew that was the hottest room in the whole house, Jessie! That's why you insisted I sleep there. You're trying to run me out!"

"Looks like it didn't work, did it? Unfortunately, you're still here!"

"Ah, to hell with you, Jessie McClure!" Jed shouted as he shot out of his chair and left the room, grabbing the small phone book on his way out.

Jessie didn't look up from her breakfast; she knew it was coming. "Sister! What was that Jed called you?" Jessie ignored him and kept eating. "What did he mean by calling you Jessie McClure? Answer me right now, girl!"

"I married that idiot, Simon. I did it to get my name back on my ranch! Now I wonder if it was even worth it!" Jessie grabbed her plate and coffee cup, slung them into the kitchen sink and started from the kitchen.

Simon grabbed her by the arm. "Now, just you wait a minute, little miss! You've got a bit of explaining to do." It never occurred to Simon that it wasn't his right to know everything she did. Jessie had become like his own daughter. That's the way he saw it. That's the way it was.

Jessie knew it, too, and slumped back down on one of the white wooden chairs. "Well, what else was I supposed to do, Simon? He wouldn't let me buy back into the ranch. You know what this ranch means to me."

Simon straddled the chair facing Jessie. "Sister, you did the right thing by marrying him. He'll be good for you, and he'll be a good husband to you. Jed's a good man."

"He's a jerk!" Jessie said rolling her eyes toward the ceiling at Simon's words of praise.

Simon thought about the two of them for a minute. "Jessie, Jed is head-over-heels in love with you and has been since the day he came here. Maybe a lot longer, for all I know."

Squirming uncomfortably around in her chair, Jessie knew she had to say something. "Simon, you have never been married. So how in the world could you possibly know anything about love?"

"I've never been married, sister; but that doesn't mean I've never been in love."

Jessie hoped this was a chance to change the subject of her hasty marriage to Jed. "You, Simon? My goodness, why didn't you marry the woman you loved?"

Simon looked uneasy and squirmed around in his own chair. "The woman I loved married someone else. Now she's dead." Standing, Simon turned his chair around and stood behind it looking down at Jessie as he forced his own painful memories out of his mind. Jessie was his problem now, and he had to contend with her. He knew what she was up to, and it wasn't going to work. "Sister, I know the look of a man in love, and I know the look of a man in pain. Jed's got the look of both. He's your husband, sister. Now, what are you going to do about it?"

Jessie propped her head in her hands and slouched against the cool wooden tabletop, her mind deep in thought. "It's his fault, Simon. I agreed to be a wife to him. I agreed to share a bed, but not once has he bothered to come to me. It's been over a week and he still hasn't shown any interest in me!" Jessie looked past Simon out the tall window into the yard.

Simon slapped the cool wood tabletop, regaining Jessie's attention. "And what sort of interest have you shown in Jed, sister? Why didn't you go to his room?"

After some stumbling over her words, embarrassed beyond reason, Jessie finally admitted what happened. "On our wedding night I did go to his room. It was dark. He was sound asleep! That's how much he cared about me as his bride."

"Somehow, I find that highly unlikely. What did you do, sister? Wait until dawn to go down to his room?"

"It was three-thirty in the morning, Simon. If he wanted me, surely he would have been waiting for me."

"Sister, Jed is a rancher. He gets up early. When you came wandering in for your breakfast that morning, Jed had eaten an hour before that. And, Miss, eh, *Mrs. Know it All*, I know your husband had been up way before that, because I saw him walking around the barn when I got up at five. What were you doing at five a.m. Mrs. McClure? Oh yes, that's right. Jessie Keegan McClure was snoozing away."

"Ben, can I ask you a question?" Ben looked up at Jed from the desk in the front office where he was scrutinizing the books he'd been working on.

"Of course, Jed, but if it's about the delivery of that irrigation equipment you ordered, I need to tell you that some parts of it are on back-order, but I don't believe those parts are crucial for the operation of the equipment. With what has already been delivered to the ranch today, you should be able to start on the installation, and within a day or so, the rest of the parts should be here."

Jed almost didn't ask his burning question. "Yeah, thanks, Ben."

Jed started to walk from the room but Ben's words stopped him in his tracks. "What did you really want to talk to me about, Jed? From the look on your face and the way you've been acting lately, you seem to be miserable. Is there something with which I can help you?"

Ben closed his books, and Jed pulled up a hard cane-back chair, propping his elbows on the gray steel desk. "Naw, Ben. Nobody can help me with my problem. It's just that since Jessie and I got married, she seems like she's more distant to me than ever."

Ben slipped his glasses atop his head in shock. Surely he hadn't heard Jed correctly. "Jed, I swear I thought you said something about being married, uh, married to Miss Jessie."

"Yeah, Ben, Jessie and I got married over a week ago, and," Jed stopped and stared at Ben in disbelief. "Hell, she didn't even bother to tell anyone about it, did she? She really doesn't give a crap about me, Ben. The only reason she married me was to get her name back on this ranch! I was hoping that once she got to know me better, she'd realize

I hadn't stolen her ranch from her. Stupid me, I had hoped she'd get to like me a little bit, but it's obvious she doesn't. She hates me more than ever. I mean so little to her that she didn't even bother to tell you she married me." Jed looked at Ben with such a solemn look, it worried Ben. Jed shook his head in wonder as he dropped his gaze down to the floor in defeat.

"Jed, she hasn't said a word to me about it, and I doubt she's told Simon either, because he would have said something to me. I'm certain of that. Since I've returned to the bunk house, he talks my ear off. I've threatened to move back to the house just to get him to be quiet."

Hoping to change the subject from his miserable, embarrassing situation, Jed made small talk. "How is it out there, Ben? You boys cool enough in this heat?"

"We're fine out there, Jed. The place is well insulated and made of rocks just like the rest of the place." Ben hesitated, a big grin covering his weathered face. "Well, the whole place is cool with the exception of the hot room you're staying in. Jessie surely fixed you, didn't she, Jed?" Ben openly chuckled as he shook his head in wonder.

"It's not funny, Ben. She's tricked me every step of the way." Jed knew he was going too far, but he was so frustrated, that he couldn't help himself. "Now, she got me to marry her and won't sleep with me. Looks like she's gonna get away with that, too."

Ben pulled his glasses back down over his nose. "Won't sleep with you, huh? Now, that's a real problem."

"Ben, you said that Aimee didn't want to sleep with you when she first married you. How did you get her to want you?"

Ben was silent for a moment deep in his memories. Then he replied, "She discovered my heart."

"What? I guess I don't understand what you're talking about, Ben. Lord, I've wanted that woman since I was a kid. I've done everything I can possibly do to get her to want me. Hell, I nearly went bankrupt over my desire for Jessie, and she still won't have me."

"There's a big difference between desire of the body and love in the heart, Jed. My Aimee nearly drove me crazy until I realized that she had to discover my heart before she could accept my body."

"I'm not much into romance, Ben. I don't know anything about writing love letters and that sort of stuff, if that's what you're talking about."

"Jed, you're a good man, a real good man, but you have to be patient with our Jessie. She tends to defy her own feelings, but under all her bluff, she's a kind, loving person. Just give her a chance, Jed. Give her some time, and one of these days she'll discover your heart, if she hasn't done so already."

"He bought the dumb air conditioner! Let him sit here and wait for Jensen to come and repair it. I have things to do!" Jessie shouted as she watched Simon walk toward the outlying field.

Simon turned and glared at Jessie. "He's busy, sister! He's putting in a new irrigation system for this ranch that *you* love so much! So, unless you want to follow me out in the fields and wallow in the mud and the dirt, I'd suggest you keep your mouth shut and wait patiently for Jensen's man to come fix that air conditioner. You stuck him in that hot kennel when there was a perfectly cool bedroom for him to sleep in, sister. Now, you can just wait for the air conditioner man to come and fix the thing, so the poor man can get some rest at night. It's the least you can do for him!"

Jessie wrapped her arms around her body, knowing she was acting like a spoiled-rotten brat, and not a good wife. Yeah, sure, she thought, she was somebody's wife who wasn't wanted as a wife. Plopping her small body down onto the porch swing to wait for the service man, Jessie could see Jed and several other men working on the irrigation lines off in the distant field. They stopped as Simon approached. Someone said something to him and then Simon joined in the work. Jessie picked up her wounded pride and hurried toward the garden to take her vengeance out on some weeds while she waited.

The air conditioner whirled in the background as Jessie peered out over the fields into the shadows of fast approaching darkness. Jed and the others had made good progress that day and were still working into the evening, and Jessie knew they would continue working until they could no longer see. Even with all the work they'd done, it still seemed there were miles more of irrigation to be laid; a long, dirty, slow job, but they'd get it done eventually. Jed McClure never gave up on something he wanted to accomplish, of that she was certain.

Mr. Jensen had told her to go into Jed's room in an hour or so after he left, check to be sure the unit was cooling properly, and call him right away if there was a problem. It had been three hours since he'd left and she still hadn't stepped inside Jed's room. Instead, she sat silently staring out into the night, wondering how she could go into her husband's bedroom where she was obviously not wanted. That hurt.

Giving up her miserable thoughts of abandonment by Jed, Jessie finally picked herself up from the porch swing and walked into Jed's room. As she opened the door, she could feel the blessed cool air embrace her sticky skin, and without hesitation, she entered. She knew the unit was working fine, but once she was in Jed's room with reason to be there, she couldn't help but snoop around his private space.

As neat and meticulous as he was about the ranches, he was a complete slob when it came to housekeeping. The bed was tumbled and unmade. A semi-clean pair of jeans was thrown over the back of a chair. Dirty socks littered the floor, and on top of a vase on the dresser laid a dirty shirt that looked like it had been wadded up and thrown there.

Jessie grabbed the jeans, hung them on a hook in the closet and put his dirty socks in the clothes hamper. She straightened his bed, fluffed his pillows, and tossed the old newspapers from his side table into the wastepaper can. Glancing around the room, she spotted the dirty shirt on the dresser and walked over to get it so she could place it into the clothes hamper with the socks. As she pulled the shirt away, she realized it was sitting atop a vase of wilted Indian blanket flowers. Next to the vase was a perfect little rose rock. It was sitting on a piece of yellow paper. Carefully moving the rose rock aside, Jessie picked up the yellow piece of paper and began to read what Jed had written:

To my wife, Jessie McClure
I found this rose rock when I was a kid
And I've saved it for you until this day.
Your ever faithful husband, Jed

A smile of pure satisfaction rested on Jessie's face. Jed did really love her. Jed McClure, her husband.

There was more mud on him than in the state of Oklahoma, Jed decided as he squished his way through the field toward the bunk house shower. Simon had told him to put his dirty clothes in the bunk house laundry and one of the new men would wash them along with the rest of the mud and clay that had accumulated on their clothes. During better times, all the ranch wash had been handled there, and Ben said things were definitely getting better. How Ben could think that was a wonder to Jed. So far there had been no significant improvements completed, but Ben said that with the added muscle in the form of the new *waddys*, the transient cowboys named for the wads of tobacco always carried in their jean pockets, things would turn around quickly. Ben didn't mention that the sale of his holdings was what had allowed all the new improvements to be implemented and provided the salaries to the waddys of the J&J Ranch.

Stepping out of the crude cement shower, Jed felt reborn as he watched the mud that had been caked on him make its way down the big floor drain. Wrapping a huge towel around his naked body, Jed picked up his boots that he'd cleaned off before his shower and headed for his room, dead tired and ready for bed.

When Jessie heard Jed's bedroom door open and close, she opened her eyes as he turned on the small lamp on his bureau. She watched him as he tried to control the defiant shock of blonde hair that limped back down his forehead every time he shoved it from his eyes. In the mirror, she could see his eyes as they darted around the room, surveying the cleanliness and settling on her clothes lying on the single chair in the room.

Shocked, he turned toward her. "Good God, Jessie! You scared the living crap out of me." For a moment Jed assumed Jessie had gotten hot in her room and had come down to his to cool off from the heat. He had no idea that Jessie was there for any other reason.

"Jessie, I know you want to stay here to cool off, but I have to tell you, I need to get some sleep so you'll have to leave. I'm exhausted, so maybe you could go on back down to your room, and then in the morning you can come back down here and sleep in the cool air-conditioning."

Jessie didn't move, just stared at her husband. "Why would I do that, Jed, when I can sleep here with you?"

Jed stood frozen with his big towel wrapped around him, wondering if what he hoped was going to happen. Was it really going to come true at long last? Then he saw the slow smile on his wife's face as she pulled back the covers, exposing her full naked breasts and her dark silky hair hanging about her shoulders. "Do I have to send you a written invitation, Jed? Or do I have to drag you into this bed with me?"

"Oh Lord, no, Jessie. Believe me, I'm more than willing." Jed dropped his towel and quickly jumped into the bed next to his beloved wife, Jessie McClure. Somehow, he knew she had found his heart.

From the grin on Jed's face at breakfast and the smitten glances cast Jed's way by Jessie, it didn't take Simon and Ben long to figure out that Jed and Jessie had made their arrangement into a real marriage. Both of them were delighted with their assumptions, but they couldn't have been more pleased than when Jed made his announcement about Sean's wheat. That really confirmed their conclusions.

"I've been thinking," Jed said, shoving eggs into his mouth and keeping his eyes on Jessie for her reaction.

Jessie giggled like a school girl. "Well, I'm glad to know you can think so early in the morning, Jed." She didn't mention that she was glad either of them could think after the night they'd just shared together.

Jed laughed and tipped his coffee cup to his wife. She smiled adoringly back at him.

Knowing exactly what was going on between them, Ben and Simon politely ignored both of them, trying not to laugh at their seemingly subtle innuendoes.

"I know we haven't gotten to the irrigation in that field behind the house yet, and I'm certain we won't get to it this year with the regular wheat planting starting soon. But I'm wondering if we just might try planting that field with those samples of Sean's wheat that you have stored in all those green jars, Jessie?" Jed couldn't wait to see Jessie's reaction.

His wife didn't disappoint him. Her mouth fell into a big O and he wondered if she understood what he was saying. "Sean's wheat! My papa's wheat, Jed? Do you mean it? Are you serious? Can we plant his wheat this year?"

Grinning like he'd just conquered the world, Jed answered. "Well, Jessie, if you'd rather wait until next year, or the next...."

Jumping up from her chair, Jessie raced around the table and threw her arms around her husband's neck. He was ready for her, and pushed back from the table enough to pull her into his lap and kiss her like the newlyweds they were, forgetting they were not alone.

The others at the table smiled at one another and made their way away from the table and out the kitchen door leaving the newlyweds to their own devices.

Even with the irrigation systems being installed, they continued to work the ground, readying it for the fall planting of the winter wheat. There had been no wheat or grain planted anywhere on the ranch in the years prior to Jed's taking charge of the Keegan ranch, and in a way, it worked out well. The ground was able to recharge its strength over the years, and now a good crop could be predicted for the future.

With the money from the sale of the Tulsa property, Jed purchased an International Harvester 151 Combine, with a side hill leveling system so that he could harvest on the hilly areas without fear of turning over. Most of the land was flat, but the field where he decided to plant Sean's wheat had never been used for any grain because it was sloped. With the new combine, Jed knew he could plant Sean's wheat in this otherwise useless piece of land. He was certain Sean's wheat was worthless, so using this piece of land was no big loss, but letting Jessie know he'd tried to grow her father's wheat, that would be worth everything.

"Even though there's no irrigation out there in that field, it seems to be fairly good soil, Jessie. Sean's wheat will do as well as can be expected there." He couldn't tell Jessie that he doubted Sean's wheat would grow anywhere.

Jessie was so excited over the prospect of having Sean's wheat planted, that she had no idea that on that same day Sean's wheat was planted, her husband would plant his own seed inside her womb.

Two months later, Jessie knew she was pregnant with what they both hoped would be the first of their bunch of little McClure brats. With his first child due to arrive next summer, Jed was beside himself with absolute joy, but equally worried about his wife and her constant morning sickness. He tried to be very quiet when he arose in the mornings so she could get some rest, but it seemed that as soon as he awoke, Jessie was awake too, and then the dreaded vomiting started.

Doc had told her to eat crackers before she got out of bed in the morning, so Jessie slept with a box of crackers right next to her side of the bed, but it seemed the crackers did no more than give her added fuel for her sickness.

Seeing his wife so sick and losing weight, Jed knew he had to do something. Doc and Miss Estelle were at a medical convention and would be gone for weeks, but there was a young doctor filling in at their clinic while they were gone; and Jed was determined that Jessie would see him. As soon as they saw the new doctor, he gave Jessie what they considered to be a miracle pill. It stopped the morning sickness almost at once, and Jessie radiated in good health.

It was going to be a good crop, anyone could see that. Sean's wheat was alive and healthy, rippling through the field like green Christmas tinsel. Jessie ran her fingers over her protruding stomach as she watched Jed step off his tractor and walk up behind her.

"How's my wife and baby doing this fine day?" he asked as he slipped his long arms around Jessie and placed his hands on top of hers resting on the womb where their child was growing.

"Your wife is fine, but your baby is wild, kicking up a storm." Jessie moved Jed's big hand down further onto her stomach and looked up at him. For a moment, he was silent, then with a blissful smile covering his craggy face, she knew their child had let his father know he was busy playing in the safety of his mother's womb.

Jed nestled his mouth in Jessie's dark hair. "Never, never in my life have I ever felt anything so wonderful."

Jessie turned and faced him, slipping her arms around his neck. "If you like it so much, then let him kick you for awhile."

With that, Jed felt the kick all the way from Jessie's womb into his stomach. "Lordy, lordy, he's so strong! He's going to be a football player with a mighty kick like that. Hey, Jessie, I think I've just come up with a name for our boy. What if we call him Evan?"

"Wasn't that your grandfather's name, Jed?"

"Yes, it was, Jessie. I was told that my grandpa Evan was as strong as an ox since the day he was born, just like our boy. You know what the name Evan means?"

Smiling at her adoring husband, she knew he would tell her the meaning whether she wanted to know it or not. It didn't matter though; Evan was the perfect name for their son. "What does Evan mean, Jed?"

"In Celtic, Evan means 'young warrior'." Jed studied Jessie's face as he waited for her answer.

Jessie felt her child give her a mighty kick and grabbed her stomach. "It seems he certainly is a warrior, if our baby is a *he*. What if our *he* is a *she*, Jed? Then what?"

"Well, there's no question about that, Jessie."

"Please, Jed! No more Jess' or Jessie's!"

"Well, I was thinking along the lines of 'Maire'."

"That's my middle name, Jed."

"And just why do you think that I love that name so much, Jessie?"

Jessie knew, but she asked anyway. "And why is that, Jed?"

Jed pretended to think about it for a minute. "Well, I guess it's because it's a part of you, Jessie Maire Keegan McClure."

"If it's a girl then, our daughter will be named Maire Keegan McClure. Is that all right with you, Jed?"

Jed pulled his wife into his arms, his child contentedly asleep between them.

"Anything in this world that you want is all right with me. God, Jessie. What have I ever done to deserve such happiness?"

Standing up on her toes, Jessie kissed her husband on his lips. "You deserve it, Jed McClure. We have a long, wonderful, happy future before us."

"A future that will last for years and years, Jessie; we'll watch each other grow old and we'll know that every age line in our faces we shared in the making. I love you, Jessie McClure."

"I love you, Jed McClure."

Content in one another's arms, Jessie turned around and faced the healthy field of wheat. "It's going to happen, Jed. Papa's wheat is going to make it."

"Yeah, Jessie. Sean was right on his last hybrid experiment. From what little you were able to salvage from Sean's experiments, we were only able to plant one acre, but this one acre looks better than any of the other wheat we've planted from any past harvest."

"Really, Jed? Is it really that good?" Jessie knew it was. She just wanted to hear Jed say it and he knew it.

"It's that good, Jessie. In fact, we won't sell any of Sean's wheat this year. Instead, we'll harvest it, save it, and then we'll be able to plant a larger area next year. We'll just keep on doing that until all our wheat fields are filled with Sean's wheat. *Then*, we'll think about marketing it."

"When will it be ready, Jed? I can't wait."

"Well, it's laid dormant all winter; now it's growing tall and green, filling out just like it's supposed to do. As soon as the weather turns warmer, Sean's wheat will turn a golden brown, and just about the time you're ready to harvest my baby, I'll harvest your wheat. Now, how's that for a fair exchange of efforts?"

"My harvest is going to be a lot harder than your harvest, Jed!"

"Yeah, my love, but your planting was a lot more fun than my planting."

Jessie pulled her husband's arms around her more tightly and smiled, secure in his love for her and their child. It was such a good life.

Chapter 7

There was no spring. As was so typical of Oklahoma's unpredictable weather, winter collided right into summer with cold nights and short hot days. As the longer days rapidly progressed, the cold nights receded into the heat, and the usual spring rains were nonexistent. Creeks, normally overflowing, rushing rivers during the spring rains, now sported only creek bottoms, crusted and broken like smashed red clay pottery.

What ponds were left were covered with blue-green algae, deadly to the cattle and other livestock. Warnings to keep all livestock and small animals from the ponds were issued, but without fences around the ponds, the small wild life fell victim to the deadly water's lure, further contaminating the ponds. The fish in these ponds, the once lively crappies, catfish and bass, now floated belly-up, or were washed onto the crusted banks in pitiful abundance.

Burn bans were implemented throughout the state, rigidly enforced by Rangers on horseback in the camping areas, and by State Troopers watching for the occasional cigarette flipped from an auto. As the relentless heat permeated the earth week after week, the farmers and ranchers knew their only hope to save their crops was rain.

Without adequate hay or grain to feed the cattle, ranchers sold their herds for whatever price they could get, losing money on every sale, depleting bank accounts for the future. Old timers lamented woes of the dust storms of the 1930's, offering startling similarities to the current day's pathetic conditions, further discouragement for the ranchers and farmers of northern Oklahoma.

Even with the extensive irrigation system installed at the J&J Ranch, the crops still suffered because there was no longer any place from which to draw the water. Sean's wheat was especially vulnerable as it had been planted in a lone pasture behind the house. It was good virile land, but it had been dry for so long Jed doubted it would survive. Amazingly, Sean's wheat withstood the weather better than the fields where irrigation had been available.

In the distance, heat lightning splattered across the sky, twisting its deadly skeletal fingers throughout the heavens; dancing, twirling, bursting in light, endlessly promising relief. Like a temptress to the barren soul, it brought no release from the despair, only more seduction and more betrayal.

"How long you think that well's gonna hold out, Jed?" Simon asked, hopelessly scouring the sky for rain.

"I have no idea, Simon. The well is deep, so I don't think we have to worry about our personal needs, but without the water from the ponds, we are shut down on irrigation. One thing though, there hasn't been a crop of any sort on these acres in such a long time, that the ground is certainly fertile."

Simon gazed out over the golden brown field of wheat. "Yeah, all those wasted years were good for something, I guess. I'm still amazed that Sean's wheat has managed to hold on like it has without the irrigation that the rest of the crops had."

"You're right on that one, Simon. Whatever experiment Sean came up with, it was of hearty stock. It's a shame we couldn't have gotten the irrigation to that section before we had to plant, but we just couldn't get it done. Besides, I had no idea Sean's wheat would actually be any good after sitting all these years. I figured it would be moldy and no use whatsoever. I just planted it to make Jessie happy, but his wheat really is an exceptional hybrid." Jed pulled his worn straw Stetson low over his eyes and just like Simon, out of habit, he scoured the sky for rain.

In the distance both men could hear the baleful mooing of cattle waiting to be fed. Jed pulled his hat from his head and wiped his forehead. Simon shuffled silently next to him. Both of them knew they couldn't hold on much longer without rain. Without the rain, the tender new grass was withering and there would be nothing to feed the cattle. Because of the drought, grain was at a premium.

Jed sighed in resignation. They were just prolonging the agony. "Tomorrow we have to take the cattle in for sale, Simon."

"Ah hell, Jed. You just got the herd started."

"I know, Simon, but there was no grain supply when I took over the Keegan ranch. I thought there was enough grass to sustain the cattle until we harvested the wheat, but I was wrong. On the McClure ranch, I had plenty of hay stocked up for the cattle over there, but not enough to handle their needs and the needs of the J&J ranch too. I've borrowed from that supply to feed these cattle until the supplies are almost depleted. It's far too costly to buy feed, so it's sell the J&J cattle or lose them all."

"Okay, Jed. I'll tell Ben to call and get the trucks out here for tomorrow. This awful drought has nearly done in all the ranchers."

"We'll be okay next year, Simon."

"What makes you so sure that next year won't be the same, Jed?"

Smiling, Jed turned to Simon. "We've got Jessie's secret weapon. We'll plant Sean's wheat."

The roaring of the cattle trucks and the mooing of the young cattle was pure devastation to Jessie as she watched the last of the cattle trucks trudge away from her home in whirling clouds of road dust. As Jed and Simon followed behind the big cattle trucks in Jed's pickup truck, Jessie waved sadly, wondering how the few waddies in the back of Jed's truck would fare after they'd been paid off and left to find new work in a more prosperous location other than the drought- stricken Oklahoma.

She smiled as she remembered what a fun bunch of cowboys they'd been, always telling jokes, never letting the miserable heat interfere with their outrageous philosophies on life. They understood Jed couldn't keep them on right now, not with the uncertainty of the crops and the sell-off of the cattle, but they said they liked it on the J&J ranch even though they had no intention of settling in one place for long. At lunch that day, they'd said that Jed was a good boss man, Simon was a good cook, and they'd surely miss everyone on the ranch. They hoped to return in the fall for the harvest, if there was one, and to see the new baby. Somehow Jessie knew she'd never see them again.

In a spare few minutes, it seemed the sounds of the trucks and the cattle were lost to the false promises of the relentless overhead thunder as it raged and threatened from the heavens above. Lightning flashed, the air was thick, heavy, difficult to inhale, and all around the world took on a slight green cast as though the heavens would open up and deliver her precious gift of water, but Jessie knew it was all just a tease. There was no rain to come to the crippled crops, withering and stunted, dying before they had a chance to live. Wiping the sweat from her brow, Jessie turned and walked back toward her home in silence.

It was a cracking sphere of light, a horrible raging from heaven that demanded vengeance from the green-hazed world below. That's the only way Jessie knew to describe what had happened. The incredible violence tossed down upon the unsuspecting ranch caused her to flee to the house for safety. A bad storm had to be coming

Holding her protruding stomach and gasping for air, Jessie waddled through the door held open by Ben who had stayed behind to work on the books. "My Lord, Miss Jessie! That was a close one. Hope those waddies riding in the back of Jed's truck are all right."

"Oh, I'm sure if there seems to be any real danger, Jed will get them out of the back of the truck. It was probably just a fluke lightning strike, Ben. A one-time clatter. I'm certain the worst is over. Lord knows there won't be any rain to follow."

"I guess we can count on that. Well, take heed, Miss Jessie. Stay in doors away from the electrical until we're sure that the lightning has moved on. Why don't you go on into your bedroom and get some rest?"

"I'm not really tired, Ben. Jed spoils me so, letting me sleep late, and treating me like I'm an invalid."

"He's just excited about the baby, as all of us are, Miss Jessie. When Doc and Miss Estelle were here last night to visit, didn't Doc remind you to take it easy?"

Jessie smiled remembering the beautiful hand-stitched green and yellow quilt Miss Estelle had brought. As soon as Miss Estelle learned she was expecting, there came a weekly supply of handmade items for the baby. Miss Estelle was as excited as if she were the baby's real grandmother, which she claimed rights to be, and that was fine with Jessie and Jed. They knew they would never find a better grandmother or grandfather for their child than Doc and Estelle Collins.

"I promise I will lie down in a little while, Ben, so don't you harp on me, too."

"I won't harp on you, Miss Jessie; but really, you need to get all the rest you can now, because in another month, there won't be much rest to be had after that baby comes."

"I will later, Ben, but I think I'll go out to the kitchen and see what I can put on for supper. With Simon gone to help Jed, he won't have time to do any cooking after they get home."

"Well, I guess you know what's best for you and the baby. As for me, I'm going down to Jed's office and work some more on the books."

Jessie smiled. "Yes, Ben. Be sure to keep all your 'Peters and Pauls' separated."

"Yes, ma'am, I certainly will." The old man acknowledged as he made his way down to what used to be Jed's old room but now was converted back into an office...a cool office with a roaring air conditioner.

It couldn't get much hotter than it already was, Jessie decided as she neared the kitchen window. At least with the window open, she could let in a little air. As she lifted the window, she noticed that for the first time in what seemed like months, there was a hearty breeze. Surely, now they would have rain.

Searching through the big ranch freezer, Jessie noticed the distinct smell of smoke. Hoping the freezer hadn't given in to the heat and collapsed, she checked and found the meat to be frozen solid. When she heard the sound of the freezer kick in from being opened too long, she knew it wasn't the freezer. Still, she knew something was wrong.

Gazing out the open window, she could see nothing wrong in the front of the house. Off in the distance, the crops were still wilted and drawn, still dying from lack of water. Hurrying to the back window of the kitchen, she saw a golden sphere in the distance, waving and dancing, flipping tiny golden flicks toward Sean's wheat.

Gasping in horror, Jessie realized the lightning had hit a tall Juniper outside the fence line. Dry, unmercifully scorched from the sun's unrepentant glare, the tree had erupted into a pyramid of fiery fury, waving its long tentacles in agony, spreading the blazing fury over Sean's innocent, unsuspecting wheat.

As she screamed for Ben to come and help, Jessie stumbled awkwardly toward the stone well house where there was always a hose connected, ready to battle the usual spring fires that devoured the fields of tall Bluestem grass that helped feed the cattle. Around the houses and ranch buildings, the grass was always clipped short, and in some cases, was rocked around the bases to keep the fires at bay; but around Sean's wheat, there was nothing to keep the fire from destroying his legacy and Jed and Jessie's future.

Grabbing the swollen water hose, Jessie screamed for Ben and pulled with all her strength toward the field that was in flame, embers embracing the tender wheat, coveting it, raping the stalks of their innocence, leaving in its wake the devastation of a past hope and a lost future.

Ben scratched his head and wondered how it could cost so much money to run one ranch, but then he knew Jed was as thrifty as he was, and was only trying to get the old ranch back on its feet as quickly as possible. There was still quite a bit of money in the ranch account, but Jed had said that he didn't want to spend any more money out of that account than absolutely necessary. It was all their money, Jed had said, and they'd all be hurt if they weren't careful.

As Ben looked over the books, he thought he heard a scream, but with the noisy air conditioner running he ignored it. After a few minutes, he swore he could hear a scream again. *Miss Jessie! My God, Jessie!*

"Well, I'll be damned! The water pump has given up along with everything else in this God awful drought," Jed growled as he watched the steam pour out of the hood on his aging black pickup.

Simon turned to look out of the back window of the truck. "There's water in the back of the truck, Jed."

"Good thinking, Simon. We'll use the water in the drinking water jug to fill the pump and we should be able to make it to Tahchee before we need to fill it with water again. While we're there settling up the sale of the cattle, Simon, will you run over to the auto parts store, and pick up a new water pump? I'll install it later back at the house."

"Sure, Jed....." Simon's answer was interrupted by the shouts of the waddies in the back of the truck.

Looking into the rear-view mirror, he could see the boys waving and shouting at him. Before he could open his door, one of them was pulling it open. "Look back there, Jed! You see what I think I see?"

Peering out over the last few miles he'd driven from his home, Jed immediately spotted the spirals of smoke which seemed to be hovering over his and Jessie's home. "Oh my God, Jessie!" he swore. *"Oh my God, Jessie!"* he prayed.

Chapter 8

"You've got a son, Jed." Doc Collins walked from the delivery area and out into the waiting room where Jed, Simon, Ben, and three waddies waited for the news of the premature birth.

Jed didn't acknowledge his announcement. "What about Jessie? Don't you lie to me Doc! If something is wrong with Jessie, I want to know it, and I want it fixed."

"Jessie took a bad fall over that rock, Jed. She fell right on top of the point of the rock and it tore into her stomach and ruptured the uterus; but with any luck, the baby will survive."

There was something Doc wasn't telling him and Jed was beginning to seethe in anger. His nerves were shot, his Jessie was without him beside her, and she didn't even know he was there waiting for her. It occurred to him that Doc didn't want to talk about Jessie and he wondered why. What was wrong! Totally out of his gentle nature, Jed grabbed Doc Collins by the lapels of his white coat. "Damn it, Doc. Don't bullshit me! What about Jessie? You tell me straight and I mean it!"

Doc gently moved Jed's hands from his lapels, and instead of letting go he held on to Jed's coarse hands. "I'm not sure, Jed, but I doubt Jessie will ever be able to have another child after this awful accident. And...."

"Oh. Is that all? As long as she's all right, it doesn't matter to me that she can't get pregnant again. We'll adopt some poor little kids that need a good home. "

Doc pulled Jed outside the waiting room away from all the inquisitive ears. "Oh, she can get pregnant again, Jed, but I doubt she'll make it through the next delivery. She's pretty well messed up. We might get her through another caesarean delivery if she gets pregnant again, but I'd hate to chance it. Jed nervously wiped his long fingers on his jeans, held his head low and spoke almost in a whisper. "We won't have any more kids, Doc. She'll just have to accept that."

"Personally, I'm amazed she did as well as she did, but she's a strong girl. Of course, I've never known her to be sick one day of this pregnancy."

Jed couldn't believe Doc didn't remember how sick Jessie was during the first months of her pregnancy. She had no idea she was even pregnant until the nausea began. "Oh yeah, Doc. Don't you remember when she first got pregnant? She was so sick, she was skin and bones. Don't you remember that?"

Doc put his finger up on his chin in deep thought. "Estelle and I were gone to that medical convention in Switzerland when Jessie was first pregnant. She must have seen that young man that took over my practice for that month while we were gone."

"Yeah, that's right, Doc. His name was Dr. Surgeon. I remember that name 'cause it struck me funny that he was a doctor with the name of Surgeon. He was a good doctor though; he fixed Jessie right up with those pills he gave her. She wasn't sick a day after that."

Listening carefully to what Jed said, Doc hesitated. "I don't recall seeing anything in Jessie's chart about Surgeon giving Jessie pills for morning sickness. Do you remember the name of the medicine, Jed?"

"Naw....I don't remember, Doc. He just gave her one pill, but it sure did the trick. Well, I guess we won't have to worry any more about her having anymore morning sickness, being as she can't have any more babies. At least we've got our boy, our perfect little son."

Jed thought Doc went whiter than his jacket. "Jed, I didn't say your son was perfect."

For the first time since Doc had come out of the delivery area, Jed knew genuine concern for his son and he felt sick as he hung his head. "Tell me, Doc. What's wrong with my boy?"

"I don't know if it's due to being born too early or what, but the little fellow is suffering from respiratory distress and...."

Knowing Jessie was all right, Jed became concerned for his son. "What can we do about it Doc? Can we send him to a specialist?"

"Jed, I've already made the arrangements to send him to the children's hospital in Tulsa, but Jed, there's more."

Never in his life had Dr. James Collins dreaded more than what he had to say next.

Jed scowled at him suspiciously. "Doc? What's wrong with my boy?"

"Oh God, Jed. Your boy was born without arms. He only has tiny flippers."

Jed McClure felt his knees give way, but caught himself and remained erect. "Oh no, Doc! Oh Lord. Oh God. Has Jessie seen him, Doc?"

"No, Jed. I thought you better be with her when she first sees him. It's going to be tough on her."

Tough on me too, Jed thought, as he shoved his blonde hair out of his eyes hiding a lone tear.

Tough on me, too.

Jed sat by Jessie's bed waiting for her to awake. Arrangements had been made for their son to be transferred to the children's hospital in Tulsa, and he knew they would be moving him at any time. Still, he had not gone to see the child. Why? He had no idea.

Slowly Jessie's brown eyes opened, and she moved her hand to her stomach and winced from the pain of the caesarean operation. "Jed, have you seen our son? They told me we had a boy, but I haven't seen him. Have you seen him, Jed?"

"No, Jessie, I haven't seen it," Jed said, trying to force a smile. It was hopeless. He gave up and stared somberly at the floor.

"What do you mean, you haven't seen our boy? Why not, Jed?"

"I was worried about you, Jessie. I didn't go down to the nursery to see it." Jed stared at the floor.

"I'm dying to see who our boy looks like, Jed? I wonder if he has your blue eyes and blonde hair? I hope so. When are they going to bring him to me? I plan on nursing our baby. You know that. He's probably starving by now."

Jed couldn't stand to hear his wife carry on about the baby she thought was normal. He couldn't take it anymore. "Jessie, it has a few problems."

Jessie tried to sit up, nearly screamed as she grasped her stomach and fell back onto the bed. "What problems? What problems, Jed?"

"It's got a problem with its respiratory system, and its having a hard time breathing. Its lungs aren't completely developed so they're moving it to Tulsa where they're able to handle it better."

Why did Jed keep referring to their child as 'it'? Jessie wondered. What in the world was going on? Jessie felt the cold chills creep up her back that only a mother can feel when she senses her child is in danger. "I want to see my baby, Jed. Right now!"

Jed laid his hand on hers. "Jessie. It's not a perfect baby. Not like we wanted. Not what we planned for."

" Jed McClure! You get our son in here right this minute! I want to see him!"

"Jessie, please calm down. I'll ring for the nurse and she can give you something to make you sleep. No sense you getting all riled up."

Jed leaned over and pushed the button and watched it turn to red. "Someone will be coming soon, Jessie."

As the nurse hurried into the room, Jessie didn't wait for Jed. "Bring me our son, right now, miss, or so help me God, I'll get out of this bed and find him!"

The nurse looked helplessly at Jed.

"Damn it, Jessie! It's deformed! It has no arms, it has little flippers! It's a freak! It's useless."

Jessie couldn't believe her ears at the words that Jed had spoken. Their child was deformed. A freak. A useless child? Oh no! No! He was born of her body, of her and Jed's love. Damaged or not, he was their child.

"Jed McClure! He's our son! Deformed! Little flippers! A freak! Maybe he's not perfect, but he's our son and I want to see him, right now! You got that, Jed McClure?"

Jed sighed deeply in resignation. It would be so much easier on Jessie if she didn't have to see it, but she was pitching a fit. He was only thinking about how this would affect her, trying to protect her, but she wouldn't have it. "Bring it in," he said to the nurse.

"No! Don't bring 'it' in, nurse! Bring in our son, nurse!" Quickly she turned toward her husband. "If you don't want him Jed, then you leave right now, and go straight to hell!" Jessie glared at Jed with eyes of fire and he knew then it was useless to deny his wife their son, or whatever it was.

"Nurse, will you bring in our son?" Jed asked, wondering how he was going to be able to look upon the tiny deformity that was their son, Evan....their young warrior with the mutilated body.

The rain came, and the crops survived; and despite his respiratory problems, Evan Sean McClure survived.

Because he had to spend two months in the children's hospital in Tulsa, Jessie was not able to breast feed her child as she had planned, but Jed was secretly happy. He didn't want Jessie to bond too closely with the little boy that he felt had absolutely no chance to survive. It would hurt Jessie too much, he reasoned, but to Jed's surprise, the day came that they were told they could bring their child home to the J&J Ranch. Jessie was delighted, Jed was skeptical, Ben and Simon were worried.

While his son was wrapped tightly in a bunting, Jed could almost picture him as a normal child, but it was at his bath time that Jed couldn't look upon his son. It wasn't because he didn't care about the boy or that he was ashamed of him, but it was because he had no idea how the child would be able to adapt to life without arms to reach, to touch, and to love. People took their arms and hands for granted to offer the slightest touch, to do the smallest bit of work. His son had no arms, only small flippers such as a fish might have. How could his son possibly fit into this world? How could his son do anything on his own? How could he survive? How could he live in a world of perfect people, all so different from him?

What Jed didn't realize was that somehow, life would compensate for his son's abnormality. Nature, God, the Almighty....whatever, whoever.... Evan Sean McClure was secured by a higher power than Jed could ever imagine.

In all ways, other than his arms, Evan was a normal baby. Jessie doted on him, always there to hand him anything he seemed to want; holding his bottle, doting over him, becoming the hands and arms for their child; and the child let her do for him as she would, and he took from his mother as he would.

The one thing Evan refused to do was to go to bed without his bottle, and after watching his beloved Jessie lose night after night of sleep sitting up holding their child, Jed came up with a baby bottle holder that could lay next to the child's face and not accidently smother him. It worked, Jessie got her sleep, and Jed was as content as he could possibly be with the lot he'd been given in the form of his son.

Several months after the invention of the bottle holder, Jessie came rushing into the bedroom where Jed was getting dressed for the day's work.

"Jed, come quickly. You have got to see this." Jessie grabbed Jed by his arm, not waiting for him to pull on his boots.

"What's so almighty important, Jessie?" Jed grumbled as she pulled him toward the nursery connecting to their bedroom. When Jed walked near his son's crib, he couldn't believe what he saw. His son, his little armless, mutilated, deformed son was holding his bottle in his mouth with his feet; and he was doing a fine job of caring for himself. That was the day Jed allowed the love for his son to enter into his own heart....and a big heart it was.

From that day on, Evan demanded his own independence and balked when Jessie tried to do the things she'd always done for him in the past. With his father, he was content to be carried about by the big man, and as soon as Jed entered a room, Evan would jump up and down, and wiggle his little flippers for his father to take him. Jed took the boy with him constantly, finding great delight in taking his son out to visit with the horses and cattle they'd purchased that spring. As long as he was with his father, Evan was content.

At the time of Evan's first birthday, he had a head of curly blonde hair, big blue eyes, and white straight teeth....two up and two down. No one who knew the happy little boy could see his deformity any longer. He was Evan, a busy, busy little baby boy.

Barring any emergencies, Doc and Miss Estelle would come to the ranch weekly on Saturday nights to check Evan's chest for congestion and stay to have dinner with Jed and Jessie. Because of Evan's toes creeping onto the table from his highchair, gone was the expensive Haviland, replaced by the sturdy everyday heavy dinnerware of ranch life.

Miss Estelle no longer wore the shiny purple dress, nor did she wear her white uniform. Instead she chose an indestructible denim skirt and matching blouse. Evan liked to stand on her lap while Doc examined him, and of course there was always the likely possibility of a sticky kiss or two from the innocent child.

Adoring the child as much as his wife, Doc kept his stethoscope meticulously sanitized after discovering that not only was it a tool to listen to Evan's lungs, but it was also Evan's favorite teething toy.

Shortly after his first birthday, Evan learned to walk. He was a typical little boy: curious, intelligent, and into everything. Like all little boys, he'd fall. For awhile he was forced by his well-meaning parents to wear a helmet, but he hated the confinement and soon to everyone's amazement, Evan taught himself to fall on his shoulders and not his head. Because of his curiosity and high intelligence, the family of the J&J Ranch quickly discovered they had to watch Evan more closely than most little boys. No one knew just what he was capable of getting into, and as he grew bigger and stronger, he got into everything.

In the kitchen, using his legs, feet, and mouth in place of his arms, Evan became the nosiest pot and pan musician Simon had ever heard, nearly driving him crazy banging the wooden spoons on the heavy pots as he sang in a voice as off-key as it was loud.

He got into Ben's office and finding Ben's favorite retractable pencil, he scribbled over Ben's meticulous ranch calculations with the pencil in his mouth, causing Ben to have to redo a month of his work.

When Evan spotted one of the waddies painting the side of the old barn red, he watched until he saw him leave, and then he escaped from the house and with paintbrush in mouth, painted everything red that he could find: everything, including himself.

He loved the garden and following behind his mother as she weeded her vegetables, he worked just as hard as she did, pulling up all the plants that his mother had so carefully weeded.

When his father was around, Evan got in no trouble. He was a perfect angel.

Each night after supper, Evan would work his way up to sit on his father's lap, stroke Jed's big hairy arm with his toes, and love him with his head and mouth. And Jed loved his son with a fierceness that he could never imagine. Evan was his son. His perfect son.

As winter pushed on, Evan would throw a small tantrum when his mother would bundle him up in a warm snowsuit, encasing his feet in shoes so he could go outside to play. Jessie knew he wanted to be able to use his feet for his hands, but she couldn't let him freeze, so she fought him daily until Miss Estelle came to the rescue. She knitted him some heavy warm stockings with pads for his feet, but she had carefully knitted small pockets for his toes so he could use his feet as hands outside in the snow.

Evan's second Christmas was a time of wonder and love for the little boy. Simon had built him a wooden rocking horse and prior to Christmas, everyone had put their hand in on the detailing of the horse from the mane and tail created by Miss Estelle, to the stirrups designed by Dr. Collins, and the palomino painting by Ben. Jed and Jessie were responsible for hiding the toy until Christmas day when all were gathered together for Christmas breakfast and the unveiling of the rocking horse. From that day on, Evan considered himself to be a waddie, and with his red, white and black cowboy hat securely on his head, the rocking of his wooden horse was never stilled.

Evan never saw his third birthday. That next spring, he developed a cold that he couldn't overcome. At the hospital his condition worsened into pneumonia, and with all the family, including Dr. Collins and Miss Estelle watching over him, the little boy faded away into the protecting arms of a higher power. His big blue eyes were closed and his beloved rocking horse was still.

The world ended for Jed and Jessie McClure.

Chapter 9

The year following Evan's death was a time of deep mourning for everyone who knew and loved the little boy. Time moved on only because there was no stopping it; but even with the moving of time, there was no escape from the empty mornings, the long days, and the horribly lonely nights.

As spring turned into summer, for the first time that Jessie could remember, her beloved Indian blankets refused to bloom. Had they gone away forever like her son, she wondered as she walked through her home like a ghost lost in the world of the living. Every night she clung to the painful memories of her beloved child, and every day brought more reminders, precious reminders. Crayon marks remained on walls, tiny knitted socks were left unwashed, a blue hair brush with blonde curls waited on a small white dresser.

"No parent should outlive their child", she sobbed, as she lay alone in her bed. It just wasn't right. Where was her son? Was there really a God in Heaven? Did he want her child so badly that he took her only son away from her and made him his son? Were God's arms of more comfort than hers? How could God be so cruel? What had she ever done that she deserved this sort of punishment?

As these thoughts captured her daily thinking, Jessie questioned her life. In her grief she blamed herself for caring so much about her papa and his wheat, his vindication of life, that she had neglected the well-being of her own child. Why hadn't she taken Evan to see Doc as soon as he got that cold? As a mother, she should have realized her son was sick. In her heart she knew she was the cause of his death. She was to blame for his poor little undeveloped lungs that finally gave out when they were put to the test of pneumonia. It was her fault they lost their little boy. With that thought on her mind, every night she'd go to bed, beg her son for forgiveness, and cry herself to sleep

Jed was going through his own trials of the heart. Why had it taken him so long to accept his son's condition? Why had the child had to prove his own worth to his father to be accepted by him? Where was his son? Who would hold his son at night? Who would love him in only the way that Evan knew how to love: his pats with his little toes, the rolling of his beautiful blonde head around Jed's chest, his sticky kisses.

As time passed, Jed hated himself more and more for denying his love for the little boy all those months after he was born. Those precious months he'd thrown away. What sort of a man could deny his own child? Had he been so selfish that he had to learn how to love from a child? Yes, he knew his son had taught him many things: love, persistence, determination, and these were only the least of the lessons he'd learned. He deserved to be punished. His little son didn't. His son Evan, his fearless little warrior, deserved to live.

"God!" he pleaded. "Bring back my son and take me instead." How could he go on without his son? How could he make it through the day, let alone the night when his empty arms craved his son's touch? To lose his son was more than any pain he could possibly conceive. To escape that pain, he spent every night outside working on something, anything to keep his mind off his son. When he had exhausted himself, he went to bed.

Each wrapped in their own private hells, Jessie and Jed grew further apart. For Jessie, she felt if she got pregnant, it would be as though she was trying to replace Evan, which she could never do, and she turned away from her husband. Jed worried that if Jessie got pregnant, he might lose her along with his precious Evan. That he could never stand, and he turned away from his wife.

The intimacy they'd shared so willingly, quickly became a thing of the past.

The happy Saturday night suppers with Doc and Miss Estelle were replaced with short, somber meals at the Tahchee Cafe. No one was ever very hungry, so the quality of the food was ignored. All of them were desperately trying to survive the memory of something lost. None of them spoke his name, but all knew.

Every Saturday night was the same. The conversation rotated around the same old things. Doc spoke of new medical procedures he'd learned and Miss Estelle spoke of her charity work. Jed talked about his horses, cattle, and crops. Jessie mostly sat silent, glum, listening to the others discuss their lives' activities. She had nothing to discuss.

Alexis Morgan came into their lives during one of those Saturday night suppers. She was tall, blonde, and statuesque. Her breasts were full, her waist tiny and her hips were a perfect size for delivering babies, Jessie noticed.

Ali was Doc's new receptionist, so when she walked into the cafe it would have been rude not to invite the comely young woman to join their somber little group. She was intelligent, witty, and beautiful, bringing certain liveliness to the foursome of regulars at the Tahchee Cafe. As time passed on, Ali began showing up every Saturday night to have supper with the group. At first Jessie ignored her witty chatter, and the sultry good looks, until one night Jessie realized that Ali had her big blue eyes focused on Jed McClure and Jed McClure was enjoying the attention.

After that realization, every time Jessie saw the young woman, it seemed Ali became wittier, more beautiful, more seductive. Jessie thought about the love she and Jed had shared before the tragedy. She remembered the wilted Indian blankets, the rose rock, and the yellowed note Jed had given her. Those memories she cherished deeply and held secure not only in her heart, but in a drawer next to her bed. Those were the things that had gotten her through the lonely nights of grief. Those were love gifts from her husband. Her husband!

She loved her husband and decided then and there that no young floozy was going to steal her husband from her while she was licking her wounds from her loss. Jessie Keegan McClure was going to get her husband's attention back....starting with that night.

After they got home, Jed headed for the barn as usual. Jessie headed right after him. She found him inside the barn, his head slouched on his chest, and she was certain he was thinking about the sexy Ali. She had her work cut out for her.

Walking up behind her husband, she slipped her arms around him and hungrily grasp his familiar scent, one that she had missed for such a long time.

Jed turned and pulled her into his waiting arms. Lord, how he'd missed the feel of his wife next to him; how he missed her love.

Jessie wrapped her arms around her husband. "Jed, I've been thinking. We need to have another baby."

"Yes, I've been thinking the same thing, Jessie. Let's go into Tahchee on Monday and see what it would take to adopt a baby."

Jessie thought about adopting a baby. She didn't want to wait through that long procedure of paperwork, and she knew that regardless of what Doc said, she was perfectly capable of carrying their child to full term. This time though, she'd be more careful. Very careful.

"I want our child, Jed."

Much to Jessie's dismay, Jed pushed her away from him. "No, Jessie. We had our child. It would be dangerous for you to have another baby, so that's not a good plan. Either we adopt or we do without a child. It's up to you."

Jessie threw her arms around Jed and held him tightly against her. "Jed, Doc said I *might* have a problem. He didn't say I would....definitely."

Jed shoved her away again. "Doc's 'mights' are good enough for me, Jessie. Now that's the end of the conversation. We adopt or we do without."

Jessie's mind whirled in decision. It was up to her. "Does that mean we have to do without each other, Jed? I love you and I miss our intimacy."

Jed sighed deeply. Lord, how he loved their intimacy. Lord, how he missed his wife. "Are you still taking that birth control that Doc gave you, Jessie?"

Jessie hadn't taken any birth control in the last six months. Jed never touched her, so what was the need? "Yes, of course," she lied. She would do anything to be intimate with her husband. She would promise anything to have another baby.

Looking into Jessie's big brown eyes, Jed was overcome with the memories of their love. "Let's go to the house, then Jessie," Jed flashed a smile she had not seen in over a year. Then he continued, "Unless you want to tussle in the hay."

During the two months that followed, sex between Jed and Jessie became more than a physical act of love. It was the balm that soothed and the herb that healed their broken hearts. Soft laughter came again, touching was anticipated, love was abundant, until Jessie broke her news to Jed.

"What did you say, Jessie?" Jed roared.

"Why are you angry, Jed. We're going to have another child, you should be happy!"

"Happy, hell! Jessie! I will not be responsible for your death!"

"I'm not going to die, Jed. Doc doesn't know everything."

"Bullshit! He knows a hell of a lot more than you do! You used me, Jessie. You used me to produce another child!"

112

"Jed, I love you. This baby is just a reflection of our love. I know that no child could ever take Evan's place, but it's time we move on. Please, Jed. Love me."

The deed was done, and there was nothing he could do about it. He had to live with it, or so he thought. After Jessie came home from her appointment with Doc, Jed found her crying in Sean's old room, her former cave. There was no baby.

And then Jed went to see Doc. And Doc lied.

"Yeah, Jed, there's this operation, a new procedure called a vasectomy. From what I've read, it's fairly painful for a few days, but after that you won't have to worry about Jessie getting pregnant....not by you anyway."

Doc made immediate arrangements to have the procedure done in a hospital in Tulsa. The first day would be prep, the second day surgery, the next three days he'd recuperate in the hospital, and then he could go home. Doc lied.

Jed told Jessie he was going to a cattlemen's convention and would be there for five days and he would be home by the next weekend. Jed lied.

The day of the surgery, Jed felt a little weird as the nurse shaved his genital area. It was almost like she was enjoying it. It was embarrassing. Then she scrubbed him so hard with a brush that he knew she was a masochist in nurses clothing. After that torture, she gave him a terrifying shot in his groin, and he knew he was going to die. When he woke up, he wished he had died. The only thought that kept him sane was that at long last he could have his beloved Jessie again. That was worth any pain that damn nurse could throw at him.

Three days later, the doctor told Jed he could go home. Jed wondered if that man was insane. He could barely walk. How could he possibly drive his truck all that way home? Jed called a cab and limped out to the waiting car. The driver told him of a motel where there were absolutely no stairs, and Jed agreed readily, checking in at the seediest motel he'd ever seen.

Jed lied some more. He called Jessie and told her the convention was lasting longer than he thought, so he had decided to stay two more days. Two days later, still in horrible pain and knowing he could not let Jessie see the swelling and the black and blue marks of his genitals, Jed decided he'd act cool toward Jessie when he got home. Since she had tried to trick him into producing a baby with her, they had barely touched anyway, so what were a few more days, weeks? Hell, the way he felt, it could be years!

Jessie had gotten birth control pills again from Doc and made certain the package was laying in the bathroom, so Jed would see that she could have sex without getting pregnant. He'd been gone a week, and she'd missed him terribly, desperately wanting to feel his arms around her as they made love to each other. Lord, how she missed their intimacy. Jed's swollen groin hurt him so badly that the clerk on duty at the motel had to carry his bag to his cab. That cost him five dollars. When the cabbie dropped him off by his truck, the cabbie threw his bag in the back of the truck. That cost him another five dollars. And then his long, painful journey began. Mile after mile of excruciating pain, the only thing keeping him going was the thought of being with his wife. Someday.

His wife was waiting for him when he pulled into the drive. He was too sore to park his truck by the barn, so he just parked in front of the house. Jed limped into the house leaving his bag in the truck. There was no way he could lift the thing. Jessie thought he was just anxious to see her and raced to him giving him a big body squeeze. Jed nearly howled in pain and pulled gruffly away from her.

Jessie hung her head in distress and then vowed she'd get him to love her when they went to bed. All week long she'd been preparing for his return. She'd gotten the birth control pills, and a red, sexy night gown. It was a slinky, satin-type of gown, with tucked sleeves, and a vee-cut down the front and back, with side slit that went above her thighs. If that gown didn't work, she'd bought a pair of black baby- doll pajamas. The pajamas didn't have any bottoms. Jed would not be able to resist. Of that, she was certain.

Jed was in bed when Jessie came out of the bathroom. She turned on the light and pranced around in front of him. He ignored her. She made every provocative pose she could dream up. He ignored her. "Turn off the damn light, Jessie. I'm too tired for your silly games tonight."

Jessie turned off the light and crawled in beside her husband. He turned his back to her. She turned away from him.

The next night Jessie wore her black baby-doll pajamas without the bottoms. Jed took one look at her, groaned and turned on his side away from her. Jessie crawled in beside her husband and slipped her body close to him. "Please, Jed. I love you," she whispered as she wrapped her arms around him, stroking him lightly.

Jed came off the bed, inwardly roaring in pain. "Leave me alone, Jessie! Leave me alone or I'll go sleep in the office away from you."

Jessie moved away from her husband and silently wept into her pillow.

The next morning, Jed was still asleep when Jessie awoke. He was sleeping on his back which was something he never did. Something was wrong with her husband, and Jessie knew it. Even if he hated her, how could he resist what she'd offered him the night before? Cautiously, she pulled the sheet down over his hips and could see that he'd removed his underwear some time during the night.

What she saw was a terrible shock. His groin area was bluish-red, and one of his testicles was swollen to the size of a baseball. Jed had contracted some terrible disease while he was on his trip to Tulsa, of that she was certain. He'd been unfaithful and had picked up the clap or some such disease that she knew nothing about. How could he do this to her? Be unfaithful with some whore? Bring her home the gift of the clap? Oh dear God. What had happened to them?

The next morning Jessie marched into Doc's office. "Hello, Jessie. You don't have an appointment today, so why are you here?" announced the ever beautiful Ali.

"I need to see, Doc, Ali. It won't take but a minute."

Ali surveyed the distress on Jessie's face. She started to tell her Doc was booked up just to antagonize her, but the truth was he'd had a cancellation just a few minutes earlier. He'd be truly angry if he found out sweet little Jessie was there to see him and she had refused to let her. She might lose her job, and Lord knows that was the only job she could find in that damn Podunk town. "Well, you'll have to wait."

"I'll wait," Jessie answered, knowing she would wait until hell froze over if need be. She had to tell Doc what she'd seen on Jed's groin area. Even though she was certain he'd been unfaithful, she absolutely had to help him. With all that swelling, he had to be in horrible pain, and that she couldn't stand. Doc would help him. He'd give him something for the pain. He'd help him even without seeing him. Jessie was sure he would. Regardless of what Jed had done, he was her husband and she loved him, even if he no longer loved her.

Ali watched Jessie, wondering if Jessie knew about Jed's vasectomy that Doc had her schedule in Tulsa. Somehow she didn't think Jessie knew one thing about it, given what she knew about the two of them.

Jessie wanted a kid. Jed didn't. Neither did she. Kids didn't fit into her picture of life, but Jed did. He was big, tall, and handsome, plus he owned two ranches so he had to be rich. All she had to do was get rid of Jessie.

"When did Jed get back from Tulsa, Jessie? I'll bet he's *worn out*." Ali giggled innocently.

"How did you know Jed was in Tulsa, Ali?"

"Oh, sugar... I saw him! I was there. "

"Why were you at the cattlemen's convention, Ali?"

"What cattlemen's convention, Jessie? There was no cattlemen's convention."

"Yes," Jessie answered stupidly. "There was a cattlemen's convention in Tulsa and that's where Jed spent last week."

"Cattlemen's convention, huh? Is that what he told you?" Ali smiled her seductive smile as though she were remembering something Jessie would rather not know. "Well sugar, if that's what Jed told you and that's what you want to believe, then I don't want to bust your poor little old bubble."

Jessie still would not give up. Ali had a job. She was working. How could she be in Tulsa if she was working? How could she possibly have seen Jed when she was working? "How could you be in Tulsa if you were working here at Doc's, Ali?" She had her. She had Ali in the lie. *Ha!*

"Oh, I wasn't working last week, Jessie dear. I was on vacation in Tulsa for the whole long week. I had a grand time but I'm just about *worn out*." She stretched out her last two words to emphasize her meaning, snickering behind her hand, hoping Jessie would see her giggles.

Jessie did see her, and she was furious. Jed had lied about the cattlemen's convention, and it was all too clear that Jed had been with Ali that whole week. Had Ali given him some disease, or was it just rough sex he'd had in Tulsa with Ali. Jessie turned to walk from the office, hoping she could make it away from Ali before she broke down in tears.

"Don't you want to keep the appointment with Doc, Jessie?" Ali smiled, owning the wicked lie she'd started.

"No, Ali, I don't. You take it. You just might need it more than I do!" Jessie answered as she closed the door behind her.

As Jessie drove home she thought about Jed and the stunning Ali with the wide hips made for popping out babies. She would be able to give Jed all the babies he would ever want. She was beautiful, curvaceous, and barely twenty-years old, and Jessie knew there was no way she could compete with Ali.

Remembering Ali's sneaky little snickers, it seemed Ali had enjoyed the little scene a bit too much. Maybe Ali hadn't been with Jed after all. Maybe Ali just wanted to make her jealous, which she had certainly done. But, she reasoned, even if Jed hadn't been with Ali, he'd lied to her about where he'd been. He hadn't been to any cattlemen's convention, she checked to be sure. Why? The only answer she could come up with was he got so frustrated with her, that he'd gone on a week-long sex spree with either Ali or some tramp, and now he was paying the price with pain and swelling in his groin!

Two weeks later a bill came from the Pink Flamingo Motel in Tulsa. The place was located in a section of Tulsa that no respectable person would be seen; and from what Jessie had discovered, that part of town belonged to the pimps and prostitutes. Was he with a prostitute at some low-life motel or had he been there with Ali? Ali seemed to know all about her husband's trip. It had to be Ali. Ali with the seductive smile and the big hips made for bearing babies.

Deep in her heart, Jessie realized that she'd lost the only man she had ever loved, and it was her own fault. She hated to give him up to another woman, but what could she give him? An adopted child? One they'd have to wait forever to hold? Wait until they were too old to remember how to change a diaper? Wait! Wait and then maybe be turned down. Then what? Wait some more? She had to let him go on with the life he'd always wanted, a life with a home filled with children. Something she could never give him. With a heart crushed like damp sand, she moved all her things to her papa's old room, shutting out the world and wrapping her cold stone walls around her.

After some time, Jessie knew their marriage was over and she knew there was nothing she could do about it. She would let Jed live his life with Ali as his wife and as the mother to his children, but he would have to get the divorce. She could never divorce her husband, the only many she had ever loved, Jed McClure.

Part 2

Chapter 10

J&J Ranch
Oklahoma
May, 1970

"Well, she's back." Ben watched Jed's reaction to his words as Jed rubbed his eyes, slipped his wire-rimmed glasses back in place and studied the ranch books laying open on the big desk in front of Ben.

In his mid-eighties, Ben was still as sharp as a tack and proud of the work he was capable of doing for Jed, although he no longer had to juggle his 'Peters and Pauls' to pay the bills. Jed owed no one anymore. He had worked hard and he'd been successful. Successful, but unhappy.

Jed had always hated bookwork, and his next comment redefined it. "I don't know why you always insist I have to go over these boring books, column by column, Ben. Just show me what the profits are, and I'll figure how to make the most money from that."

"You've made enough money over the years, Jed. You have everything you could ever want. Everything, except one thing. Now it looks like that 'one thing' has come home."

"Damn it, Ben. I'm trying to decipher your chicken scratches and make some sense of all this paperwork." Jed pretended to show great interest in the books for the first time that Ben could remember. Ben knew otherwise.

"What are you going to do about her, Jed?" Ben rubbed his wrinkled brown face and studied the middle-aged man who had become like a son to him over the years. They had all been through a terrible and hard time together these past few years; but they had helped one another overcome the grief of losing little Evan, and then they'd survived the devastation of Jessie leaving them all. Ben never knew what happened between Jessie and Jed, Simon didn't know either. It was just such a bad time after little Evan died. Everything was mixed-up and confused. Emotions were so raw.

And now she was back; back with a little blonde-haired, blue-eyed boy who was younger than Evan had been when he passed on at two-and-a-half-years of age. This little boy was more likely around a year or so, it seemed to him. The child's name was Danny, Jessie said. No one dared mention it, but Daniel was Jed's middle name. That couldn't possibly be an oversight. That was the name on their marriage license. Jessie knew exactly what she was doing when she named her child after Jed. Maybe he wasn't the child's father, but she wanted him to be.

"What do you think about her baby, Jed?" Ben sat with his hand over his mouth, amused and anxious to see Jed's reaction.

Jed slammed the books closed, shoved his wire glasses in his shirt pocket and glared at Ben. "I don't think one damn thing about her baby, Ben. I told you a long time ago when she left me, I washed my hands of that woman and anything else she does. So, leave it the hell alone!"

Ben grinned and pulled out a sheet of paper. "Sure Jed, and by the way, here's that private investigator's last bill for checking up on that woman you've washed your hands of, and anything else *she* does.

"I don't think we should pay him, though. He didn't even know she had a baby and that blonde hair of Danny's is hard to miss." Jed started toward the door, so Ben quickly got in his next shot. "Oh, and Jed, did you realize she named her baby Daniel McClure? Don't you think that name has a lot of significance?"

Jed grabbed his worn Stetson and walked out the door, slamming it behind him. Ben laughed softly and hurried down to the kitchen to tell Simon these latest developments.

Pulling out years of boxes of Christmas presents he'd never used, Jed finally found what he'd been searching for during the last twenty minutes. He placed the *No 8 Neo-Aviator* full-mirrored sun glasses on his face and wrapped the gold temples of the frame around his ears.

Studying the increased darkness in the room, he wondered if anyone would suspect why he was wearing these big bug-like sunglasses when he wasn't in the sunshine. But he knew that if he didn't hurry, he'd be late for supper, and Simon got real cranky when he was late for supper, especially when Simon had been preparing some special meal for the return of the elusive Jessica and company. Jed flipped off the bedroom lamp, stumbled over a stool in the infernal darkness of his *Neo-Aviators*, picked himself up and found the door.

"What's the matter with your eyes, Jed?" Simon asked as he placed a big platter of Chicken Alfredo on the table. Jed ignored him as he watched Jessie and her little boy through those dark sunglasses. That's why he'd spent all that time and effort finding the things. He wanted to observe her and the child without Jessie knowing he was watching her.

Now he discovered it was so dark, he could barely find his plate, let alone watch Jessie.

Ben tried not to snicker out loud as he watched Jed, watching Jessie, who was watching her son tear into the bowl of noodles with his tiny hands. Jessie wiped the little boy's hands with a damp cloth, cut up his noodles, and shoved a spoonful into his screaming mouth. The child stopped screaming, and chewed with his tiny mouthful of teeth. "Sorry for the noise and the mess. Danny gets so hungry that he devours his food."

Simon and Ben responded with a nod of their heads. Jed glared through his mirrored sunglasses, which he had no idea reflected Jessie's face as he observed her. It didn't take long for the others to figure out what Jed was up to, but Jed didn't seem to realize that with those mirrored lenses, everyone could see exactly where he was looking.

Ben spoke first trying not to laugh. "If your eyes are bothering you, Jed, we can dim the lights. Simon, dim those overhead lights so Jed doesn't have to use those dark glasses."

Hurrying to turn down the overhead lights, Simon and Ben both laughed as they watched Jed fumble around his plate with his fork. "Turn those damn lights back on," Jed growled slamming the sunglasses from his eyes onto the table. As he looked at the mirrored glasses he saw his own reflection and knew that Ben and Simon were on to him. They knew he wore them so he could watch Jessie without her seeing his eyes scrutinizing her. After that, Jed kept his eyes focused on his plate and never once lifted his eyes toward Jessie or her child.

One morning, a few weeks later, to Jed's absolute horror, neither Simon nor Ben were in the kitchen when he arrived for breakfast. When he smelled coffee, he figured Simon was making breakfast as usual. He wasn't. She was.

"Good morning, Jed. Here, let me get you some coffee." Jessie said as she left her child in his high chair and hurried toward the coffeepot.

Jed watched as the little boy shoved his hands into his oatmeal and then shoved the sticky oatmeal into his mouth. Jed ignored him and stared out the window.

"Daa," the little mouth said through mouthfuls of oatmeal. Jed ignored him. "Daa!" the little mouth repeated watching Jed with great interest

Jessie set the coffee down in front of Jed and stopped to kiss the top of her son's blonde head. Jed ignored both of them until he felt the first fistful of oatmeal hit his cheek. "Daa," said the little boy.

"What the hell?" shouted Jed. More oatmeal came at him.

"Oh, I'm so sorry, Jed!" Jessie cried grabbing a sticky damp cloth and rushing over to wipe the oatmeal off Jed's cheek. Seeing there was oatmeal in his hair, she quickly grabbed his head and began wiping his hair of the sticky cereal.

"Leave it alone, Jessie." Jed snarled pulling from her reach, the wet oatmeal dropping down onto his forehead. With his own napkin, he wiped at his sticky hair not realizing that as it dried it formed harsh peaks on his head causing him to look like some weird, slimy lizard.

Jessie couldn't look at him. She knew she'd break down laughing and he would get mad, so she hurried from Jed toward her child who was slapping oatmeal around his high chair tray.

"Lord, Danny. You are the worst little boy," Jessie cooed as she loosened the tray, wiped the oatmeal from the child and sat him on the floor. "He definitely has a mind of his own. He can't talk yet, but when he wants something he goes after it."

Jed didn't answer. He didn't care about her or her child, he told himself. The sooner they were gone the better. Both of them!

Danny pulled his tiny body up from the floor, wobbled like an old drunk, and eyed Jed curiously. "Daa!" said Danny as he toddled toward Jed.

Jed tried to ignore the little boy but Danny wouldn't have it as he pulled on Jed's leg. "Daa!" he demanded. Jed kept on ignoring the tiny hands that wrapped around his leg. "Daa!" Danny screamed demanding Jed's attention.

Why in the hell didn't Jessie do something about her kid? Jed wondered. Couldn't she see that the little brat was bothering him? No, of course she couldn't see! How could she? She was busy cooking bacon and frying eggs. It was up to him to defend himself against that twenty pounds of demonic energy pulling on his pant leg.

"Daa!" Danny repeated.

"Move. Go away, kid." Jed whispered quietly, so Jessie wouldn't know he had paid her child any attention whatsoever.

"Daa!" replied Danny.

Jed moved his legs out of the little monster's grip and turned away from him. Peering out the window into the distance, Jed ignored Jessie and her demon spawn. He knew the child was trying to crawl up his chair because he felt the movement of those tiny feet on the spokes of his chair, but he continued to ignore him. Danny's movement was still, and Jed hoped he'd just leave him alone. He thought about leaving the kitchen, but even though he denied it, the pull to be close to Jessie was more than he could resist. So he stayed, hating Jessie, but chained by the love they had once known.

Things were quiet, and Jed settled back to enjoy his coffee while observing Jessie, who was unaware that he was watching her.

"Daa!" Danny demanded. Jed felt the tiny hands grab him in his crotch and latch on with his tiny fingers.

"Son of a bitch!" Jed shouted. Danny screamed and fell to the floor.

"Oh shit!" Jed said as he quickly hit the floor and picked up the screaming little boy.

"Danny! Danny, are you all right?" Jessie shrieked as she raced across the room to her child held securely in the arms of Jed McClure.

"Daa," said Danny as he smiled a toothy grin up at Jed, as he clutched Jed's big shoulders in his tiny hands.

"Yeah, I know." Jed said to the little boy as he ran his fingers through the soft blonde hair of Daniel McClure. "You don't like to be ignored, do you little man?"

Just as Jessie had suspected, Jed could not ignore Danny for too long. Danny wouldn't allow it. She had never planned it that way. She thought Jed would see what a good and loving little boy Danny was, and Danny would charm his way into Jed's heart. She had no idea Danny would take to Jed the way he did. Of course, she should have known better, because Evan had adored Jed just the way Danny did. What was it about Jed and children? How did children sense that someone was inherently good when there was no way to tell them? She certainly had never pushed Danny to go to Jed. She felt lucky Jed hadn't kicked both of them out, but she knew in her heart he never would. Maybe Danny knew something about Jed's big heart, too.

It all started on a bright spring morning in June. For some reason, Simon and Ben no longer joined Jed, Danny, and her for breakfast. It was like they purposely waited until they were finished eating. Then they came in later. It was strange. But that's the way it was.

Normally, she fixed oatmeal for Danny, and toast, bacon and fried eggs for Jed. Jed never thanked her and she didn't expect it. He didn't talk to her, and she didn't expect that either, but with Danny that was something else. There was a connection between the two of them, and it wasn't just on Danny's part.

As soon as Jed walked into the kitchen, Danny demanded to be let out of his high chair and pitched a fit until he could get to Jed and crawl up on his lap. In time, as soon as Jed walked into the kitchen, he would walk directly to Danny, wipe his breakfast off him and carry him over to sit with him. When Jed would take a piece of toast and dunk it in his egg, Danny would grab one of Jed's pieces of toast and dunk his toast in Jed's eggs. When Jed took a bite of egg, Danny would open his mouth for his share. When Jed took a sip of his orange juice, Danny wanted a sip too, and when Jed lowered his glass to Danny, he slobbered all over Jed's glass of orange juice. It was nearly nauseating.

From then on, Jessie started fixing Jed an extra egg, an extra piece of toast, and she fixed a sippy cup of juice for Danny. She didn't say anything to Jed about Danny, nor did she apologize for her son's monopolizing the big man's early morning breakfast. Breakfast was the one time of the day, the only time of the day, she ever saw Jed smile.

One rainy morning, Jed came into the kitchen earlier than usual carrying a denim jacket with a faded blue flannel lining. Jessie hadn't even started the coffee. Danny, still in his creeper pajamas, was busy pulling pots and pans from under the cabinets.

"Oh Jed, I'm sorry. I haven't even started breakfast." Jessie hurried to her son and grabbed a large skillet from him. Danny began to squeal as though that skillet was his favorite toy.

Jed didn't answer just walked toward Danny. When Danny saw him coming toward him, he pulled himself up and toddled toward Jed as usual. Without a word to Jessie, Jed grabbed the little boy up in his arms and wrapped the big jacket around him, covering his head and ears in the warmth of his jacket. The only thing peering out was Danny's face, his big blue eyes open and ready for adventure.

"What are you doing, Jed?" Jessie asked as she watched Jed near the back door with her son in tow.

Jed ignored her as he pulled open the back door to the kitchen. "Where are you going with my son, Jed? Answer me right now!"

Danny gasped as the wet wind caught his breath. Jed smiled down on the little boy. "It's time Danny met my cows and my horses, if that's all right with you, *Jessica?*"

Jessie smiled at Jed, and almost detected a rare smile before he reverted back to his usual scowl saved only for her. "It's all right with me, Jed. Oh, I've been meaning to ask you. Would you prefer something different for breakfast? Maybe, pancakes? How about an omelet? Maybe you would like...?"

"Toast, bacon and eggs are fine," Jed interrupted. "Danny and I like our eggs sunny-side-up, just like always."

As Jed left the kitchen with her son in tow, Jessie felt a rush of overwhelming happiness in her heart for her son and for the man she'd loved all these years. But along with this happiness came an incredible sorrow. One day she would be forced to leave this home that she had loved her entire life, and this man she had loved for nearly as long.

As the chill of autumn whirled it's golden leaves around the ground, cooling it, and readying it for the planting of wheat, everyone knew winter would not be far behind. Jessie had come in May, just as her beloved Indian blanket covered the road-sides with vivid hues of purple, red and yellow. It was almost like it bloomed only for her return, as though waiting for her homecoming. As the biting, chilly days appeared now, the Indian blankets seemed to have lost their zest for life, going into seed, and waiting for the next year to sprout up all over again, offering vivacious color to the dreary road-sides.

Over the past months, Jessie had adapted her own life exactly as it had been before she left five years ago, with the exception that she didn't go into town during the day, and she didn't sleep in her husband's bed at night. Still, being back on the old ranch, she found a peace that she thought she had lost forever.

She really hadn't planned to stay as long as she had at the ranch. It was too dangerous to stay in one place too long, and she knew it. Even out on the remote ranch, the neighbors quickly discovered that she was back. If the neighbors knew, it was only a matter of time before they found her and Danny, and she would be damned if she would ever give up Danny. So every day, she promised herself that next week she would pack her and Danny's things and move on. Next week never came and Jessie stayed on at the place she'd left her heart five years ago.

As expected and eagerly anticipated, the nippy days of autumn gave way to the warmth of Indian summer. This was Jed's favorite time of year and it was right on schedule with the planting of the winter wheat. It had taken him some time to develop the amount of seed needed to sow the wheat on both ranches, but from the small crop saved from Sean's burned out wheat of years ago, he had managed to plant all his wheat fields with Sean's hearty hybrid. To his amazement, Sean's wheat had adapted beautifully to the uncertain weather of Oklahoma. No matter if the winters were cold and snowy, or cool and rainy, the wheat flourished.

As Jed visualized the wheat he realized that Jessie had never seen all those beautiful fields of wheat waving in their rich brown promise of prosperity. She'd come home just after he'd harvested the wheat last spring, and she never had a chance to see it glowing in its golden majestic splendor. And as much as he hated himself for his foolishness, he couldn't wait for next year so she could see what he'd accomplished with Sean's wheat.

Smelling the aroma of coffee, Jed quickened his step. It wasn't for the coffee he hurried, and he knew it. It was to feel the warmth of those chubby little fingers as they grasp onto his own large calloused hands, to smell the sweet odor of milk on the child's breath, to press Danny's blonde hair onto his own lips. There was no getting around it, he loved that child. Jessie's Danny. He tried not to dwell on the fact that Danny wasn't his biological child and that Jessie had her baby with another man. What he had was between him and Danny, not Danny's mother. No, Danny's mother had nothing to do with it.

"Kachuu!" Danny sneezed, snot running down his nose. Shoving his hand into his nose, Danny examined the clear liquid on his hand.

Just as Jed walked into the kitchen, he saw Jessie rushing toward Danny. "Oh Lord! Danny, are you sick?"

Jed beat Jessie to her son's side and grabbed him up into his arms, wiping his face and hand with a paper towel. It seemed to Jed that Jessie hovered over the little boy too much. If he coughed she got out a thermometer, if he got the slightest bit warm, she doused him with cold cloths, now he sneezed and Jed wasn't sure what poor Danny was going to have to put up with, but he was certain it would be something awful. A child had to get used to the germs of everyday life, so his system could fight them off. She couldn't keep Danny in a protective bubble. Jessie was paranoid about that little boy.

"Jed, I think he's sick!" Jessie said as she tried to retrieve the little boy from him.

"It's just allergies, Jessie." Jed growled turning away from her. "Have you been gone so long you don't remember how bad the fall allergies are in Oklahoma?"

Jessie hovered around Danny with a tissue to wipe his nose. Jed turned his back on her and walked toward the window with Danny, while talking softly to the little boy.

Trying to peer over Jed's shoulder to examine Danny was unsuccessful. Jed corralled the boy in his arms and held him away from his over-protective mother.

Jessie gave up. Then she remembered what she wanted to talk to Jed about. "When I was in Tahchee last night doing some shopping, Jed, I stopped by Doc's house and there was no one home. It looked as though no one lived in Doc's and Miss Estelle's house anymore."

"Why'd you do that?" Jed answered, ignoring her, as he walked away from the window and sat down at the table, settling Danny down on his lap.

"Well, I've wanted to see Doc and Miss Estelle since I've gotten home, but every time I've driven past their house at night, I never saw a light on, so I decided they must be asleep."

Handing Danny his sippy cup, Jed tried to take a sip of coffee. Then he eyed Jessie cautiously, changing the subject. "What I was asking you, *Jessica*.... is why you always do your shopping in the middle of the night?"

Jessie ignored Jed's question. "I drove over to Doc's office building, and there was a sign on the door that said his office was closed until further notice. What in the world has happened? Did they go on vacation?"

"They're not on vacation! It's none of your business what they do, so just leave them alone."

Turning off the skillet on the stove, Jessie allowed the popping bacon grease to cool before she put the eggs in, then she eyed Jed. "Just because I left the people here, doesn't mean I don't still love them because I do, Jed, every single one of them."

Jessie knew she shouldn't have admitted that, but it just slipped out. It was so hard to be with Jed day after day, watch him love her child as he did, and not be able to touch him and love him the way she wanted. Being near him was almost worse than being away from him. But she knew that it didn't matter where she was really, because when she lived in Colona, she couldn't stand being without him there either. In the evenings when she was sure he was in the house, she had to call every once in awhile just to hear his voice. That's all she'd lived for the past years until she got Danny.

Crossing over to the table, Jessie sat down across from Jed. As usual he wouldn't look at her but continued to play games with his hands for Danny's benefit. He cared for her son, but he certainly didn't care about her. That was obvious. "Jed, can't we call a truce for awhile?"

"No, we can't." Jed continued to play with Danny, ignoring Jessie's sorrowful face.

"Do you want me to leave? I will if that's what you want."

"Jessie, you know I don't want you to take Danny off somewhere to some God-forsaken place where I can't see him! Is that going to be your big threat over me? If I'm not falling all over you, you'll take this little boy away from me?"

Jed held Danny to him protectively, both arms enclosing the child.

Jessie got up from the table and walked behind him out of his sight. She looked down on his silver blonde hair, and before she knew what she was doing, she wrapped her arms around his neck, knowing he couldn't push her away and hold Danny, too. "I'm so sorry, Jed. I know you hate me. I was responsible for the death of your son."

Jed didn't move. Feeling the warmth of the woman he once loved and the softness of her child bouncing on his lap was almost more than he could tolerate without grabbing her, comforting her, and giving her all the love he still felt for her. But he didn't. He remained stiff and unyielding. She had let another man love her. She had let another man father her child. That, he could not tolerate.

Still, he had never known that she felt responsible for the death of their child. She'd never said anything about it. She cried all the time back then but who didn't? Regardless, that was a horrible guilt to carry around. One she didn't deserve.

Jed didn't say anything as he felt Jessie bury her head in his hair. He still wanted her. He still loved her and he knew he'd never stopped loving her. Finally, she pulled away from him and walked across the kitchen.

"Sit down a minute, Jessica, over there." He pointed to the chair opposite him. "There's something you need to be told."

Jessie returned to the chair across the table from Jed, feeling unwanted and stupid to have grasped onto his neck, starving for his slightest touch, envious of her own son.

Cradling Danny in his arm, Jed gave him his sippy cup again. "Do you remember when you first got pregnant....with Evan, I mean? Not when you were pregnant with Danny."

Jessie couldn't believe her ears. Jed thought she had been pregnant with Danny. He thought she had slept with another man and had a child with him. Well, what else could he have thought? She'd never said anything different to anyone, not even Simon. As much as Jed used to love her, he would have considered that an unforgivable slap in his face, a betrayal of the love he'd once known for her. Gradually, Jessie began to understand how Jed felt toward her. He was jealous. He was hurt just like she'd been hurt when she left him. Sadly, she looked up at him as he began to speak, not knowing what to say or how to tell him what had really happened. One thing she did know was that she could never tell anyone how she got Danny. If anyone found out where she was, they'd come after her. They'd take Danny and she couldn't let that happen. No one was going to take him away from her.

"Jessie, do you remember those pills that young doctor gave you when Doc and Miss Estelle were gone to that convention?" Jed made his fingers into a triangle and Danny tried to play peek-a-boo through his hands.

"It was only one pill that I took, Jed. Don't you remember how sick I was? And that one pill fixed me right up." What in the world was Jed asking her about some medicine she took so many years ago. Without that pill, she couldn't hold anything on her stomach without throwing up. Surely, he remembered all those crackers she had to eat in bed before she could even stand up in the morning.

"Daa!" said Danny. Jed looked down at the innocent little boy and nestled his mouth into Danny's golden blonde hair, inhaling his baby scent, treasuring these early morning trysts with the little child. And his mother.

Jed ignored Danny's comment and continued on in reply to Jessie's remarks. "That one pill sure did fix you up, Jessica. It fixed up our son, too. What that stupid doctor gave you while Doc was gone was a drug called Kevadon. Now, do you understand?"

Shaking her head in wonder, Jessie answered. "No, Jed. I've never heard of a drug by that name."

"Have you ever heard of a drug called Thalidomide, Jessie? It was the same thing."

Jed saw Jessie's face go white. She almost fell out of her chair, but caught herself. "No! No, Jed. That horrible drug was banned from use in.....Oh God, it was banned in 1961! I got pregnant in 1960. I didn't know it was bad for our baby, Jed. I didn't know." Jessie laid her head down on her arm on the table and began to cry, long sobbing gasps of grief.

Jed's heart ached for her. Still, he wouldn't go near her. He couldn't.

Danny, seeing his mother crying, began his own heart-wrenching cries of sympathy. He wiggled off Jed's lap, toddled over to his mother, and with some innate intuition began to pat and love his mother to comfort her.

Jessie was off in her own world of hysterical grief and didn't seem to notice the little boy's efforts. Not knowing what was wrong with his mother, Danny toddled back to Jed and grabbed his big hand. "Daa!" he shouted. "Mama!" he pleaded.

Jed couldn't stand it any longer. He leaned down picked up the little boy and walked toward Jessie. With one arm around Danny, he leaned down with his other hand and pulled Jessie up to him, holding Jessie and her son against him.

"Jessie, listen to me." He whispered in her ear. "I have to tell you what really happened to our son."

"Oh God, Jed, I know what happened. I took that terrible medicine, and I caused Evan's deformity." Jessie held one arm protectively around Danny. The other arm she held on to Jed for support sobbing openly into his shirt.

"No, no, Jessie. You weren't responsible for any of it. It was that young doctor, that Dr. Surgeon, who caused all Evan's problems. Doc said he'd been given samples of Kevadon, but after doing some research on it, he didn't trust that drug and so he sent his samples back to the drug company who issued them.

"Dr. Surgeon was a hotshot young doctor who wanted to get ahead in the business as fast as possible. Hoping he'd get in good-standing with the big drug company who'd given him those samples, he readily passed them out to us without qualms, or doubts about it. Later that month after studying more on the drug, he realized the potential harm it could do, and he was afraid he'd get sued by us. He was afraid we'd have some problem with our child, so he erased everything from Doc's files concerning his distribution of those pills."

Jessie gasped and clutched her chest, barely able to breathe as she listened to Jed speak.

"Not finding any evidence to show that you had taken that drug, Doc said he could never understand what caused Danny to be born without his arms. He said he knew you did everything possible to take care of our baby."

"But I took that pill, Jed. I was just given one pill, but I did take it."

"Yeah, Jessie, I know. I remember when you took it and I was all for it. You started feeling better right away."

Jessie pulled away from Jed. Twisting a damp paper towel around in her hands, she wondered why something so ancient could be remembered so easily and with so much pain. "Well, Jed, how did Doc finally discover that I had taken that awful drug when there was nothing in my files?"

"We talked about it later on, and I told him about that one pill you took from Dr. Surgeon. Doc confronted Dr. Surgeon, even sent him a certified letter, but Dr. Surgeon would never admit he gave you that pill. Doc did some additional research on him and he is certain that's exactly what he gave you. He'd given it to another couple before us. Their child had similar problems."

Jessie looked up at Jed with eyes flooded with tears. "That horrible drug might have caused his lack of arms, but I was responsible for the rest of his problems"

Not knowing what to think, Jed answered her. "Jessie, how could you be responsible for Evan's respiratory problems. You had nothing to do with that."

"Jed, for God's sake! Our baby wasn't ready to be born that soon. His lungs weren't developed! When I was acting the fool, running around trying to save Papa's wheat, I fell and that's what brought on the early delivery. I was to blame."

"No, you weren't to blame, Jessie," Jed answered. "According to Doc, you were almost 37 weeks along, and Evan's lungs should have been developed well enough. He told me that there was no reasons for Evan to suffer from respiratory problems other than you being given that damn Thalidomide. He said that after further investigation, it was discovered that women all over the world had given birth to babies just like ours, missing limbs, respiratory failure, blindness, and the one thing they had in common was that all the mothers had been given the drug Thalidomide. It was pulled from the market and that rash of tragedy stopped."

Pulling away from the man she loved, Jessie was in shock. All those years she'd blamed herself for their son's death, all those long-wasted years. "It wasn't my fault then, Jed? I didn't kill our boy?"

"No, Jessie. It was just a terrible tragedy. The drug companies thought they had come up with some great new product to help with anxiety, nervousness, morning sickness and that sort of thing. They had no idea of the damage it could cause. They pulled it from the market as soon as those effects were determined." Jed continued to hold Danny, but patted Jessie with his other hand. Jessie sniffed and wiped her eyes on her sleeve.

"Mama", said Danny patting his mother's arm as he'd seen Jed do. That was the first time she'd ever heard Danny call her mama. Smiling down at her son through her tears, she reached to take him from Jed's arms.

"No." Danny said clinging to Jed's strong arms. Jessie let him go as he wanted. Seeing that his mother was all right again, Danny patted Jed's big arm. "Dada," said Danny looking up with adoration in his eyes at the big man holding him and his mother.

"Whatever you say, Danny; whatever you say." Jed whispered to the little child he thoroughly adored.

With Danny devouring more than his share of Jed's breakfast, he settled comfortably into Jed's arms, his eyes drooping in contentment. Jessie smiled at both of them, as contented as her son.

"Jessie, there's something I want to show you. Do you suppose between those two old coots, they might be able to babysit one sleepy little boy for a little while?"

Right on cue, as though they'd been listening at the door, Simon entered the room followed by Ben. "And just which two old coots would you be referring to, Jed? If you're referring to Ben and me, then you address us as virile young men or you can find someone else to do your bidding." Simon laughed as he pulled Danny from Jed's arms and settled down with a cup of coffee that Ben had set in front of him.

Jessie moved toward Simon with her arms out to take the child from him. "Simon, I'll take him and put him in his bed. He's been up for quite a while, so he should sleep for some time."

"No, you will not take this child from me, sister. I never get to hold him. Now, get out of here and go do whatever it is you're bound to do."

Jessie patted Danny's sleeping head. "Simon, Danny's going to get awfully spoiled if someone is always holding him."

"Well, I'd say that is someone else's problem. Not mine. Now, get on out of here before your racket wakes up this baby

Chapter 11

Climbing into Jed's two-tone blue truck, Jessie realized she'd been wrong about the truck. It was a car. Or, she wondered, was it a truck-car? Whatever it was, it had to be the biggest auto she'd ever seen.

"I've never seen a car quite like this one, Jed," Jessie said running her hand over the smooth seat which she thought must be covered in ivory leather, or it was the softest vinyl she'd ever seen. Leather seats were too rich for her meager salary, so she really didn't know the difference.

Pulling the door closed behind her, she watched as Jed hit some buttons and the warm car was immediately cooled by air conditioning, of all things. Only very rich people had such luxury in Colona, Illinois. Of course, there was little need for such a thing there. The weather was so much cooler.

Jed couldn't resist bragging on his new Jeep. "Yeah, this is a Jeep Wagoneer, the finest SUV made, I think, anyway. It's a true four-wheeler with an independent front suspension, a powerful overhead cam engine, and automatic transmission, which, hell, I didn't need, but it came with it so I got it. Watch this!" Jed fumbled with another control. Down went his window. He hadn't even rolled it down. In fact, she couldn't find the knob to roll her window down either. "Hit that button over there, Jessie." Jessie pressed on the button and like magic, her window went down. She didn't have to fool with rolling it down like she did in her own car. That was amazing! Jed hit another button, and the window went back up. She hit her button and her window went back up, too. In his enthusiasm to show off his car, Jed forgot to scowl and openly smiled at her. Feeling the warmth of his smile, Jessie radiated one of her own back to him.

"Now, listen to this!" Jed hit something on the radio and the most powerful blare of music she'd ever heard poured out of the radio. He turned the radio off again. "This little baby has everything. Those seats you're sitting on, those are real leather and so is the steering wheel cover. Watch this." Jessie watched as Jed played with some buttons under his seat, and his seat moved automatically. He grinned in delight, and then while he was driving down the long lane, he hit another button on the steering column, and the steering wheel moved up and down. It scared Jessie to death but she hung on for dear life as Jed rammed the gas pedal down on the SUV.

"Wait until you feel the ride! Why you can't even tell you're driving down a bumpy road in this baby. And if we get stuck, I just put it in four-wheel drive and off we go."

Jessie smiled at Jed's enthusiasm. He reminded her of Danny with a new toy, but he was at least talking to her and for that she was grateful. "You seem to have done very well over the years, Jed."

"I have," he grumbled, resuming his sour disposition. After some time, Jed pulled over to the side of the road and got out. Not knowing what was expected of her, Jessie started to step from the auto.

"Stay there, Jessie. It's muddy out here." Jessie climbed back inside the SUV as she was told, and watched as Jed crawled over a fence, leaned down and picked up something beside the fence that looked like wheat. Then he returned back to the SUV and took his place behind the wheel.

"You know what this is, Jessie?" Jed handed Jessie the golden-brown, stubby stem, overflowing with popped pods of wheat.

"Well, of course I recognize this, Jed. It's papa's wheat. There's no other wheat quite like his wheat anywhere in the world."

"Yeah, I figured you'd never forget Sean's wheat." Jed put the SUV in gear and soon they were climbing their way to the top of a hill overlooking the J&J Ranch on one side and the McClure Ranch on the other.

Jessie hung on to Sean's wheat as though it were a beautiful bouquet of flowers, instead of a spindle of wheat pulled from the ground. It was stupid, she knew it was stupid, but Jed had crawled over a fence to get it for her, and she appreciated it. Besides, it was the only thing he'd given her in such a long time.

Slowing the powerful SUV to a crawl, Jed brought the big car to a complete stop. Pulling up the emergency brake, Jed exited from the car. "Now you can get out, Jessie." Quickly exiting the car, Jessie followed Jed toward the crest overlooking the landscape below.

"See those fields over there on the J&J Ranch?" He didn't wait for Jessie to answer. "And see all those fields over there on our McClure Ranch?"

Wondering if he realized that he still referred to the McClure ranch as "our" ranch, Jessie smiled. She didn't comment though, she was just happy to be with him when he wasn't grumbling at her, or worse, ignoring her completely.

Waving his hand toward the distance, Jed turned and looked at her. "All those fields out there have been harvested and plowed under, but before you came home last spring, they produced bumper crops of Sean's wheat. And where do you think that wheat came from, Jessie?"

Jessie started to answer but Jed interrupted. "Remember when you were pregnant with Evan, and that lightning hit that tree and caught Sean's wheat on fire? You said you were foolishly running around trying to save Sean's wheat."

Feeling the sad memories of a past lost, Jessie hesitated to speak. Jed continued. "Well, Jessie you did save Sean's wheat, some of it, anyway. After you left me...." Jed cleared his throat and continued. "Well, sometime later, I noticed what wheat hadn't died had replanted the next year. It was just amazing. So, I started babying it a little bit, and to my astonishment that wheat took off growing. It took me some time, but over the years I was able to plant all those fields out there with Sean's high-quality wheat.

"The ranch made a fortune off his wheat, and it was all because you believed in your father. I made so much money off his wheat, I paid Ben back all the money he'd given us, plus interest. He refused to take it, but I insisted. When he finally did accept the money, he donated it all to children's research in Evan's name. Hell, Jessie, there's a whole wing down at the children's hospital named after Evan. Children from all over the country can go there and be treated for next to nothing, and it was all because of your efforts, our little boy's ailment, and of course the generosity of Ben White. Now, Jessie, tell me again how foolish you were to believe in Sean's wheat. "

Jessie was so relieved that in her happiness she forgot herself and threw herself into Jed's arms. For a minute Jed seemed to hesitate, as though he still loved her, but quickly he shoved her away from him remembering that she had been unfaithful to him. That he couldn't forgive. Just the thought of Jessie being in another man's arms was heart breaking to him. Why did she do it? Why did she throw away everything they once had together? Why?

"It's time to go, Jessie." Jed said gruffly.

"Yes, of course," Jessie answered, knowing he could never forgive her for what he thought she had done. She couldn't tell him about her past. No, she'd just have to live with his resentment. One day she'd be forced to leave. It was better he didn't love her.

Jed and Jessie climbed back into the truck. Knowing he was showing off, Jed allowed his Jeep to climb down the back of the hill side where there was no road, just an old beaten-down path of little bluestem grass. As he expected, his Jeep performed admirably.

Surveying the area below, Jessie got a chance to oversee the McClure Ranch. It appeared someone was living in Jed's old house. Even from that distance, Jessie could see someone moving around the yard. "Who is living at the McClure house, Jed?"

Jed remained close-mouthed and didn't answer her. Jessie noticed a grimace on his face and wondered what she had said to spoil his good mood. It was just a simple question.

Realizing his mistake at letting Jessie get close enough to see his old home and the occupants puttering around the yard, Jed tried to bypass the area near the McClure Ranch by plowing through a small gully and found he'd gotten them stuck in heavy mud from the previous nights wash of rain. "I'll get us right out, Jessie. I just have to lock in the hubs."

Jed exited the car to lock in the hubs. Not knowing what the hubs were, Jessie exited also. Still wondering about the inhabitants of the McClure Ranch, Jessie started walking toward the McClure house while Jed fiddled with the hubs to put them into four-wheel drive. Coming up from the driver's side of the car, Jed shouted after her. "Come on Jessie. We're ready to go." She didn't answer him, so Jed pulled the car out of the gulley and drove up next to her over some small rocks and tangled Indian grass. "Jessie, get in the car, or you'll find yourself walking home."

Jessie continued to walk down the hill toward the McClure Ranch, ignoring Jed following behind her in his Jeep, and as she walked she wondered about Jed. He had stayed at her house all these years instead of moving back to his fine home. Why? Were their memories binding him to the old house, as they'd bound her all these years? Yes, he couldn't let them go any more than she could. Stopping in her tracks, she walked back toward the Jeep and stood next to Jed's window. "Who is living over there, Jed? There are two people out in the yard, and I swear they look like Doc and Miss Estelle!"

"Just get in the truck, Jessie. It doesn't matter who lives over there."

Leaving Jed to follow in the truck behind her, Jessie ran down the hill. Then she stopped and waited for him to catch up to her. When he did, she jumped into the passenger's side of the truck. "Jed, it is Doc and Miss Estelle! Why didn't you tell me they lived so close? Please take me to see them. I've missed them so much!"

Jed continued on down the hill, but instead of turning right toward the McClure house, he turned left and headed back toward the J&J Ranch. "Doc and Miss Estelle don't want company, Jessie. That's why they moved into the McClure house. They wanted to be away from people."

"Well, I think that's the strangest thing I've ever heard. I know they would want me to stop by, Jed. And Lord knows, they'll be thrilled with Danny."

"I don't think so, Jessie. Just leave them alone. If they wanted company, they would have stayed in Tahchee. Out here in the country, they don't have to be bothered with people stopping by."

"I'm not just *people*, Jed! They treated me like I was their own daughter. Miss Estelle said that if she'd ever had a daughter, she'd want her to be just like me. That's how close I was to Miss Estelle. I loved her, and I loved Doc."

Jed scowled at Jessie as he thought about what she had just said. "Yeah, sure Jessie, Doc and Miss Estelle were just some more of those *people* you loved for the last five years and never once... not once, did you bother to come back to see! Oh no, Miss TV reporter, you were too busy making a name for yourself in Colona, Illinois. You didn't have time to bother with the likes of us dumb Okies back here in Oklahoma! You were too smart to think about us!"

"Jed McClure! You know that's not true. I called you at night at least once a month just to hear your voice! You had to know that was me calling!"

"And how was I supposed to know that, Jessie? How was I supposed to know it was you calling me in the middle of the night, waking me up, ruining a good night's sleep, and yet, you never said a damn word! That used to infuriate me when you'd call like that!"

"If it made you so furious, why didn't you have the telephone number changed? You knew it was me, Jed. You wanted to hear from me, as badly as I wanted to hear from you!"

Jed slammed the Jeep into park and glared at Jessie as he hung onto the steering wheel. "The difference is, Jessie, I never did hear your voice."

"But you knew I was thinking of you, didn't you, Jed?"

Jed turned and with a mighty grab, pulled Jessie toward him over the wide seat. "Damn you, Jessie. Damn you for leaving me!" Jed kissed his wife with all the pent up passion he'd hidden for the past five years. He kissed her hard, wet, finally easing into the familiar love they'd both missed for so long.

Remembering Danny, he shoved her back toward her seat. "Who is Danny's father, Jessie?" Jessie leaned over and put her hand on his arm, stroking him gently. "I can't tell you that, Jed. Does it have to matter that much?"

Putting the Jeep Wagoneer into gear, he tromped on the gas. "Yes, Jessica! Unfortunately, it does matter quite a bit to me." Jed slammed on the brakes again and glared at Jessie. "Unless you forget, you were still married to me when you took up with some other man and had a child with him! That, Jessica, is something I can never forgive you for doing to me."

Jed was silent for a moment, eaten up with jealousy. "Was he there all those times you called me, Jessica? Was he lying next to you all sated from all your love making when you thought to call me? Or did he get some sort of perverted amusement listening to you call me while he laid there naked beside you? Is that what happened, Jessica?" That vision of his own wife with some other man was more than he could handle. As he put the big vehicle back into drive, he sighed deeply as he pressed on the gas pedal. "Ah, hell! I don't give a damn what you did, Jessie. It just isn't worth my worrying over anymore."

Tears filling her eyes, Jessie peeked at Jed and saw the set determination of his jaw. He would never forgive her until he knew the truth, that awful truth that had her running from Colona in the middle of the night. How could she ever tell him what really happened? He couldn't possibly understand how much trouble she was in. And if he did find out, he'd want to help and possibly get hurt in all this mess. It was just better to leave it alone and suffer his anger and his rare episodes of warmth. Besides, she would leave next week. Yes, she would leave next week.

Next week came and went, and so did the week after that and the week after that. Soon Christmas was upon them, and Jessie wanted Danny to be able to enjoy the holidays at the ranch during the Christmas season. Being on the run was no place for a little boy, especially during the Christmas Holidays. Danny was two-years old. He'd just turned two, but she hadn't said anything about his birthday.

That would just bring up a lot of commotion, and Jed would get started all over again about her having some ridiculous lover. He was her one and only lover. Didn't he know that? What a stupid man he was to not realize how much she loved him, how much she had always loved him. But he didn't, so Danny's birthday had been ignored, but not Christmas! Never Christmas! Danny would have some sort of Christmas even if it killed her!

For as long as she could remember, Simon would make a big pan of "Lesoignoi", meaning Lasagna for Christmas Eve, and then he'd laugh and say that's what Sean had always called it. "Lesoignoi, imagine that," Simon would say. "Why, my Italian mother would turn over in her grave if she ever heard her signature dish called Lesoignoi. Of course, she'd never heard an Irishman like Sean Keegan pronounce it either." Simon would tell that story every Christmas Eve, and every Christmas Eve he'd roar with laughter; and although all of them had heard that same story many times, they'd all laugh with Simon. Simon said that his mother was a tiny Italian and his father a big Swede, and he'd gotten his mother's stature and his father's coloring. He said he was a mongrel, just like Ben. Ben, with his proud heritage didn't think that was too funny, and seeing Ben's scowl, Simon would laugh even louder.

In memory of his Swedish heritage, every Christmas morning the house would be filled with the delectable smell of Simon's Kanelbulle, a cinnamon roll made from cardamom dough, and Christmas dinner would be Christmas ham and Swedish potato and onion casserole. That's the way it had been as long as she could remember, and that's the way it would be for Danny, at least for now.

Jessie had some plans of her own. She would make a big batch of chocolate chip cookies, and she would take a plate over to Doc and Miss Estelle. That she was determined to do. All this time she'd been home and not once had Doc or Miss Estelle come to see her. They had to know she was home. Everybody locally seemed to know she'd come home. Still, she went to town late at night because it was the safest time to go. She'd seen a few of her old friends out late at night, and they said they'd had *right hurt* feelings because she hadn't contacted them when she came home.

Maybe Doc and Miss Estelle had *right hurt* feelings because she didn't go to visit them. Maybe that was it. Jed had *instructed* her to leave them alone, but what did he know? It wasn't like he had some grand social life. He never went anywhere socially.

Pulling out a large mixing bowl, Jessie found her old recipe book from years ago and located her favorite recipe for chocolate chip cookies. Danny was taking his afternoon nap, and she decided this was the perfect time to begin her Christmas cookies without him under foot. As she measured and poured, beat and stirred, she began to hum ancient Christmas carols that she'd sung years ago. Hearing the kitchen door open, she turned and smiled at Simon as he entered the kitchen whistling the song she'd been humming.

"It's almost like old times, isn't it, sister?" Simon caught himself, worrying that Jessie might think he was bringing up Evan. "I didn't mean to bring up old memories, sister. I'm sorry."

"Oh Simon, I have finally realized that I was not responsible for Evan's death. I have a little boy who needs me now and wants me to be happy, so I won't torture myself with that sort of needless pain any longer. I try to remember Evan for what he was, a brave, young warrior."

"That he was and God love his soul, he was a happy little boy. Sister, you know we all want you to be happy, too. That's all any of us ever wanted. Jed, too."

Jessie stopped to slap Simon's fingers as he stuck them into her cookie dough. "I know that, Simon. I do. I just wish Jed could understand why I had to leave."

"None of us ever understood why you thought you had to leave, Jessie. That's the worst thing you could have done to any of us who loved you."

Jessie turned to look at Simon. "Simon, I couldn't have any more children. Jed wanted children, and I knew that Ali, Doc's receptionist, was willing, ready, and able to do what I couldn't. I knew there was something between Ali and Jed. She told me as much one day in his office. So, I left. It nearly killed me to leave, but I didn't want to be in their way. Every single day I expected to receive notice of a divorce from Jed. Every morning when I opened the mail I held my breath. I just hated to think he would send me a divorce notice through the mail."

Simon slapped the table so hard it made a hollow sound. "And you never did receive that divorce notice did you, sister? And you know why, Miss Know It All? Jed loved you. He never took one good look at that little hussy that worked for Doc. He always loved you. Damn it! He still loves you."

Before Jessie could answer, she heard Ben open the kitchen door. He must have overheard the conversation. Ben stopped and smiled at his old friend, Simon. "Miss Jessie, Simon's not right on many things, but in this one, he knows what he's talking about. Jed McClure has never stopped loving you."

The late morning temperature had quickly dropped, and the overhead clouds were threatening to turn the rain into some pretty heavy snow.

"Now that's what I call a mighty pretty Christmas basket, sister. Lordy, it's filled with my favorite chocolate chip cookies, some fudge, divinity, and what are those other little things over there?" Simon poked his finger into the basket through a break in the clear plastic wrap surrounding the basket.

Jessie pulled the basket out of Simon's reach. "Never you mind what those little things are, Simon, and keep your fingers out of that basket."

"What! I thought that basket was for me." Simon pretended to be outraged. "Well, if it's not for me, then who you giving it to, sister? Ben? You better not be making that old scallywag a basket and not making one for me."

"It's not for Ben and it's not for Jed, Simon. If you must know, I'm going to run over to Doc and Miss Estelle's for a minute and give this to them. I've neglected seeing them, Simon. I just feel awful about that."

Losing his playful attitude, Simon shoved the basket toward the back of the counter, his voice lowering into a harsh tone. "Does Jed know you're going over there, sister?"

"For heaven's sake, Simon! Where I go is none of his business."

Simon faced her like he'd done so many times when she'd done something naughty as a child, and he'd caught her in the act. "It most certainly is his business, if it concerns going over to Doc's."

Jessie took in a deep sigh of frustration and let it out no less despondent. "Simon, what in the world is going on? Every time I mention Doc and Miss Estelle, everybody acts like I'm speaking out of turn! Why can't I go visit them? They're like my family."

Feeling his own frustration, Simon put his arm on Jessie's. Then he pulled her to him and hugged her. "Sister, Miss Estelle has been ill. Doc doesn't want anyone to upset her, so out of respect for his wishes, everyone stays away."

"Simon, you know yourself that when a person doesn't feel well, they need close friends to comfort them. No, I wouldn't expect just any old acquaintance to go over there, but Miss Estelle told me many times, that if she ever had a daughter, she would want her to be just like me. In fact, she told me one time that she considers me to be her daughter. Now, how can I turn my back on that dear sweet woman? She needs to see me, and I need to see her. And that's the end of it, Simon. I have Danny down for his nap, and Ben has promised to babysit. I swear I won't stay long. I'll leave as soon as I see her getting tired, but I'm going, Simon, and I'm going right now." Jessie picked up her basket and hurried from the kitchen.

"Just where do you think you're going, Jessica?" Jed pulled open the door to her yellow Fiat as she was getting seated in her car. Jessie glared up at Jed and realized that Simon must have raced to find him as soon as she left the kitchen.

"I'm going to take some Christmas treats to Doc and Miss Estelle, Jed. This time you won't stop me!"

Jed stared off into the direction of his old home on the McClure Ranch. Doc had come to him over two years ago and asked if he could rent the old house there in the country. He said Miss Estelle was ill and the country air would be good for her. Of course he had agreed, but absolutely refused to charge them any rent. He told Doc he would be delighted to have them stay there and keep up the house and the yard. He worried that vandals would desecrate the place without someone staying there, and he had welcomed the thought of having his old friends for neighbors.

During the past years since Jessie had left, he hadn't seen much of them and he'd missed them. He thought having them live so close would be the chance for all of them to get together again, even without Jessie, but things had not turned out the way he'd planned.

That was an understatement, he thought, remembering the first time he went over there. Lord, it had been so awkward.

He hadn't known what to expect, but he surely didn't expect the reception he got. He hadn't been invited into the house, nor was he offered even a cup of coffee. Miss Estelle was not to be seen anywhere, at first. Finally, he spotted her through the window. He was shocked.

He'd gone over there many times since then, but it was never a social call. No, it was never a social call. He only went there to help Doc in whatever way he could with the upkeep of the place. And he always called ahead. Always.

Spotting the Christmas basket in the backseat of her car, he wondered how he could allow Jessie to witness what he'd seen over at Doc's. Then he wondered how he couldn't. "Can't you just respect their privacy, Jessie? Do you have to stick your nose in their business?"

"I'm not sticking my nose in their business! Unlike you, Jed, I care about people and their feelings! For God's sake, it's Christmas! I've tried and tried to get over to see them, and always for some reason, I'm not allowed to go there. Can't I go for a few minutes, and offer them at least a basket of Christmas cheer? They have always been so good to me. I miss them! I love them, Jed."

Dropping his head to his chest, Jed breathed deeply. Jessie would go over there one way or another, with or without him. It was best for her if he was with her. "All right, Jessie. I'll take you over to Doc's and Miss Estelle's, but I need to call first to let them know I'm bringing you over to see them. Will you at least wait until I do that, Jessie?"

"You don't need to babysit me, Jed. I know my way there."

Jed forced a smile. "Well, maybe I'd like to wish them a happy Christmas too, Jessie. I'll go with you as soon as I call ahead and clear it with Doc. Now just wait a minute, and I'll be right back." Jed opened the back door of her car, reached in and grabbed the plastic wrapped Christmas basket with the beautiful red bows, and took it back into the house with him. Jessie stared after him in amazement.

In long strides, Jed walked back where Jessie was waiting none too patiently. "Doc said for us to come this afternoon around two o'clock, Jessie. I said that would be just fine."

Jessie wanted to tell him that she hadn't invited him to go with her. He would just ruin her happy visit by sitting there scowling at her like she was some sort of tramp, but she didn't say that. There was no need to get him started on her again. It was Christmas. A time of peace she'd hoped. Now he was going to ruin this one little act of joy she was trying to share with two people she loved very dearly. "Why? Why do we have to make an appointment to go there, for God's sake? All I wanted to do was run over there and bring my basket of goodies. I wouldn't stay long! I just wanted to see them for a minute."

"Doc said he and Miss Estelle had been working outside when I called, and she was in a dither because she wanted to be dressed appropriately when you came. You know how Miss Estelle is, Jessie. She'd fastidious about her appearance. Her dress has to be just so-so, every hair has to be in place, you know that. She's probably soaking her fingernails in bleach right now after working in her garden this morning."

Jessie got out of her car and slammed the door with a mighty thrust. "I thought you told me that Miss Estelle was ill? How can she be working in the yard if she's ill?" Jessie felt a tiny flake of snow hit her hand, then another and another. "And besides that, it looks like it's going to snow. The ground's hard and nearly frozen. Why would she need to work in her garden at this time of the year? I think you're lying to me, Jed McClure! I think you're hiding something from me! And speaking of hiding! Where's my basket?"

Jed ignored her and walked toward the barn. "We'll take my Jeep, when we go to Doc's and Miss Estelle's. He knows my car and will see that it's us."

"Damn you, Jed McClure! What has recognizing your Jeep got to do with it? And where in the hell did you hide my Christmas basket?"

Pulling the door to the barn closed behind him, Jed left Jessie fuming by her little yellow Fiat.

Two o'clock was a long time coming for both of them, but it passed quickly while they were at Doc and Miss Estelle's. There was something wrong there, and Jessie knew it.

Closing her door of the big blue-over-blue SUV, Jessie waited for Jed to pull away from Doc and Miss Estelle's before she began to speak. "Well, if you ask me, I think Miss Estelle looks just fine. She's just as beautiful as ever and certainly does not look to be one bit sick. Her hair is still the same dark auburn and shines as though she brushes it at least 100 strokes a day."

Jed wondered if Jessie had really seen Miss Estelle or had she just seen what she wanted to see. Surely, she had spotted the gray hair protruding from under that wig of Miss Estelle's.

"When I'm her age, I hope I can wear my clothes as well as she does now. She must be nearly seventy, but she certainly doesn't look it. My heavens, she was wearing that same purple dress she wore almost ten years ago at our first dinner together, and it was still a perfect fit." Jessie continued to ramble on about how well Miss Estelle looked.

Pulling out onto the blacktop road that would take them back to the J&J Ranch, Jed thought about Miss Estelle and her shiny purple dress that she had worn that day, and wondered if Jessie noticed anything different at all about Miss Estelle. Obviously, not.

"Personally Jed, I think Doc is the one who could stand to see a doctor. Did you notice how yellow his skin is?" Not expecting Jed to answer, she continued. "And he seems so nervous. He never let Miss Estelle answer any question I asked her, and he was constantly grabbing her hands. He wouldn't even let her check her appearance in the mirror. What's the matter with him?"

"Maybe he thinks you should mind your own business, like I told you to do."

Jessie continued on, hating to agree with Jed but it did seem Doc was trying to get rid of them just as fast as he could. And Miss Estelle didn't act like she cared whether they were there or not. She ignored them. It was a weird visit.

"I think something's wrong between Doc and Miss Estelle, Jed. Every time she looks at him she frowns. If I didn't know better, I would think she's grown to hate Doc. Why in the world would she hate the man that has loved her for so long?" Jessie hesitated for a moment and then continued. "You don't think he's been hurting her do you? No, Doc would never do that, but sometimes when people get older...."

Jed cut Jessie off. "Jessie, will you leave those poor people alone and let them live out their final days the way they want to do? Didn't you hear Doc say he was glad we came but he was afraid the visit was too much for Miss Estelle? Can't you understand that they don't want to see you anymore, Jessie? For God's sake! Just leave the people alone."

"Oh no, you don't, Jed McClure! Don't try and make me think I'm imagining things! Something's wrong over there, and I intend to find out what it is! Miss Estelle needs me, and I'm going over there when you're not around to stop me!"

Hearing that threat, Jed knew the only thing he could do was to lock Jessie up in the house and he knew he'd play hell trying to do that, so he decided to try and put her off while he came up with something else to detour her. "Will you make me a promise, Jessie?"

"What promise, Jed?"

"Will you stay away from them until after New Year's? We'll go back then. How's that sound to you?"

"Oh, that would be wonderful, Jed. We'll go back on New Year's Day and we'll bring Danny with us. They'll love meeting Danny."

Jed pulled his big SUV up to the front door of the J&J Ranch, let Jessie out, and sped off to the garage by the barn.

Chapter 12

Jessie had told Jed and Simon to not get her or Danny anything for Christmas. She didn't say anything to Jed because she didn't expect him to get her anything anyway. She told them that her reason for not wanting them to give her presents was that she didn't need anything. She said that she had planned on getting exactly what she thought Danny needed for Christmas, and she didn't want him any more spoiled than he was already.

What she didn't tell them was that when she was forced to leave the ranch, she wouldn't be able to haul a lot of extra things with her. Her car was too small to carry anything except Danny, her, and the bare necessities. One day they'd track her down, and she'd have to run again. Receiving no extra presents was best.

Ben and Simon had agreed even though they didn't like the idea one bit. They argued that Christmas was a time for children to be loved and spoiled. What was wrong with that? Still, Jessie insisted she knew what was best for Danny, and he would have a fine Christmas without a lot of toys. Besides, she had gotten him a large collapsible ball that she could deflate quickly, and small picture book.

One thing she absolutely could not resist was a pair of tiny cowboy boots that she found at the big store where she shopped at night. Fretting over the purchase, she wondered if this was a needless extravagance on her part; but giving into the temptation, she decided that Danny needed a new pair of shoes anyway, and these boots wouldn't take up any additional room in the car when they had to leave. As she located Danny's size on the shelf, she spotted a small toy gun with a holster and wondered what a cowboy would be without his guns. As she threw the boots and little toy guns in her cart, she discovered the cutest little tan cowboy hat. It looked just like Jed's big Stetson that Danny loved, but she knew she didn't dare get that hat for Danny. When Jed wasn't wearing his hat one day, she discovered it had slobber marks all over it, and it had some definite baby teeth marks on it, too. She had planned to brush out those marks so Jed wouldn't see them, but he had come back into the house for his hat, and she hadn't had a chance to clean it. He just grabbed his hat and plopped it on his head, and didn't appear to see the destruction Danny had caused to his new Stetson. If Jed saw Danny's hat so similar to his own, Jessie thought it might remind him of Danny's handiwork on his expensive Stetson. That could possibly ruin Christmas. No, it was best to just leave that hat for Danny on the shelf.

Long ago, the gift-giving routine at the ranch had stopped. All of the men had everything they could possibly want, and gift giving among them had become repetitive. Eventually, it died away as so many other traditions had done over the years without a woman around to instigate them. What Ben and Simon had found, and Jessie didn't understand, was that with her and Danny around again, they missed the holidays. Jessie and Danny had brought life back to the old ranch, and Ben and Simon had missed it sorely. They would buy presents for Danny and Jessie anyway, they'd decided between them. Danny would have a little cowboy shirt and toddler jeans they'd seen, and a furry little pony he could hold while he slept. Jessie would receive a soft pink cashmere scarf. Small presents, but Jessie and Danny would have something from them on Christmas morning.

To Jed, Christmas had become nothing more than another day. He was not a church-going man, and without Jessie and his son with him, he had ignored the day completely. He had tried to ignore the day, anyway. He knew it was Christmas, but he dreaded the holiday and all the happy memories he'd known before his life had gone to hell....before Evan died and Jessie left him.

In the years past, Ben and Simon had insisted on getting him presents. Finally, they seemed to sense how the day upset him, so they'd given up the gift tradition, and eventually the holiday became no more than any other day at the ranch for all of them. For that he was grateful.

Now, here was Danny. It would be the first Christmas that Danny would remember and even though he wasn't Danny's father, he loved the little boy. He wondered what he could give Danny to make this a special Christmas for him.

Jed grabbed his flannel-lined jean jacket, put his tan felt Stetson on his head, and headed to Tahchee in search of the perfect present for Danny. In the first store he shopped, he found something he knew Jessie would love, if he'd been shopping for her, which by God, he wasn't. Still, he knew it was something that would mean a lot to her. It would mean too much! He ignored the gift and moved on.

As he searched the store for something for Danny, his mind kept going back to that one small thing he knew Jessie would love.

Eventually, he found himself staring down on it again. It was a small oval picture located in the Oklahoma Wildlife Section. He picked it up and ran his fingers over the gold gilded frame. It was a small oval picture, flooded with the bright orange, red, and purples of the Indian Blanket which Jessie loved so much. Scripted in gold and black at the bottom of the page were the words:

Like the Indian Blanket,
My Love
Endures Forever

With a scowl Jed put the picture down and went on to the next store.

He searched every store in town, but nothing seemed right for Danny. In the back of his mind, he knew exactly what he wanted to give the little boy. That's why it was so hard to come up with a present that could possibly equal that gift. The problem was he didn't know if he had the courage to bring up all those old memories, or if Jessie was ready either.

Without finding a present for Danny, Jed made one final stop and then drove on to the end of town where he spotted that big all-night store where he knew Jessie shopped. Browsing through the farm supplies, he spotted something he couldn't resist. It was a child's tan felt cowboy hat that looked exactly like his big Stetson. Danny loved his big hat and would insist on wearing it when he took him out to see the horses in the mornings. It was so big on Danny that he could barely see from under it, but that was their routine and he wasn't about to tell Danny he couldn't wear the hat. Jed removed his hat, smiled and caressed the tiny teeth marks marring his fine new Stetson. Alongside the teeth marks was evidence of teething slobber and something that he was certain was baby snot. It was just Danny. Danny cutting some new baby teeth on his custom- made Stetson.

Christmas Eve was just as Jessie had hoped it would be. Simon's lasagna was as good as she remembered, and just like always, they laughed as he told his story of Sean and his first taste of Italian lasagna.

After eating their fill, Jessie put Danny down for the night in his crib in her room. She left the doors of the bathroom and her room opened so if he should cry, she would hear him. On the kitchen table she assembled a small Christmas stocking. Walking from the kitchen to the den, she laid it under the Christmas tree that Simon and Ben insisted on having.

All of them, except Jed, had been in on the decorating of the small tree that day. Jed had gone into town and hadn't returned until supper. When he returned though, he seemed surprised and happy to see the tree, grabbing Danny up in his arms and pointing to all the pretty decorations as though he had done the job himself. And of course, Danny seemed to think he had.

As Jessie slipped her presents under the small tree, she gasped as she heard the front door open, the brisk winter air filling the living room off the entryway. Simon and Ben had returned to the bunkhouse for the night, and Jed had gone to bed earlier.

"Who's there?" she managed to say.

No answer, just a lot of noise.

Gathering up her courage, she approached the entryway. "Who's there? I have a gun and I'll shoot!"

"Good God, Jessie! That's the stupidest thing I've ever heard," Jed said struggling through the hall way with a large object covered with a heavy blanket. "Do you realize that if I had been a burglar, I would have shot you and asked questions later? How was a burglar to know you had a toy gun in your hand?"

Jessie ignored his question and placed the tiny gun back in its holster. "I thought you went to bed. What are you doing here?"

Struggling through the door, Jed looked at Jessie sitting near the tree and remembered the Christmases past, those happy times way back then. "This thing isn't heavy; it's just so awkward to carry. Close the door behind me, will you Jessie?"

Jessie got up from the floor and pushed the door shut wondering what Jed was doing; but before Jed had pulled the blanket from it, she knew exactly what it was.

Jed explained. "I want you to understand one thing, Jessie. I didn't bring this out to upset you, I just..."

Not waiting for him to finish, Jessie interrupted. "I know what that is, Jed. That's Evan's rocking horse."

"That it is, Jessie. Is it all right with you that we give it to Danny?"

"Jed, truly I am delighted that you would allow Danny to play with Evan's toy. He'll be very careful with it. I'll see to that."

"And what the hell fun is it in being careful, Jessie? This toy is Danny's now. He can do with it what he wants."

"No, Jed. Danny can play with it, but if we have to leave suddenly, he can't take it with him." In a sudden burst of old memories, Jessie hadn't realized what she said.

Jed pulled the blanket from the rocking horse and examined it for wear. It was still in perfect condition except for some wear around the stirrups. Evan hadn't lived long enough to put many scars on his favorite toy. Finally, Jed stood and faced Jessie standing next to him.

"Why would you have to leave suddenly, Jessie? Why would you ever leave here again?"

"It's a long story, Jed. It's best you don't get involved."

"Get involved? Get involved? Lord Jessie, I've been involved with you since I was twelve- years old. So, how can I not be involved now?" Jed pulled Jessie into his arms and held her to him, embracing her, wishing he could somehow protect her from whatever fear controlled her. "Are you in some sort of trouble, Jessie? Is that it?"

When Jessie didn't answer, he shoved her away from him, "Or are you running from your child's father? That's it, isn't it? You got into it with your lover, and took off with his child. Now, you're afraid he'll come after you and take Danny. Well, let me tell you this right now, Jessie, he's not taking Danny away from here! And neither are you! That little boy is happy here! I don't know what sort of a life he's had in the past with you and your lover, but Danny is safe here. He loves it here, and by God, nobody is taking that poor little boy off to an uncertain future!"

"Oh Jed, I know you love Danny. I know you want to protect him, but...."

"It's not just Danny I care about, Jessie. You know that, or at least you should."

Jessie walked toward Jed and threw her arms around him. "I love you, Jed. I know you don't believe this, but I have always loved you."

Jed didn't pull away from Jessie, but slipped his arms around her and held her close.

"Why can't you just leave my past where it belongs, Jed? Leave it in the past. Why can't you forgive me without having to know everything that I've done in the last few years? Just tell me you forgive me without question, Jed. I know you still love me."

Looking down on Jessie, finally Jed did understand that she loved him. Whatever she had in the past with her lover was over. That he could handle. What he knew he could never handle was the day she would leave him again. "Jessie, will you promise me right here and now, that you will never leave me again?"

Jessie pulled him close to her. "Oh Jed, I can't promise that. You just have to trust me to do what I think is right for Danny."

Pulling away from the woman he had always loved, Jed walked dejectedly from the room.

Christmas day had been filled with a tumultuous array of emotions for Jed and Jessie. There was joy for Danny and his discovery of Santa Claus and his wonderful "horshie", but there was also the terrible heartache of their loss of another little boy who had loved the same rocking horse as much as Danny did now. But they survived the day, and for that Jessie was indeed thankful.

The day after Christmas brought a flurry of snow, sparkling and twirling in the sunshine, skipping and dancing upon the frozen ground. It wasn't heavy enough to pack, just enough fluff to remind everyone that it was winter in Oklahoma. Jessie bundled Danny in a warm coat, his new boots, a thick knit hat and his big tan cowboy hat over the knit hat. It had been quite an effort to get him away from his "horshie", but promising him he could play outside in the snow took his mind off the rocking horse he loved so dearly.

"Jessie," Ben called. "Someone wants to talk to you on the telephone. The operator said it was a person-to-person call. The caller won't speak to anyone but you."

Jessie went white as the snowflakes falling outside the house. Whoever wanted to talk to her had to be calling long distance. How did they find her? She'd been so very careful. Walking toward Ben, Jessie put her hand over the mouth piece so the caller couldn't hear her. "Ben, tell them I'm not here. Tell them I've never been here. Please Ben."

Ben stared at her a minute, then lifted the telephone and began to speak. "I'm sorry. Who did you say you wanted, operator?" There was a silence and then Ben spoke again. "Beg your pardon, ma'am, but I misunderstood with whom you wanted to speak. We have no Jessie McClure at this house. I thought you said 'Jed McClure'."

Ben laid the telephone back into its cradle and faced Jessie. "Miss Jessie, are you in some sort of trouble? Is someone searching for you and you don't want them to find you. Is that what is causing you such anxiety?"

Trying to act nonchalant, Jessie breathed a sigh of relief. She and Danny were safe for awhile longer, anyway. "No Ben, I was just surprised someone was calling me. I didn't think anyone knew I was here, and I'd just like to leave it that way." Fingers shaking nervously, Jessie managed to get Danny's hands into his mittens, and then with his hand clutching hers they walked out into the bright sunshine of a cold and beautiful snowy day.

Watching Jessie and Danny as they played outside the window, Ben heard the office door close, and he looked up to see Jed walk into the room.

"What's she up to, Ben?" Jed asked walking toward him.

Ben explained her reactions to the mysterious telephone call. "She's hiding from someone, Jed. She's absolutely terrified that someone will find her and Danny."

"I know. I heard the call on the extension in my office. Hell, I don't know what to do for her, Ben. She won't tell me anything, so I can't help her." Jed moved next to Ben and watched Jessie and Danny playing in the snow.

"I'm going to talk to her," Simon said as he entered the den from the kitchen. "I was listening on the extension in the kitchen. Someone's after our Jessie and she's scared to death."

Jed nodded in agreement."I'm not sure she'll tell you anything, Simon. I think she's so scared that she has no idea what to do or what to tell us. What I do think is that we better come up with some way to protect her, from whatever or whoever is scaring her half to death. I think I'll start by accompanying her on her little night time shopping sprees."

"How you gonna do that, Jed? She leaves at all times of the night, and we never know when she's going."

"She can't leave if I fix her car so that she can't go anywhere unless she asks me to help her," Jed answered, as he watched Jessie throwing snow in the air outside and Danny trying to do the same.

Simon laughed. "You're damn sneaky, Jed."

Jed smiled. "Sometimes you have to be sneaky, Simon. Ben handled it well by telling the telephone operator that he had made a mistake, that there was no Jessie McClure here, but we still don't know anything whatsoever about who's got her so terrified."

Simon pushed the two men aside as he took his place between them to watch Jessie and Danny playing out in the snow. "I think it's got something to do with Danny, Jed. I asked her once about Danny's father and she wouldn't say anything about Danny except that he was hers. Somehow or other Danny is involved, I'm sure of it, and that's what's got her so scared."

"Maybe the boy's real father has custody, and he's trying to take Danny away from her," Ben said.

Simon turned and glared at Ben. "Jessie's a wonderful mother! And besides, with the laws the way they are, you'd have to be a pretty lousy mother to have your child taken away from you. If anything, Lord knows Jessie is too protective of Danny. Just look at the way she's got that poor kid bundled up with two hats on his poor little head! No, I'm sure it has nothing to do with her being a neglectful mother."

All three men shook their heads in agreement. Jessie was a good mother. There was no question about that.

Ben turned toward Jed. "Well, we can start screening all the calls, and Jed you can accompany her shopping, but what are we to do if someone shows up out here?"

"It's simple. We won't let them in the house!" Simon said. "Jed doesn't keep that shotgun mounted over the door to shoot friends, now does he?"

All three men shook their heads in agreement again. If they had to, they would use force to protect Jessie and Danny. No one was going to hurt them. Of that, they all agreed.

As they watched Jessie and Danny start walking toward the house, the three men scattered off in different directions to do their chores of the day. Jessie would never know they would all be watching over her and Danny night and day.

The next day the phone rang before the sun was up. Immediately on the alert, Jed grabbed the phone and heard the other extensions being picked up. Simon and Ben were waiting. "Jed McClure," Jed answered. Immediately, there was a click and a dial tone from the unknown caller on the other end of the phone.

This same episode happened later in the morning. Jessie didn't attempt to answer the phone, and no one would have let her anyway. When Simon answered the phone "McClure Ranch" shortly after lunch, he got the same empty dial tone.

A few minutes later the phone rang again. Jed had put up with it long enough and his temper was showing. "What the hell do you want?" he shouted, but there was no dial tone hang-up.

It was Doc in a voice so shallow Jed could barely make out his words. "Jed. Can you come and help me?"

"Sorry, I didn't mean to be rude, Doc. I thought that was a crank call."

"Jed, I'm down on the floor. I can't seem to get myself back up. I hate to bother you, but can you please come and help me."

Sure, Doc. I'll be right there. Hang tight a few minutes, and I'll be there as soon as possible."

"Thanks, Jed. And Jed, don't bring Jessie. It's not a good time."

"I understand, Doc. Don't worry, I'll come alone." Jed put down the phone and grabbed his coat and hat hoping he could escape without Jessie finding out where he was going.

Jessie threw open the door to Jed's office. "What's wrong with Doc?"

"Jessie! Were you listening on the extension?"

Jessie ignored the question. "Why doesn't he want me to come, Jed?

"We've got too damn many phones in this house." Jed grumbled as he pushed past Jessie.

Don't they like me anymore? What have I done?"

Hearing the pain in her voice, Jed stopped to wipe a dark strand of hair from Jessie's face. "This is not about you, Jessie. Doc just needs some help from me, that's all."

"Then, let me go too, Jed."

Jed rushed past Jessie and hurried out to his big SUV, leaving Jessie to wonder and wait in his wake. There was something strange going on at Doc's and Miss Estelle's, she was certain of that. Jed knew what it was, but he wasn't about to let her know anything. Slipping her coat on as she walked toward the front door, Jessie was determined she was going to find out. Maybe Doc didn't want her around, but that didn't mean Miss Estelle didn't need her.

Crossing over to the kitchen she called in a soft voice to Simon. "Simon, I'm going to run an errand. Will you listen for Danny? I just put him down for a nap and he's sleeping soundly. He should be asleep for another hour?"

"Sure, sister, I'd be happy to take care of the little tyke. You just go on and do whatever you have to do." Simon rushed to the window to watch Jessie, knowing she couldn't use her car. Jed had disabled it before he left for Doc's. After watching her efforts to start the car in vain, to his horror she jumped out of the car, popped open the hood, and began messing with the engine.

Racing out the door, he called to her. "Sister, what do you think you're doing? You best wait until Jed comes home so he can fix your car for you."

"I can fix my own car, Simon. Surely, you remember what it was like living in Colona, Illinois. You had to learn to take care of yourself or someone would take care of *you* in a way you wouldn't like." Jessie laughed and slammed the hood of the car shut.

Trying to stall for time, but freezing without his coat, Simon wrapped his arms around his cold body and tried to act casual. "Of course, I remember what it was like there. I was born and raised in Colona. It was *my* hometown." Trying to stall Jessie, Simon continued. "I never could understand why you went to live in Colona, Jessie."

"You just answered your own question, Simon. It was *your* hometown! Since I had no other place to go, I thought I might find some of your family there." Simon looked worried and Jessie laughed teasingly. "I never did find anyone to claim you, Simon. Oh well, it seemed like a good plan at the time." Jessie jumped in her car, slammed the door, and the engine immediately started. As she put her car in gear, tires were spinning, snow was flying, and in no time at all, Jessie's little yellow car was racing down the road like a bumble bee flying into a wall full of pollen. And then she faded out of sight.

Shivering from the cold and from his bitter memories, Simon walked back inside the house.

As soon as Jessie opened her car door at Doc's and Miss Estelle's house, she could hear the shrill screaming of Miss Estelle. Hurrying toward the door of the farm house, she didn't bother to knock but raced on into the house. From the entryway, all she could see was Jed's back. All she could hear was the screams of Miss Estelle.

"Jed, my Lord! What is going on over here?"

Jed turned and glared at Jessie. "Jessie! I told you to stay home!"

"Well, I didn't!" Jessie answered as she shoved past Jed and saw Doc lying on a small sofa in the den. "Oh Doc, what happened?"

Doc's head was lying on a tan brocade pillow which was covered in blood. He tried to get up but groaning he fell back onto the sofa in a daze. In the background, Miss Estelle's screams continued in a crazed incoherent voice that Jessie could not understand. It sounded like she was swearing absolute filth, but Jessie knew that couldn't be true. She doubted that Miss Estelle knew what a filthy word was.

Jed was bending over Doc with a cold washcloth washing the blood from his face, as Jessie started toward the door where she knew Miss Estelle had to be. Jed looked up at her, a firm sorrow on his face. "Jessie, Miss Estelle is having a bad day. You need to go on home now and leave these folks alone." Jessie put her hands on her hips and glared at him in retaliation. Almost in a prayer, Jed whispered, "Please, Jessie. Just go on home."

Ignoring his pleas, Jessie tried the doorknob and discovered Miss Estelle had been locked inside the room. "Did you lock this poor woman inside this room, Jed? What a cruel thing to do to her. She's hysterical with worry about Doc, and you've locked her away from him! What in the world is the matter with you?"

Turning the lock on the door, Jessie entered the room and could not believe her own eyes. Miss Estelle was pacing the room like a caged animal in flight. Her eyes were wild, darting around the room like a feral cat; her hair was wiry, brittle and gray hanging in unkempt ropes down her back, her body odor was putrid, and she was completely naked.

Ranting and raving as she was, Miss Estelle hadn't noticed Jessie when she first entered the room, then she turned and spotted her. "Anne!" she screamed. "Anne, you have to help me." Miss Estelle was completely unaware she was naked as she continued to scream at Jessie. "That old man out there has taken James from me! I can't find your father, Anne. That old man keeps saying that he is James, but I know he's lying! He's old! That old man is not James! James is a young man! I had to do something to find James, so I hit that old man really hard with a big statue, and I think he's dead!"

"Oh, no, Miss Estelle. Doc is...."

Miss Estelle raved on, "I've searched all over this house, but I still couldn't find James! Then that other man came! He shoved me in here and locked the door! Anne, you have got to help me find your father. Anne! Help me!" Grabbing Jessie by the arm, Miss Estelle tried to pull her out of the room.

Jessie stood firm in front of the door, not knowing what to make of the situation. Jed had evidently locked her in there while he tended to Doc's head wound, so Jessie grabbed a sheet and tried to put it around the naked, overly-distraught woman standing in front of her.

"Miss Estelle, I'm not Anne, I'm Jessie. You always said I was like a daughter to you. Surely, you must remember me."

Miss Estelle ran her fingers through Jessie's dark hair. "Jessie? No, you weren't named Jessie! You're my Anne. My little girl! You're all grown up now, but I'd know you anywhere."

"No ma'am. I'm Jessie McClure. You don't have a daughter, Miss Estelle! You never had a child."

With almost inhuman strength, Miss Estelle lunged at Jessie and wrapped her hands around her throat. "Liar! Liar! You bitch! You're just like that old man out there that's taken my James from me. Tell me where my James is you little slut, or I swear I'll kill you! Tell me, damn you! Tell me!" Miss Estelle continued to scream as she increased the pressure on Jessie's throat.

Jessie felt dizzy, everything was going black. Then she heard Jed's voice. "I'm going to take Anne into the kitchen and make some lunch, Miss Estelle. I'll fix you both a nice picnic lunch. Would you like that?" Jessie could feel Jed dragging her from the room, all the while speaking in a calm controlled voice to Miss Estelle. As she was pulled through the door, she heard Miss Estelle's screams again as Jed closed the door and locked it behind them.

Jed cradled Jessie in his arms, then settled her into a big overstuffed chair and examined her throat for bruises. "You okay, Jessie?" he asked.

Doc was coming around slowly, and then as though he'd had an adrenalin shot, he jumped up, the cold washcloth falling from his head exposing a deep gash and a big purple lump on the back of his head. "Oh, Jessie, I'm so sorry. Are you all right?"

Jessie sat up and stared at Doc. "I'm fine, Doc." Not knowing what to ask about Miss Estelle, Jessie repeated softly, "I'm just fine."

"Good...good. Telly didn't mean to hurt you, Jessie. Poor sweetheart, she just doesn't recognize her own strength." In the background they could hear Miss Estelle throwing furniture around the room, swearing in vile contempt, and calling for James to come to her.

Jessie rose from the chair and walked toward Doc, gently pulling his head forward so she could examine the gash on the back of his head. "Doc, what else should we be doing for you?"

Doc picked up the cloth and handed it to Jessie. "Maybe you could put some ice in this cloth for me Jessie."

"Of course, I will Doc." Jessie hurried from the room, but listened outside the door as the two men began talking quietly.

"Jed, I hate to ask this of you, but I just can't handle her by myself anymore when she gets like this. I...."

Watching Doc was breaking Jed's heart, so quickly he interrupted. "I'll help you, Doc."

"Telly's latest rant started because I tried to put clothes on her. I don't know if she has a problem with her stomach and that's what causes her to resent wearing clothes, but I can't keep her dressed. She rips off her clothes and tears them into shreds."

Doc hesitated for a moment and then continued. "Good God, Jed. Poor Telly is completely naked. How can I ask you to help me with her? Oh Jed, I'm so sorry to ask this of you."

Jed stood up, walked to the old man and held out his hand to help the old man to stand. "What do we need to do to calm her, Doc?"

"I need to give her a shot to knock her out, Jed, and I can't hold her down and give the shot at the same time. Maybe we can throw a blanket over her so you don't have to see her naked. She'd be so embarrassed if she knew."

Jed steadied the old man onto his feet. "I wouldn't think of looking at Miss Estelle as naked, Doc. She's sick and that's the way I look at her."

"Thank you, Jed. I'll get my bag and we'll go in there together. I know she thinks I took her James away from her, so I'm sure she will come charging at me. When she does, do you think you could grab her from behind by her arms and hold her so I can try and give her the shot?"

Without hesitation, Jessie could hear Jed reply, "Absolutely, Doc."

As Doc tried to speak, they could hear something crash against the wall. The screaming and swearing had started up again. "I'll have to give her the shot in her hip, so maybe we could tie her legs somehow. I'm worried she'll kick me and knock the shot out of my hands as I try to inject it. I have only one shot left."

"She can't kick you if I hold her legs, Doc." Jessie said as she hurried into the room. Doc looked shocked, but Jessie continued. "Doc, I love Miss Estelle. She's sick and I will do anything on earth to help her."

"Thank you, Jessie," he whispered, wiping his eyes. "Miss Estelle has always loved you so very much, too. Thank you, Jessie. Thank you, Jed."

The house was finally quiet as Jessie poured everyone a cup of coffee and they all collapsed in the big friendly kitchen. It had been quite an ordeal to get Miss Estelle calmed down with the shot, but between the three of them, they had somehow managed. Miss Estelle was now dressed in her warm nightgown, sleeping like the angel she truly was, and the house was quiet.

In a slow determined voice, Doc began to tell the story. "Telly has a condition known as Alzheimer's disease. I saw it coming on years ago, but I had hoped and prayed it wouldn't get this bad."

Jessie patted Doc's arm. "I'm so sorry, Doc. This must be awfully hard on you."

"Don't worry about me, Jessie. It's Telly I'm so worried about. Some years back, I noticed she would forget to do simple things, things like making patient's appointments that I'd told her to make; ordering supplies that we needed for the office, those sorts of things. So, after work, I'd play memory games with her, but my memory games didn't help.

"Things progressed until she could no longer work in the office. She couldn't tell a band aid from a scalpel. I tried everything I could think of to save my precious Telly. I studied everything I could find on the disease, constantly searching for new breakthroughs, but there were none to come. Desperate to help her, I put her on a strict diet and fed her vitamins by the handful. I continued memory games with her nightly, and when she began to get agitated, I would sing lullabies, or read love sonnets to her. In time she didn't know what day it was. Poor Telly didn't even know if it was night or day.

"She became obsessed with mirrors. Not recognizing her own face, she would get upset when we'd leave the house to go outside. She thought we were leaving someone inside the house, so I had to take down all the mirrors."

Jessie looked where the mirror had been the day they had visited. The mirror was gone and in its place was a shadow of where it had been before. Evidently, Doc had taken it down as soon as they left.

"One day when I was at my office, I got a call from a neighbor. Telly was out in the yard doing the gardening, and she was completely naked. I rushed home, got her in the house, and cancelled all my appointments until I could find someone to come and stay with her.

"I found a woman who had all the proper references for the job, so I hired her. Soon I discovered she was a thief. I closed down my office again and hired another woman with even better references.

After a few weeks, I came home early and the woman was passed out drunk. I found Telly down the street in the neighbor's yard.

"Because Telly was getting so strong, I hired a male nurse from the hospital. I knew this young man and paid him a hospital salary to stay with Telly. After a few months, I started noticing black and blue marks on Telly. I couldn't be sure if he was abusing her, or was hitting her back in self-defense. I let the young man go, closed down my office again, and notified all my patients that I was retiring.

"I didn't know what to do anymore. We had wonderful friends, and when they heard Telly was ill they offered to come and stay with her for a few hours, but I couldn't let our friends see my Telly like that, so I refused. I told them that Telly didn't like for me to be gone from her, but I didn't tell them the truth. No one needed to know about her violent rages, the vile words she shouted at me. I had no idea my darling Telly even knew such words, and there she was, screaming them at me. No, they all thought we were living a simple quiet life in loving devotion. No one had a clue what was going on. Our old friends said they understood, but how could they? I couldn't understand. How could this woman who once loved me so dearly, tell me she hated me and accuse me of killing her husband?

"One day I saw Jed in town as he drove past my house. I had Telly safely sleeping inside, so I waved to Jed and he stopped to chat for a moment. I remembered he had a house in the country away from people, and I wanted to get Telly out of town as soon as possible. I just couldn't bear to let the whole town discover her condition and talk ugly about this wonderful woman. She could not help what had happened to her. It was not her fault her poor brain had gone haywire. So, that's when I asked Jed if we could move out to his old place. He agreed. I closed down my house and now I take care of Telly myself. When I go into town every few months for supplies, I have always knocked her out with a shot that would keep her safe until I returned. Unfortunately, just recently I found it's losing its effects.

"I just don't know how much longer I can handle her. I can't put her in an institution to be treated like some demented animal. If she were the one that was sane, and I was the sick one, she would never do it to me. No, I cannot trust her welfare to anyone but myself. She is still the Telly that I have loved all of my life."

Doc took a long swallow of coffee, and a suffered a deep sigh of defeat, which was followed by an uneasy moment of silence.

Jessie leaned over and patted his arm in sympathy. "Doc, do you know who she is referring to when she calls me Anne?"

Doc's face went white, then he sighed again. "Anne was our child."

"Your child, Doc?" Jessie asked. "I didn't know you had a child. Miss Estelle never said...."

Doc interrupted her. "Telly and I have been in love since we were children. Our parents didn't pay us any attention, just thought it was puppy love, but it wasn't. When we got into our teens, our love became of an intimate nature. Telly's parents didn't like me. They thought I would never amount to anything and like the good parents they were, they wanted the best for Telly. They had no idea just how far our love had gone.

"When Telly was sixteen, they moved away. I never saw her again until she came back to me years later. I had never known that Telly was pregnant. That's why they moved away. Telly delivered a little girl six months after her family moved from Tahchee. Our little girl. She named her Anne. Within an hour of her birth, Anne was taken from Telly and given to some couple from out of state. She never saw her again.

"After Telly graduated from nursing school, she came back to me. We tried and tried to have another child, but it was not to be. Our child was gone, and by the time we tried to adopt, they told us we were too old. So we both threw ourselves into helping the community in whatever way we could.

"After Telly got to know you, Jessie, I think you became her surrogate daughter. Your family became her family. When Evan died, it nearly killed her. And then when you left...well, she missed you terribly."

"Oh God, Doc. Do you think I am responsible for her decline?"

"Oh no, Jessie. You didn't cause it. Something in her brain caused it. We may never know what causes that awful disease, but that's what it is. Alzheimer's is just a dreadful sickness that robs good people of their dignity, destroys precious memories, and leaves loved ones guilt-ridden and painfully alone. Even though the body of the one they love is still living, the minds of their loved ones are dead, or worse, hopelessly volatile like my Telly. It's a horrible disease. There's no cure. There's no answer."

Jed spoke, his deep voice steeped with sincerity. "Doc, what are you going to do about her?"

"I don't know, Jed. I had been giving her pills to keep her under control, but recently she's become very suspicious of me. She thinks I have killed her young husband and have taken his place as an old man. Because she always seemed so agitated, I started watching to be sure she took the pills I gave her. Then one day I found she'd been shoving them to the side of her mouth, and when I wasn't looking, she'd spit them out on the floor by the side of the bed by the wall. How is it possible that they can lose their minds and yet, be so clever?"

Doc shook his head in frustration. Jed and Jessie said nothing. Finally, he continued, "What's ironic about the disease is that the person with it looks totally healthy. Sometimes, as with Telly, their strength becomes superhuman, and it is almost impossible to control them." Doc looked directly at Jessie, pleading with his eyes for her to understand and be able to forgive the woman he loved. "Jessie, Telly doesn't mean it. She doesn't mean to be unkind or to hurt you. It's just something in her brain that has gone astray."

Jessie got up from her chair and put her arms around Doc's neck, careful to not touch his wound on the back of his head. "I know, Doc. I understand."

"Jessie, I just want you to try and remember Telly, Miss Estelle, the way she was the first time we came to check on Ben and had supper with you and Jed. Remember how beautiful she was? Telly was such a classy lady. Please try to remember her that way."

"Doc, to me she will always be Miss Estelle, a fine lady. Before I met her, I thought that being a lady meant being a stuck-up snob. After I got to know her....her kindness, her warmth, her goodness....that's when I learned what being a lady was all about. Doc, I didn't learn those things in that finishing school I went to. I learned them from Miss Estelle."

Doc brushed the tears from his eyes. "Thank you, Jessie. She would want you to remember her like that."

The next morning the phone rang just as Jed was finishing his breakfast. "Sit still, Jessie. I'll get it." Sliding Danny from his lap, Jed hurried to the phone wondering who was waiting on the other end. Defenses up, he growled, "Jed McClure. Oh, good morning, Doc. Is everything all right with you and Miss Estelle?"

Jessie heard Doc's voice in the distance on the phone. She couldn't hear what he was saying, but she heard Jed say, "Sure Doc. We'll be there about one o'clock. See you then."

"Is there something we need to do to help Doc, Jed?" Jessie asked.

Jed returned to his chair and Danny crawled back up on his lap. "No, everything seems to be fine. He didn't even mention yesterday. He did ask if you and I could come over this afternoon about one o'clock. He said that he found something to give Miss Estelle, and she has calmed down completely. He said he wants us to see what a wonderful woman she really is, so we can remember her that way."

Taking a last sip of coffee, Jessie looked at Jed in wonder. "Does that seem a little odd to you, Jed? Maybe Doc has decided to put her in an institution, and...."

"He's not putting his wife in any damn institution, Jessie! He loves her."

"That's not what I meant, Jed. I know he loves her, but just how much can one person take? He's got to be exhausted."

"Well Jessie, I know this is hard for you to understand, but some people mate for life. They stand by one another when things go bad. They're not like you....run off, take yourself a lover and go on about your business, not giving a crap about people that love you. Oh hell, no! Being faithful to one person, not running off and leaving them alone, that's something you could never understand!"

Walking toward Jed, Jessie leaned down and pulled Danny from Jed's lap. As she started from the room, Danny on her hip, she turned and faced him. "Shut up Jed! You don't know what the hell you're talking about, so just shut the hell up!" Rushing from the room with her son in her arms, tears in her eyes, Jessie slammed the door behind her.

"Jessie, get in my car, damn it! The roads are slick with ice, and that piece of crap bumble bee you drive hasn't got the tires to handle this weather."

"My car made it just fine all over Illinois in a lot worse weather than this, Jed McClure!" Jessie stumbled to her car, nearly fell, but finally managed to regain her step. When she got to her car, she discovered the driver's door was completely frozen shut. Staggering her way around the car, she tried the passenger's side door, and it opened. Crawling over the seat, Jessie settled down into the driver's seat and tried to start the car. The car did absolutely nothing. She got out, nearly fell on the ice again, and pulled up the hood.

"What in the hell have you done with my battery, Jed!" she screamed.

Jed lowered his window. "Don't worry about the battery. Just get over here and ride in my car." Jed raised his window back up.

Struggling to stand on the snow covered ice, Jessie shouted at the closed window. "I don't want to ride in that damn fancy car of yours! I want to ride in my own car!"

Jed lowered his window again and shouted at her. ""That's just tough, Jessie! Either you drive with me, or you can stay home. It's up to you!"

Watching Jessie struggle to not fall, Jed almost felt sorry for her. Almost, sorry.

"Bastard!" she shouted as she crawled up into the warmth of the big car.

"Put on your seat belt, Jessie," Jed warned. "We don't move until you do."

Jessie locked her seat belt into place and the SUV plowed through the ice and snow as though it was a summer day. When they neared the end of the drive, she noticed Jed began to slow the big car sooner than normal. Finally, they came to a slow stop. Pulling out onto the highway, Jessie felt the car swerve in the ice and was secretly glad they were in Jed's big car with him doing the driving. She had lied about driving around Illinois in her beat-up car. The few times she'd tried it in the snow, she had gotten stuck, and she wouldn't even think of venturing out on the ice. In the city, that's when you called a cab. But, Jed didn't need to know that.

"Knock louder, Jed! I'm freezing out here."

"Well, why the hell didn't you dress warmer? Who ever heard of wearing tennis shoes in this sort of weather?" Jed snorted his disgust as frosty air escaped his mouth.

Jessie let loose with her own frosty air. "My tennis shoes have good traction for walking on the ice!"

Jed turned and eyed the shivering woman behind him."Yeah, and is that why you fell on your ass getting out of the car!"

Shoving past him, Jessie turned the doorknob into the kitchen and the door opened. "Jessie you can't just go walking into someone's home!" Jed argued through a frosty breath.

"They invited us here for one o'clock! It's one o'clock, I'm here, and I'm going in!"

Jed pushed past Jessie. "Be quiet, Jessie. They'll hear your big mouth."

"Well, duh! Isn't that what we want?"

Ignoring her, Jed called softly, "Hey, Doc. We're here."

No answer.

Jessie called in a louder voice. "Doc. It's Jed and Jessie McClure. Did you forget you invited us here for one o'clock?"

Silence.

"Jed, there's something wrong. I can feel it."

"Yeah", he answered as he stomped his boots on the rug by the door. "Doc! Where are you?"

No answer.

Cautiously, Jed and Jessie made their way from room to room in the old house until they came to a closed door at the back of the house. "This is the downstairs bedroom that my parents used." Knocking softly, Jed called after Doc again. Still, there was no answer.

Slipping under Jed's arm, Jessie turned the doorknob. Fearing the worst, Jed pushed Jessie back. "Jessie, don't go in there. They must be sleeping. I'll take a peek in there myself. You go on back to the kitchen, and I'll be right there."

Shoving past Jed, Jessie pushed the door open and walked into the warm, cozy, bedroom, the windows flooded with sunshine. Then she spotted them. "Oh, God, Jed." she gasped. "Are they....are they asleep or....? Moving Jessie behind him, Jed walked quickly toward the bed.

Miss Estelle and Doc were lying on top of a beautiful hand stitched quilt surrounded by the colors of the rainbow. Both were dressed in their familiar professional attire.

Doc wore his dark horn rimmed glasses, his physician's white coat, dark blue dress trousers, a starched white dress shirt and a blue bow tie. His hair was neatly combed, his shoes were polished until they glistened in the sunshine, and he was dead.

Miss Estelle's makeup was flawless, her skin plush, her eyes closed. Her hair, obviously a wig, was pulled back into a neat up-do at the back of her head, and her white nurse's hat was settled properly in the raven hair. Still as slender as a young woman, she wore the same crisp white nurse's uniform she'd always worn, her white cotton stockings fitted perfectly over her slender legs, her stark white nurses shoes tied in perfect bows, and she was dead.

Hands joined together in the love they had always shared, Doc and his beloved Telly looked as happy as when they served their adopted community so many years ago. Now, in death, they had once again found each other.

Soft tears rolled down Jessie's face as she looked down on them. She heard Jed clearing his throat to gain control of his own emotions. "They are together, aren't they Jed?"

Jed stood at the foot of the bed staring at the two lovers holding hands into eternity. "Yes, Jessie. Doc could never leave the woman he loved. They are together as they were always meant to be at long last."

Jessie sat at the kitchen table, sobbing softly. Jed stared blankly out the window. When they heard the coroner's wagon pull into the driveway, they waited patiently to show him to the room where Doc and Miss Estelle lay. Jed explained to the coroner, John Sikes, how Doc had called them earlier that day.

"Doc knew what he was doing," Jed explained. "He wanted someone to find them as quickly as possible after their deaths, so he called my, uh, my wife and me and asked us to come at a time he was sure they'd be dead. My God, that took a lot of guts."

The aging coroner made a few notes and then he looked at Jed. "I knew about Miss Estelle having Alzheimer's, Jed. I had called Doc one time when I saw her out in the yard gardening in the nude. By the way, did you know Doc had cancer?"

Jed was shocked. Jessie clasped his arm for strength. "No....Oh God, no."

"At most, Doc had another few weeks to live. He'd gotten weak and couldn't handle Miss Estelle anymore, and I'm sure he worried what in God's name was going to happen to her when he was gone. Surely, he knew she'd be locked away in an institution, and Lord knows what would happen to her there. They had no other family to care for her, never had any children."

Remembering Doc's story about his and Miss Estelle's baby was not something to be shared with anyone else, so Jed and Jessie didn't say anything. They just stood silently watching.

"I remember them when we were all kids." The coroner continued, "Those two were never apart. Very few people ever find a love that lasts a lifetime, but those two had it. Theirs was truly a classic love story." The coroner sighed deeply. "He was a good friend and one hell of a good doctor. And Miss Estelle, why you couldn't find a better, more kind lady in this entire world before she became ill."

Jed and Jessie agreed.

"It looks to me like this is a clear case of murder-suicide," John Sikes said as he examined both bodies with Jed and Jessie watching from the foot of the bed. "If you look here, you can see where Doc must have injected Miss Estelle with a lethal dose of something that put her to sleep so she'd never wake up again. I'm certain she went peacefully."

Moving Miss Estelle's arm slightly and then moving Doc's, the coroner continued. "It appears Miss Estelle is in a more advanced state of Rigormortis than Doc, so it seems to me he waited to be sure she was dead before he killed himself. As I said before, this is surely a murder-suicide, but I wish I didn't have to report it that way. It sounds so harsh. It really was a mercy killing. Doc was just trying to take care of Miss Estelle as he'd always done. I wish we could just say that Miss Estelle had an incurable disease and she died. Doc knowing he was dying too, decided to die with her."

"Miss Estelle died a long time ago," Jessie said. "In her mind, she thought she had lost her beloved husband. That's when she died."

"Do you agree with that, Jed?" the coroner asked.

"Absolutely. The way I see it is Doc found Miss Estelle dead. He knew he was dying too, so he just took the short route to be with Miss Estelle. It's as simple as that."

"Okay, Jed and Jessie, this is the way I'll report it. Doc never called you to come to the house this afternoon. You just happened to stop by and found them dead? Is that what we agree on?"

"That's exactly what happened." Jed answered.

"Because of the ice storm, we stopped by to check on Doc and Miss Estelle and found them both dead." Jessie repeated. "It was tragic, but that's what happened."

"Then, that's the way it will be reported." John Sikes said. "No one will know any different."

Jed and Jessie watched as Doc and Miss Estelle were driven away in the coroner's wagon.

Jessie turned down the heat.
Jed locked the doors.
They struggled through the ice and snow to the big blue SUV.
They drove home in silence.

Chapter 13

"I'm just so sorry to hear about Doc and Miss Estelle, Jed."

Jed slumped down in the chair in front of the big steel desk in the office where Ben was working on the books. "Yeah, well now they will be at peace, together forever." Jed didn't say anything about it, but Ben looked awfully tired to him. It worried him. Ben had to be eighty- years old or so, and he still insisted on handling all the paperwork for the J&J Ranch and the McClure Ranch too. Jed decided that it had just become too much for the old man to handle and he wished there was a way to get him to give up the chore.

Sitting quietly, as he watched the old man it seemed as though Ben had drifted off into his own little world. Then he spoke softly. "What I wouldn't give to be with my Aimee for just a day. An hour, A minute."

"After all this time, you still miss her that much, Ben?" Jed asked, placing his hat on the desk.

Slipping his glasses atop his head, Ben stared at Jed without bothering to answer. He sighed deeply. Jed had been the loneliest person on earth until Jessie returned. Now she was back and they still weren't together as they should be. That was something he would never understand.

Glancing up, Jed saw Ben staring at him in wonder. "What's wrong, Ben?"

"Oh nothing, Jed," he said. "I was just thinking what a fool you are."

"A fool? Why do you think I'm a fool, Ben?" Jed asked, shoving the hair from his eyes. "Did I make a mistake on the bills I gave you? That's what came in this month and...."

Ben suddenly came alive, slapping the top of the desk, scattering papers in his wrath. "It has nothing to do with bills, Jed, and you know that."

Glaring at Ben, Jed answered him. "I'm not a mind reader, Ben. If you have a problem with me, then spit it out."

"All right, Jed, I'll be more than happy to tell you what's on my mind. It's Jessie."

"Jessie? What's she got to do with anything?"

"You foolish man! She has everything to do with everything! She loves you, and Jed you know good and well, you love her too."

Jed stood, grabbed his hat, ready to leave. "I'm not going to allow myself to get trampled by that woman again, Ben. I gave my soul to Jessie years ago, and she walked out on me and stayed away from me for five years."

"Did you ever bother to find out why she left, Jed? No, you did not. You scrutinized every movement she made for the last five years, and yet you never once asked why she left."

"Ben! Do I have to spell it out for you? She didn't love me, so she left!"

"Why you're even more stupid than I thought, Jed. Stupid! Yes indeed."

"All right, Ben. You think you know so much, then what the hell happened? Why did my wife run off and leave me? Ben, Evan had just died, we couldn't have any more children, and she just ran off and left me to go on however I could without her."

"That's why she left you, Jed. She couldn't have any more children and she knew how you wanted a big family. It seems a Miss Alexis Morgan led her to believe that she had spent a week in Tulsa with you, and that she was more than willing to provide you with a large family; if you could only get rid of one problem, that problem being your wife Jessie."

Jed slammed his fist down on Ben's neat desk, sending papers and pencils flying again. "Ali? Ali Morgan? I would never give that little tart a second look. How could Jessie ever believe something like that? I spent a week in Tulsa, all right! I sure as hell did! And you know why, Ben?"

Not allowing Ben to answer, Jed kept right on ranting. "I didn't want to lose my wife in child birth, Ben. She was so damned determined to provide me with a child that she even tried to trick me into getting her pregnant. The thought of losing my wife, my Jessie, nearly killed me. I did the only thing I could think to do. I had one of those painful ass vasectomies and it damn near killed me. And I did all that so I could have a good marriage with Jessie; but she left me anyway!"

"Yes, and now you have her back, Jed! After five years, you have the woman you love back, and you're too stupid to accept the love she offers you!"

"Love! Love me? She doesn't love me. You say this woman loves me, but how can you forget that she was unfaithful to me during those five years that she was off on her little jaunt?"

Ben motioned for Jed to sit back down. Angry and frustrated, Jed slumped back down into the chair like a love-sick schoolboy. When he looked as though he'd settled down and would listen, Ben continued. "Jed, I've explained to you what I recently learned was the reason for Jessie's leaving, and we know that was just a big misunderstanding. Will you please tell me exactly how you know your wife was unfaithful to you during those years? Or did you forget that I paid the bills for all those years that you had that investigator in Colona watch every move she made? Did you ever once get a report that she had a lover, a boyfriend? Hell, Jed, Jessie never even had a date with a man, let alone slept with one! So, how can you accuse her of being unfaithful?"

"What about Danny, Ben?" Jed asked scowling at Ben. "She has a child and she says he's her son."

"Honestly, I don't know about that, Jed. As soon as Jessie arrived here with Danny, I contacted the fellow in Colona and asked him to investigate whether she adopted a child. There's no record of such an adoption, and where she got Danny no one knows, but I can assure you she was never unfaithful to you, Jed. It's not in a woman like Jessie's nature to love one man and sleep with another. Well, maybe some women would, but I've known Jessie since she was a little girl, and there has only been one man in her life. And believe it or not, that man is you, Jed McClure."

Jed sat silently twirling his hat around his fingers, deep in thought. "I do love Jessie, Ben. I've never stopped loving her and I really don't care about Danny's father either. She says she loves me. That's what she says, but if it's true, why won't she commit to stay with me. Why does she insist she will have to leave one day? If she really loved me, she would tell me whatever it is that's making her run, and let me handle it for her. She doesn't need to suffer whatever trouble she is in all by herself. I can help her. She just doesn't trust me enough to talk to me about it, and I'll be damned if I'll open myself up to getting my heart crushed again! She'll just walk out on me again just like she did before."

"Maybe she won't be here next week, Jed, but she's here now. What I wouldn't give to know my sweet Aimee was just down the hall from me, and I could go to her, touch her soft face, and love her. Oh God. What I wouldn't give. Jed, if Doc had been given the chance to be with his Estelle like she used to be, if only for just a few minutes, do you think he would have demanded more from her? No, Jed. He would have taken those precious few minutes he'd been allowed and savored them for what they were, a precious gift."

"But this is different, Ben. Jessie has a choice. She can stay with me or she can leave. She has a choice!"

"Maybe she does and maybe she doesn't, Jed; but if it was me, and my Aimee was here for however long she could stay, I wouldn't question it. I'd love her today for as long as I could, and I certainly wouldn't waste our precious time worrying about tomorrow."

Danny squalled and Jessie walked back and forth trying to calm him as he squirmed miserably in her arms. As she walked trying to comfort her screaming son, she watched the snow falling outside the den window, and wondered how she would be able to get to Tahchee to get some more diapers with the weather like it was.

"What's the matter with Danny?" Jed's voice was soft and warm as he spoke to her and she wondered why the change in his attitude toward her. Then she realized that anything that concerned Danny was a concern to Jed. It had absolutely nothing to do with her worries.

"Danny's teething and it's caused his little bottom to be sore."

"What are you doing for him?"

Jed pulled Danny from her and Danny went right to him wrapping his arms around Jed's neck. For once she was glad Danny wanted Jed, and her aching arms certainly did appreciate him taking a turn walking the screaming child.

"I let him soak in a bath of oatmeal water, and I put some baby cream on him, but nothing seems to give him relief."

Jed walked toward Jessie and handed Danny back to her despite Danny's screams of "Dada". "I think I have something in the barn that might help."

"Oh Jed, for God's sake! You want to put *something from the barn* on Danny?"

"It doesn't look like what you're doing is working, Jessie." Jed didn't raise his voice, he just seemed eager to help. She was grateful and tired. Danny hadn't slept in two nights and she and Danny were both worn out.

Jed threw on his warm Shearing sheepskin jacket and started out the door, the snow blowing into the entryway from the porch. In a matter of minutes, he returned, a big jar in his hand. "Lay him down on the sofa, Jessie, and pull off his diaper."

Grabbing a heavy blanket, Jessie threw it on the leather sofa and laid Danny on top of it, Danny screaming as she pulled his pajama bottoms and his diaper from him. Jed stuck his hand into a big jar of cream, worked a big glob of the white cream into his hands to warm it, and then began to rub it onto Danny's fiery little bottom. Immediately, Danny stopped his wailing, his eyes drooped from lack of sleep.

"What was that stuff, Jed?" Jessie asked as she began to refasten his diaper, and then stopped. The cream and cold air soothed his rear, but it also caused him to wet his diaper.

"It's something I put on the cows udders when they get sore. Works like magic."

"Yes, it certainly does." Jessie looked around the room helplessly. "Jed will you watch him while I try and find a clean diaper for Danny?"

"Are you out of diapers, Jessie?"

Not answering, Jessie hurried from the room. She had one clean diaper left out of all those diapers she'd bought the last time she went to Tahchee. Fearing the bad weather, she had bought an extra supply that should have held her over through the storm, but she hadn't planned on Danny cutting teeth and having such diarrhea. Why in the world they didn't make the good old cloth diapers like they used to make, the kind you could wash and reuse. She knew they probably made them, but she certainly hadn't found any. The disposable ones were convenient, but it certainly was a pain if you ran out. Remembering the trip from Colona, Jessie cringed.

Finding two clean diapers, Jessie threw on her warm jacket and hurried back to the den where Danny was sleeping contently on the leather couch, Jed sitting next to him. Simon had walked into the room and was bending over looking at Danny.

"Jed, I hate to ask this of you, but do you think you could baby sit Danny until I get back from Tahchee? I won't be gone any longer than it takes me to run to the store and come right back."

"There's a storm going on out there, Jessie. Can't it wait until morning?"

Jessie quickly replaced Danny's soiled diaper with a clean one. Going into town during the day was not something Jessie would do. She had to go tonight or wait until tomorrow night. She had no choice. "Jed please, just this once do we have to argue about it?"

Simon said something to Jed that Jessie couldn't hear, and then Jed answered her. "No, we don't have to argue about anything, Jessie. Simon has offered to take Danny out to the bunkhouse with him for the night and bring him back tomorrow in time for breakfast. I'll drive you into town."

"Oh Simon, I can't ask that of you. Danny's been sick and..."

"And I know how to take care of a sick child, sister. I took care of Evan plenty, and I know what to do. Besides, if he gets to fussing, I'll stick him in bed with Ben," Simon chuckled. "Now, go on both of you."

Throwing a big blanket around Danny, Jed picked up Danny. "I'll carry him out to the bunkhouse for you, Simon. The snow's let up, but it's still treacherous."

Jed turned and smiled at his wife. "Jessie, give me a minute to warm up my Jeep, and then come on out. And put on some boots instead of those tennis shoes. The four wheel drive is great, but if we start to slide on the ice, it will do little good. Your feet could get mighty cold in those tennis shoes if we get stranded."

"Oh Jed, I hate for you to go out in the middle of the night in this weather. I thought I had plenty of diapers, but I've never seen Danny have so much trouble teething. I hate to bother you, Jed."

Followed closely by Simon carrying the last clean diaper and a jar of white cream, Jed smiled as he walked out the door carrying a sleeping Danny. "It's no bother, Jessie. Just think of it as an adventure."

"Adventure?" Jessie gasped. She'd had enough adventure in Colona to last a life time.

It looked to Jed like Jessie had bought enough diapers to last till Danny was a teenager; but she said until she could get him potty-trained, she wasn't taking any more chances on getting stuck in a snow storm without diapers.

Bag after bag of diapers Jed hauled into Jessie's bedroom, and as he watched her stacking the packages under a changing table he slipped a small package on the table next to her bed. "Are you okay now, Jessie?"

"I'm fine. Thank you, Jed," Jessie answered as she walked toward him and put a kiss on his cheek.

"All right, then. Good night, Jessie." Jed pulled the bedroom door closed and walked through the bathroom, the kitchen and down the long lonely hallway to what used be their bedroom, he remembered sadly.

Glancing at the clock by his bed, Jed noticed it was almost the beginning of a new day. Dawn would come quickly. Pulling his boots off, he threw them across the room and tossed his heavy gray socks on top of them. Standing, he unbuttoned his shirt and flung it across a chair. Slipping out of his jeans he tossed them on top of the shirt. Sitting down on the side of his bed, he slipped under the covers and lay staring up at the ceiling for a few minutes thinking about Jessie and Danny.

Ben had been right. He was always right. Remembering Ben's words, Jed thought about Jessie and how much he loved her; how he'd loved her for as long as he could remember. Savoring those things, he knew that if he could have Jessie with him for just one night, lying beside him, loving him as his wife, he would not demand more of her. He would take whatever she was able to give and be grateful.

Flicking off his lamp, he rolled over and tried to sleep, but sleep was elusive. He wished he could say the right things to Jessie, the things that would let her know how much he loved her; but he couldn't. It was his stupid pride. He was such a jerk, and he knew it. She had shown her love for him over and over, and what had he done but demand more than she could give him. He really was a fool.

As Jed lay with his arms over his head staring at the bedroom ceiling he wondered what Jessie was thinking right now. What was she thinking about the gift he'd left for her? Would she understand how much he really loved her? Was that silly little gift enough to make up for all the hurt between them?

Jessie slipped out of her warm boots, laid them to dry on a dirt catcher, and slipped on a pair of fur-lined moccasins. Walking to her closet she pulled her sweater over her head, folded it neatly, and placed it on a shelf. Stepping from her moccasins, she slipped her jeans down her long lean legs, placed the jeans on a hanger, shivered, and replaced her warm moccasins on her cold feet. Grabbing a clean flannel nightgown from another shelf, Jessie pulled it over her head and buttoned it close against her throat.

Settling down on the side of the bed, she leaned to turn off the lamp by the bed and spied a plain brown paper bag. No one would come in her room when she wasn't there, she knew that, but someone had been in there. The only person she knew of was Jed. Picking up the brown paper bag, she studied the outline of the name of the store imprinted on the front of the small sack.

Inside the brown paper bag was a small box. On the outside of the box was the word, "REMEMBRANCES". Carefully opening the box, Jessie pulled out the colorful picture of the Indian blanket flowers and ran her finger around the gold gilded frame. At the bottom of the picture were the words written in gold and black:

Like the Indian Blanket,
My Love
Endures Forever

Jessie lay down in her bed, caressing the gilded frame and ran her fingers over the colorful flowers. Jed loved her, he had always loved her. She had known this, but there was so much hurt between them she had wondered if they could ever find their way back to one another. Was this his way of letting her know what was in his heart, even though he didn't have the words to tell her? Was Jed ready to love her again? She wasn't sure, but she was going to find out. With Danny sleeping with the two old men out in the bunkhouse, this was the perfect time.

Throwing the blankets from her bed and shivering as she put on her warm moccasins, Jessie pulled the door closed to her bedroom as she walked through the bathroom, the kitchen and down the long hallway to Jed's bedroom, their bedroom, she remembered sadly.

Knocking softly, she called his name.

Jed didn't know when he'd fallen asleep. He was dreaming that Jessie was calling to him, but he knew it was just a dream until he heard his door open. "Jed, are you awake?"

Pulling up from under his covers, Jed leaned over and turned on the lamp next to his bed. Rubbing the sleep from his eyes he spotted his wife standing in the doorway in a long white flannel nightgown. "Jessie, are you all right?"

"Oh Jed, I'm sorry. I didn't think you'd be asleep yet. It's nothing, I'll come back later." Jessie started to leave the room.

Sitting up straight in bed, Jed was immediately awake. "No, no, Jessie. It's fine. I wasn't asleep. See, I'm wide awake"

178

Venturing further into the room, Jessie noted the disarray of Jed's bedroom and smiled. "I just wanted to thank you for the gift, Jed. It means so much to me."

Fumbling, not knowing what to say, Jed answered, "Well, Jessie....I....well, I know how much you always loved those Indian blanket flowers and I well..."

Interrupting her husband's jabbering, Jessie felt awkward, wondering why she even came to him. "All right then. I guess I'll go back to my own room."

Jed realized why his wife had come and he wasn't about to let her leave. Not now. Not while they still had a chance. "Now, Jessie, why would you want to go back to your room to a cold bed when you can sleep in here with me where it's all toasty warm?"

Hesitating, but knowing what was in her heart, Jessie stumbled over her words. "Jed, I can't.... I can't promise you that I can stay here at the ranch forever. Can you....can you possibly understand that? Can you accept me being with you here tonight...without a guarantee for tomorrow?"

Throwing back the covers, Jed grinned seeing the longing in his wife's face. "However long you can stay is fine with me, Jessie. I won't push you, I promise." Jed remembered her words to him from a long time ago. "Now, do I have to send you a written invitation, Jessie? Or do I have to drag you into this bed with me?"

"Oh no, Jed. Believe me, I'm more than willing." Jessie jumped in the bed next to her husband, reveling in the warmth that she had craved for so many years.

Jed worked the tiny buttons of his wife's night gown down past her chest. "Do you really need this to keep you warm, Jessie?"

Pulling the gown over her head, she tossed it across the room where it landed on top of Jed's clothes. "Absolutely not, Jed. You're all I've ever needed."

At breakfast the next morning, no one needed to tell Ben and Simon that Jed and Jessie had faced their problems and accepted the love they both had denied themselves for so long. There was no big grin on Jed's face and no smitten glances from Jessie, but there was a feeling that radiated between them: a devotion that embraced everyone it touched, a mature responsible commitment, a coming home.

Later that day, when Jed and Jessie moved all of Jessie's things back to their old bedroom, no one said anything about that either. It was only natural, at long last.

"You think she bought enough diapers, Jed?" Simon laughed as he watched Jed try to struggle through the door carrying a changing table loaded with packages of disposable diapers. "Here, let me help," Simon offered as he grabbed several packages of diapers threatening to topple from the table.

Jessie was busy hanging her clothes back into her side of the large cedar closet of their shared bedroom, and Danny was busy rearranging Jessie and Jed's shoes and boots at the bottom of the closet, stopping only long enough to try and shove his foot into Jed's big boots.

The phone rang. "You want to get that, Simon?" Jed asked, glancing quickly at Jessie.

"Sure thing, Jed," Simon answered as he walked toward Jed's old bedroom that had been converted into Ben's office. After hearing Simon answer "hello" several times, Jed knew who was calling. It was the same mysterious caller as always. Someone was still after Jessie, but who was it, he wondered. He started to say something to Jessie, but remembered his promise to her and kept quiet as Simon walked back into the room.

"Jed, I've been thinking," Simon said.

"Yeah, Simon, I've been thinking, too." Jed answered.

The open door was pushed open further and Ben walked in. "Jed, I think we need to get an unlisted number for the ranch."

"We can do that Ben. In fact, we'll get two separate lines. One line will be listed for the ranch only, and one line will be unlisted for our personal use. The calls for the ranch will go directly to the office, and will be picked up by a recorder which we'll monitor. If any of us are out somewhere and need to call home, we'll use the private number which will go to all the other phones in the house. Maybe we can cut off some of these nuisance calls."

Jessie stopped fussing with the clothes that she was pretending to straighten as she listened to Jed, Ben and Simon try and work a solution to her dilemma. There was no solution, she was certain of that, but at least this might solve the phone calls. They were after her, and they had found her. It was only a matter of time before they showed up. Then she would have to leave.

Chapter 14

Hearing the sound of a car pulling up in the driveway outside the bunkhouse, Simon thought Jed and Jessie had returned from supervising the sale of Doc and Miss Estelle's personal property at the McClure house, but it wasn't. Peering out the half-opened door of the bunkhouse, he noticed two men walking toward the door of the ranch house. One of the men was tall and lanky; the other was squat and muscular. Both had an air of self-importance that riled Simon. It was nothing that was noticeable to most people, but it was a certain familiarity of their mannerisms that caught Simon's eye; a swagger, a swank, something he remembered from the Colona hoods who used to stake out the street corners at night.

Simon watched as Ben opened the ranch house door. As Ben began to talk to the two men, it became very evident to Simon that what he suspected was definitely true about those two thugs. If their mannerisms didn't reflect who they were, the shouting in their thick, harsh accents certainly did. Those boys were from Colona and they were after Jessie, or him.

The two men argued with Ben for a moment, and it appeared Ben threatened to call the police because as quickly as they arrived, the two men headed back to their cars. As they pulled out of the driveway, Simon noted the Illinois license plates on the car.

Closing the door behind him, Simon gasped a sigh of relief that they had gone. He hadn't been to Colona in nearly forty years, but when he left there, he left his past behind for good, at least that's what he had hoped. He'd done what was required of him at the time, and then he washed his hands of the whole place, leaving it to his younger brother to handle the city and its problems. His brother had done a good job until his death. That's just about the time when Jessie arrived in Colona. That's when all the crap started up again. Now the city was more corrupt than ever and he knew just how bad a city could get if left to the devices of the gangsters. Hell, yes, he knew. He'd dealt with gangsters all of his life.

The bunkhouse door opened and Ben entered. "Did you see those two bums, Simon?"

"I saw them. What did they want?"

"They were looking for Jessie! I'll bet those two are the ones who have been behind those mysterious telephone calls all this time. I'm sure they were from Colona, Simon, because they had an Illinois license plate. Jessie shouldn't have to put up with this type of harassment! I mean calling all the time was bad enough, but now they've starting showing up at her home. You were from Colona, Simon. Can't you do something about this? "

Ignoring his old friend's comment, Simon didn't answer as he opened the bunkhouse door and walked out into the drab February day.

Tromping up and down his ragged garden, Simon stopped occasionally to pull a weed, or toss a branch. He hadn't had time to work the area yet, and it was still mostly a bramble of last year's left-over foliage, a few corn stalks, and some tangled vines. As soon as the ground was workable, he would ready it for planting. He always liked to get his onions, carrots, and Irish potatoes in the ground by the middle of February and that time was fast approaching. Some folks said you should plant lettuce, broccoli, and cabbage at the same time you plant the onions, carrots and potatoes, but he didn't believe that. Since he'd lived in Oklahoma, he'd seen many a cold snap that would kill off the above-the-ground vegetables. Since he'd lived in Oklahoma....

Simon's mind tried to ignore the memories that circulated around his brain. They would only cause him pain. He knew that. He pushed them away.

Maybe next week, he would get started turning the ground, he decided, as he fought his worries. Maybe this year he'd try planting....

What if those thugs came back again when Jessie was here? What could he do?

There is nothing I can do!

What if they tried to take Danny?

There is nothing I can do!

Why? Why can't you help them?

Damn it! There's nothing I can do without letting Jessie know about me!

Beets! Yes, beets. They would grow well during this time of year. He had never tried beets before. The truth was he couldn't stand beets. Danny might like them, though. That little boy and those tiny fingers sure would make a mess with them. Danny....

What if those thugs came back and took Danny when Jessie was alone?

Oh God!
What if someone hurt Jessie to get to Danny?
Oh Lord!

As Simon worried, he wondered what would happen if Jessie knew about the real Simon, the man he'd left in Colona. How could he protect her without destroying the love he knew she felt for him, the love he cherished with all his heart? He had done some horrible things in his past, but he'd left all that in Colona buried right along with the person he used to be. Now, it seemed as though his past had finally surfaced, creeping up from the ground like a corpse escaping its' morbid grave.

In some far-off corner of his mind, he knew he could take care of Jessie and Danny. He could make those goons go away; but in order to do that, he would have to take on the depiction of the man he used to be. Would she hate him for the things he'd done in the past. Could he live with that? How could he give up the love she had known for him? Could he do it?

Simon continued his tromping up and down his garden, pulling weeds and tossing sticks. It didn't help. Maybe it was the arrival of those two thugs. Maybe it was the cold February day so much like the day he'd first met Sean Keegan. It didn't matter whatever it was, his memories still controlled him.

With his mind scurrying around his past life, Simon smiled as he remembered Sean Keegan. Sean was such a good friend, and to this day, he still missed him. He'd never met anyone quite like the wiry little Irishman. He was a good man, a good friend, a responsible boss, and a fair person.

Sean's ranch had been nearly scalped by the dust storms of the 1930's, but he was always working on some sort of plan to pull the ranch out of the trouble it had encountered during that awful drought. Simon had always thought it was a shame Sean couldn't see the results of his last experiment with the wheat, but he died before it could be planted. A massive heart attack, the Doc said. After that, everyone just forgot about Sean's wheat, everyone, except Jessie. She never gave up on her father's dream, and when she married Jed, he made everything right again for her and for the ranch.

When they lost Sean, Jessie was only twelve-years old, still a baby. She needed her father, and Simon decided to make it his responsibility to be a substitute father for her. It wasn't hard for him to step into the role, because he had loved that child from the moment he had first met her when she was barely knee-high. He could never take Sean's place, he knew that, but Jessie needed someone to help her. And in his opinion, her mother was next to worthless.

That wife of Sean's was never good enough for him and that was a fact. She wasn't worthy of wiping Sean's boots but Sean could never see it. He adored her. No one else did, though. She was always putting on airs, acting like she was such a grand lady. She wasn't. She was just a snob. She even insisted little Jessie go off to that awful school to be a lady like her. Thank God it didn't work.

Simon's mind wandered to the day he'd first met Sean. He'd left Colona the year before. Hoping to get away from anything remotely similar to Colona, he'd settled on Tulsa, Oklahoma. After doing some research on the city, he discovered it was a progressive city that had somehow managed to maintain small-town warmth. Well, that's what he'd read anyway; but when he'd decided to open his Italian restaurant, he had no idea that the people of Tulsa would not love his way of cooking. What he learned all too quickly, was that if food was not boiled, broiled, or barbequed, the citizens of Tulsa avoided it.

After one year of business, he'd found himself standing on the street corner offering free plates of lasagna to anyone who was willing to try it. Nobody even stopped to taste it. Frustrated and broke, he went back into his restaurant and began packing away his pots, pans and spices. He didn't know why he bothered; he didn't have any more money to start over, and he had no place else to go. And he'd be damned if he would go back to Colona. He'd lost his soul there. Now he needed to find it again.

As he sat at one of his tables, alone, a miserable failure, he heard a voice with the strangest accent he'd ever heard. "Do ye got fod here, mon? Ur do ye jus put oot a sign claimin' such a thing to lur the sturving foks into yer den?"

Simon couldn't believe it. A customer! A real live customer! After a whole year of waiting, he finally had a customer. The very day he was closing his doors, he had a real customer.

Watching the wiry little red haired man near him, Simon was reminded of an Irish gnome statue he'd seen in a yard in Colona. He was dressed in green work pants, a green work shirt, and unlike the cowboy booted Tulsans, he wore laced brown high top boots, with his green work pants tucked inside the boots. He wore his strange red and green plaid narrow brimmed hat pulled down over his ears, his fiery red hair spurting out from under the brim as though it had a mind of its own. Simon knew then, that the man's choice in hats certainly said something about its bustling owner.

"Veel, ye got foid here lad, or du ye jus plan to stan here an envy me hat. Tis a foin hat, it tis, but I be a sturvin mon with no time for foiliry."

Completely overwhelmed by the little man, Simon's brain raced back to his lone pan of lasagna that he couldn't give away. "I'm sorry mister. All I've got is one pan of lasagna left, but you're welcome to that. In fact, I'll bring out the whole pan, and you can eat your fill on the house."

"On de house, ye say. Lesoignoi....hmmm. Veel, I expects moi taste boids kan't be ta choosey, now can dey?"

"Lasagna, mister," Simon said as he filled a plate with the food. "It's called lasagna."

"Veel jeh, dat's vat I said. Lesoignoi."

Simon gave up on the pronunciation and watched the man scarf down his food. For a small man, he could put a horse to shame when it came to eating.

"Dat's de best Lesoignoi I had in moi loif ." Simon wondered just how many times, if ever, the little man had ever had *lesoignoi*.

"I won' be a comin' back te toin soon, but I veel stop by next toim I be in Tulsoi."

"I won't be here, mister. Today's my last day in business. Nobody wants my lesoignoi. Hell, I can't even give it away. I'm giving up and moving on to find some other way to make a living other than trying to earn a living cooking."

"Sa mon, ken ya coik anyting 'cept lesoignie?"

"I can cook anything you can think up. I can cook Italian, Swedish, and some French. I can cook Polish, German...."

Sean interrupted him. "He mon, can ye cook cowboi foid?"

"I can sure try."

"Ye need a joib? 'Cas I need a coik."

"When do I start?"

"Noi."

Simon grabbed his coat. "Let me grab my pans and my spices and you got a new cook. Well, I guess that's what you said."

"Dats vat I sid. I need a coik. Veel, come on wid ya. Ve vant to reach my ranch before soiper, so ye ken show off yer fancy coiking ways. Me bois veel be sturvin to deth."

As Simon hurried from the kitchen, pots, pans and spices in a large box, he stopped. "I need to tell you up front, mister. I've got a past."

"Soi do meself. By de vay, me name's Sean Keegan."

"No, you don't understand, Sean. I have a bad past."

"Ve all got bod pasts in oin vey or tother. Vat's yer name, lad?"

"Simon. Simon Hanson." For some reason, Simon knew Sean Keegan was a man he could trust, and without realizing it, he heard himself spilling out his miserable past. "Sean, I'm responsible for the killing of two people."

Sean didn't look the least bit shocked. "And did dey desoivre it?"

"Yes, Sean. They were very evil people."

"Den ye probly did the woild a big favoir."

That's all Sean said, and that was the last time he mentioned it.

Simon smiled as he remembered the day he and Sean drove up to the Keegan Ranch with his pots, pans, and spices tucked safely in the back of Sean's truck. That's the day he met Ben White who eventually turned out to be another good friend. That's the day he met Jessie, the little child he grew to love so dearly. That's the day his soul began to mend.

Simon wiped his face as he walked toward the main house after he finished planting the large garden. Given the fact that beets made such a mess, and the added fact that he hated them, he had not planted them but decided on asparagus instead. Entering the large den of the house, he heard Jessie and Jed talking in their bedroom. Not wanting to interfere with their privacy, he started to walk down to his domain, the kitchen.

"Wonder what the state police want?" Simon heard Jed say. Simon hurried into the dining hall and pushed back the curtain to take a look himself. Sure enough, it was a big black and white police cruiser, and it was pulling right up to the front of the house.

In an excited voice he heard Jessie speak. "Oh Lord, Jed. I'll bet they're here for me. Oh God! I knew they'd come. I knew it. I've got to get Danny and me out of here."

Simon could hear a lot of commotion and then he heard Jed again. "Jessie, just what do you think you're doing with those suitcases?"

Then he heard Jessie. "Oh to hell with those things. Jed, I've got to get out of here with Danny right now. As soon as we can, I'll come back and get the rest of our things."

"Jessie, for God's sake! There's a police cruiser racing up the lane right now. How do you possibly think you can get past him?"

Hearing Danny start to whine from being awakened from his sleep, Simon decided Jessie must have pulled him from the bed. "I'm going out the back door, Jed. I'll sneak out before they get a chance to find us, but please Jed, if you love me, keep them occupied for a little while so I can have a chance to escape."

"Jessie, listen to me! I'm not going to let anyone hurt you, and nobody is taking Danny away from here, so just settle down and let me handle this! It's too damn bad I don't *know* what I'm up against because you won't tell me, but you have to trust me on this. I'll take care of it!"

Simon heard Jessie begin to gasp in her sobs. He knew she was scared to the point she was nearly hysterical. Then he heard Jed again, soothing his wife. "Calm down, Jessie love. I'll see what they want, and I'll get rid of them. But Jessie you have got to tell me what this is all about. Ben said there were two thugs out here looking for you a few weeks ago."

Simon couldn't hear what Jessie said, but he figured she was denying knowing anything about those two because then he heard Jed losing his patience. "Damn it, Jessie, I know you heard Ben talking about those two thugs. You ignored him, but I know you heard him. Your face turned as white as a sheet."

"Jed, you promised me," Jessie fumed.

"I know I promised you that I wouldn't insist you stay if you couldn't, but Jessie I lied. I'm sorry about that, but I just can't let you run off some place without me being there to protect you. I love you more than life, you should know that. God, I have loved you all my life and I will love you until the day I die. And Jessie, I don't know what Danny is to you, but whatever he is to you, he is to me."

"He's my son, Jed. My son!"

"And Jessie, I'm your husband! That makes Danny my son, too. I love you, and I love Danny as though I was his biological father. Now, do you honestly think I could let you fight this, whatever it is, by yourself? No Jessie, we're in this together: you, me, and Danny. I just wish I knew what the hell was going on."

"Jed, you don't know these people. They're bad people. Oh Jed, I'd die if anything happened to you. You just have no idea...."

"Jessie, we can't live like this anymore; always hiding if anyone comes to the door, shopping at night so no one sees you. My little love, you know what I'm saying is true. You have got to let me help you. I'm your husband, for God's sake. You have got to tell me what this is all about. Who or what is it that has you so terrified?"

The angry banging on the front door interrupted Jed, and in a few minutes Simon heard the door open and close. Jed had gone outside to face the police without a clue as to what he was up against.

Pulling back the blinds in the office, Ben peered out at the police car parked in front of the house. Scratching his wrinkled chin, he wondered what would bring the state police all the way out into the country. Surely, this area couldn't be under their jurisdiction. If there was some problem, why didn't the local sheriff come out to the ranch? Actually, all he had to do was call, and Jed would have come into town. There was no need for the state police to come out to the Keegan Ranch. Something was wrong, and something told him that Jed, or Jessie, was going to need some legal help.

As Jed walked out onto the front porch, the sun was shining brilliantly, warming the snow and ice with its kiss of warmth, sending steady streams of water from the overhang of the porch roof. Sidestepping the cold wells, Jed walked out into the yard, through the melting snow, and approached the officer in the brown shirt and gray trousers. The officer was wearing his brown Stratton sheriff's model hat pinched so low in the brim, Jed could barely see his face, and he felt a genuine uneasiness as he faced the man.

"What can I do for you officer?" Jed asked expecting the man to identify himself.

He didn't. "Whose car is that parked down there? That yellow Fiat?" The officer strode arrogantly down the driveway toward Jessie's car.

Jed didn't answer as he heard the door close behind him. Then he heard Ben's rich baritone voice. "Before you approach any further on this property officer, we'll need your name and purpose for being here."

The tall officer stopped in his tracks and whirled around to see who was addressing him in such a stern authoritative voice. Seeing the aging black Indian standing on the porch, he turned and faced him, obviously angry at the old man's interference. "And just who the hell are you old man?"

Holding on to the porch column to support his dominant stance, Ben replied in his best courtroom voice. "My name is John Ross, Officer. I am Jed McClure's attorney." Ben could feel his strength faltering as he faced the police officer. "Now, once again sir, I ask you for your name, your badge number, and the paperwork that authorizes you to come onto this private property."

Forgetting his ruse, the officer glared at Ben. "I don't have to give you squat, old man! I'm here to bring Jessie McClure back to Colona. I'm certain that's her yellow Fiat parked down there." Ignoring both Jed and Ben, the tall man kept on walking down the drive toward Jessie's car.

Behind them Jed heard the distinctive, mechanistic sound of a pump action Remington 870 shotgun being cycled into play. Then in a no-nonsense voice he heard Simon. "If you don't want to listen to Mr. Ross, then maybe you'd like to hear what Miss Remington has to say."

Simon moved from the doorway down the steps and stood fearlessly in front of the officer. As the officer moved toward the old man, Simon lifted the gun and aimed it directly at him. "I think if you know what's good for you, you'll go on back to Colona. When you get there, tell your boss that Salvatore Johansson sends his regards."

The officer's jaw dropped noticeably as though he couldn't believe what Simon had just said to him. He started to say something, but changed his mind as Simon raised the shotgun again. Without turning away from Simon, he backed his way toward his police cruiser. Struggling to get the door open, he jumped inside and sped away.

Jed turned and looked at the two old men facing down hell to protect what they loved, both still holding their rigid, defiant stances. Then he started to laugh. "Salvatore? Simon, how the hell did you get Simon out of Salvatore?"

"How the hell did you get Jed out of Jess?" Simon answered.

"Touché old friend, you've got me there." Jed said as he ushered Ben and Simon into the house and closed the door. "That was mighty ballsy of you two old coots to step up to that cop like that." Smiling, Jed thought about the two old decrepit men facing the police officer without so much as a minute's hesitation. They had been defending their own, and as old and decrepit as they were, he knew it would take a lot to defeat them.

Simon stopped to mount the shotgun back over the door. "Yeah, Jed, you don't ever want to underestimate the power of us two old coots. Ben's got the brains, and I've got the moxie. You can't beat a combination like that."

Remembering the reason for all the drama, Jed started toward his and Jessie's bedroom, but Jessie was waiting for them in the den where she had been watching the scene play out in the driveway. Danny was sleeping in their bedroom.

"I'm so terribly sorry. I never meant to involve any of you in this mess." Tears ran down Jessie's face as Jed pulled her into his arms, and she sobbed quietly into his chest.

Jed held her tightly, stroking her dark hair. "Jessie, you promised you would tell us what's going on. We can't help you if we don't understand."

"Jessica Keegan McClure!" Ben said somewhat agitated. "Jed's right. We have to know what you're hiding so we can help you. We don't want to have to fight off the entire police department without knowing what they want with you."

Jessie continued to seek the safety of her husband's broad chest as she continued her sobbing and ignored the inevitable.

"Enough crying, sister," Simon said abruptly in a harsh voice that Jessie had never heard him use before. "That fellow that was just here was a Colona boy, Jessie. How do you explain that? What's he doing all the way down here in Oklahoma looking for you?"

"How did you know he was from Colona, Simon?"

"Didn't you see the small tattoo between his thumb and his forefinger, sister? I spotted it right away. It's the mark of a Polish gang in Colona."

"Yes, I did see it, Simon. But I had no idea you would recognize it too."

"Those fools have worn that same stupid tattoo since before I left Colona. Now, what's this all about, sister? I know this has got something to do with Danny, so I think it's high time we heard the whole story of how you got Danny."

Turning to look at him, Jessie saw the anguish in his aging blue eyes, and knew it was time to tell her story. As much as she dreaded telling it, they had to know. She had been selfish and stayed too long with the people she loved. Now they were involved. Even if she left, the police would hound them. It was time.

"Yes, of course you're right. I didn't mean to involve all of you but now that I have, I owe it to all of you to tell you the whole miserable story."

Everyone settled in the same room, the same chairs, and the same places, where so many years ago, Ben had told the story of his family and his life, and his reason for coming to the ranch. Then Jessie began her story.

"As you all know, after I left....the ranch, I had gotten a job as a columnist writing advice on etiquette for the small newspaper, *Colona At Large*. After the first six months, I was given more serious assignments, and was covering some pretty big crime stories. That was good for me, because it kept me busy and eased my loneliness for all of you.

"About a year later, I was offered a job as a reporter at the local TV station in Colona. I had worked there for some time when Carl, my stepbrother, spotted me on TV. I had no idea Carl was anywhere near Colona, but I guess he came there for the same reason I did. He had no place else to go. Anyway, he found out where I lived and came by my apartment right away. With him he brought a pretty, blonde, blue-eyed woman....actually, she looked like a young girl to me. But anyway, he introduced me to Sara and said they wanted to get married. He said he was broke right then, but that he would be coming into some money in a few months. I asked him why they couldn't wait until he got the money to get married, and he said they were going to have a baby, and he wanted to be a good father to his child. It was obvious to me that the girl, Sara, was completely taken in by Carl. She was so very young, so very stupid.

"I didn't dare ask Carl how much money he needed. If I had, I knew he would have wanted everything I had saved to put down on my apartment. I told him I could loan him five-hundred dollars. He said he had to have at least a thousand dollars. He hounded me constantly; showing up at my work, calling me late at night, and in general, driving me insane. Finally, just to get rid of them, I gave in. I told Carl that I expected him to pay me back, and of course, he assured me he would, but he never paid me a dime. There was always some excuse why he couldn't pay me back. Later I found out there was no child. It was all just a con to get my money.

"Some time later, I was given an assignment to investigate child prostitution down in the bowery section of Colona. It was a thriving business for the pimps, but of course, it was a horrible beginning and almost a death sentence for any young girl forced into that life. My newspaper wasn't interested in getting these girls arrested. Heavens, they weren't even interested in getting the pimps arrested. What we wanted to learn was why these girls were forced into such a horrid lifestyle. What could we, as a community, do to help these poor girls?

"Well, I got my facts, and I learned a lot more than I ever wanted to know as I trudged the back streets of that filthy city. Some of the older women were willing to talk to me, because they had been on the streets for years and didn't care if they lived or died anymore. Most of them said they preferred death to the life they now endured.

"They didn't spare me on the details of their lives, and I heard stories so horrible that I couldn't sleep nights. Most of those poor girls thought they were escaping a miserable home life, only to discover they had fallen into a way of life where there was no escape. Quickly hooked on drugs by the environment they sought for safety, they became virtual sex slaves, living toys for men who touted respectability by day and perversion by night. It was awful.

"Anyway, one blustery, snowy night as I was getting into our news van, I spotted a pretty young girl who looked very familiar. It was Sara working the streets as a common prostitute. I left the guys in the van and raced over to her. I got her to come over to our van and out of the cold, by paying for an hour of her time. Her story was just pitiful. She looked even worse. She said that she and Carl had gotten into the drug world. He was a two-bit player for one of the gangs of the city and through that gang she had been introduced to crack. To put it bluntly, she became a crack whore. I didn't condemn her, but she let me know in no uncertain terms that she didn't want anything to do with me. She was doing just fine, she told me, as she slithered back out onto the cold streets in a skirt cut up to her rump, a disgusting filthy excuse for a sweater, her fake zebra jacket and her high heels with no stockings on that miserable freezing night.

"I felt awful as we drove off and left her there on the street, because it was too cold for man or beast out that night. Obviously, it wasn't too cold for some john, because I saw a car pull up and Sara climbed inside. Heaven only knows what happened after that.

"A year later, I got a call from Sara. She was in prison for armed robbery and drug possession. There was absolutely no way that Sara could have pulled off an armed robbery, I knew that. I was certain she was taking the rap for that no good bum, Carl. I asked her about that, but she flatly refused to involve Carl and said she wouldn't talk to me if I kept bugging her about Carl. Finally, I gave up and listened to her story.

"She had been there for over six months she told me, and being nearly nine-months pregnant, she was scared to death. The oldest daughter of a preacher, I guess some of her early teachings finally got through to her. She said that she wanted to be married before she had her child, so she had contacted Carl when she first found out she was pregnant. His advice to her was to get rid of it. She said she told him it was his and she wanted to keep it, to make a life for them away from the city of Colona and all its corruption. He just laughed at her, told her to keep her mouth shut and leave him alone.

"About that time the police picked her up, and she spent the rest of her gestation in prison which I know was a blessing. It took her off the streets and out of the drug world. In prison she was able to get the care she needed to deliver a healthy baby. To make a long story short, she wanted me to take her baby until she could get out of prison in two months. With her written permission, I did take Danny. I took him the day he was born and I named him Danny. I loved him. I was his mother. I would do anything to keep him with me, but still I knew that one the day Sara would come to claim him. I thought about leaving Colona with Danny, hiding him, but I had nowhere to go. So I waited, dreading the day Sara would come for Danny, but she never came for him. I knew Sara had gotten out of prison and had been out of prison for almost a year, but I never saw her again, not until I identified her at the morgue.

"I didn't know what or where Carl was, and I didn't give a damn. As far as I was concerned, he gave up his rights to the child when he told Sara to get rid of him. Unfortunately, Carl came looking for me, and naturally, he was in trouble. He said he was going to give Danny to one of the gang leaders for his girlfriend who couldn't have a child. Danny was to be a payment for a debt Carl couldn't pay back."

Jessie stopped telling her story long enough to stop and gasp, "Can you imagine that? My precious little boy was to be a down payment on a debt. A debt! I knew it was for drugs and I didn't care about that. I didn't care if the gang killed Carl either. I was not giving up Danny, and I told Carl he couldn't have him.

"Carl pitched a raving fit. I thought he was going to kill me. It was Danny or him, he said, and he'd be damned if it was going to be him. About that time Danny woke up and started crying, and Carl made a bee line for his room. He grabbed Danny out of his bed and started out the door. If I had owned a gun, I would have killed Carl myself. Instead, I begged him to let me pay off his debts, and he agreed. I found out how much he owed the gang leader, mortgaged my apartment, traded in my nice car for the one I have now, and gave Carl the money in lieu of his giving up his rights to me for Danny, which he did in writing. I contacted a lawyer and everything was done legally and above-board, I thought.

"I had no idea Carl hadn't paid his debts with my money. I found out later that he had spent it on a lavish time of women, drugs and God only knows what. Several months later, I identified him at the morgue, just as I had done Sara.

"A week later, I was contacted by this goon while I was at work at the newspaper. He told me Danny belonged to his boss. He said I had to give Danny to them or they'd find me at the morgue with my brother. I told him that I had legally adopted Danny, and the papers had been filed at the courthouse. He laughed at me. My so-called lawyer was on the take from his boss. That's how they found Danny. That crook took my money, pretended to file the papers, and notified that crook Leon Suluski what had happened.

"I couldn't go to the police, because the town was so corrupt that I had no idea who was on the take to the gang world. All I knew was that I couldn't let that goon's boss take my little baby son. I didn't know what else to do, so I came home."

Simon was the first to speak. "You did right, sister. Let me ask you this though, what do you know about this Leon Suluski?"

"I don't know much about him personally, Simon. He keeps his personal life quiet. I do know that he is the head of the most powerful gang in Colona."

"Not the *most* powerful gang, sister. There's another group, or I suppose you could still call them a gang....anyway, the gang I remember is much more powerful than that bunch of street trash that Suluski runs."

"Simon, I worked the crime stories in Colona. There were a few small gangs, but the Poles of Colona, or the POC as the called themselves, they control that town."

"Well, most likely you don't know of this other gang, because now it's run by families of some of the state legislators. From what I've learned, one of them is running for a Senate seat, and with the influence of his family, I have no doubt he'll win."

"Simon, surely you're not talking about the Marino family. Why, they're the most respected family in Colona. They own half of the town. They're the only family that has a son with political ambitions. No, it can't be the Marino's. I would have known if they had gang connections."

"Would you, sister? How would you know about such things if these people didn't want you to know?"

"Surely, someone would have said something to me."

"You were in Colona for five years, sister. There was a lot of history that happened in Colona long before you ever got there."

Giving his words some serious thoughts, Jessie continued. "Well, the only other big name in Colona is Johansson."

Jed's eyes glanced toward Simon. He was certain that Johansson was the name Simon had mentioned to the police officer that had caused him to nearly drop his teeth. Yet, as long as he'd known him, Simon had referred to himself as Simon Hanson. Jed couldn't help but wonder if anyone in that place was using their real name. His was Jess and called himself Jed. Ben White was really John Ross. Simon's real name was Salvatore Johansson. Who was next?

"Bingo, sister. You made an "A" on your test. Put Marino and Johansson together, and you get and 'A+'."

"But Simon, that's impossible. The Marinos and Johanssons don't even associate in the same circles."

"They don't have to, sister. Blood is thicker than water."

Jed interrupted. "What's all this got to do with Jessie and Danny, Simon? We still don't know how we can protect them other than putting up a fence around the whole ranch and I'm not sure that could keep them out."

Simon ignored Jed. "Sister, Leon Suluski was my age. He'd be an old man now. What does he want with Danny?"

"I'm not talking about Leon Suluski the father, Simon. He has a son, Leon Suluski Junior. He's the one that's in charge of organized crime now. He probably doesn't know anything about Danny personally, but in Colona there's all these little gangs of criminals each controlling their share of the pie, the total pie belonging to Leon Suluski Junior."

"So, you're saying that Suluski has no interest in you or Danny, but because this has happened to of one of his gang leaders, that makes Suluski involved."

"Yes, Simon."

"What's this gang leader's name, sister?"

"Ed Petrotski."

"I never heard of him, must be a newcomer."

"Simon, he's been around for years. How long has it been since you left Colona?"

Hesitating to answer, Simon was afraid Jessie would put two and two together.

"Simon?" Jessie repeated.

"Forty years, sister. It's been forty years since I left that awful city."

Jessie was silent for a minute, staring down at the floor in deep thought. "Simon, did you...."

Simon didn't wait for her to continue. "I still have some friends in Colona, sister. And I still have some debts to be collected. I'll make a call to Colona and see what can be done."

"Simon, that's not possible. I know you mean well, but no one can help me. They'll be back. Danny and I need to leave for awhile. Maybe I should go to Mexico or Canada....maybe I should..."

Jed interrupted. "You need to stay right here, Jessie. You and Danny are not leaving."

"Jed's right Jessie," Simon said. You have to trust me on this. I can take care of you and Danny. The people I know in Colona will force those thugs to call off their dogs. As long as you stay here with us, you will be protected. I promise you that."

Jed was dumbfounded at all he was hearing. "Simon, I think you know a lot more than you've ever told us about Colona and its people."

Ben nodded to Simon. "Go on Simon. It's your turn. Let's hear your story."

"Simon, I've got a feeling you're hiding something from me that you don't want me to know, but I want you to understand that I love you and nothing you have ever done will change that. If I can understand your connections with Colona, then maybe I won't be so afraid. Please Simon, tell me what you know about these people."

After giving Jessie's anxious face some thought, Simon answered. "Yeah, why not? I guess it can't hurt anyone anymore, but first I have to make those phone calls."

It was obvious to Jessie that Simon was putting off telling his story as she watched the old man walk from the room. A few minutes later, they could hear him speaking in Italian, and even though he had the door closed; Jessie knew he was angry. He wasn't shouting, but he was speaking in a voice so cold and so authoritative, that if she hadn't known better, she would never have believed it was Simon Hanson speaking.

Expecting to see Simon return after he hung up the phone, Jessie was surprised to hear a door open and close. As they all sat there waiting, they spotted Simon through the big window hurrying down the porch to the kitchen, bypassing all of them and their many questions.

Chapter 15

As Jessie, Jed, and Ben watched, it seemed to take forever for Simon to prepare supper. He chopped every piece of celery until it was almost fine. He did the same with the onions and the green peppers. Then he put the ground meat in a large skillet and stirred and stirred until Jessie thought she would pull her hair out. At the rate Simon was preparing supper, it would be tomorrow before they got to eat, or before they heard the rest of his story. Anxiously, Jessie watched as Simon poured tomatoes over the meat and stirred and stirred and stirred some more.

Trying to prompt him to speak, Jessie tried to make small-talk, but hearing Danny fussing, Jessie knew Simon had timed it so that he was able to put off the telling of his story until later, and she wondered what he was hiding. Simon was such a sweet, gentle person. What could he have possibly done that was so bad? Nothing, she was sure of that. There was not one ruthless bone in Simon's body.

Before Jessie had a chance to stand up, Jed was on his way to get Danny and she knew there would be no story telling until Danny was in bed later. Whatever Simon was putting off telling them, he had timed it perfectly.

Simon dragged out supper as long as he possibly could. His was a story that was not only painful to remember, it was a story of when he was forced to become someone he had never wanted to be. That man was a hard man, a cruel controlling man, a man he had never liked. But he had forced himself to become what he detested. It nearly tore him apart, but he did it. When he finished his obligations, he left Colona forever, burying his past behind him.

They were waiting for him, he knew that. Jessie, Jed and Ben were waiting to hear his story, and he wondered how could he sugar-coat it, to make it sound better? He couldn't, he knew that. Once Jessie discovered who he really was, she would recognize his name as one of the most ruthless gangsters that Colona had ever produced.

Simon Hanson....Salvatore Johansson. One in the same. How could Jessie ever forgive him? How could this young woman, who he'd loved like she was his own child, ever understand what could drive a person to do the things he'd been guilty of doing?

"Is there a word you haven't read in that newspaper, Simon?"

Jessie asked as she, Jed, and Ben sat waiting for Simon to tell his story. "Whatever happened to you in Colona was in the past, Simon, but I think all of us need to know about it so that we can understand."

Simon folded his newspaper, removed his glasses and set them on the table next to his chair in the den. There was no getting out of it. Everyone had collected around him after Danny had settled down, and now they were waiting for his story. He had to finally let them see the real monster he had been years ago. The fact that he had never wanted any part of it, that didn't matter. He had done those things for revenge of his blood family. Now he would pay for it with the love of his adopted family.

Settling back in his chair, Simon knew he could put it off no longer. "Way before prohibition began, there were only two gangs in Colona. The North side gang was run by the Italians and the Southside gang was run by the Swedes. There wasn't much fighting between the two gangs because they both respected one another's territories and kept an equal distance apart.

"Both sides dealt in gambling, small-time extortion, and the control of the sale and flow of liquor in their own territories. Labor racketeering and the police departments were controlled according to the boundaries as established. Malone Street ran straight through the city and was the half-way point that separated the two gangs. Neither side crossed past Malone Street to the other side without permission. If you chose not to respect Malone Street as your stopping point, you might wind up in the river. That, everyone respected.

"The two sides got along as well as could be expected for gangs. The only problem they really had between them was the personal relationships between some "would be" young lovers. That was strictly forbidden. Any young man and woman who crossed that line found themselves forced out of the city or worse. Not many chose that path.

"In January, 1920, everything changed. Prohibition was enforced in the United States. Every state in the union went dry; breweries, distilleries, and all saloons were forced to close their doors. Women were big proponents of prohibition because many had witnessed the influence of liquor on husbands, fathers, and brothers who turned mean while under the influence of alcohol. Some had watched their families fall into ruin because of alcoholism.

"I suppose prohibition served that purpose well enough, but on the other hand, it put an awful lot of people out of work. When people don't have work, they don't have food and when a man can't feed his family, he's liable to do anything to take care of his family whether it's legal or not.

"Booze had always been, and booze would always be, and so out of nowhere came the bootleggers, the moonshiners, the rum runners and the bathtub gin. People made beer and wine at home and sold it for a few dollars to help them get by. Most all of the doctors readily gave out prescriptions for whiskey to get their cut. They called it 'for medicinal purposes' and these prescriptions could be readily filled at the local drugstores where the druggists got their cut of the action. It seemed everybody was on the take in one form or another in Colona.

"There was twice the number of speakeasies as there were legal bars before prohibition and that's where the gangs and the mobsters made their easy money. Either they supplied the booze to the speakeasies, or they owned, or controlled the businesses where the booze was sold.

"The twenty's and prohibition were a lucrative period of time in Colona, and just as things were handled before prohibition, the Italians and the Swedes controlled their own turfs. With the exception of a few minor problems between the two gangs, Colona flourished from its speakeasies and gambling businesses. But even with that, Colona was not a dangerous town back then. The Swedes and the Italians kept it as clean and safe as could be expected, so the young rich kids came from Chicago on the weekends to spend papa's dough and have a good time. Hell, they even brought their sweethearts once in a while. It was that safe.

"Things were going along just fine in Colona, and all of a sudden everything went nuts. As though it happened over night, along came a group of second-generation Polish looking to escape the factories and farmlands of their parents, and to cash in on the illegal sale of alcohol. The fact that Colona was run by two local gangs meant nothing to the Poles. They gained control over the outer perimeter of the city, and as they gained in power, they forced the Northside and Southside gangs closer together, basically squeezing them out of power. The more they were squeezed, the more inner fighting happened until both the gangs realized something had to be done if any of them were to survive. That's when they joined forces and began to push back, crippling the efforts of the Polish invading gangs.

With the Northside and Southside gangs joining together, the Poles were quickly pushed back outside the city, and a relative peace was regained within the inner city. Realizing the delicate bond between the Italians and the Swedes could be broken at any time, it was decided among the two united gangs that the union would be sealed by the marriage of the two first born gang leaders' children. This turned out to be my Swedish father Joseph Johansson and my Italian mother Amina Marino. My parents were married in 1922 and by the end of that year, I was born.

It was always assumed I would take over control of the Swedish-Italian gang when I grew up, and I was groomed well for the event, but my heart was never in it. I enjoyed the simple things of life. I loved working in the Italian kitchen of my mother, or visiting my aging Swedish grandmother helping with the making of her breads and sweet delicacies.

I detested the meetings and the politics of the Inner City Nationals or ICN as my family called themselves. To me they were just my Swedish and Italian family. As I learned the family business, I hated some of the things we were required to do to protect our city. I could never understand why they couldn't see that my younger brother was much better suited to run the family business than I was. To me it was obvious. To my family it was my duty, one I dared not refuse. I was told that before I was born, it had been decided that this was to be my duty. I had no other choice. So along with learning the family business, I went to college, studied Economics and Business and hated every minute of it. When I had free time, I would cook Italian sauces and knead dough into fancy breads escaping the drudgery of the family business.

When I was in college, I met Alenka, and we fell head over heels in love. Yeah, you guessed it. She was Polish. She was as unacceptable to my family as I was unacceptable to hers. To make it worse, her uncle was Leon Suluski, Sr., my family's mortal enemy from the 1920's.

Knowing we could never be together in Colona, Alenka and I planned to run away from Colona and marry. I didn't give a hoot about the family business, and Alenka was more than willing to leave with me. Then, before we could make any real plans, I was drafted and sent off to war. It was 1942, and we were at war with Hitler's Germany. I knew I had to go. When I came home on leave six weeks later, I found my Alenka had been married off to a member of the Polish organization, a man named Nick Nowaskowski. I was heartbroken, but there was nothing I could do about it. She refused to see me, but I wouldn't give up. When I did finally get to see her, she told me she no longer loved me and was happy with the man she married. I was devastated, but I went on with my life as miserable as it was.

I found out later that she had lied about her love for me to protect me from her family. I also found out her husband had been very abusive to her, and she had run away from him. With no place for her to hide, he found her and brought her back to live with him. She meant no more to him than an animal, and from what I learned later, he treated her much worse. When I found that out, I vowed that when I got home again, I'd find her and we'd run off together, whether she was married or not.

"I never got a chance to go home again. That next week I was shipped off to fight in the war. After suffering a shattered leg at Faid Pass in southern Tunisia, I came home from the war for good. At that time, I discovered that Alenka had been killed. *My Alenka* had been killed!

"What I soon discovered was that she had been forced to marry this man, this Nick Nowaskowski. When he discovered she was not a virgin he hated her for that. I was told that he felt he had been cheated by her uncle when he agreed to marry her.

"Eventually, I found proof that her husband had arranged Alenka's killing. I was furious. I was so furious that without even a body guard, I went to see her uncle Leon Suluski. He claimed he knew nothing of the details of the killing, but I knew he did. Alenka had given herself to me, and that was unforgiveable to the Polish organization. I promised him, then and there, that I would personally destroy him and his organization.

"I went back to my home and took my designated place as head of the family. I spent the next five years of my life fulfilling my promise to Leon Suluski. By the time I was through with them, the Polish organization was of no more significance than a pimple on a goat's butt. The city was again under the control of the ICN, and I demanded my brother take over the family business which had been made into a legal corporation. I was done. I was finished, I told them. I'd done everything they expected of me, and I wanted out. My brother was more than happy to take control, and I got the hell out of Colona. I headed as far away from that type of life as I could find, winding up in Tulsa, Oklahoma."

Jessie stood in front of Simon. "Simon, in all my investigations and studies of the history of Colona and its gangs, I never heard of you, Simon Hanson. I know that at one time there were two notorious gangs called the Northside and Southside gangs, but they had nothing to do with you, did they?"

"Sister, did you ever hear of a gangster named Salvatore Johansson? He was a murderer."

"Of course, Simon, everyone knew about him. He was a gangster of the 1940's. How did you know him?"

"Know him? Know him? Sister, I was him."

Jessie nearly collapsed, so she settled herself back on the sofa.

Simon stood staring down on Jessie. "I'm sorry, sister. I had hoped you would never find out about me, but I cannot allow that bunch of thugs to destroy your life."

Jessie looked up at the small rotund man she had loved since she was a little girl. Gathering her inner-strength, she stood and faced him. "Simon, I read about those two people you were suspected of killing, that man and his fiancé."

"Yes, Jessie? What about them? I did kill them."

"Did you know who they really were?"

"The man I killed had been married to my Alenka. He's the one that killed her. I had no qualms about taking his life. An eye for an eye and so on...."

"What about his fiancé, Kristen Adams, Simon? She was killed with her future husband on her wedding day in that car bomb. What about that?"

"She wasn't supposed to have been in the car with him, sister. I swear it. The wedding was scheduled to be for two o'clock. I had no idea the woman would be with him at one o'clock, a good hour before the scheduled wedding. Trust me, I have suffered over that for years. One thug killing another was no big deal to me, but killing an innocent person was something I could not forgive myself for doing. After I learned an innocent had been killed, I quit the family business and left town. No one could ever prove I had them killed, and of course my family was behind me."

"Did you ever discuss those two people with your family again, Simon?"

"It was all hush, hush, Jessie. I left Colona and I wanted my past buried behind me. I have talked to my family over the years, but I refuse to listen to anything about the past. They know that and never bring it up. They still respect what I did for the family. They know it cost me my soul."

Jessie stood and walked over to the old man slipping her arms around him. "Killing those two people did the United States a big favor, Simon. Several years later, it was discovered that those two people were not Polish at all. They were German's involved in espionage for Hitler's Third Reich."

It was Simon's turn to nearly collapse. "Sister! Where did you ever learn that?"

"It was my job to do research, Simon. I spent hours in the libraries looking up people's pasts, and by some quirk of fate, I came upon the name Nick Nowaskowski of Colona, Illinois. I got to reading up on him, and discovered he'd been killed in 1943 in a gangland killing. It seems it was later discovered he was a German plant in the Polish gang of Colona.

"The German's figured with all the unrest within the gangs of Colona, no one would ever notice him. They thought he would just be considered another gang member, a nuisance at most, and he could continue spying unnoticed. With the close proximity to Chicago, it was planned he could get information regarding the Chicago water supply and it would only be a matter of time before the entire city was destroyed. There was one catch, though. He was supposed to marry a woman named Kristen Adams, who worked in Chicago at the water company and could get him access into the water plant. That plan was squelched when he was forced by the POC to marry a Polish woman by the name of Alenka Suluski. The article said that she died sometime after the marriage. It was insinuated that she was murdered for political reasons."

Simon openly gasped. "My Alenka? My Alenka was murdered for political reasons?"

"Yes, Simon. Your innocent Alenka was the biggest deterrent possible to half of Chicago being destroyed. With the marriage of Nick and Kristen and his access to the water supply, it was almost a given that soon their dastardly plan would have succeeded."

"Sister, are you telling me that Nick Nowaskowski's fiancé was a German spy, too?"

"That's right, Simon," Jessie answered. "Both of them were graduates of Hitler's school of hate in Germany. You were actually a hero. You did the United States a great favor by eliminating both of them."

"Well, I'll be damned," Simon answered. "I'll be double dammed."

True to Simon's word, the mysterious telephone calls stopped and never again did anyone come to the ranch looking for Jessie or Danny. Sometime later, Simon told Jessie that he had learned through his connections in Colona, that Danny's adoption papers mysteriously reappeared at the Colona courthouse, and his family saw to it that they were properly filed as they should have been two years prior.

At long last, Jessie was legally Danny's mother. As soon as Jessie and Jed heard the news, they agreed that Jed should file for adoption as Danny's father. That adoption went much smoother than the one Jessie had been forced to endure and all the residents of the J&J Ranch settled into a secure future, all the residents except one.

Several months later, Ben didn't arrive for breakfast at his usual time, nor could he be found working on the ranch books in Jed's office. When they found him, they discovered that he had passed away peacefully in his own bed in the bunkhouse. And from the soft smile on his face, it was obvious that he had once again found his beloved Aimee

Chapter 16

"I think it's time we have another baby, Jessie." Jed said wrapping his arms around his wife as they watched their little girl hugging her baby doll close to her chest, while traipsing along after her big brother, Danny.

"I couldn't agree more, Jed. Telly has outgrown the baby crib, and we can move her into the bedroom next to Danny."

Jed smiled and kissed his wife on the top of her head. "How about we start working on this baby tomorrow, Jessie?"

"How about we start working on it today, Jed?"

"I'm ready whenever you are, my love," Jed answered as he stood and held out his hand to his wife. "Do you think Simon would mind babysitting for a while?"

"Are you kidding, Jed. He is the ultimate grandfather. He spoils both of our children rotten."

As Jed went to find Simon, Jessie's mind wandered back to the day they got their baby girl, Telly, named after Miss Estelle.

Oh, what a day that was.

"Mr. and Mrs. McClure, I do have your petition for adoption, but you see we have no children for adoption at this time. Well, we have *none* that you would want to adopt." These words were spoken by John Whitcomb, a man who would become an integral part of their large, unusual family in the future years.

He was a small man with withered legs kept hidden as he handled his job in his wheelchair from behind a large Family Services no-nonsense steel desk. Glancing past the imposing desk, Jessie could see there was a certain look in his eye that almost seemed as though he was searching for something deep inside them.

She was certain Jed could see it, too, as he addressed the man. "Let's not stand on ceremony, John. I'm Jed and this is my wife, Jessie. We want another child. We're good parents to the little boy we have, whose name is Danny. We adopted him several years ago and now we both feel we would like to have another child. Actually, we'd like to have a house full of kids. Surely, there are children who need good parents such as we are. We have a large ranch, it's safe for children to play, and we have more than an abundance of love to give."

"Yes, yes, Mr....Jed. I'm sure you are both wonderful parents, but we have long waiting lists of parents hoping to find that perfect child."

Jed reached over and grabbed Jessie's hand and held it as though he was examining it as his mind raced backward a few minutes. "I don't understand your first statement, John. What did you mean when you said you have no children for adoption, *none* that we would want'? What does that mean?"

John Whitcomb pressed his fingers together, almost in prayer. *Every once in a while potential parents came along who could....*John came out of his thoughts and answered the two people seated in front of him. "People come in here looking for the perfect child, one that looks like them; a little boy with blonde hair and blue eyes, or a little girl with big dark eyes and dark hair. You know what I mean. Everyone wants the perfect child."

"John, my wife and I have agreed that we would be willing to foster a child if we cannot adopt. Is there a possibility we could do that?"

"Fostering a child is a heartbreaker for most people, Jed. They get so attached to a child, and then it's pulled from them when the natural parents are deemed capable to care for them again."

Jed dropped his head as Jessie leaned over and took his hand again. "We can handle it, John. Our little boy is growing like a weed, and that's good. What's bad is that we now find ourselves with empty arms. We're desperate for another child....for however long we can keep it."

John pushed his hand through his thinning hair and wondered again....*rarely, but every once in awhile, some really extraordinary people came along. Were these the ones?*

"Well, I do have one little child, she's about three-months old, but let me warn you, she is not perfect."

Jed snapped to attention. "What do you mean, she's not perfect? What's wrong with her?"

Taking a deep sigh, John answered. "Well, you see, she has a club foot."

Jed laughed and squeezed Jessie's hand. "A club foot?"

"Yes, yes. Well, I'm sorry, I...."

"We'll take her!" Jessie said.

John looked up in disbelief at the two eager faces in front of him. "Well, Jed, Jessie....that's not all that's wrong with her."

Jessie was beside herself she was so happy, and she knew Jed felt the same as he squeezed her hand. Then Jed asked what they both were wondering. "So, what else is wrong with this baby, John?"

"She's part Indian."

"We'll take her!" Jed said.

"That's not all, Jed. I know you both think you can overlook a lot of imperfections, but don't get too excited just yet. There's more that's wrong with this little girl."

By this time Jed and Jessie were standing up holding each other in their excitement. "What else, John? What else is wrong with the little girl?"

"Nobody wants this little girl, Jed. She was abandoned when she was just a few hours old, and she has been living in an orphanage since she was born."

"Spit it out, John. What's wrong with the child?"

"Oh Lord. I hate to tell you this. The child is part black. She's a Black Indian."

"We'll take her!" Jed and Jessie shouted together.

"We want to put in for her adoption right now, John," Jed said squeezing Jessie's hand.

"Can we take her home today?" Jessie asked turning to wrap Jed's arm around her .

"How can you know you want to adopt her as your own child? You haven't seen her, and Lord knows she's not perfect." John asked rubbing his chin in wonder.

"Not perfect in whose eyes, John?" Jed answered. "She's...."

Jessie interrupted her husband. "John, she's absolutely perfect for us. Now when can we see our daughter?"

John smiled knowingly. These two were the ones. Yes, indeed. Every once in awhile you found people like Jed and Jessie. It was rare, but thankfully, there were still people like them who could see the perfect in imperfection.

Epilogue

Over the years John Whitcomb came to know Jed and Jessie McClure very well, becoming a regular visitor at the J&J Ranch. Every time there was a throw-away child, a misfit, an imperfection, he turned to Jed and Jessie. Over time, Jed and Jessie had fostered nine neglected children, and had managed to adopt six of them.

Jed finally had his big family of brats running all over the place, all of them a multitude of colors, disabilities and imperfections. The only thing they had in common was that none of them were perfect, deeming them unacceptable to most people....those everyday people who saw with their eyes and not with their hearts.

About the Author

Brenda Brouillette Dawson was born in Mississippi, raised in Illinois, and now resides in Oklahoma.

Season of Magenta is her first novel to be published, ensuring all dreamers that love has nothing to do with age and that love's zap can happen when least expected...even to the most unlikely people.

Brenda's second book, *Season of Regret*, is a book she started years ago, and discovered she lacked the life experience to finish. She has plenty of experience now, and all of her books are available through e-stores, Amazon.com, and

http://2firespublishing.weebly.com/
http://brendabdawsonauthor.weebly.com/

Please enjoy a complementary chapter of Dawson's,

Season of Regret

Prologue

June, 1973
"Grime's Book Nook"

Tulsa, Oklahoma

It wasn't that she was erotic. No, she wasn't erotic at all. She was all about desire and denial, pain and passion. That's how the reporter from *The Times* described her work. Another reporter from the *Tulsa Journal* said she captured lost love as though she'd been a victim of untold betrayal.

Charlie knew all about betrayal, too. She'd taught him well.

She was writing under a different name: a fake name, a pseudonym, but it was her. He didn't need to see her face to recognize her. He would know her anywhere, even though her hair was blonde now and cut short.

Her hair was dark then, beautiful and long, really long, and it hung down her back in glossy panes of radiant mahogany that almost touched her waist. But she was just a kid way back then; barely seventeen.... back when she was his wife.

But that was before Kevin, Vietnam, and that awful accident

Chapter 1

May 27, 1962
Martineau, Illinois

It was so damn hot, the devil went back to Hell to cool off.

Charlie chuckled as he remembered Judd Brown having said that at lunch. He sure was right on that one.

Sweat ran down Charlie's face, dripping like a leaky faucet and saturated his neck and chest. Without a hint of breeze, Charlie wiped his tanned face with his faded red kerchief and pulled the cloth around the short blonde hair at the back of his neck. Knowing it was useless, he tried to brush away the dirt from the itching hay captured under the neck of his grimy blue t-shirt. The sweat mixed with the hay was driving him nuts, but he knew if he pulled his shirt off over his blonde crew cut, he'd just itch worse; so he just kept on pitching hay, itching, sweating, and swearing.

It was June and the summer season hadn't even began, but Charlie figured if the past spring was any preview of what was to come, it would be one long hellacious hot summer.

Swinging his long leg forward in his steel-toed black work boots, he kicked some of the loose hay toward the raised door of the hayloft and wiped his filthy hands on his washed out jeans. Grabbing his pitchfork, he pitched another load of the itchy hay from the hayloft door to the few cattle gathered below.

Then he spotted her. Of course, he always watched for her. Always. And now he was delighted that while he was working, he could take his mind off the itch of the hay and focus on that incredibly sexy girl swinging in the old rubber tire that hung in the huge oak tree.

Charlie's wide mouth exploded into a grin as he watched her pump her lean legs back and forth causing the tire to move with every stroke of her young body. It wasn't that she was beautiful like a movie star, but she did remind him somewhat of Marilyn Monroe. Well, Marilyn Monroe with dark mahogany hair. No, she wasn't beautiful in the classic sense, but there was something about that girl that caused his mouth to drop open every time he saw her. She just drove him nuts.

Charlie ran his hand through his sopping wet hair and thought about his favorite fantasy: that gal with those firm legs wrapped around his eager body.

He'd seen her often enough at the old swimming hole where all the kids went on Sunday afternoons to cool off from the heat. Charlie recalled how he'd nearly killed himself showing off for her, but she never paid him any attention. One day he'd done a fancy dive from the top of the peak, sunk so deep into the hole he thought he'd never come to the top of the water; and when he did finally make it up, all he saw was her sexy backside heading toward her father's truck. He'd nearly died for her and she still didn't notice him.

But then everyone knew she was one stuck-up girl; and man, did she have a spiteful mouth! Nobody dared ask her for a date. Nobody wanted her to laugh in their face. But even so, half the guys down at Harley's Tavern claimed they'd had her. Charlie wondered how that could be true, since she never dated anyone. Well, there was that stupid Kevin McCall, and he was a joke.

Yeah sure, she was Big Gus Heinrich's daughter and Charlie knew he was "a nobody", but he could still look. He wasn't dead. God, he was only twenty-years old, and nobody was going to stop him from watching her. Especially since no one knew he was watching her.

Charlie smiled a mischievous smile and continued his steady watch as she leaped from the swing, her long dark mahogany hair whirling in the breeze as she pranced toward the two-story white farmhouse with its' gaudy blue gingerbread trim. Setting his pitchfork down, he lost himself in the gentle sway of her rounded hips enclosed in tight blue jeans rolled half-way up her legs. Covering her ample breasts was a big white men's shirt tied in the front just under her stomach, the latest style of the teenage girls. She looked good in the jeans, but they definitely made her look heavier than she usually looked, and Charlie was an expert on her looks; her body, anyway. She sure didn't look like the rest of the skinny young girls that chased after him. This gal was sexy as all get-out.

Determined to check her out further, Charlie leaned his long body so far out of the upper door of the barn that he nearly fell. He caught himself and grinned. Falling out the window would be worth it, if he could get some sympathy from her; but he knew she'd just laugh at him and leave him laying there in the dirt. He continued to smile anyway, watching the swaying of her sexy rear-end and fantasizing all sorts of immoral thoughts about her.

It had been some time since he'd seen her wear her red poodle skirt with all that crisp crinoline under it to make it poof out. He especially liked that outfit, because he could look at her legs; long, sexy and tan against her white socks and white buck shoes. Sometimes she wore a red sweater with a fancy white lace collar, or sometimes she wore a white cotton blouse with a red chiffon scarf knotted about her neck. But, regardless of whether she wore the sweater or the blouse, she always wore a thick cinch belt to show off her small waist. Charlie stopped and thought about that for a minute. She hadn't worn that outfit for some time. Now it seemed she always wore the same dull blue jeans and baggy white shirt.

Of course, Charlie knew it was a well-known fact that the girl always did exactly as she pleased and didn't give a peddling damn what anyone thought about her. Everyone in Martineau knew she was a hellion. They also knew that her father, Big Gus Heinrich, had absolutely no control over her. Judd Brown, who'd been the top hired hand for Big Gus forever, said the girl's mother had died at her birth, and so she had been shipped off to be raised by Gus' sister, Katrin. Kat died when the kid was about ten-years old, and she'd been sent to live with another of Gus' sisters, Helga Reinhart, and her brood of ten kids. Rumor had it Helga ruled with an iron hand and eventually the girl rebelled and ran away. After they found her, Judd said Gus sent her to a private school, but she was soon expelled from that fine institute of learning. The reason given was that the girl was incorrigible. It was also rumored that even with all of Gus' money, none of the other schools would take on his hopeless daughter. She was sent home to her father, and Gus had been stuck with her ever since.

Charlie put down his pitchfork and grinned a lazy grin, still visualizing her butt as she walked toward the old farmhouse; but his lazy grin quickly changed to shock as he saw the girl topple over and fall to the ground. Charlie jumped from the barn window onto the hay below and managed to land on his feet. Gaining his balance, he raced across the yard to where she lay crumbled on the ground.

She didn't look like she was hurt, so he slipped one arm around her shoulders and the other under her knees. That's when he discovered her big secret. The oversized shirt and blue jeans were gapping wide open, and Charlie could see that the girl was pregnant, for God's sake; and she was pretty far along if her bulging belly was any indication, and he knew it was. Big Gus was going to have a fit, and he did.

"What the hell do you mean she's pregnant?" Gustav Heinrich roared as Charlie lowered Gus' daughter gently onto a wooden chaise on the front porch and began fanning her with a newspaper.

Gus Heinrich was a big man, a mountain of a man. There wasn't anyone for miles around that could equal the size of him, and there wasn't an ounce of fat on him. He was all hard flesh, muscle, and bone. Even the big jowls of his stern jaw were solid, vividly proclaiming his staunch German heritage.

Of one thing Charlie was certain, he never wanted to tangle with Gus Heinrich. Even so, he knew the girl was in big trouble; and he wasn't about to just dump her on the porch and leave her there.

"You don't believe me Gus, then take a gander at her big belly," Charlie spit back at his boss, as he lifted her shirt and stared up at the gigantic man with the golden gray hair.

"Get your eyeballs off my girl's belly, you ignorant ass." Gus was so angry Charlie thought the large man was going to have a stroke. After a few minutes Gus seemed to calm down, but Charlie knew it was just the quiet before the next storm.

Gus glared at Charlie as Charlie glared back. He dropped the shirt back over her stomach, and the two men stood silently on either side of the girl wondering what to do.

Reluctantly, Gus broke the silence. "Ah, hell," he sighed as he reached down and pulled the shirt back up over his daughter's swollen stomach. "Maybe she's got a tumor or something like that."

"Maybe," Charlie answered, but he knew better. "Better have a doc check her out Gus, 'cause either she's got one hell of a big tumor or I'd say she's pretty far along with a kid. Either way, she needs a doc."

"Ah, hell," Gus sighed again, as he watched his daughter stir in her unconsciousness.

Knowing there was nothing else he could do for the girl, Charlie started down the wooden steps of the porch, but was stopped by Gus' angry voice. "Hey you, boy! Don't you be saying nothing about this to the rest of the work crew! I'll fire your ass if I so much as hear one word about my daughter." As though to give it more credibility, Gus added, "And I'll see to it that nobody in a hundred miles hires you either, so you keep your damn mouth shut about this until I can figure out what to do with her. You understand, boy?"

Charlie understood well enough but refused to acknowledge the futile threats. "Name's Charlie Barnes, Gus, not 'boy'."

"I know what your name is! Just you keep your mouth shut. I'll find out who did this to my girl, have a quick weddin' and nobody will know any different."

"It might not be too easy to prove who the father is, Gus." Charlie wiped the sweat from his eyes and peered up at the huge man hovering over the small girl on the chaise. He knew his comment would bring out the worst in Big Gus, and it did.

"What the hell's that supposed to mean, boy? You suggesting my girl's a tramp? I'll knock your teeth down your throat for a comment like that." Gus ignored his daughter struggling to come out of her faint and stomped down the steps after Charlie.

Charlie held his ground as Gus approached him, his

hambone arms swinging in rage, perspiration clearly visible under the arms of his gray cotton work shirt. Charlie knew he was no match for the big man who towered over him by half a foot and outweighed him by over fifty pounds, but still, he defiantly faced the big man.

"Gus, I'm not downing your girl, but you damn well know she's a handful. Hell, she's everybody's favorite topic of conversation down at Harley's Tavern." Charlie paused wondering if he'd get a punch for that comment. It was the truth, though.

Gus came running after him, but he didn't throw a punch. He just stood there, sweat running off his massive jowls causing small wet splatters on his gray work shirt. "My girl don't go to no tavern. She's only seventeen."

"I know it, Gus, but half the guys in the bar claim they've had her." With that comment, Gus did swing his big hambone arm at Charlie and caught him on the jaw. Gus grabbed Charlie around the head, but instead of pulverizing Charlie further, he loosened his grasp on Charlie's dirty, sweating blonde head, and seemed to be meditating some place deep inside his mind.

Quickly, Charlie took the opportunity to distance himself from Gus, his problem daughter, and the heavy swing of his hambone arms. As he approached the barn, he could still hear Gus moaning, "Ah, hell."

After Charlie entered the barn, he turned and looked back at Gus. He was still standing where Charlie had left him staring up at the sky, but now the girl had managed to sit herself up on the chaise and was looking around in confusion. Charlie ignored both of them. It was their problem, not his.

Big Gus Heinrich searched the sky above and whispered the name that meant everything to him. "Rose." Rose, his delicate little French flower, skin as soft as the petals that were her name, hair as dark as the earth from where her namesake came, a sweet gentleness that was her heart. Rose, his Rose. Rose Gillian, his tiny, precious little Rose....his only love.

He had fallen head over heels in love with the girl when they were just kids. Head over heels. Never once in his wildest dreams did he ever think she'd consider loving him, but she did.... a big old work horse like him. She loved him. She loved him. She loved him and he had betrayed her. "I'm so sorry, my beloved Rose, " Gus whispered.

Wiping the tears from his eyes, he turned to face the product of their love, Gillian Rose.
May 28, 1962

"Charlie, Big Gus wants to see you. Get on over to the house real quick. He's hotter than hell about something and I guess it's got to do with you." Judd Brown looked totally disgusted with his latest hire as he watched Charlie turn off the tractor and climb down from the big red machine. "Charlie, damn it! You ain't been here more than three months and already Big Gus is   fuming over you! What the hell have you done now boy?"

Charlie groaned over the 'boy' reference, but let it go. He owed Judd Brown, the tall thin foreman for Gus Heinrich. Judd had gotten him the job with Gus, but he was certain it wasn't due to Judd's concern for him. No, he was positive Judd had been sweet on his mom for a long time. After her John died, her useless husband, there was always prime meat wrapped in white freezer paper showing up on his mother's doorstep. Charlie was sure the mysterious meat had been Judd's doing, so Charlie was grateful to him and treated him with the utmost respect. But the man he and everybody else worked for, Big Gus Heinrich, he had no respect for that man....no respect, whatsoever.

The other workers all seemed to like and respect Big Gus, but Charlie had no idea what there was to like or respect about the man. They all said Gus was a good man, but to him Gus seemed to be a big tyrant with a ton of money. Charlie had no use for his sort at all, but Gus signed the paychecks and until something better came along, he'd keep his mouth shut.

"I haven't done one thing to piss Gus off, Judd. Honest."

Charlie thought about Gus' pregnant daughter and wondered if someone had guessed the truth about her. He hadn't said anything to anyone, but he knew he'd get blamed anyway. Anything that got broken or left unfinished was blamed on him. It had been that way since he started working for Big Gus. That's just the way it was with Gus and Charlie knew it. Why Gus disliked him so much was a mystery to him, but then Charlie didn't like Gus either. Maybe Gus could sense that, he thought, but he didn't care. As soon as he found another job, he was gone. To hell with Big Gus Heinrich!

"Get on over to the house and see what he wants. I don't envy you his rage, Charlie, whatever you did."

Charlie started to protest but knew it was useless. Slowly, he made his way over to the back door of the big ugly house where he knew true hell was waiting for him. But it wasn't.

"Come on in, Charlie Barnes." Using his full name without swearing, Charlie decided Big Gus Heinrich must have something planned for him. Something bad. Something really bad.

Gus motioned for Charlie to sit at one of the big chrome and yellow vinyl chairs and poured Charlie a large glass of ice tea. That's when Charlie knew Big Gus was planning a doozy of a wallop for him, but Charlie was hot and tired, the kitchen was cool, and the frosty tea was too inviting to refuse; so he gulped a big swallow, cleared his head and wondered what Gus was up to. It didn't take long to find out.

"I've been thinking about my daughter's situation, Charlie Barnes. She confessed that she's almost five month's along with child, and that's a big problem. But there's an even bigger problem, Charlie Barnes. The boy that has done the deed to her is off doing service in this great country of ours and can't be located at this time."

Gus thought about lamenting on Charlie doing his duty in the military, too, but right now he needed Charlie to do duty here at home, whether he liked it or not. And Gus didn't like it but what was a father to do? His only child was pregnant and most of the decent young men had volunteered for the military, as was their obligation.

According to the radio that morning, the whole world was in turmoil; and the great United States of America was gearing up against the threat of Castro's Cuba, the communist Soviets, and some place called North Vietnam. With so many decent young men answering the call to arms, that left only the dregs of society; namely, Charlie Barnes. And whether he liked it or not, Gus knew he needed Charlie Barnes. Something had to be done, and as far as Gus could determine, Charlie Barnes was the only available answer to his daughter's dilemma.

Gus ground back his hostility and tried to smile at the young man sitting at his kitchen table enjoying his ice tea, long legs leisurely stretched out in front of him, looking cool and comfortable while he should have been out sweating in the bean fields or even serving his country, which at least was honorable. But, Gus knew the boy wasn't honorable. None of the men in his family were worth a damn. All of them had been lazy, irresponsible losers. That's why Glory, Charlie's mother, had lost her few acres of land. That's why he had it now.

Gus had spent many hours wondering what he could offer the boy that would entice him to agree to his plan; maybe a new truck, he'd thought. Hell, a new truck would be an easy fix, too easy. Money? He had plenty of money to offer, he reasoned, but somehow, that young man didn't look like he could be bought off with money.

His future? Yeah, Charlie Barnes' future. What did he want to do in his life?

Gus circled the small kitchen and wondered how to begin. "Charlie Barnes, have you ever thought about what it would take for a young man to be sure of a good future? What would it take for you, Charlie Barnes?"

Charlie was getting a bit sick of hearing the man constantly repeat his full name, because he knew the old geezer could barely stand looking at him. Gus was up to something and he was trying to lure Charlie in, but Charlie wasn't stupid. Even talking in his most gentle voice, Gus was doing a sorry job of being respectful to the name of one Charlie Barnes. He was acting like he was interested in him personally. No, Big Gus was up to something. Charlie decided to wait him out and took a long satisfying drink of the ice cold tea and watched the sweat build up on Gus' forehead.

"Charlie Barnes, I know a lot of things about you. Your mama had you out of wedlock and that makes you a bastard. I know your stepfather was a no good, lazy drunk who lost your mama's little bit of land left to her. I know you ain't got one pot to pee in nor a window to throw it out of, Charlie Barnes."

Charlie listened as the big man strolled nervously about the kitchen, recalling every bad thing he could ever remember about Charlie's family. He didn't miss anything, so Charlie shut out the drone, except for the part about his step dad losing his mother's only inheritance. Those eighty acres had been Charlie's future; his big plan to begin a good life for him and his mom. How was he to know John hadn't paid the property taxes until it was too late, and Gus had gobbled it up dirt cheap for the back taxes?

That loss had been really tough on his mother, Glory. That had been the only home she'd ever known. Living in town like she was, Charlie knew she must have felt the loss of country living something awful, but he also knew she never felt any loss over that no-good John. It was almost a relief when he was coming home drunk one night, fell asleep at the wheel, and was killed. Nobody missed that mean, lazy drunk. Nobody!

"So, I ask you, Charlie Barnes, is that the way you want your own future to be? You know I'm the sort of man who's always looking to help out young people who want to make a better life for themselves. So again, Charlie Barnes, what do you need to make a good life for yourself?"

Charlie avoided the big man's distressed gaze. What a con job. The only person Gus Heinrich ever helped was Gus Heinrich. What was he up to? If they were going to play games, Charlie could play games with the best of them. The sweat from the iced tea glass had loosened some of the grime from his hands, so Charlie wiped his hands on his worn jeans before he made his announcement for the dreams of his future. Useless dreams, but Gus had asked.

"I want my mother's land back."

Gus openly gasped, didn't even try to hide it. Illinois land was sacred, the best farmland in the world and the most scarce. No man in his right mind would let that fine fertile black ground go, not that the old Barnes place was all that good of land for grain farming. Half of it was full of rocks, but it would be fine for raising a few head of cattle. He'd always wondered why John didn't put in cattle, but that would have been work.

He'd have to haul out some of those rocks, and John was too lazy to do work that hard.

Gus stroked his big jowls and reviewed his options. Those eighty acres were useless for grain farming, but that land was adjacent to his own land. It made for an easy access to the main road for his trucks hauling grain to the grain elevator when it was time to sell. That's the reason he was so determined to keep the land. He had to have that right-of-way or lose half of his grain driving through that damn rough creek by his house; and when it rained, that made it impassable. And then, there was that big pond over on the Barnes place that made a good run-off for the rain. He could easily run his trucks through there without getting stuck.

Gus thought about the situation for a moment. No, he'd never let that land go. He'd waited for years for John to slip up on the taxes on that land, and he did. And he was there, cash in hand.

What to do, what to do? What could he offer this boy, the only obvious answer to his daughter's problem? Schooling. The boy was smart, or so Judd had said. Schooling?

"Don't you want to go on and finish your schooling, son? Get a fine education at one of them big universities?"

Now it was 'son'. Charlie listened as Gus rambled on about a fine education which Gus had never been able to acquire and how sorry he was about that. Charlie was doubtful about Gus' educational desires, but let him ramble on while Charlie tried to figure out what the big man was up to. It really didn't matter. Sitting in Gus' big cool kitchen, drinking iced tea was better than sweating his butt off in the fields. Charlie looked up from his comfort and saw Gus glaring down at him, still smiling his fake fatherly smile. What did Gus want from him?

"Now son, I can't give you that particular piece of land. You know better than that, but I can give you almost any other thing you want, if you're willing to do just one little service for me."

Here it comes, Charlie grinned. They were finally getting somewhere, and Charlie was well aware Gus was in desperate need of his services, whatever they were. "And what would that one little service be, Gus?"

"Now son, keep in mind, this is only a temporary fix. It's not a lifelong commitment."

Would the man ever get on with it?

"Charlie Barnes, you're the only one who knows about my girl and her situation." Gus' bushy-blonde eyebrows rose considerably as he dared to continue. "I need someone to make her a wife, so that she doesn't deliver a bastard child."

Gus checked Charlie over for shock and then continued. "You, of all people, know what it's like being a bastard, Charlie Barnes. Kids making fun of you. Folks looking down their noses at you. Decent parents not letting their daughters date you."

Charlie had run into that sort of rejection before, but not often, and it had never bothered him that much. Years back, being a bastard carried a lot of shame, but after the last war, things had changed....times had changed. People were more accepting and less judgmental. And he'd never had any trouble getting a date.

Like a blast, Gus' words hit him. "Someone to make her a wife." Good lord, Gus wanted him to marry that fiery hellion of his. Hell no. He wouldn't do it. Dreaming about her was one thing. Taking her for a wife was something else. Charlie placed his empty tea glass on the table and pulled his weary body up from the sticky yellow vinyl.

"Don't mean any disrespect, Gus, but I think you've been out in the sun a little too long, or else my hearing is bad. Did you just ask me to marry your daughter?"

Gus had worried that maybe it would be a problem convincing the boy of the urgency of his daughter's situation. Hell, if she'd had a mother, she could have told her about her problem sooner. They would have had time to think about what to do. But there was no way she would have told him about it. He and the girl just weren't close. Never were. They never had a chance to be close.

Gus' thoughts came back to the situation at hand. He had to get that boy to agree to marry Gillian for his grandchild's sake. The child's mother had made a mistake but there was no need for an innocent babe to suffer for it. No, he couldn't put his grandchild through that shame.

"Well, it wouldn't be a permanent marriage, Charlie. You'd give the babe a name; even a seedy name is better than no name at all."

Gus saw Charlie flinch and knew he'd almost blown it, but he kept on. "Now Charlie, don't go getting all uppity on me. You know what I say is right and true, don't you? I mean, your name isn't like it was something to be proud of, so why the hell would you mind putting your name on my daughter's babe?"

"And just why would I do something like that, Gus? You asked me what I wanted in my future and I told you. I want my mother's land back. You said that was impossible, so what's there to talk about? Nowhere in my future plans do I see me taking on a wife and a kid that isn't even mine, so I'd say this discussion is over. Thanks for the tea, Gus. I'll be on my way to see Judd to collect my final pay."

But Gus wasn't done yet. He knew Charlie Barnes would be a hard-sell, and now he was forced into his next plan. "Hold on a minute, Charlie."

After talking to Charlie Barnes for awhile, Gus had a new appreciation for the tall, flaxen- haired young man. He was a tough character: smart, cool headed, just what Gillian needed. Besides that, he'd seen them peeking at one another, both acting like they could care less what the other one did, but not being able to stop themselves from looking either. They'd be good for each other. They just didn't know it.

Gus stopped the young man as he pushed the screen door open. "Come on back here and let's work out this situation." The screen door squeaked shut again and cautiously, the tall blonde man returned to his seat at the kitchen table.

"I don't know how you feel about my daughter, Charlie, and it really doesn't matter. All you'd have to do is live in the same house with her for let's say a year. Next June. Yeah, stay with her until next June. That'll be a respectable time after the babe's birth and then you can divorce her."

Live in the same house with the girl? Was this man insane? It would drive him wild being close to that gal every day. Sleeping in the same house with her, being alone with her all the time? The thoughts he had about her when he watched her were bad enough but being with her all the time? Good God! She'd either kill him or he'd kill himself over his desire for her. "I don't think so, Gus. No offense, but living with your daughter would drive any normal man nuts."

Gus felt the sweat dripping off his big jowls. Charlie was a lot tougher than he thought he'd be. Not realizing Charlie's hidden passion for the girl, Gus decided that Gillian's wild reputation was what was putting Charlie off, and Gus was well aware her character was his fault. Every bad thing that had ever happened to his child was Gus' fault and he knew it. Endless nights he'd suffered over how he'd failed her, over and over. He'd even failed her before she was born. God, how that thought hurt, but he was responsible.... responsible for everything. This time he couldn't fail Gillian. This time he'd make it right for her.

"Charlie, the old Beaupre place is for sale. Hell, that place has got one hundred acres, twenty acres more than that old place of your ma's. I could buy that for you, son." Gus circled the table, barely breathing. The boy was a damn hard-sell.

"Gus, that land is across the state line in Indiana; and besides, its twenty acres of swamp and the rest is sandy loam. They've reduced the price on that place over and over. You must think I'm stupid if you think I'd ever settle for something like that. Give it up, Gus. Let the kid be born out of wedlock and accept it. There's no shame in being an unwed mother anymore. Things aren't like they used to be. Things have changed."

But to Gus, some things would never change and he knew it all too well. He wouldn't let this happen to Gillian or his grandchild. He owed this to Rose. He couldn't let her down like he did before. Not again.

Gus was getting desperate. He knew he would have to go ahead with his last ditch plan. He certainly didn't want to, but he had no other choice. "Okay Charlie, you drive a hard bargain."

"It's my mother's place or none, Gus. Simple as that." Charlie stopped in his tracks as he crossed the kitchen toward the back door again. What had Gus said?

"Now just wait a minute, Charlie. I'm willing to let you have the old Barnes place but we'll have to sign a few conditions."

Charlie eyed Gus with suspicion. What was the old coot up to now? What conditions?

"You drive a hard bargain, Charlie Barnes, but I think I've come up with a solution that will benefit both of us. You marry Gillian, and after a year, you get the old Barnes place back."

Charlie couldn't believe his good fortune. This was just too good to be true. Finally his mother could move back out to the country where he was sure she wanted to be, and he could start building up the herd of cattle that he had always wanted.

Gus could see the gleam in Charlie's eyes and he knew he was sucked in. Gillian would have a proper husband and a name for her child. But the truth was, Gus loved his wayward daughter, and more than anything he wanted her to be happy. The more he saw of this young man, the more he knew he'd be good for Gillian. Maybe his only child could find happiness with this young man. It was worth a shot. Gus decided to sweeten the pot.

"I'll tell you what, Charlie Barnes. You make my girl happy to the point that after a year she wants to stay married to you and doesn't want a divorce from you, then you not only have the old Barnes place, but I'll throw in that forty acres north of it. Plus, Charlie Barnes, when I die, you get everything I've got to boot, and a beautiful wife and a readymade family. Hell, son, I can't think of a better offer than that and the conditions are simple."

Charlie couldn't believe his ears. All he had to do was marry the girl of his dreams, get her to fall in love with him, which he was certain he could do given the opportunity. All the girls around town liked him. He'd had endless offerings from the women, single and married alike. If they thought he was that hot, surely that young girl would fall under his charms, too. Yeah, he'd have her all legal, willing in his bed, and he'd have his mother's place back, and he'd have all Gus' other properties to boot. Man, what an offer. It was almost too good to be true. Maybe it was too good to be true. Conditions? What conditions?

"Go on, Gus. What conditions are you talking about?"

Gus knew he had Charlie chomping at the bit. He just had to be careful how he worded it. "If after a year, next June, Gillian decides she doesn't want you, she'll be free to divorce you. Oh, I'll still give you enough money to buy a small piece of land someplace else, but naturally, you'll give up all rights to any of my property. You can't ask for a better deal than that, Charlie Barnes. My daughter has a name for her babe, I won't have a bastard for my first grandchild, and Charlie, you'll have the means for a good future. Now what do you think of that generous plan, Charlie Barnes?"

Charlie tried to show indifference to Gus' plan; but in truth, he felt excitement all the way down to his boots. He'd have his mother's land back without her lazy, drunken husband to destroy everything he tried to accomplish. Sure, it would take some work. A lot of work, he knew that, but instead of putting the land into crops, he'd clear out all those rocks and raise a fine head of cattle on that eighty acres. And if he could get the girl to fall for him and want to stay married to him, Gus would give him that forty acres north of his mother's old place and he could increase his herd even more. Gus never did anything with that land because it wasn't tillable soil, but it would be good for cattle to graze. Oh, yeah!

Angus. Black Angus, he thought. He'd get some calves and with a decent amount of care, some day he'd have a big herd of prime Black Angus cattle. Sure, he'd have to keep on working for Gus, probably for a few years. But what was a few years compared to his future? When he came to work that morning, he had no future whatsoever. Now he had the whole world. He'd have to support the girl and her kid, but with what was left, he could put that into his cattle.... his own cattle. What an opportunity he'd been given. How could he refuse? This was an offer he'd always regret if he didn't accept it.

Gus saw the look of pure anticipation on Charlie's suntanned face and knew his daughter's plight had been solved. Feeling the weight of the world being pulled from his shoulders, Big Gustav Heinrich grinned and offered his hand to seal the deal. Charlie accepted it.

Things were going to finally turn around for Charlie Barnes he thought as he shook the hand of his future father-in-law, Big Gus Heinrich.

Made in the USA
Charleston, SC
17 April 2012